TOTO

THE DOG-GONE AMAZING STORY OF
THE WIZARD OF OZ

To Anoushka ~ M.M.

To Caroline ~ E.C.C.

michael morpurgo

Illustrated by
Emma Chichester Clark

TOTO

THE DOG-GONE AMAZING STORY OF
THE WIZARD OF OZ

HarperCollins *Children's Books*

CONTENTS

PROLOGUE

———◆———

I Was There...

That was how Papa Toto always began his story: "I was there." There were seven of us puppies, and that's a lot, and I was the littlest. Papa Toto always called me Tiny Toto. Whenever Mama lay down in the basket to feed us, my brothers and sisters just trampled all over me to get to her first. Mama hardly noticed me, I was so small, but Papa Toto did. He always saw to it there was a place for me, and when the others pushed me off,

he'd nose them away to make room for me. Without Papa Toto I guess I wouldn't ever have had enough milk, would probably never have lived to grow up at all and tell the tale.

Papa Toto's tale was the best part of every day for me. Papa Toto would wait until Mama had climbed out of the basket and gone out of the house with all the people folk. Like Dorothy, who Papa Toto loved almost as much as he loved me. And that wasn't just because I was the littlest and the best-looking but because I was the only one who was always still awake at the end of his story. We didn't see too much of him during the day. He was out most of the day on the farm working alongside Dorothy and Uncle Henry and Aunt Em, plowing and sowing. Of course Papa Toto didn't do all the chores himself—that was people folk's work—but he did drive the cows, keep an eye out for snakes and wolves and so forth, and chase rabbits and rats and mice whenever and wherever he found them.

And on the lazy hot days he'd just hang around, making sure Dorothy didn't come to harm. "It's what I'm for," he'd tell us. "Wherever she goes, I go. But now you littl'uns are around, Dorothy says I got to look after you from time to time, give your mama a break from you. But I don't want none of your wiggling and clambering and tumbling out like you do, and no chewing on my tail. No tinkling in the basket, y'hear. Dorothy don't like it when you tinkle on the floor neither. And don't go pestering me for food, cos you ain't going to get none—I've told you time and again that's what your mama does, not me. You just lie still and go to sleep."

But lying still only ever happened when we were all fast asleep, and Papa Toto had his own special way of getting us to do that. He'd be telling us one of his stories, and sure enough, pretty soon all the wiggling and clambering and the tumbling stopped, and we'd all be lying there still and listening, all seven of us. And then, one by one they'd all drop off to sleep and in the end I'd often be the only one left awake, because I always wanted to hear what happened in the end. The way I saw it, there wasn't much point in listening to *the beginning of the story if you didn't hear how it finished. Of course, I knew what happened in the end—we had all heard Papa Toto's stories often enough. But it was the way he told them that kept me awake, kept me listening, like he was there inside the story, and I was right there with him.*

Even so, I've got to say—but don't you go telling him now—I did doze off during some of his tales. But there was one story I stayed awake to hear from beginning to end, the one about the Wizard of Oz, the one he always began with: "I was there." Papa Toto especially loved telling that story, and we loved hearing it. The way he told it you just had to believe every last word of it. Of course, I never believed it afterwards. But I wanted to. It was funny and frightening, and sad and silly, and weird and wonderful, and so amazing and exciting that I never wanted go to sleep, however warm and snug and full up with milk I was. That was Papa Toto's best tale, the one I longed for, the one I never fell asleep in. He'd climb into our basket in the corner of the room, turn round and round, and then lie down carefully, trying not to squash any of us, but he always did, and this time it was me. "Sorry, Tiny Toto," he said, nudging me gently with his cold, cold nose. He waited until all the squealing and squeaking had stopped, until we were all snuggled up to him, and ready for the story.

"I was there," he began, and those magic words sent shivers down my spine. It was going to be the Wizard story. "Dorothy and me were both there. She never tells Uncle Henry or Aunt Em this story any more, because they won't believe her. She told me that one day, when she has children of her own, she'll tell them, because children know how to believe. Well, pups are children too, right? So I can tell you. Think of that: you little pups will know this story before any people folks know it, except Dorothy, of course, and me."

We were all silent, snuggled up together, all of us lying there, waiting, waiting. Then Papa Toto began.

"Well, little pups, my tale begins in this very house, in this very room, in this very basket…

CHAPTER ONE

—•◆•—

A Giant Monster of a Twister

I was lying right here, deep in my dreams in this very basket, when I was woken up by the sound of the wind roaring and howling around the house, rattling the doors and windows, shaking the whole place. I never heard a wind like it. The door blew open. So I got up and went outside. Everyone was rushing around, Dorothy trying to shut the hens into the hen house, but they were skittering about all over the place.

They didn't want to go inside, of course they didn't. It wasn't getting dark yet. The hens never go to bed before dark. What was Dorothy thinking of? Uncle Henry was driving the cattle into the barn, but they didn't want to go in either, and he was calling for me to come and help him, but I had sleep still in my head and didn't want to. Anyway, he was managing well enough on his own, I thought, without me. Aunt Em was trying to shut the barn doors, but the wind wouldn't let her. She was blown off her feet and went rolling over and over, like tumbleweed. Dorothy saw what was happening, left her hens and ran to help Aunt Em up on to her feet, and together with Uncle Henry they managed to shut the barn door.

Then they did some more chasing round, getting old Barney, our plow horse, into his stable, rounding up the pigs—and that wasn't easy either—and all the while they were hollering at each other about a great storm coming in, and how the clouds were dark in the north and how that was a bad sign.

"If I'm not mistaken, there's a twister on the way," Uncle Henry was bellowing. "Or else I'll eat my hat."

And then suddenly he didn't have any hat on his head any more. It had blown away. So I went after it.

I love a good old hat chase, especially when there's a wind blowing over the prairies in Kansas. As Uncle Henry often says, maybe other folks in other places invented the wheel and writing and all that smart stuff, but in Kansas we invented the wind.

Anyways, I went chasing that hat of Uncle Henry's just about all over Kansas, and caught up with it down by the creek where it landed in the water, and I dived right in, grabbed it in my teeth and trotted back home, head high, tail high, pretty darned pleased with myself.

I've always been like that. If I'm chasing after something, hats especially, I put just about everyone and everything else out of my mind. But now the chase was over and I could hear Dorothy screaming for me to come home. I could see her now, standing on the veranda of the farmhouse, and right behind her, and nearly right above her, came this giant monster of a twister just a-roaring and a-raging, towering up into the sky, taking the barn with it, making splinters of it, and the fences too, and the rain tub, swirling and swallowing everything. Well, I ran. I took the steps up the veranda in one bound, jumped right into Dorothy's arms. "Where've you been, Toto?" she cried, hugging me to her and running into the house.

I showed her the hat in my mouth, shook it for her to be quite sure she noticed how smart I had been!

"You rescued Uncle Henry's hat!" I was so pleased that she was pleased. "You are such a smart Toto. Don't you drop it now. We got to get ourselves safe out of this storm, or else we'll be blowed to smithereens. Aunt Em and Uncle Henry are waiting for us down in the cellar. But I couldn't really leave you behind, could I? I ain't going down there without Toto, I told them. And now I got you, that's where we're going, right now. I know you don't like it down in the dark, Toto, but it's safe down there, so like it or lump it, you're coming with me."

She was right, I hated it down in that cellar. Never did like the dark, still don't. I could see the trapdoor open on the far side of the room. I could hear Aunt Em and Uncle Henry hollering for us to hurry up. Dorothy managed to get the front door shut against the wind, with the house shaking all around us, shaking so bad I thought that old twister was going to make splinters of it any moment. Cups and saucers, jugs and plates, smashed on to the floor. Drawers flew open, knives and forks and spoons, kettles and pots and pans, rattled and crashed, chairs and cupboards and dressers tipped over.

I was never so scared in all my life. We were halfway across the room when the strangest thing happened. The trapdoor slammed itself shut, and all of a sudden the shaking and the roaring, the whistling and wailing, simply stopped. I heard Aunt Em and Uncle Henry still calling for us from down below in the cellar, but their voices were becoming fainter with every moment.

Then all was silence.

The whole house was
swaying now, and we were
swaying with it. Dorothy fell on
to her knees but never let go of me.
She crawled to her bed in the corner,
and we curled up there, holding on
to one another, wondering what had
happened, what was going to happen.

"We're floating, Toto!" Dorothy cried.
"Floating on the air right in the middle
of the twister. We're flying, Toto."
She called out for Aunt Em
and Uncle Henry. But
there was no reply.

"We're all alone," Dorothy said, her voice trembling a bit. "But don't you worry none. I'll look after you, Toto. You know I will."

And I did know that, so I wasn't worried, not as much as I had been anyway. There was blue sky outside the window now, and we were flying up and out of the clouds. There was hardly a sound. I wasn't frightened at all any more. I did feel a little sick though, what with all this floating

around in the air, especially when the house lurched and tipped and rocked about.

"We'd best lie down, Toto," said Dorothy, "and close our eyes, then we'll feel better."

So that's what we did, and pretty soon, what with all that gentle swaying and rocking, we were both of us fast asleep, her arm around me, my head in her lap, Uncle Henry's hat right beside me. She'd told me to look after his hat, so that's just what I was doing.

CHAPTER TWO

Landing in the Land of the Munchkins

I always slept on Dorothy's bed—Aunt Em and Uncle Henry didn't like me to, but I often snuck up on to her bed when they were asleep. Then Dorothy was happy, and I was happy. We breathed together. I think sometimes we dreamed the same dream together. I was usually awake before her. She was a bit of a sleepyhead. But this time we were woken up together by the same jarring, crashing bump. We sat up at once. The house didn't like it any more than we did. The whole place groaned and creaked around us. And then we heard nothing for a while except the sound of whispering outside the farmhouse door. Strangers!

I don't like strangers, especially not whispering strangers. I leaped off the bed, barking as fiercely as I could, just to let them now how terrifying I can be, which is never easy for me because as you know, little puppies, I am a small black dog with a yappy kind of a bark. Very likely you'll be much the same when you grow up. I can point my tail, make the hair stand up along my back like a bottle brush, and I can bare my teeth. I can frighten rats and rabbits and cats and so on. But if I'm honest, the most frightening thing about me is probably my cold, cold nose. Wake up Dorothy or Aunt Em or Uncle Henry, with my cold, cold nose, and they shriek like blue murder. Of course, my nose was no use to me with these whispering strangers on the other side of the door. But luckily they couldn't see how small I was. I barked and growled as

deep as I could, howled like a bloodhound, snarled like a wolf.

Dorothy was beside me, and she could hear the whispering too. "Who's out there?" she cried.

"Only us," came a friendly voice at last. "We are the Munchkins!"

Dorothy opened the door and I went bounding out, barking my head off. I was so amazed by what I saw that I stopped barking at once. Standing on the grass just beyond the veranda steps was the strangest crowd of people, every one of them with a round-brimmed hat, dressed in azure blue, and all the size of children—Dorothy's size—but with grown-up faces. All of them looked like men peoplefolk, except one, a little old lady, and she had long white hair. Her face was as wrinkled and brown as an autumn leaf. She was the one who spoke first. She was pointing at me, which was rather rude, I thought.

"What is that?" she asked, wrinkling her nose. "And who are you?"

"I am Dorothy," Dorothy told her. "And this is Toto, my dog, and my best friend, and he does not bite."

"I never saw such a dog before. An odd-looking creature," the strange lady went on. "But if he is your best friend he is most welcome, as you are. We all want to thank you from the bottom of our hearts."

"What for?" Dorothy asked.

"For coming here and saving us, of course! For killing the Wicked Witch of the East, my dear."

"Killing her! But I've never killed anything in all my life," Dorothy protested. "Toto here will go after a rabbit or a mouse, maybe, or a hat. But that is his nature; what dogs do. I've never killed anything. I wouldn't hurt a fly or a beetle or any living creature."

"Well, maybe you haven't, but your house has," replied the old lady. "Look, over there!" She was pointing at the corner of the house. "See those two feet sticking out from under the house? That is all that is left of her, the Wicked Witch of the East. Her two pointed feet and her two red shoes. She's done for. You squashed her good, or rather your house did."

"Oh my goodness!" cried Dorothy. The tears were coming, and she could not stop them. "I'm so very sorry. I can't believe it, I never meant to do such a terrible thing."

But the strange old lady shook her head. "Don't be upset, my dear, you have done a good thing, though you didn't know it. It's the Wicked Witch of the East, who was cruel and terrible. She was the wickedest witch that ever lived. Think of it this way: your house has saved many lives."

Dorothy looked uncertain.

"You must believe me, my dear. Your house did us all a great favor," said the old lady. "Didn't it, Munchkins?" All the Munchkins whispered their appreciation, nodding very vigorously and clapping most enthusiastically.

"You can see they are happy, as I am too," she went on, "because these poor unfortunate Munchkins have slaved for that horrible Wicked Witch of the East, day and night all their lives. They were under her wicked spell, which is now all over, because she is dead, dead as a doornail."

"So she really was a witch? She could put spells on people?" Dorothy asked.

"Yes," replied the old lady. "But witches are not all wicked like she was. I am a witch myself, but I am not a wicked one, am I, Munchkins?" And all the Munchkins whispered amongst themselves—their whispering sounded like a wind blowing through the trees—and then shook their heads all together. "I can make spells, as all witches can," she went on. "But I make only good spells."

"You are a real live witch?" gasped Dorothy, stepping

back a pace, and wiping the tears from her cheeks.

"Oh yes, my dear, I am the Good Witch of the North. But there is nothing to be frightened of," she said. "You should have known my dear sister, the Good Witch of the South. She was killed by another Wicked Witch, the wickedest witch who ever lived, and the sister of this one you squashed with your house. Another reason I have—we all have—to thank you. She and I, we did all we could to help and protect good and kind people like the Munchkins, to save them from the Wicked Witches of the East and the West. We wanted to set them free, but our power was not strong enough. And then out of the blue your house comes falling down out of the sky and squashes the Wicked Witch of the East, and now the Munchkins are free, thanks to you."

"I don't understand," Dorothy said. "My Aunt Em back in Kansas, where I live, she says that all witches are make-believe, that they are only in story books, and not real at all."

"Well, your little dog thinks I'm real, don't you?" the old lady said. And it was true. I was sniffing her hand and she smelled real enough to me, quite sweet, like syrup. I like syrup. "Nice dog. Cold nose. I like a dog with a cold nose that wags her tail. Where is this Kansas place you came from? I have not heard of it."

"Toto is a he not a she," said Dorothy. "And Kansas is—I don't know—up there somewhere in the sky, I suppose. It's where we live, Toto and me, and we want to go home. I mean, you folks look really nice, and I can tell now, like Toto can, that you are a good witch. But we don't have real witches, good or wicked, unless they are in books, and Aunt Em says they can't do much harm in books.

"I mean, you just close the book, and poof! The wicked witch or the magic-making wizard, or whatever, is gone. Aunt Em and Uncle Henry will be mighty worried on account of the farmhouse flying off with us in it. Can't you please help us get back home?"

"Well, I can't do it," said the Good Witch of the North. "But there is someone I know who might..."

"Oh please, do tell us!" said Dorothy. "I so wish to go home."

"There is a wizard we know," the Good Witch of the North went on thoughtfully. "Isn't there, Munchkins?" The Munchkins all trembled terribly at this and whispered frantically. "He is called the Wizard of Oz. He is a great and terrible and powerful wizard, and he lives far away in the Emerald City, down the yellow brick road, which is a very long road. No one is wiser, I have heard. No one is smarter. He knows everything there is to know.

He'll know for sure how to get you back to your home in this Kansas place—though why you ever should wish to leave this beautiful country of ours, I can't imagine, especially now that you have killed the Wicked Witch of the East. Look around you. This will be such a happy country now after what you have done, as happy as it is beautiful. And believe me, the Munchkins are the kindest folk who ever lived."

Until then I don't think either Dorothy or I had even noticed just how beautiful this place where we had landed was. Everywhere we looked there were grassy meadows full of wild and wonderful flowers, and forests of towering trees, luscious fruits growing from them, and leaves all the colors of the rainbow. There were bubbling, sparkling streams, humming bees and fluttering butterflies. And every bird that flew overhead was like a bright jewel, and sang so sweetly. Gone was the flat, gray land of the prairies of Kansas, the dusty tracks, the cruel wind, and the tumbleweed.

"It is so beautiful," said Dorothy, "but home is home, and home is best."

"You're so dog-gone right," I woofed.

Just then the Munchkins began to whisper and point excitedly at the corner of the house. "All gone, all gone," they muttered in unison.

Those pointed feet sticking out from under the house had gone, disappeared, vanished entirely. Only the Wicked Witch's red shoes were left. I went to sniff around—my nose tells me so much more than my eyes ever do. Dust, all I could smell was dust. I picked up a shoe and carried it back to Dorothy,

who sat down right away and put it on. "Just the right size," she said, "and so comfortable it's as if they were made for me."

"They are yours now, my dear," said the kindly Witch of the North. "The nasty Witch of the East always wore those shoes because there is magic power in them.

"But magic obeys only the heart of the one who uses it. Your magic would always be a kind magic, because you are kind, I can tell. Please stay and help us."

"I would..." said Dorothy, and I could hear the wobble in her voice, so I knew she was going to cry. I know Dorothy so well. I always knew—I still do— when she is happy before she is happy, when she is sad before she is sad. "And I do love my new shoes, truly I do... but I do so want to go home. Aunt Em and Uncle Henry are the only family I've got. Please tell me how to get back home. If you are a good witch, you must know the way."

But all the Munchkins were shaking their heads and crying because she was crying. I touched her leg with my cold, cold nose and wagged my tail and looked up into her eyes to comfort her.

"There is only one thing to do, Dorothy, my dear," the old lady said, stroking Dorothy's hair and wiping her eyes with her handkerchief. "You must go to the Wizard of Oz, who knows everything. You must follow the yellow brick road."

"Follow the yellow brick road?" echoed Dorothy.

"Yes," said the kindly Witch of the North. "To see the Wizard of Oz."

"You called him terrible. Is he a good man or a wicked man?" Dorothy asked.

"He is terribly powerful, but everyone says he is a good wizard. However, I have to say I have never met him. I don't even know what he looks like. No one does. But if you want to go home to this *Kansas*, he's the only one who can help you. It is a long way to go, but an easy road to follow. Just follow the yellow brick road, and you will find the Emerald City. But look after yourself—there will be great dangers on the way. Remember, the right road is never the easy road. But you will look after her, Toto, won't you? Can you be ferocious and fierce?"

I growled my best to show her, straightened my tail, and rose up the hackles along my back like a bottle brush. I bared my teeth. The Munchkins shrank back in horror and fear, and I was, I am ashamed to say, rather pleased with myself about that. *I may be small and funny-looking,* I thought, *but I can still make like a wicked wolf when I need to.*

Dorothy tickled the top of my head with her fingers, which is always her way of telling me to calm down and be nice. The Good Witch of the North bent forward and kissed Dorothy softly on her forehead. "The mark of my lips will stay there for as long as you need protection.

Now you have a kiss from the Good Witch of the North, no one who sees it will dare harm you. And you have good magic in your red shoes. Be brave, Dorothy, my dear. Look after her, Toto. Goodbye now. You follow the stream through the trees, and you'll soon come to the yellow brick road."

She turned around three times on her left heel and simply vanished into thin air. The Munchkins bowed silently, and went off over the grass meadow, whispering among themselves and looking back at us as they went, before they too disappeared into the long grass and the flowers. I thought at first it was the flowers themselves that were singing. But it was Munchkins, I'm sure of it.

"Follow the yellow brick road," they sang. "Follow the yellow brick road."

"Well then, Toto," said Dorothy, "up we get and off we go! Home is home, and home is best."

"You're so dog-gone right," I woofed.

CHAPTER THREE

A Real Live Walking, Talking Scarecrow

*B*y now, my little puppies, I was getting pretty hungry, I can tell you…

I was especially missing the sausages that Aunt Em always made for breakfast. Uncle Henry would often sneak me one under the table; Dorothy too. But Aunt Em never. I do love my sausages.

I tried many ways to let Dorothy know. I sat down right by her all polite and tail tucked in, and touched her with

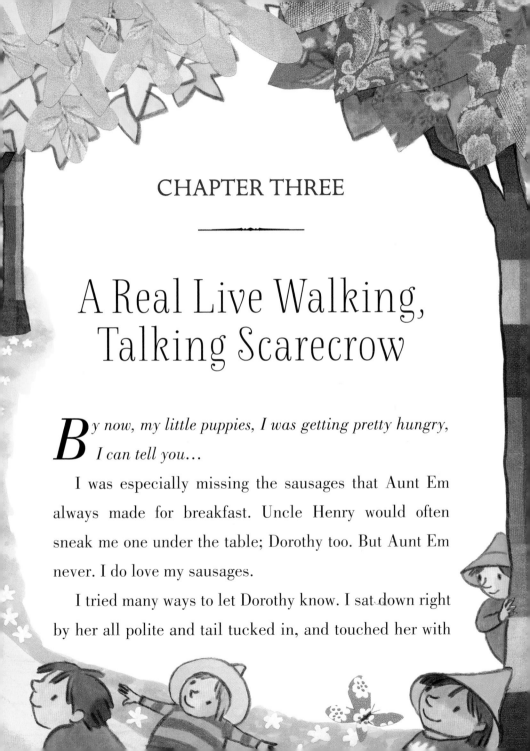

my cold, cold nose. That didn't work. I looked up at her as plaintively as I could—and I can do plaintive pretty darned well when I want to, little puppies—and all the while letting my tongue hang out and dribble. I did a bit of whining and whimpering. I tried pawing her leg. But she was just too busy to pay me much attention.

"Not now, Toto," Dorothy said. "Can't you see I'm getting myself dressed and all cleaned up for our long walk down the yellow brick road?" She was putting on her favorite dress, of blue and white checks. "Doesn't it look fine, Toto, with my new red shoes?" she said, twirling around to show me. "And look," she said, tying her bonnet on, "better still with my bonnet that Aunt Em made especially! And my basket too for sandwiches. We've got to have sandwiches. And we'll put Uncle Henry's hat in the basket too, so we won't forget it."

I sat there, telling her with my eyes as best I could that I really wasn't that interested in her bonnet or her basket, that my tummy was gurgling and groaning with hunger.

Finally, finally, she got the message. "Oh, Toto! I'm sorry. Don't look so sad. Aunt Em had some ham and bread in the kitchen. I'll soon find something for you." Now she was talking! She made ham sandwiches on the kitchen table. There were broken plates and dishes scattered all around us; everything was topsy-turvy. That twister had surely made a dreadful mess of the place. Dorothy had a sandwich and I had one too. I had lots! She made a few more for the journey. I thanked her with my eyes, with my dribbly tongue, and with my cold, cold nose. "Now we have to find the yellow brick road," Dorothy said, "which will lead us, so that kind Good Witch said, to the Emerald City and the Great and Terrible Wizard of Oz. I don't much like the sound of 'terrible', Toto. But just so long as he can help us get back to Kansas, we don't care how terrible he is, do we, Toto?"

So she picked up her basket, now with Uncle Henry's hat in it, and packed it with some more sandwiches. Sadly there were no sausages.

Off we went then, shutting the door behind us, following the stream, where I stopped to have a long, cool drink. Dorothy said I made a lot of noise with my lapping, as if I wanted to drink the whole stream. Well, the water was lovely, and I love to lap.

We walked on and on through lovely leafy orchards of apples and pears and peaches and plums, where Dorothy helped herself and filled her basket, being careful not to squash Uncle Henry's hat.

To be honest, I'm not that fond of fruit, never have been. And, at last, there ahead of us lay the yellow brick road, golden in sunshine, stretching away over the hills into the distance as far as the eye could see. "Come along, Toto," Dorothy said. "That's the way we go, that's our way home to Kansas, back home to Aunt Em and Uncle Henry."

So there we were, the two of us, Dorothy carrying the basket over her arm with the ham sandwiches in it, and the fruit she picked on the way, making our way along the yellow brick road. She was happy, I could tell, skipping along, and singing as she went. So I was happy too, because she was, and because we were on our way home, with a little bit of luck.

All the Munchkins we met along the way could not have been kinder. They all seemed to know what we had done, or the farmhouse had done, how we had squashed the Wicked Witch of the East and set them free. They gave us shelter for the night. They honored us, feasted us royally. There was dancing and singing wherever we went. I loved playing with the children, and they made a great fuss over me, squeaking with laughter when I jumped for their balls or leaped into the stream after their sticks. The Munchkins would hang garlands around our necks, before setting us on our way again the next day, waving us off, wishing us well. Those Munchkin folk thought I was the funniest thing they had ever seen—I don't think any of them had ever seen a dog before. The babies and toddlers in particular loved me, pulling my tail and ears, never too hard. And I'd let them, because it didn't hurt, and they'd giggle and gurgle and shriek.

And they all loved Dorothy too, because they knew she was a kind and good witch—she had to be, they said, because she had killed the Wicked Witch of the East, which was good, and set them free, which was good. And they also said there were blue checks in her dress, and blue was the Munchkins' favourite colour. They too all wore blue dresses or blue jackets and trousers, blue hats, and blue socks and shoes. So for many reasons they felt Dorothy was one of them. They loved her when she danced, loved her when she sang. I have to say, I have always thought Dorothy sings a bit shrilly and squeakily for my liking, and she sings a little too often as well, but they seemed to like it.

But once we were on our way again, down the yellow brick road, Dorothy fell silent. Dorothy wasn't often silent. Something was wrong.

She soon told me what it was. "No one seems to know how far it is to the Emerald City, and all the Munchkins say we should be very careful, that everything may look mighty pretty on the way, but there will be dangers ahead, that we have to be brave, and I'm not sure I'm all that brave, Toto. And they all seem terribly frightened of the Wizard of Oz, whenever they speak of him. I don't know why. But we have to find him, Toto, don't we? He's the only one who can help us get back to Kansas. And I want to see Aunt Em again and Uncle Henry. So we'll just have to be brave, won't we, Toto? We'll walk on down the yellow brick road for as long as it takes and we won't be frightened, not of anyone, not of anything, and especially not of the Wizard of Oz." That's how Dorothy always cheered herself up, by talking to herself, or to me—to both of us mostly.

So on we went, under the hot, hot sun, Dorothy skipping along, singing rather too often, and me trotting along cheerily at her heels, wagging my tail to keep happy and keep her happy too. After a few miles we sat down by a stream to rest. She was dabbling her aching feet in the cool of the stream, and I was lapping up all the water I could.

"Look!" cried Dorothy suddenly. "Over there! A scarecrow! Like we have at home on the farm." And sure enough a little further down the stream, standing in a field of ripe corn, was a scarecrow, but he was not at all like the poor old stuffed sack of a scarecrow we had back home, with Uncle Henry's dirty old hat and dusty old jacket, and his smelly old pipe stuck in his mouth.

No, this was the grandest looking scarecrow I ever saw. He had real eyes and a real nose and a real mouth. He even had sticks for ears. He was dressed like the Munchkins, entirely in blue, wore the same kind of round, wide-brimmed hat they did, that was pointed at the top, and was blue like everything else he wore. He had actual boots on him too, like the Munchkins, blue ones, and blue socks too.

"Why, he looks almost alive!" cried Dorothy. "What a fine scarecrow!" We got up and ran down along the riverbank to get a closer look. Dorothy was right. He was the finest scarecrow I ever saw. He wasn't at all lopsided and weather-beaten like the poor old fellow back home. This one stood up straight and tall.

As we came closer, we could see he had a pole stuck under his jacket at the back, fixing him securely to the ground. He was standing there stiff and still, but he was so real-looking, so alive-looking. I ran up to him barking at him. He never moved, so I knew he had to be a scarecrow, a fine scarecrow, but a scarecrow like all scarecrows, a stuffed-with-straw man.

"Hello, little dog," he said suddenly.

The scarecrow spoke!

He was alive!

Dorothy looked at me. I looked at Dorothy.

"'Scuse me, sir," Dorothy said, "but did you speak?"

"I did," came the reply. His voice sounded how you would expect a scarecrow to speak, with a rather husky, dusty voice. Dorothy didn't seem to know what to say. I did. I just went on barking untill she shushed me. Then she said what all people folk seem to say when they don't know what else to say. "How are you doing, sir?"

"Not so good, I'm afraid," said the scarecrow. "I mean, all I do is stand here all day and all night. I don't just scare away crows—that's my job—I scare away everything and everyone. It gets a bit lonely, if I'm honest. I'm not complaining, mind you. My Munchkin farmer comes out to see me from time to time and tells me his troubles, says he likes talking to me because I'm a good friend and I listen. Back home, he says, no one listens to him."

"Poor you," Dorothy said. "Can't you move? Just walk away?"

"I wish, how I wish. See this pole stuck up my jacket? Well, it's hammered deep into the ground behind me. So I'm stuck here, can't move."

"Have you asked the farmer to let you go?" said Dorothy. "Uncle Henry's a farmer and he's very kind. Most farmers are, in Kansas."

"Oh, I've asked him," said the scarecrow. "But he says he made me so I belong here, that I have a job to do, and besides he likes my company."

"That doesn't seem very fair," said Dorothy. "Wouldn't you like to be free?"

"More than anything," said the scarecrow. "But how can I get myself off this pole? I can't move."

"We'll soon fix that," Dorothy told him, "won't we, Toto?"

"Toto?" the scarecrow asked.

"That's my dog's name, and I'm Dorothy," Dorothy said, tugging at the pole, and wiggling it back and forth, to and fro. "Have you got a name?"

"Just Scarecrow," said Scarecrow. "It's what I am, just an old scarecrow stuffed with straw. You'll never get that pole out of the ground, Dorothy. It's very kind of you to try. Maybe you could lift me off? I'm very light, you'll see." So Dorothy reached up, put her arms right around him and lifted him clear of the pole, then set him down on the ground in front of her. I expected him to fall over, but he didn't. He shook himself down, pulled his coat straight and arranged his hat. "There," he said, "that's much better. I feel like a new scarecrow. You've been so good to me, Dorothy. Thank you so very much." He looked down at me, as if he was rather nervous of me. "Does that dog bite?" he asked.

"Never," Dorothy replied, which was not quite true. "And anyway, Toto likes you. I like you."

"And I like you too, both of you," Scarecrow said. "So where were you off to this fine day, if I might ask?"

Dorothy told him where we had come from and where we were going and why, and all about the Great and Terrible

Wizard of Oz who could do just about everything, make anything happen, because his magic was so powerful. Scarecrow didn't seem in the least bit frightened by the mention of the Wizard of Oz, as so many of the Munchkins had been.

"I wonder," he said, "might I come along with you perhaps? I've been standing here in this field for a week or two now, and I've never done any walking.

I'd love to go for a long walk, wherever it takes me.
It would be good for me, loosen me up. And I should
love to have new friends."

I was sniffing at Scarecrow now. He smelled just like
the barn back home in Kansas, a good familiar smell,
a strong whiff of Uncle Henry's trousers, and
pipe tobacco, and rather of mice too. I like
mice and rats, to chase I mean. Dorothy
was right, I did like Scarecrow, and I
liked his smells! "Of course
you can come with us, can't
he, Toto?" said Dorothy.
"I think that would be a fine
idea. Let's go, shall we?"

So the three of us set off down
the yellow brick road that
wound its way into the far, far

distance, the two of them chatting away beside me as we went. "Maybe you can help, Scarecrow," Dorothy said after a while. "You see, Toto and I, we do not know this country at all. This yellow brick road looks as if it will go on forever. Do you happen to know how far it is to the Emerald City?"

Until now Scarecrow had been walking along quite happily, but suddenly he stopped and stood there, shaking his

head sadly. "I wish I could help you, Dorothy," he said, "but look at me. I know nothing. I am made of straw, all of me, my legs, my arms, my body, and worst of all, my head. I have no brains in my head at all, only straw. Maybe the Great and Terrible Wizard of Oz, if he can do just about everything he wants to do, like you say, could give me some brains? I want brains in my head like you, so I can know things, understand things. Everyone thinks I'm stupid, and I am, I am."

"No, Scarecrow, you're not," Dorothy said, holding his hands and looking up into his eyes. "You are good and kind and gentle, and Aunt Em says that's more important than anything else, doesn't she, Toto?"

I jumped up on Scarecrow's leg and licked his hand, to make him feel happier. And that's when I smelled a stronger whiff of mice and rats in his straw, and so I snuffled at him with my nose, growling just a little, because I was so excited. I get like that when I smell a rat or a mouse.

"He's growling at me," said Scarecrow.

"Don't be afraid," Dorothy told him. "Toto won't hurt you."

"Oh, I'm not afraid of dogs, Dorothy," Scarecrow said. "I'm not afraid of anything—oh, except fire. I really don't like fire. I can't think why, but I don't like fire at all. Maybe fire and straw don't agree with one another somehow. I don't know. That's my trouble, Dorothy, that's what's wrong with me, you see? No brains. I don't know anything."

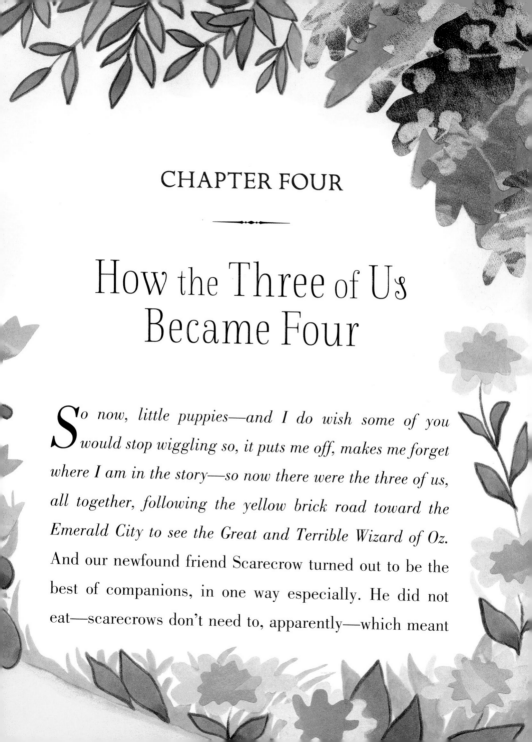

CHAPTER FOUR

How the Three of Us Became Four

*S*o now, little puppies—and I do wish some of you would stop wiggling so, it puts me off, makes me forget where I am in the story—so now there were the three of us, all together, following the yellow brick road toward the Emerald City to see the Great and Terrible Wizard of Oz. And our newfound friend Scarecrow turned out to be the best of companions, in one way especially. He did not eat—scarecrows don't need to, apparently—which meant that Dorothy and I could share those few sandwiches that were in her basket, so there was more for each of us, more for me!

And like Dorothy, Scarecrow loved to chatter away, to tell stories. There was never a dull moment. I sniffed and snuffled along the roadside as we went, loving all the new smells of this strange place, missing some of the old whiffs of course—no whiff of rabbit here, no whiff of squirrel, or hedgehog, no whiff of sausages, either. But I didn't mind, I had Dorothy and Scarecrow to listen to as we walked along.

Walking, it soon turned out, wasn't at all easy for Scarecrow. He kept staggering around and tripping over and falling. "I am not used to this walking game," he explained as Dorothy helped him up yet again on to his feet. "I am used to standing still. But don't worry. It doesn't hurt when I fall over, not one bit."

Dorothy took his arm anyway to steady him, to help him on, but mostly I could see it was because she liked him. She talked to him more about how we had got here and all about home and Kansas and Aunt Em and Uncle Henry, and about how much she missed them and how much she wanted to go home. "Home is home," she said, "and home is best."

"You're so dog-gone right," I woofed.

"And besides," said Dorothy, "Uncle Henry must be missing his hat by now. We have to get it back to him."

"Hat?" said Scarecrow.

Dorothy took Uncle Henry's hat out of the basket and held it up.

"It's a long story," said Dorothy, and she gave it to me to carry for a while. Made me feel right at home trotting along with Uncle Henry's hat in my mouth. "We've just got to get home, that's all."

"Well, if you'll forgive me for saying so, Dorothy," Scarecrow said, "I can't imagine why you would ever want to leave this beautiful country, to go back to that gray old Kansas and those horrible twisters. From the way you tell it, it sounds a most dreadful place. I mean, just look around you. Isn't this the most lovely of places, with the kindest of people? And you want to leave it and go back to that wind and all that tumbleweed? I don't understand you at all, I really don't. But then I don't understand anything, do I? I wouldn't, would I, because I have no brains. My head is stuffed with straw like the rest of me. Well, I think it's lucky for Kansas that you want to live there, because you are a good and kind person. And countries need good and kind folk. Lucky Kansas! Lucky Kansas!"

And Scarecrow skipped along with Dorothy for a while, both of them, chanting "Lucky Kansas, Lucky Kansas" over and over, until Scarecrow tripped and stumbled and nearly fell over himself again. They were a bit breathless after that, and so they sat down to rest by a stream.

I wasn't breathless at all, so I went exploring. There was a smell about the place I recognized, the same smell as Uncle Henry's saw back in the barn at home, the same smell as his scythe and his great heavy sledgehammer. It was definitely the smell of metal. But strong though the smell was, I couldn't see anything that was made of metal anywhere. I followed the scent of it, but lost it. So in the end I got fed up looking and went to sit down with them by the stream, where I found Scarecrow telling Dorothy his story.

"Truth be told, I was only made a week or two ago," he was saying. "The Munchkin farmer who made me, painted me ears and eyes to hear and see with, a nose to smell with, and a mouth to talk with. He took great care. He said he thought I would like to see how the rest of me was made as he was making me. He's a very thoughtful and good man, as I think I've told you. And it was interesting, if a little strange, to watch the rest of me coming together, taking shape, my arms and legs and body being stitched up and stuffed, then all my clothes put on me. The part I didn't like so much was when he stuck a pole up the back of my jacket, and carried me out into the field, then hammered me in and left me, telling me to be a good scarecrow and frighten off all the crows so they didn't fly

down and eat his corn.

"I was pretty good at it too at first,
frightened them all silly I did. But then this old crow came
flying along and landed on top of my head. 'You don't fool
me,' he cawed. 'You're not a real Munchkin at all. You're
nothing but an old sack stuffed with straw, aren't you, not a
brain in your head. Couldn't hurt a fly, could you? Doesn't
matter whether you be a bird like me or a man like a
Munchkin, you've got no brains. Now if you had brains, you
could be of some use. As it is, you're just a brainless,
worthless scarecrow, no use to anyone.' And of course, that
old crow was right. Soon he was helping himself to the corn
all around my feet, and there was nothing I could do about
it. Then all the birds for miles around arrived and were
pecking away happily. I couldn't even do my job, not
without a brain, could I? The poor old Munchkin farmer
was nice enough about it. 'Not your fault,' he told me.
'Maybe I didn't make you right. Not your fault you haven't
got any brains, is it?'"

Dorothy tried to cheer him up, as best she could. "As soon as we get to the Emerald City, as soon as we see the Great and Terrible Wizard of Oz, we'll put that right," she said. "You'll see. You'll have your brains. Don't let's be downhearted. Up we get and off we go."

So on we went.

Now people folk—and scarecrows actually—don't seem to see so well in the dark as we dogs do. So it was me that found the cottage in the wood, or rather my nose did, I should say. I've got a good nose, just about the best nose there is, if I say it myself. That metal scent I'd discovered a while before, well, I picked it up again, and it led me right to the door of this cottage, which was rather strange as it was built entirely of wood, and when we went inside I saw that all the furniture inside was made of wood as well. I was really puzzled by that. But Dorothy and Scarecrow were delighted with the place. We were so tired with all that walking. All we wanted to do was sleep. It was dry and clean, and there was a soft bed of dried leaves in the corner for Dorothy and me. I curled up beside her. Scarecrow stayed standing by the window. He said he preferred to stand, he was used to it, and didn't sleep anyway.

"I don't understand what sleep is for," he said.

"You will," murmured Dorothy beside me, already half asleep, "just as soon as you have some brains. And you soon will have. Goodnight, Scarecrow."

"Goodnight, Dorothy," he replied. "Goodnight, Toto."

I woke up early. Scarecrow opened the door for me, and out I went to explore the woods. That metal smell was stronger still.

I had to find out what it was, but the scent took me round in circles and brought me right back to the cottage. Dorothy was up, searching the cottage for something to eat. The sandwiches and the fruit were all finished by now. Her basket was empty apart from Uncle Henry's hat, and the cupboards were all bare. All she could find was an oilcan on a shelf.

"We can't eat oil, can we? We shall have to find food somewhere soon, I'm so hungry," she said, going outside. "Or we'll starve. Come on, we're bound to find some fruit or some nuts. There are trees everywhere here." So we walked off into the woods looking for fruit or nuts, anything we could find. But there was nothing. "These are just forest trees," Dorothy said. "Not fruit trees or nut trees. What are we going to do?"

I thought, when I first heard it, that it was Dorothy groaning with hunger, but it wasn't. She was looking at me, and so was Scarecrow.

"Did you groan, Toto?" she said. The groaning was louder now, and closer. It wasn't her doing it, not Scarecrow, not me. And then through the trees, I saw something ahead of us in a clearing, a-glinting it was, and a-shining. It was something metal! I know metal when I smell it. My trusty nose! It never lets me down! I was off, following my nose.

Dorothy and Scarecrow were coming along some way behind, so I got there first.

In the clearing stood a man made entirely of tin, an axe raised above his head, and about to chop down a tree. It was half chopped down already. He stood as still as a statue. But then the tin woodman groaned. I ran up to him. He smelled like Uncle Henry's saw, like his scythe, like his hammer, yes, and like his axe too. I bit the man's leg then, just to let him know that he wasn't to harm Dorothy. It hurt my teeth, so I didn't do it again. I barked instead, loudly, sharply, pointed my tail, bared my teeth, made my hackles rise like a bottle brush all along my back, just so he got the message.

"Oh, hello, little dog," said the man of tin, and I backed away, frightened. Though I suppose I should have been used to strange talking creatures by then.

Dorothy was so brave though. She walked right up to him: "Was it you groaning?"

"I've been standing here like this, groaning for a year

or more," he replied, "and no one has ever heard me before. I am so glad you came." His voice echoed and boomed inside him as he spoke.

"Are you stuck or something?" Dorothy asked. "Why is everyone around here so stuck? Can we help you?"

"That is kind of you," he replied. "I need to be oiled. My can of oil, it's in my cabin. I should be so obliged if you would fetch it for me."

"I saw it, I know where it is," said Dorothy. "I'll fetch it. Don't go away." And off she ran back through the wood.

"I may be brainless," said Scarecrow, "but I don't think you could go away, Mr Tin Man, even if you wanted to, could you?"

"Quite right," said the tin man.

While we waited for Dorothy, Scarecrow and the tin man chatted away as if they had been friends for a long time, comparing notes as to whether it was better to be made of tin or straw.

"Well, at least you can't rust up like me," said the tin man. "I don't like rain."

"Well, at least you can't catch fire like me," said Scarecrow. "I don't like fire."

Dorothy was soon back, and she got going at once, oiling the tin man's neck so he could begin to move his head, turn it this way and that, shake it, nod it. Scarecrow took hold of his head and helped to loosen it gently. Then Dorothy oiled his arms and his legs, and his hips as well. Soon he could move his knees and his elbows quite freely, and could lower the axe, wiggle and wriggle and jiggle just about everything he needed to. He danced up and down in sheer delight. "You have saved my life, my dear friends," he said. "But what are you doing here in the forest? How did you find me? My name is Tin Woodman. I live in that cottage. But who are you?" So they all shook hands there in the forest, and introduced themselves. I have to say, I felt rather left out at that moment. So I reminded Dorothy I was there, loudly.

"Toto was the one who found you, Tin Woodman," said Dorothy. "I'm sorry he bit you, but he gets rather excited sometimes, I'm afraid." And then she told him the whole story of how we were there in the Land of Oz, and how we were on our way to see the Great and Terrible Wizard, who knows everything, and can do everything, and who could help us get home to Kansas. "Home is home," said Dorothy, "and home is best."

"You're so dog-gone right," I woofed.

"What *I* need is not a home but a heart," sighed Tin Woodman. "If only I could come with you, I could ask him, couldn't I? He could give me a heart. He's a kindly sort of wizard, isn't he?"

"I hope so," said Scarecrow, "or I'll never have any brains."

"Of course you can come along," said Dorothy. "The more the

merrier—as Aunt Em always says when she's collecting the eggs. As for the Great Wizard of Oz, let us hope he is kind, but I have heard he is also terrible."

"Oh, I don't care. This is the very best day of my life!" cried Tin Woodman happily, and off he clanked through the trees, dancing a little jig as he went. "I can walk, look at me! I can dance, look at me! And I have new friends, and I'm going to have a heart. With a bit of luck." He stopped and turned around. "Don't forget the oilcan, Dorothy. If I get caught in the rain, I'll rust up and go all stiff again, and I don't want that."

So Dorothy put the oilcan in her basket, and off we went after Tin Woodman until we came out of the wood at last and found the yellow brick road again, me trotting along in front, tail waving, nose to the ground sniffing out whatever smelled interesting. And in this place every smell was more than interesting. But nothing here smelled quite like Kansas. Even the rats and mice smelled different, even more whiffy. To chase they were just the same. I've never caught any, not one in all my life, but they're such fun to chase.

I stayed quite close to Dorothy and Scarecrow. I didn't want to get too close to the Tin Woodman. He was clanking along quite clumsily, still not used to walking, I could tell that.

He was all arms and legs, walking a bit like a puppet on a string. I didn't want to get under his feet. But it turned out to be very lucky that he was with us, because it wasn't very long before the yellow brick road had narrowed and the trees had grown so thick on either side that the branches blocked the way. Dorothy and I sat down, not knowing quite what to do.

But Tin Woodman chopped a way through for us, singing as he did so in time with his chopping. He was never jollier, I discovered, than when he was chopping.

I'm telling you, my little puppies, Tin Woodman could chop even better than Uncle Henry, and Uncle Henry is pretty darned handy with that axe of his. I mean, the yellow brick road had been grown right over by the forest on either side. We would never have got through without the tin woodman and his axe, so we were mighty pleased to have him along.

Once a way through was cleared, Dorothy clapped her hands, and we all got ready to be on our way again. "Up we get and off we go!" she said. "Down the yellow brick road!"

CHAPTER FIVE

———— ◆ ————

How a Jolly Woodman Became a Tin Woodman

A little while later, we were all walking along together, Tin Woodman, Scarecrow, Dorothy and me, when Dorothy asked one of her questions. She loved asking lots of questions back home, and she was no different now. When I come to think about it, I guess I use my nose, and Dorothy asks questions. I suppose that's just how we each of us find out about the world around us. "We know how and why Scarecrow came to be made of straw," she began.

"But how come you're made of tin, if you don't mind my asking?"

"Not at all," replied Tin Woodman. "I wasn't like this always you know. I was a regular sort of a woodman, like my pa, a forester. We lived in that cottage in the woods, Pa, Ma and me. Life was hard, but life was good. We kept ourselves warm through the long winters, always had just about enough to eat. That forest provided all we needed. Then one sad day a tree fell on Pa, as he was cutting it down, and he died. I looked after Ma after that, until she died too a few years later, and then I was all alone. You know something, you never know what lonely is until you are really alone, alone all day, alone all night, with no one to talk to. I talked to myself a little, sang when I worked, just to keep myself from getting too sad. But I was sad.

"Then one day I got lucky. I was taking my wood to the charcoal burner in the forest, when I met his daughter, Angelina, who had just begun to work with him, and she smiled at me and I smiled at her. That's how these things often get started. Well, soon enough the two of us had decided we wanted to marry and be together. Her father was fine about it, but her mother disapproved of me, said her daughter deserved better than me, a man from the town with some money and good prospects, not a poor woodman who lived in the forest and chopped wood all day.

"Well, we told her we were going to get married whether she liked it or not. Do you know what that mother of hers did? She went to the Wicked Witch of the East and made a deal. She told the Wicked Witch she would give her two sheep and a cow if she would somehow stop the two of us getting married. And the Wicked Witch of the East—who was, if you didn't know it, just about the wickedest witch there ever has been in all the world—she put a spell on my axe, without me knowing, of course.

"I thought I was just being clumsy when the accidents began to happen. I was out in the forest one day, chopping wood as usual, when the axe slipped out of my hand and cut off my left leg. Well, what was I to do? If I was going to marry Angelina, I needed to set myself up, and build a house for us. I needed to keep working. So I went to the tin-smith in town, and got him to make me another leg. It was a perfect fit, almost as good as the one I had had before. I could work again. But the next time I went out chopping, my axe slipped again, and I chopped off the other leg.

"Well, I wasn't going to give up, was I? I got the tin-smith to make me another new leg. Back to work I went. But that axe of mine seemed to have a mind of its own, and I had accident after accident. I lost one arm, then the other, and then I lost my head too, cut it right off. But every time the tin-smith mended me, new tin arms to go with the legs, a new tin head, I thought nothing could go wrong now. But then that cursed axe slipped again, and cut me in two, cut the heart right out of me. The tin-smith saved me yet again, gave me all the joints I needed, so I could move around, move everything just as well as before—well, almost. It's amazing what people can do these days. 'Just keep them well oiled,' he said, 'and you'll be fine.' But the tin-smith also told me he couldn't make a heart of tin, that my body would always be hollow. I would be empty inside—there was nothing he could do about that.

"Angelina still loved me well enough, even though I was all made of tin now, but when I told her I had no heart inside me, that was more than she could bear, and her love for me died. Maybe I should never have told her, but I reckon you have to be honest and true with those you love. There was many a day afterwards when I wished I had never told her. After we parted, I didn't just feel empty inside, my whole life seemed empty."

I was thinking then about what it would be like to lose Dorothy. Just the thought of it made me feel awfully sad and empty inside.

"I never thought I would," went on Tin Woodman, "but in time I got over it, and became quite happy with my new clanky tin body. It shone in the sun and everyone noticed me in town. Everyone heard me coming, and I liked clanking about. When I danced it made everyone laugh. That's what got rid of my sadness: laughter, other folk's laughter. I learned to laugh again. Now I was Jolly Woodman once more to my friends—and with a difference: I was Jolly Tin Woodman. I liked being different. I was proud of being different. And, what's more, I sang better now that I was tin, my voice booming louder. I liked to hear it echoing out through the forest as I worked. It didn't matter if my axe slipped any more. It couldn't hurt me now. It just clanked and bounced off.

"There was only one problem, I discovered. My joints. If ever I got wet, they would stiffen up and rust. So I knew I had to keep an oilcan handy all the time, which I did. But then one day I forgot it, left it in the cottage by mistake one morning when I went out to work, and I was caught out in a sudden thunderstorm. I don't like to be out there in the open when there's lightning around. Lightning likes tin, did you know that? I don't know what it is, but if there's lightning around, it seems to want to seek me out.

And if it strikes me, and it has too, well, it hurts—my, how it hurts. It burns me, scorches me.

"I wanted to run home, to get my oilcan, but I didn't dare. I stayed under the trees and just got wet, dripping wet.

"And the storm raged on and on, rained cats and dogs. Anyway, it wasn't long before my joints stiffened up, and then they rusted, neck first, shoulders, hips, knees, ankles, and soon I couldn't move at all. So that's how come you found me a year and more later, stiff as a poker, and all rusted up. But standing there for so long gave me time to think. You have to keep hoping, I told myself, hoping and dreaming. It was my dream and my hope to have a heart again one day, and then you came along, my dear new friends, and now I'm off to see the Great Wizard of Oz to ask him for a new heart. Won't a new heart be wonderful?"

"Not as wonderful as brains," Scarecrow told him. "Brains are more useful than a heart, for a fool like me would not even know what to do with his heart. Give me brains any time."

"But I promise you, Scarecrow," said Tin Woodman, "brains cannot make you happy, not without a heart. And happiness is the most wonderful, most important thing in the whole wide world."

But I was thinking not of hearts or of brains but of sausages. Happiness for me was sausages.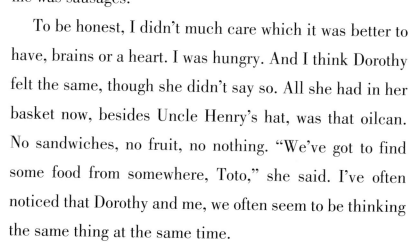

To be honest, I didn't much care which it was better to have, brains or a heart. I was hungry. And I think Dorothy felt the same, though she didn't say so. All she had in her basket now, besides Uncle Henry's hat, was that oilcan. No sandwiches, no fruit, no nothing. "We've got to find some food from somewhere, Toto," she said. I've often noticed that Dorothy and me, we often seem to be thinking the same thing at the same time.

I think it's because we know each other so well, and that's because we love each other so much.

CHAPTER SIX

───◆───

Be Afraid, Be Terribly Afraid

*N*ow, *my little puppies, I'm afraid this part of the story can get a tad frightening. But don't you worry about it none. After all, it can't be so bad if Papa Toto is here to tell the tale, can it? And here I am, right here. Tiny Toto, you come and snuggle up a little closer, there's a good boy. On we go then.*

The further we walked, the darker the world about us seemed to become. Very little sunlight found its way through because the trees grew so tall and thick on either side of the yellow brick road. Well, you couldn't hardly call it yellow any more. The road, what little you could see of it, was covered in leaves and branches and twigs. If there were any birds around, they had stopped singing. The quietness of the forest was eerie, and I was glad to hear Tin Woodman's clanking steps, and his cheery singing and humming. He kept my spirits up, but I needed more than a song to keep me going. I kept looking up at Dorothy with my eyes, telling her what I was after. "Food, I need food," I was trying to say. "Anything will do, anything. How about one of these?" I picked up a nut from the road to show her.

"Hazelnuts!" she cried, bending down to gather all she could. Tin Woodman and Scarecrow helped her, and soon there was a whole pile of them. "We have to crack them open," said Dorothy. "Tin Woodman, would you be very kind, and stamp on these for us? Toto and me, we are so hungry."

"Easily done," he replied, and with one stamp he cracked them all. So Dorothy and I feasted ourselves on all the nuts we could eat. It wasn't much, but it was a lot better than nothing. Neither Tin Woodman nor Scarecrow wanted any of them—eating just didn't seem to interest them. So the nuts were all for us. Dorothy filled her basket with all the hazelnuts and chestnuts and walnuts she could find, and on we went, much happier now, both of us. I was trotting on, and she was skipping along, and singing too. Tin Woodman and Scarecrow joined in after a while. Strange sound they made together, but they seemed to like it. Life was good again, despite the shadowy gloom and the drizzly mist all about us. But soon enough the singing stopped, the skipping and trotting slowed to a walk, then a weary plodding.

"My feet ache. My legs ache," Dorothy said. "I don't like to complain—Aunt Em said I shouldn't—but how far is it to the Emerald City, do you know, Tin Woodman?"

"I have no idea," he said, stomping on, and clanking

loudly as he went. "My pa went there once. I don't like to frighten you, but I remember he did say this was dangerous country to travel through, so it's a good thing there are four of us. We can all look after each other, can't we? I'm not afraid, so long as you look after that oilcan, Dorothy. Scarecrow doesn't have a brain, so he can't be scared. You have to have a brain to be scared."

"Fire," said Scarecrow. "I don't like fire at all. I'm not scared of it, I just don't like it. And Dorothy told me she was once kissed by the Good Witch of the North, so no one can harm her. So she's got nothing to be scared of. That only leaves Toto. Do you think Toto is frightened?"

I growled at that, just to show everyone I was scared of nothing and no one, which wasn't true of course, but none of them were to know that, except Dorothy, who knew everything about me.

"Toto may be small, but he's very brave..." said Dorothy, "...well, mostly. We can all look after Toto, can't we? That's what friends are for, isn't it? Nothing and no one will ever hurt you, Toto. Promise."

It was just as Dorothy said these last words that we heard a terrible roaring from the forest, and before we had time even to run, a huge lion leapt out of the trees right in front of us. "Be afraid," he roared, "be terribly afraid."

In a trice, the lion lashed out with his paw and Scarecrow was sent flying. And then he did the same thing to Tin Woodman, sending him sprawling on the road with much clattering and crashing. Then the lion turned on Dorothy, and roared mightily. Until now, I had just stood there too shocked to move, but I didn't at all like the way he was looking at Dorothy, so I went for him, charged at him, making like I was a wolf, barking wildly, tail pointing, back bristling like a bottle brush. No one threatens my Dorothy. I'd show him!

That was when the lion rounded on me, and opened his great mouth and roared at me with all his sharp white

teeth, with all his horrible bad breath. Any moment I knew I'd be a dead dog. But then Dorothy rushed forward and gave him a big push and slapped him on his paw.

"Naughty, naughty lion," she was shouting. "Don't you dare bite my dear little Toto. How could you? You should be ashamed of yourself, a great big lion like you attacking a sweet little dog. You nasty, nasty lion. Put your claws away this minute." I don't think I had ever seen Dorothy so furious. To my amazement, the lion did not attack her or me, but shrank back, whining pitifully and rubbing his nose with the side of his paw.

"You didn't have to push me," the lion cried—and he was crying, really crying. "I wasn't going to bite him."

"But you were trying to, weren't you?" Dorothy said. "You're a bad, bad lion. Look how small little Toto is, and how big and strong you are. You're just a big horrible bully, and a coward too, what's more. And what did Scarecrow ever do to you, or Tin Woodman? Why did you need to knock them about like that? How could they hurt you? One is made of nothing but straw, the other of nothing but tin. And they're nice, kind folk, too, and they're my friends. You're a cowardy, cowardy custard, that's what you are."

I was still barking at him for all I was worth, so that the lion should know I was agreeing with everything Dorothy was telling him. The lion sat back and put his paws over his ears. "Don't be so angry with me," he said. "You frighten me so."

"How can you be frightened of little Toto?" Dorothy asked him. "I mean, look at him. He's so small and sweet. And you're a ginormous, humongous lion! You're supposed to be the king of beasts! And you really are a coward, aren't you?"

"I think I must the be the most cowardly lion that ever lived," the lion said sadly. "I can roar. I can bare my teeth, but at heart I'm just a softie.

Even when I'm out hunting, a deer only has to stamp her foot at me and I run. That's why I go hungry a lot. I have always been like this, and it makes me so sad, so unhappy. I know a lion is supposed to be brave. My mother and my father brought me up to be like that, but I'm not. I think I was born like this, with no courage inside me. You mustn't ever tell anyone, but I am useless as a lion, not one ounce of courage in my whole miserable body." And then the lion was weeping so piteously that I stopped barking and Dorothy went to put an arm round him to comfort him.

"Have you got any brains, Lion?" Scarecrow asked him.

"I think so," the lion replied. "Why do you ask?"

"Because I have no brains at all," Scarecrow said. "My head has no room for a brain, it is stuffed with straw. I'm going to the Great and Terrible Wizard of Oz in the Emerald City to ask him to give me some brains, so I can think."

"And I am going to ask him for a heart," said the Tin Woodman, "so I can feel again, like I used to before I was just tin."

"And I'm going to ask him if he can tell Toto and me how to get back home to Kansas," said Dorothy. "Home is home, and home is best."

"You're so dog-gone right," I woofed.

"So, might I ask him for some courage, do you think?" asked Lion. "Would he do that for me? Then I could be a real lion."

"Why not?" said Dorothy. "Come along with us, Lion. Just so long as you don't eat us, we'd be more than glad to have you, wouldn't we? You can help Toto frighten away anyone who tries to hurt us on the way. Would you do that for us?"

"Of course," said Lion, wiping away the last of his tears. "I shall pretend to be the bravest lion there ever was. Like this." And with that he roared so loudly, and bared his teeth so horribly, that we forgot for several moments that he was just pretending.

So now there were five of us, Dorothy, Scarecrow, Tin Woodman, Lion and me, off to see the Great and Terrible Wizard of Oz. They all seemed to think he was a wonderful and wise wizard, Dorothy too, but I wasn't so sure. He sounded a bit scary to me. I mean, he wasn't called 'terrible' for nothing, was he?

And talking of scary, Lion loped along beside us, not scary any more at all, but as friendly as you like. I liked him. I so wanted to be big and strong like him, with a roar that terrified the world. And he liked me too. "Toto, my friend," he said as we walked along, "you may be small, with little legs and little teeth, but you stood up to me to protect Dorothy. You have the courage of a lion already, a real lion."

But if I'm honest, from time to time when he looked down at me, licking his whiskery lips and showing me his great teeth, I couldn't make up my mind whether he was smiling at me or thinking of me as his next meal. Lion may not have been brave, but he was smart. He seemed to know what I was thinking. "I'd never eat you, little Toto," he said, "nor Dorothy, nor Tin Woodman, nor Scarecrow, because you are my friends. I like you too much. And besides, I have decided none of you would taste very nice. I'm most particular about what I eat, I can tell you." I was much relieved and very pleased indeed to hear it.

Friendly though I was now with Lion, I liked above all to be alone with Dorothy. She would tell me all her hopes and fears, and I would listen, or at least pretend to. Often we would find ourselves walking ahead together, Lion and Scarecrow and Tin Woodman far behind us.

"I like our new friends, Toto," she told me once, "but every night I dream of Kansas and home and Aunt Em and Uncle Henry. Do you think they are all right? Won't it be nice to go home? I'm not complaining, mind you. I have lovely new red shoes, three new friends, and you, Toto. I have you, my best friend in all the world." She looked over her shoulder, and went on in a whisper. "They are strange companions, Toto, aren't they? I mean, did you see how upset Tin Woodman was when he stepped on that beetle and squashed it by mistake? Cried his eyes out, didn't he? He had tears running down his face. Did you see? I had to wipe them away, and then oil his jaw so it didn't rust up again. He was so sad. Well, you can't be sad if you haven't got a heart, can you?"

I told her with my eyes that I agreed, that I didn't know what they were all fussing about so much. It seemed to me too that Scarecrow wasn't brainless at all, he just thought he was. And I wouldn't have minded betting

either that deep down Lion was as brave as any other lion in the world.

I told her something else with my eyes too, and my tail. "I'm so hungry," I told her. "I could do with a sausage or two!"

"Me too," she said.

CHAPTER SEVEN

Lost in the Forest of the Cruel Kalidahs

Well, I can tell you this for sure, little puppies, everyone was mighty glad to have Lion with us after that, because every mile we walked on down the yellow brick road, the forest around us grew thicker and darker and scarier. Lion would let out a dreadful roar from time to time just to warn off anyone or anything that might be lurking in the forest that night, which might spring out suddenly and attack us. We'd left the Munchkins and their lovely countryside well behind us by now. There were no kind Munchkins to take us in and give us shelter and food, so that night for the first time we had to camp out. Tin Woodman chopped up enough wood to make a blazing fire, so at least we were warm, and Lion insisted a good fire would keep all the wild animals away, but that we had to keep it going, and keep the flames crackling. "Even the cruel Kalidahs don't like fire," he said.

"What are Kalidahs?" Dorothy asked.

"You don't need to know," Lion replied in a whisper, looking around him nervously. "And I don't want to talk about them. They frighten me silly." He lifted his head and sniffed the air. "I am rather hungry. I smell deer. I think I shall go and catch my dinner."

"Oh, please don't kill a deer," cried Tin Woodman, "I couldn't bear it. I shall cry if you do, then my jaw will rust again."

Lion said no more about it, but kept licking his lips at the thought of a meal, which only reminded me of how hungry I was. "If we go to sleep, Toto," Dorothy said, as we lay down together near the warmth of the fire, "then we won't feel hungry any more." That sounded like sense, but I knew it wasn't true. Once I am hungry, I am hungry even in my dreams. I have had more sausage dreams than hot dinners—if you see what I am saying.

Scarecrow was so kind to us. Even though he didn't like coming anywhere near the fire, he brought armfuls of dry leaves to cover Dorothy and me as we lay there.

"Sleep tight," he said, and then went to stand guard with Tin Woodman at a safe distance from the fire. Lion snored us to sleep, and by the time we woke the next morning Scarecrow and Tin Woodman had collected a pile of nuts for our breakfast, and cracked them open too. I had never much liked nuts until now, but perhaps I had never been so hungry as I was that morning. Dorothy and I wolfed some down—so to speak—while Tin Woodman and Scarecrow filled the basket with more nuts.

Dorothy oiled Tin Woodman's joints to make him feel

looser after all the damp dew of the morning, and off we went on our way.

It wasn't long before we came to a great chasm that cut right across the road. The forest was impenetrable on both sides—impenetrable, in case you don't know, means the forest was so thick you couldn't find a way through it. Sometimes, little puppies, long words are best, and it makes me feel good to use them. Anyway, all you need to know is that there was no way for us to go. We stood on the edge of the great wide chasm and looked down, which made me feel a bit sick. It was too steep to climb down on our side, and too steep to climb up on the other side.

"Now what?" asked Tin Woodman.

We all thought about it for a long time. It seemed hopeless.

"Well, I think," Scarecrow began slowly, "I think this. We can't fly over, can we? So logically, either we will have to stop and stay where we are, or we'll just have to jump it. Nothing else to do."

"How clever you are to think of that," said Dorothy. And Scarecrow looked suddenly so pleased with himself, and so happy.

Lion said then: "I'm a pretty good jumper, though I say it myself. I could jump this chasm—I think."

"And when you jump, Lion, do you think you could carry us over on your back, one by one?" asked Scarecrow.

"I could try," Lion replied, trying his very best to sound brave. "But you'll all have to hold on very tight to my mane," he went on. "You first perhaps, Scarecrow. You're made of straw, aren't you? So you must be the lightest. If I can't jump across with you on my back then I can hardly do it with anyone heavier, can I? Up you get,

Scarecrow. Let's get going before I can change my mind. You ready? Hang on!"

Then to everyone's amazement, mine too, Lion didn't do a running jump. He just loped up to the edge of the chasm, stopped for a moment or two, and then, as if he had springs in his legs, just took a great leap and landed easily on the other side.

"How did you do that?" Scarecrow gasped.

"Springing is what lions do," Lion said, and as if to prove it, he sprang back over at once to fetch Tin Woodman, who climbed on his back and clung so tight that Lion had to ask him to loosen his grip because he couldn't breathe. When they landed on the other side, Tin Woodman fell off with quite a clang and a crash. But he was soon up on his feet and waving across at us quite happily. All was well. Then it was our turn. Somehow Dorothy managed to hold me tight and hang on to Lion's mane at the same time.

For a moment, as Lion leapt over the gaping chasm below us, it seemed as if we were really flying! By the time we landed I had my eyes closed. We were all safely across!

Dorothy said what we were all thinking. "How brave you were to do that, Lion!" And Lion looked suddenly so pleased with himself, and so happy.

But our troubles were not over. On the other side of the chasm, the forest was even darker still. Even though it was still morning, the sky was almost as black as night. The yellow brick road led on ahead of us, our only comfort in the gloom around us. Lion lifted his head to sniff the air. So I did too. I didn't like what I smelled, didn't like it at all, but I didn't know what it was. "I smell Kalidahs," whispered Lion. "They are near, and they are many. Walk softly, as softly as you can." Tin Woodman did his best, walking on tiptoe. He clanked softer now, but he still clanked. He couldn't help himself.

"What are they like, these cruel Kalidahs?" Dorothy asked.

"I don't think you want to know," whispered Lion, looking about him anxiously.

"I do," said Dorothy.

"Well then," Lion said, "since you ask. They have heads like tigers, bodies like bears, and claws as sharp as… I don't want to think about their claws. Believe me, you never want to meet a Kalidah. If they hear us, we are done for. We must all be as quiet as mice."

"I'm doing my best," said Tin Woodman. "But it's not easy being tin, you know." Then quite unexpectedly, and most unfortunately, the yellow brick road seemed simply to stop. It began again further on, but on the far side of a deep black hole in the road.

"Oh no!" cried Dorothy. "It's another chasm, like the last one, only wider and deeper. We'll never be able to jump this one."

Lion agreed. He stood there on the edge of the black hole, shaking his head. "I'd have to be a kangaroo to jump this," he said, "and I'm not."

Scarecrow was standing beside Lion, scratching his head, which he always seemed to do when he was thinking. "Tell you what. I have an idea," he said. "You see that big tree over there? Now if Tin Woodman could cut it down for us so that it fell right across, then we could walk over, couldn't we? Simple." We all looked at Scarecrow in utter disbelief.

"What a great idea!" Dorothy said.

"Not a great idea," Scarecrow told her, "just a simple one. I haven't any brains, but I do have simple ideas from time to time."

"I don't think you're simple at all," said Dorothy.

"Hurry," said Lion, lifting his nose and sniffing the air again. "The Kalidahs are close." I lifted my nose too.

Rotten eggs! If these Kalidahs smelled like rotten eggs, then they were very close indeed.

So Tin Woodman got to work right away chopping down the tree, and soon it was toppling across the ravine, falling with a huge crash, and making just the bridge we needed. One by one, we ran across, trying very hard not to look down. I was almost across with Dorothy and Scarecrow, but Tin Woodman and Lion were behind us and only halfway across when we all heard a terrible snarling and growling. Out of the trees they came, charging toward the bridge, toward us, two ferocious-looking Kalidahs. Monstrous they were, half tiger, half bear.

"Get across," cried Lion, turning to face them and roaring his defiance. "I shall stay here and fight them off. Go. Go. I won't let them pass. Don't worry. Go!" So we did as he said and ran for it until we were all safely across. When we looked, we saw Lion was still there on the tree trunk over the black hole, roaring his worst, flashing his claws, shaking his mane, baring his teeth. But I could see, we all could, that the Kalidahs were coming closer all the time, about to pounce on him. There were two of them, and one of him, and they were each twice his size, with claws as big and sharp as Uncle Henry's scythes back home in Kansas.

Suddenly Tin Woodman had his axe in his hand, and was chopping away at the branches of the tree on our side of

the black hole. "Lion!" cried Tin Woodman as he chopped. "Listen to me, Lion. I shall chop six more times, and then the tree will fall down into the ravine. On the fifth chop, turn and run back to us as fast as you can. You hear me?"

"I hear you," cried Lion. "I am not that good at counting, but I will do my best! Keep chopping." One chop, two, three, and everyone was counting out loud now to help Lion, me too. The Kalidahs were almost on him, and he was still roaring at them.

Four.

Five...

"Run, Lion! Run!" we all shouted. Lion turned and raced back along the bridge.

Six!

The tree was shaking, slipping, falling. At the very last moment Lion leaped to safety.

Down into the rocky depths of the black hole went the tree, and those dreadful Kalidahs with it.

Lion took a deep breath. "My poor heart is pounding with fear. I thought we were done for, but it seems we shall all live a little longer after all."

"I rather like that idea," said Scarecrow. "To live a little longer, I mean. With or without brains, I don't think I should like not to be alive." And Dorothy clapped her hands and told them all how wonderfully smart and brave they had all been, and I barked and barked until my head ached with it, telling them exactly the same thing.

It's a funny thing, but I reckon that fight with those horrible Kalidah creatures turned out to be just about the best thing that could have happened to us. After that, we all felt like one big family. True, a strange sort of family. Every one of us was mighty different from the other, about as different as we could be, but we all knew that if we stuck together everything would turn out just fine. Together we had beaten the Kalidahs, together we would reach the Emerald City, whatever dangers we might have to face on the way. We would face them together.

Lion and I padded along together ahead of the others, the best of friends, on the lookout for trouble, and behind us came the rest, arm in arm, sometimes singing as they went, Tin Woodman's great feet clanking on the yellow brick road. There never was a happier band, except for two things—I was getting mighty fed up by this time with eating nothing but nuts, and Dorothy's singing wasn't getting any better either.

CHAPTER EIGHT

———•◆•———

One Bad Situation After Another

We all thought nothing could ever be more dangerous than the cruel Kalidahs. But none of us had reckoned with poppies. Yes, poppies, little puppies, I am not kidding you. And first we had to cross a raging river and rescue poor Scarecrow, which wasn't easy either. But I'm getting ahead of myself, aren't I? Mustn't do that. Now where was I? Oh yes.

Things were looking pretty good. We followed the

yellow brick road for quite a while, and it led us gradually, gradually, out of the dark of the forest and into bright sunlight and grassy flowery meadows with singing birds and fruit trees humming with bees. There was lots of fruit to eat now, plums, pears, peaches, all we wanted—all Dorothy wanted anyway, she's crazy about fruit. It was better than nuts, made a change at least, but Lion and me, we had hunting on our minds. There were rabbits everywhere now, and deer flitting through the trees. Dorothy didn't like me catching rabbits, and Tin Woodman and Scarecrow would have been very sad if Lion had brought back a deer to eat. Both of us knew that, so both of us ate fruit and had to be happy with it, but whenever I lay down to sleep I dreamed of rabbits—rabbits for me were almost as good as sausages. And Lion dreamed of deer—he told me so.

For days and days we walked on down the yellow brick road, until one morning we came to a rushing river, with no bridge across it, not that we could see anyway.

We just had to get over it somehow. There on the other side the yellow brick road began again, the road that would take us to the Emerald City and the Great Wizard of Oz. "How are we ever going to cross this?" Dorothy said, shaking her head. "Toto can swim, but I can't."

Scarecrow scratched his head for a moment or two, and we knew then that he was going to come up with one of his brilliant ideas. "Simple," he said, "a no-brainer. A raft. Tin Woodman cuts down a tree or two, and we build a raft."

So that's what we all did, and that was how we came to find ourselves a while later floating across the river, Tin Woodman and Scarecrow each with a long pole, pushing us, guiding us toward the far bank. But we soon realized we were in trouble. We weren't floating across the river—we were being carried down it. Scarecrow and Tin Woodman were doing their best with their poles, pushing with all their might, but it was no use. The current was sweeping us downstream, and the river was running faster and faster all the time, swirling us around and around.

"Oh no," cried Tin Woodman, "we shall end up in the river, or worse still in the land of the Wicked Witch of the West, and she's just like the Wicked Witch of the East was before you squashed her, Dorothy. She makes bad magic. There never was a wickeder witch. She'll make us her slaves. Then we'll never get to see the Great Wizard of Oz, and I'll never have a new heart."

"And I will never have the courage I should have," said Lion.

"And I will never have any brains," said Scarecrow. "We have to push harder, Tin Woodman, as hard as we can!" And with that Scarecrow plunged his pole deep into the river, down into the mud, and pushed with all his might. But there it stuck fast. Scarecrow should have let go of his pole, but he didn't, he wouldn't. So he found himself clinging on to the pole in the middle of the swirling river, watching us drift further and further away from him on the raft.

"We have to save him!" Dorothy cried.

"First we have to save ourselves," said Lion. "I shall swim for the bank. Tin Woodman, you hang on to the tip of my tail. I will dive in and pull the raft across. Whatever you do, don't let go of my tail."

So Tin Woodman grabbed his tail. And in Lion jumped. I could see at once he needed some help. I barked at Dorothy and she understood right away.

If Lion can swim in that swirling river, I thought, *then so can I.*

Dorothy knelt down on the edge of the raft, grabbed my tail, and in I jumped after Lion. Soon I was paddling for the shore like crazy alongside him. I was getting pretty puffed out, I can tell you, but somehow we made it across the river in the end, towing that raft, with Dorothy and Tin Woodman on board, all the way. Our troubles were by no means over though. We may have reached the other side, but we had drifted a long way downstream by now. There was no sign of poor Scarecrow clinging to his pole in the middle of the river, no sign either of the yellow brick road. It was not a good situation.

"We have to find Scarecrow and rescue him!" cried Dorothy. "We can't go on without Scarecrow, we just can't."

"Well, there's only one thing to be done," said Lion, who was shaking himself dry in the sun, showering us all, and somehow making at the same time a great rainbow around his mane and head, like a rainbow crown. "If we walk back along the river," he went on, "we should soon find him, and the yellow brick road as well."

I shook myself dry, hoping to make a rainbow too, but I didn't because I didn't have a mane. I so wanted to be like Lion, be brave like him, roar like him, have teeth as big as him, make rainbows like him. When he bounded off along the riverbank, I followed him. We all did, all of us worrying we might be too late, that Scarecrow might already have been swept away.

As we came round a bend in the river, I saw him first.

"Help!" Scarecrow was crying. "Help me, please. I can't hold on much longer."

He was slipping down the pole, his feet already almost in the water. All of us looked at one another. There was nothing we could do to save him. He was too far away, the river was running too fast, we were too late.

Just then, the most wonderful thing happened. Floating down on his great wide, white wings, there came a stork. He landed right beside us on the riverbank. "You all seem rather upset," he said. "Is there anything I can do?"

"Our dear friend Scarecrow," Dorothy explained. "He's stuck out there in the river on that pole, and we can't help him."

"Scarecrow, you say?" the stork said. "We birds don't usually like scarecrows. But he looks like a nice sort of a scarecrow, so I'll rescue him for you if that is what you'd like. He's only made of straw. He shouldn't be too heavy.

Come on, wings! Do your thing. Off I go, up, up, up, and away!"

The stork lifted off and with a few strong beats of his wings he was hovering out over the pole in the middle of the river.

He grasped Scarecrow by his arm, then carried him back, setting him down gently in amongst us.

I never in my life saw so much hugging. Tin Woodman cried and Dorothy had to dry his tears quickly, oiling him again, before his jaw went stiff on him. I leaped up into Dorothy's arms and joined in all the hugging, only I do licking a lot better than hugging.

Lion was up on his hind legs, his huge paws on Tin Woodman's shoulders, smiling toothily, very toothily.

Luckily he had his claws hidden away or else he would have scratched Tin Woodman all over.

The stork hopped up and down, cackling all the while. "I like to make people happy," he cried. "But I must go now. There are babies waiting for me in my nest. So long, you guys. Be happy."

"We are, we will be," cried Dorothy. "Thank you ever, ever, ever so much."

Off he flew, and Dorothy clapped her hands. "Let's not waste time!" she cried. "Up we get, and off we go!"

I woofed, and the others laughed. They loved me woofing.

On we went along the river, Scarecrow arm in arm with Tin Woodman and Dorothy, all of us smiling, all of us searching for the yellow brick road. This was the most beautiful countryside we had been through, brilliantly colored flowers and butterflies and birds wherever we looked. We were all so happy, happy to be together again, and on the right side of the river.

So when we saw the field of red poppies on the hillside ahead of us, and beyond it the yellow brick road, we cheered and barked and roared and clapped and clanked, all of it with joy. Never had we seen a prettier sight! All we had to do was cross that poppy field, and we'd be on our way again to the Emerald City and to the Great and Terrible Wizard of Oz.

The poppies were head high for me as we walked up over the hillside. Dorothy kept rubbing her eyes and yawning as she went (which I thought was rather odd). She was obviously quite sleepy, and then suddenly I was too. And Lion was as well (which I also thought was rather odd).

He was yawning—I never saw so many teeth in all my life! But I was too tired to care. When Dorothy lay down to sleep, I lay down beside her.

Tin Woodman kept trying to shake us, to wake us up, to help us back on to our feet. "You mustn't go to sleep. You mustn't. It's the poppies making you sleep. You go to sleep now, you'll never wake up! Up, on your feet! We have to walk on!" he was shouting at us, shaking us.

But my eyes felt heavy. I could hardly keep them open. Everything began to go dark.

"I like poppies," I heard Lion murmuring. He was lying down right beside me, but his voice seemed far, far away, as if in some dream. "Toto and Dorothy are falling asleep, so I will too. I'll have a nice long sleep. I think I could sleep forever."

"Up, up, Lion!" cried Scarecrow. "On your feet!" And he was pushing at Lion with all his might, shaking him and shaking him. Tin Woodman was helping him too. "It's the poppies, they're making you sleepy. We have to get out of this poppy field before it's too late. Tin Woodman and me, we can carry Dorothy and Toto. But we cannot carry you, Lion. You are too heavy for us."

"Don't you feel sleepy too?" murmured Lion.

"The scent of the poppies cannot affect us," said Tin Woodman. "There are some advantages to being made of straw and tin. Please get up, Lion, please!"

I felt myself being lifted up and carried then. I don't know if it was Tin Woodman or Scarecrow who got me out of there. But get us out they did, me and Dorothy both. All I know is that when we woke some time later, we were lying in soft grass by the river, a gentle breeze wafting us awake. Tin Woodman was there kneeling over us, Scarecrow too. But when I woke up completely and I looked around, there was no sign of Lion anywhere.

"Where is Lion?" Dorothy asked, sitting up. "What's happened to him?"

"He is lying out there in the field of poppies, fast asleep," said Scarecrow sadly. "But he won't last long, I'm afraid. Stay there in among those deadly poppies and you never wake up."

"We couldn't carry him out, Dorothy," Tin Woodman told her. "Lion is too heavy. Scarecrow and me, we tried and we tried. We couldn't move him. We may not be seeing Lion again, I'm afraid. I'm so sorry, Dorothy."

CHAPTER NINE

How Lion was Saved
by a Mouse—or Two

*D*on't go getting yourselves all upset now, little puppies. *Things are never as bad as how they seem. Lion is going to be all right, you'll see. You just listen up and you'll hear how it happened.*

We were lost. We were still looking for the yellow brick road, and couldn't find it, when we saw this great tawny wildcat come a-bounding toward us, a-snorting and a-spitting like wildcats do. But he wasn't after us.

He was chasing a little gray field mouse who wasn't doing him any harm. Well, I don't like cats, never have done, wildcat or not. That wildcat was mighty big, and the little gray field mouse, he was, well… little, as well as being kind of cute too, so I reckoned that wasn't fair. And besides, I wanted to chase that mouse myself, which is why I started running and barking at that wildcat, telling him exactly what I thought of him.

He didn't hang around.

Wildcats don't like dogs any more than we like them. Difference is, they're plum scared of us dogs, and if I'm honest I don't think he much liked the look of the fearsome axe that Tin Woodman was whirling about his head. That old wildcat, he took off and I went right after him. When I came back, the little mouse was hiding behind Tin Woodman's leg, all shivering and shaking he was.

"Is he gone?" he asked.

"You're safe now," said Tin Woodman, "thanks to Toto."

"How can I ever thank you?" said the mouse. "If there's ever anything I can do for you in return, you only have to ask."

"Isn't he sweet?" said Dorothy, crouching down beside the little field mouse.

"He? He?" squeaked the mouse. "I'm not a he! I'm a she, and I am not just any old mouse either. I'm Queen of all the field mice."

"Oh, I'm so sorry, Your Majesty," said Dorothy, and bowed. Tin Woodman bowed. Scarecrow bowed. I didn't bow. Dogs don't bow to anyone.

At that moment, there was a scurrying of tiny feet, and suddenly all around us were hundreds, thousands of mice, all of them leaping up and down and squeaking, so happy to see their queen was still alive. I'd never seen so many mice. Back home in Kansas, I'd have been after them at once, I can tell you that. I love a good mouse chase. I was sorely tempted. But luckily for them, there were so many I couldn't make up my mind which one to chase and, before I could decide, Dorothy picked me up and was holding me tight.

"No, Toto," she whispered in my ear. "Don't spoil it. You've been a very good dog up until now. But I know you only chased off that big nasty wildcat because you wanted to chase the mouse for yourself. The others don't know that. They think you are a hero. I know you're just my lovely, naughty Toto!"

That's the whole darned thing about Dorothy: she knows me far too well.

Scarecrow was scratching his head again, so we all knew an idea must be coming, "S'cuse me, Mrs Queen," he began thoughtfully, "or Ma'am, or Your Majesty—never do know what to call queens—but you said that if ever there was anything you could do for us in return for Toto saving your life, just ask. Well, I'm asking. You see, our dear friend Lion is lying fast asleep over in that field of poppies, and if we don't get him out of there right now, he's going to sleep himself to death and never wake up. Trouble is, he's far too heavy for us to carry him out of there. We've tried. So I thought—Mrs Queen, Ma'am, Your Majesty, whatever—if all your thousands and thousands of field mice would lend us a helping hand, that we could, between us perhaps, manage to get him out of there and save him. He's a lovely lion. Wouldn't hurt a mouse, I promise you. I thought that if each one of your thousands of mice could find a little piece of string, or cotton or hair even, we could tie all of them together and make a strong rope; and then Tin Woodman here could cut us out some wheels and maybe make a cart big enough to carry him, and we could haul Lion out, and he could breathe good clean air and wake up and not die at all. What do you think?"

Everyone was speechless after this, simply gawping in amazement at Scarecrow; me too.

"Brilliant," cried Dorothy, clapping her hands in delight. "You're a genius, Scarecrow!"

And I woofed and woofed to tell him how smart I thought he was too.

"What's a genius?" Scarecrow asked, rather bewildered. "It's not a word I know. I'm not smart with words. No brains, you see." Everyone laughed at that, the mice too, and Scarecrow had no idea why. Then we all hurried away to carry out Scarecrow's master plan. The mice fetched all the little bits of string and cotton and hair from miles around and wound it all tight into a strong rope. Tin Woodman cut down a tree and made it into the four wheels we needed, then chopped and chopped until the cart itself was all made and ready.

"Ready to roll?" said Scarecrow. "Let's roll!"

All the field mice took hold of the rope, the mouse Queen and Dorothy and Tin Woodman too, as well as Scarecrow and me—I got it in my teeth—and we all of us pulled. We pulled and we pulled, and slowly, ever so slowly, the wheels began to turn and the cart moved, and off we went back to the field of poppies. There we found poor Lion lying fast asleep in among the flowers, snoring deeply. The longer we stayed in that deadly field, the more dangerous it was—we all knew that.

So we worked fast and we worked hard, all of us together, thousands of us, pulling and heaving, shoving and tugging, until at last we had hauled Lion up on to the cart.

It was nearly done. We still had to pull the cart out of the field as fast as we could. But I was beginning to feel drowsy again, so was Dorothy, so were the mice. Time was running out for every one of us, but if we were going to save Lion, and save ourselves too, we had to do it.

So we just took hold of that rope again and we heaved. Yes, sir, we heaved that old cart out of that deadly field of poppies and into the sweetest, freshest air you ever did breathe. We breathed it in deep, coughing and spluttering, but we had done it, we had got him out of the poppy field.

Lion lay there, his eyes closed, and still, so still, too still.

"Breathe!" cried Dorothy. "You've got to take a breath!"

I had to do something. I licked his nose, his eyes, his ears. I woofed at him. He didn't move. Not a twitch.

"Oh no!" cried Dorothy. "Are we too late?"

Lion opened one eye.

"Oh!" he said. "I was having a very odd dream about mice." Then he saw the mice all around him. "Or maybe it wasn't a dream…"

Soon Lion was sitting up, and looking around him, all sleepy still and bleary-eyed he was, and rubbing his face with his paws. We had saved him! He lay there now only half asleep in the back of the old cart, and we all joined hands and danced around him, singing for joy. Barking for joy in my case; I don't do singing.

"What's up?" he said. "What's all this singing? You woke me up."

"We did," cried Dorothy, happily. "We did, didn't we?"

"Good job everyone," said the Queen of the field mice. "We'd better be going. Let us know if we can ever help you again, won't you?" And off they scampered.

"Thank you so much," Dorothy called after them.

"What are friends for?" came the faintest reply.

We waited a while down by the river for Lion to wake

up completely. "I had a funny dream," he told us. "There were lots of mice in it, and Tin Woodman was making a cart—I'm sure I don't know why…"

"We do, don't we?" Dorothy laughed. There was a whole lot of laughing as we walked on our way through the flowery meadows. Between them, Dorothy and Scarecrow and Tin Woodman told Lion everything that had happened.

"Well I never!" said Lion when they had finished. "That's so strange, because it's exactly what happened in my dream. Is that weird or what?"

On we walked, until we found the yellow brick road again, and soon after we began to notice that all the fences were green, emerald green, the houses too, and even the people wore green clothes and hats, not sky-blue like the Munchkins. They looked just like the Munchkins, sort of small and round, not blue though and not quite as friendly. They didn't smile much, nor whisper and chuckle among themselves like the Munchkins had.

It was evening time by now, and darkening. There were

plenty of houses, plenty of faces at windows looking out at us, but no one invited us in, as the blue Munchkins had. So in the end Dorothy decided that if they wouldn't do it, we had to invite ourselves.

"We are tired out, right?" she said. "And we're hungry, right? Aunt Em always says you should invite strangers in, be hospitable. It's only good manners. Poor Toto hasn't had a proper meal for ages, have you, Toto?" She was right enough there! She marched right up to a farmhouse door and knocked.

"What do you want?" came a woman's voice from inside.

"S'cuse me, ma'am," Dorothy began, "but we are awful tired and hungry. Can you help us, please?" The door opened just a little, and a face appeared. She was an old woman, rather thin and sickly-looking, with a green shawl round her shoulders. She eyed us all, looked us up and down.

"A lion, a dog, a tin man and a scarecrow, and a girl,"

she said. "Does that dog bite?"

"No, ma'am."

"Does that lion eat people?"

"No, ma'am."

"And does that tin man and that scarecrow fella eat a lot? Cos we ain't got much."

"No, ma'am. They don't eat anything," said Dorothy. So the old woman opened the door. "Come along in then, and mind you wipe your feet. I only got porridge." The porridge was steaming hot and sweet with maple syrup, just how I like it best, just how Dorothy likes it too. Lion wasn't so keen. He wrinkled his nose at it.

"There's oats in there," he said. "Oats are for horses, not lions." So I ate his bowl too, every last lick of it.

"Well, Toto," said Dorothy to me. "That was just like Aunt Em's porridge, wasn't it? Just like home. Oh, home is home, and home is best, isn't it, Toto?"

"You're so dog-gone right," I woofed, licking my whiskers again.

"Where are you folks off to?" said the old woman, sitting down at the table with us when we had finished.

"We're going to the Emerald City to see the Great and Terrible Wizard of Oz," Dorothy told her.

"Are you indeed?" she said—she spoke rather croakily. "Well, that Emerald City is a fine and beautiful place all right, so bright and so beautiful it hurts your eyes to see it. But you won't see the Wizard of Oz. No one's ever seen him. No one even knows what he looks like. You hear different tales. Some say he looks like a bird, or a cat, or an elephant even. With just one click of his fingers, I heard, that old wizard can be just about whatever he wants to be. I mean, after all, he is all-powerful, isn't he?"

"Well, I wonder what he'll be when we meet him," said Dorothy.

"Don't you listen, girl?" snapped the old woman. "You won't meet him. No one does. Anyways, why in tarnation do you want to see him so much?"

So each of us told her why. She listened, nodding, and after a while thinking about it, she said: "He could do the heart, the brains and the courage, I reckon, but even the Great and Terrible Wizard of Oz could hardly get you and that dog of yours back to Kansas, not if he don't know where it is. I ain't ever heard of the place. Where in heck is Kansas?"

"It's somewhere," said Dorothy sadly. "I know it must be because Toto and me live there, it's our home."

"Well, just don't go counting on the Wizard of Oz for anything you want in this life," said the old woman. "That's all I can say. All I know is that if you want something bad enough, you got to go out and get it for yourself. And I got to warn you folks—cos you seem like nice enough people—that old Wizard of Oz can be mighty mean sometimes, that's what I heard."

Dorothy hugged me extra tight that night as we lay down by the old woman's fire. She kept whispering in my ear. "We will get home, Toto. Don't you worry, we will get to see Aunt Em and Uncle Henry again, whatever that old woman says."

CHAPTER TEN

Face to Face with the Great and Terrible Wizard of Oz

*T*hree of you asleep already! I reckon there's some of you little puppies who still don't know the end of my tale. Never stayed awake that long, have you? And that's a kind of a shame, because as Tiny Toto will tell you—and he never goes to sleep until it's over, do you, Tiny Toto?—he knows the end is just about the best part, and the most frightening too, not frightening enough to give you nightmares, but *frightening enough to be exciting. And we're coming right now to the moment we met the Great and Terrible Wizard of Oz, which was scary enough, I can tell you!*

We were all up early the next morning. We said our goodbyes and thanks to the old woman—who had turned out not to be such a bad old stick after all—and were soon off on our journey again, following the yellow brick road. As the sun rose, we could see a green glow in the sky.

"Look, it's the Emerald City!" cried Scarecrow. "We're almost there!" And linking arms with Tin Woodman and Dorothy, off they all skipped ahead of us, so that Lion and I had to trot along to keep up. As we came ever closer, we saw the city was surrounded by towering green walls, and set in the wall were great green gates studded not with nails but with glittering emeralds that dazzled our eyes. The gates swung open as we approached and there stood the Guardian of the gate, small and green like everyone in these parts, but he wore an especially smart green uniform, with emerald buttons, and had a twirling green moustache that stretched across his face, from ear to ear. He stood before us, fingering his moustache.

"Yes?" he said. "And you are?"

He seemed rather an officious little man.

Dorothy explained very patiently and very politely who we were and that we'd come a very long way to see the Great and Terrible Wizard of Oz and how she would be very obliged if he would take us to see him.

"You do know," said the Guardian, "that if you do not please Oz, if he finds you foolish,

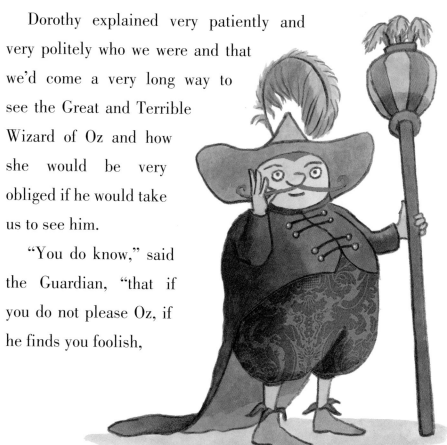

if you waste his time, he will be very angry indeed, and when Oz is angry, he can be—how shall I put this?—most unpleasant, shall we say. With a click of his fingers, every single one of you could become nothing more than a puff of smoke. Poof! Poof! Poof! Poof! And Poof! The dog too. Five puffs of smoke. Think about that. You are well warned. But since you have asked to see him, I must take you to him. That is my duty." He opened a green chest beside him and took out a pair of green glasses. "Each of you must wear a pair of these, or else you will be blinded by the glare of our magnificent Emerald City. I have glasses of all sizes, for lions and dogs too." Then putting on a pair of glasses himself, he said with an imperious wave of his hand: "Follow me, and do not on any account remove your glasses." And so we entered the Emerald City.

"I just hope we're doing the right thing," whispered Scarecrow.

"So do I," said Dorothy.

As we walked down the street, I was looking into the shop windows. Green hats, green shoes, green dresses. Then I spotted something I liked: sausages, in a butcher's shop, green sausages. I'd have eaten any sausages by now—whatever their color—I was so hungry. They looked so good, and I'd never had green sausages. I had to lick my lips to stop myself from dribbling. Lion, I noticed, was doing the same. That was all Lion and I were thinking of as we walked on into the Emerald City. We weren't thinking of the Great and Terrible Wizard of Oz.

We were thinking of sausages, lovely delicious green sausages.

I didn't like wearing those glasses at all, little puppies. I mean, dogs in glasses! We caught sight of ourselves in a shop window. Believe me, we looked stupid. But all the same, it was a good thing we had those glasses on, little puppies, I can tell you. As I walked through the streets of the Emerald City, I had a peek over the top of them. I never saw anything so bright and shiny in all my life. The whole city glittered and sparkled in the sun. And of course everything was green, and I mean everything: green cobbles on the streets, green lampposts, green horses, green carts, and the people didn't just wear green clothes, they had green skin too. The lemonade on the street stalls was green, so were the children drinking it, and the popcorn and caramel apples and cotton candy green too, all of them.

The Guardian with the twirling green moustache led us on through the bustling streets, and everywhere we went, people pointed and stared at us as if we were strangers from another world—which I suppose in a way we were, Dorothy and me anyway. They seemed quite afraid of us. Tin Woodman and Scarecrow waved at everyone cheerily, so no one seemed to be afraid of them. But I could see they were really terrified of Lion. I can't imagine why. He just looked funny in his glasses, not frightening at all, as he padded along beside me.

"Nice place, Toto," he said, "nice people too. But green's not my favorite color.

I'm hungry. I so want some of those green sausages."

"Me too," I told him with my eyes.

We came at last to the gates of the Palace of Oz, right in the centre of the city. The Guardian led us through the door of the palace and up a grand staircase into a huge hall where, of course, all the chairs and tables and carpets were green, the chandeliers too. "Wipe your feet," he told us. "The Great and Terrible Wizard of Oz does not like strangers anyway, but he particularly hates strangers with dirty feet."

So we wiped our feet and our paws very carefully so as not to upset the Great Wizard. We had to wait in this hall for some while, all sitting side by side on a green sofa, me on Dorothy's lap because I had kept wandering off around the room, just to snuffle about and explore, and the Guardian had said that the Great and Terrible Wizard of Oz did not like snuffling dogs, that snuffling dogs made him angry.

Everything the Guardian said about this great

and terrible wizard did not sound good at all. By this time, all of us were getting really worried. He sounded so scary. I was trembling with fear. We all were, Lion most of all. I was so glad I was on Dorothy's lap, that she was stroking the top of my head and talking to me. "It'll be all right, Toto," she was whispering. "He can't be that terrible, he can't be." But she was humming now, so I could tell she was worried too.

Soon we were all humming, me as well in my own way, until the Guardian with the green and twirling moustache told us off. "Stop that dreadful noise at once. The Great and Terrible Wizard of Oz hates humming." So we sat there in silence, waiting and trembling, and Dorothy hugging me so tight I could hardly breathe. We seemed to be sitting there forever, before we heard a gong sounding, echoing so loud through the palace that the walls and windows and the chandeliers seemed to shake with it.

"The Great and Terrible Wizard of Oz will see you now," said the Guardian. "Remember to bow low, very low," he added, "when you see the wizard and when you leave too."

"What will he look like?" Dorothy asked nervously.

"Whatever he wants to look like," replied the Guardian rather impatiently. "And another thing," he went on, "you speak only to answer his questions, and you do exactly as he says, understand? And don't gasp in astonishment at anything, and particularly do not say 'Wow!' He hates gasping and he hates 'Wow.' Argue and he will get angry. And if he gets angry, he will only have to click his fingers, like this—poof!—and you will go up in a puff of smoke, and that will be the end of you. Many strangers before you have gone in there and ended up as puffs of smoke." He led us to an arched doorway and opened the door. "In you go," he said. So in we went, slowly.

We found ourselves waiting in a vast room, green of course, with a high-vaulted ceiling, studded with brilliant emeralds so bright it hurt my eyes to look at them even through my glasses. At the far end of this great room, on a dais draped all around with green velvet, was a throne of green marble, and there was something or someone sitting on it, but we were too far away to see what or who it was.

"Bow," whispered Dorothy. "Bow very low." So they did. Not me though. Dogs don't bow to anyone, and anyway I couldn't because Dorothy was carrying me.

"Approach!" came a booming voice that echoed around the room. So we did, slowly. The something or someone on the throne turned out to be just about the weirdest thing I ever saw. It was a head, a massive bald head, that filled the throne. It had no arms, no legs, just a great head with a mouth and eyes and ears. It looked something like a giant egg, pearly-white and smooth, and not a hair to be seen. "Like a grumpy sort of Humpty Dumpty," Dorothy whispered. "I'm not afraid. I'm not afraid. I'm not afraid."

She kept saying this to herself as we walked slowly and trembling toward this strange and enormous head on the throne. The face frowned, the eyes glared, the mouth moved and spoke.

"I am the Wizard of Oz, Oz the Great, Oz the Terrible. Oz the All-powerful. Who are you? What have you come for? Speak!"

"I am Dorothy," Dorothy answered, her voice firm and full of courage—which surprised me and made me very proud. "And these are my good friends, Toto, Tin Woodman, Scarecrow and Lion."

The bald head leaned forward. "Those red shoes you are wearing," the mouth said. "Where did you get those from?"

So Dorothy told him our whole story, from the day the twister picked up our farmhouse in Kansas; the house falling accidentally on the Wicked Witch of the East in the land of the blue Munchkins, how the Good Witch of the North had kissed her and had given her the Wicked Witch's magic red shoes to protect her and us; how we had crossed deep black holes and rushing rivers, and had even escaped the cruel Kalidahs; how the Good Witch of the North in the land of the blue Munchkins had told us that the only way we could ever get home to Kansas was to go to the Emerald City and ask the Great and Terrible Wizard of Oz to help us; how Lion longed to have courage, how Tin Woodman so wanted a heart, and how Scarecrow yearned to have some brains. She told it all very fast and it was a bit jumbled.

"Could you help us please, sir?" Dorothy asked, rather breathlessly when she had finished. "I so want to go home, and so does Toto."

"And I so want to have courage," said Lion.

"And I so want to have a heart," said Tin Woodman.

"And I really want some brains," said Scarecrow.

"Please, sir, we'd be ever so grateful," said Dorothy.

"Turn round," the head commanded us, blinking slowly three times, "while I think about this. I don't like strangers looking at me while I'm thinking, and mind you don't turn back until I tell you."

So we all did as we were told and turned round. We stood there, wondering, waiting. Then, after a while, came another voice from behind us, a woman's voice this time.

"Very well, you may turn and gaze upon me now." And when we turned round the giant head was gone, and in its place on the throne sat the loveliest and most radiant of ladies, in a long green gown of finest silk, with shining green hair and on her head, a crown of glorious emeralds. We all gasped.

"Wow!" we said all together.

Although I'm thinking mine sounded more like "woof".

The lovely lady frowned at us. "Do you all want to be poofed into puffs of smoke?" she said, lifting her hand, her fingers ready to click.

We all shook our heads. "Please no!" cried Dorothy. "We didn't mean it, honest."

"I can see you are honest," the lovely lady said. "But don't do it again. No more 'wows,' understand? Now tell me

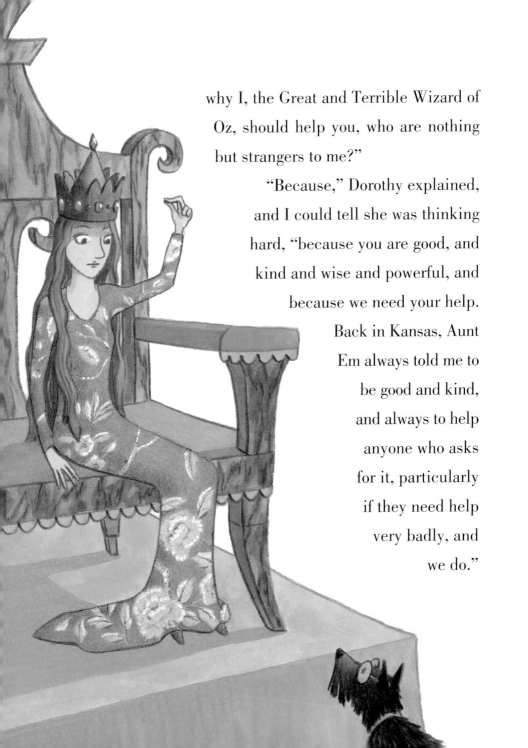

why I, the Great and Terrible Wizard of Oz, should help you, who are nothing but strangers to me?"

"Because," Dorothy explained, and I could tell she was thinking hard, "because you are good, and kind and wise and powerful, and because we need your help. Back in Kansas, Aunt Em always told me to be good and kind, and always to help anyone who asks for it, particularly if they need help very badly, and we do."

"Turn round again then," said the lovely lady, "while I think about it. I don't like anyone looking at me while I'm thinking."

So we turned around again, and waited, and waited, none of us daring to look before we were told to. "I have thought about it," came a voice, after a while, but not a woman's voice this time, in fact hardly a voice at all, more a raging roar. "Turn round now!" So we did, in fear and trembling, and saw sitting on the throne a most dreadful-looking beast, as big as an elephant, with the head and horn of a rhinoceros, with green woolly hair covering its whole body, with five eyes in its head, five arms and five legs. We almost gasped but stopped ourselves just in time. We almost said 'wow' too, but managed not to, only just. "I have thought about this," growled this terrible beast, "and I have decided I will help you, but only if you help me."

"How can we possibly help you?" Dorothy asked. "You are the Great and Terrible Wizard of Oz. Surely you can

do anything you wish? You can even change what you look like, click your fingers, and make puffs of smoke of us. How can we possibly help you?"

"No one asks the Great and Terrible Wizard of Oz a question," roared the beast. "Have you no manners? I ask the questions, I say what is to happen. Understand? Or do you wish to be puffs of smoke?"

"No, please," Dorothy begged. "Don't be angry. We will do whatever you want us to do, or try to anyway."

"Very well, that is better," growled the beast, but his growl was slightly gentler now. "You have already got rid of the Wicked Witch of the East, which was good. Now you will find and do the same with the Wicked Witch of the West. Get rid of her. You have the power—even my great powers cannot overcome her spells. Yours can. You told me you have been kissed by the Good Witch of the North. And I see the mark of it still on your forehead, so you cannot be harmed. And you have those magic red shoes. Wear them, and you will have all the power you need to dispose of the Wicked Witch of the West. Do this for me, and bring me proof you have done it, and I will help you get home to Kansas, you and your dog. Tin Woodman can have his heart; and you, Scarecrow, can have your brains; and you, Lion, you can have the courage of the king of the beasts. All this I promise you. Now, turn and go. And don't look back!"

We turned and walked the length of that room together, and all the time I was thinking: *Don't look back, Toto, don't look back.* But I'm never very good at doing what I'm told, especially when I don't want to do it, so just as we reached the door, I had a crafty, sneaky look behind me. The head on the throne, the lovely lady, the horrible beast, had become a great ball of flaming fire. "Toto!" came a thundering voice filling the room, filling the whole palace as we walked out.

Uh, oh, I thought. *Now I'm in trouble, big trouble.*

"Toto, you looked back!" roared the Wizard of Oz. "You are a naughty dog, a very naughty dog, and I should be very angry with you. And I am. But although I am the Great and Terrible Wizard of Oz, I can be kind and merciful when I like to be. So for Dorothy's sake, for she is a kind and honest girl who loves you like a best friend, I will not make a puff of smoke of you—this time!"

Well, as you can imagine, I did not look around again. I was mighty pleased after that to get out of the Palace of Oz alive, and soon we were on our way back to the city gates through the streets of the Emerald City. At the gates, still trembling after all that had happened, we handed our glasses back to the Guardian with the twirling green moustache. "Where are you off to now?" he asked us as he opened the gates to let us out.

"West, I suppose," said Dorothy, "because somehow we have to find and get rid of the Wicked Witch of the West. We don't want to, but we have to, or the Wizard of Oz won't help us."

The Guardian laughed at that, laughed loud and long, laughed fit to bust. "You, do away with the Wicked Witch of the West? What, a tin man, a scarecrow, a slip of a girl, a trembly lion, and a little bitty dog?" I nearly bit him then just to show him, but Dorothy told me not to.

"Pay him no attention," she whispered to me. "He's a rude, rude man."

"We won't be seeing you again then, will we!" the Guardian sneered, twiddling his twirling green moustache. "That Wicked Witch of the West will have you all for breakfast. She'll see you coming a mile away through her all-seeing eye. She sees everyone coming, and once she's seen you, you don't stand a chance. She'll send her horrible creatures after you."

"We'll show her," said Dorothy, linking arms with Tin Woodman and Scarecrow. "Won't we?"

"Yes, Dorothy," they said.

"Yes," I told her with my eyes. But we only agreed with her to make her feel better, to make us all feel better.

They all felt as I felt, I could tell. None of us believed we could do it, none of us. But all of us knew we had to try.

"Which road do we take?" Dorothy asked the Guardian with the twirling green moustache. "How do we find this witch?"

"There is no road," replied the Guardian. "Just go west toward the setting sun, and believe me, she will find you with her all-seeing eye. As soon as you are in her country, the country of the yellow Winkies,

she will know you are there, and she will either destroy you or make slaves of you, whichever she feels like doing. She magics her horrible creatures out of dust, out of thin air—you won't stand a chance against them."

"Oh, stop trying to frighten us," said Dorothy, stamping her foot at him crossly. "It's not fair and it's not kind. We are going. I have the kiss of the Good Witch of the North on my forehead and the red shoes of the Wicked Witch of the East on my feet. Nothing the Wicked Witch of the West can do can harm us. That's what the Great and Terrible Wizard of Oz told us. Oh yes," she went on, "and by the way your moustache is far too long and twirling, that's what I think. You should cut it. You'll be a much nicer person altogether with a shorter moustache, not so proud and hoity-toity, not so unkind!"

"Do you really think so?" said the Guardian, fingering his moustache rather nervously now. He seemed very upset and taken aback. "Maybe I shall then, if you say so. Pardon my rudeness, please. I did not mean to be unkind.

I must say, you are the bravest people I've ever met, for the Wicked Witch of the West is the wickedest witch there ever was. I wish you well. I wish you all the luck in the world. You will need it." And off he went.

"Well," said Dorothy, clapping her hands to cheer us all up. "Up we get and off we go!"

And so off we went, westwards toward the country of the yellow Winkies, toward the country of the Wicked Witch of the West, where her horrible creatures would be waiting for us. It was hard to be cheerful. But Dorothy wanted us to be, so we were, or so we pretended to be.

CHAPTER ELEVEN

The Wickedest Witch There Ever Was

*N*ow this part does get quite alarming, little puppies. So, if you don't want to hear it, now's the time to put your paws over your ears. That's what Lion used to do whenever things became too frightening for him.

We had no road to follow, only the sun. The grass was soft to walk on, and there were daisies and buttercups everywhere. The birds were twittering and cooing, the larks trilling as they rose into the blue above us, and along the sparkling streams the dippers were dipping and kingfishers flashing by. It was the most beautiful countryside we had walked through in all our long journey.

It was hard to believe anything bad could happen to us in this country. Our spirits rose, our steps quickened. By now we had left the Emerald City far behind us; and were up in the hills, where suddenly the way was full of stones, and rockier altogether, which made for harder, rougher walking. Tin Woodman often stumbled to his knees and had to be helped up. Dorothy took his arm, but then she would stumble, and he would have to help her up. Higher and higher we climbed, the sun beating down on us, every hill steeper than the one before, and now the wind was howling around us. Soon we were all tired out. We found a more sheltered place out of the wind, in amongst the rocks, where a carpet of soft thrift had grown. We lay down to sleep, all of us huddling together.

Even Scarecrow lay down with us, which was unusual. "I don't like wind," he said. "I'm so light I could get blown away."

We had just settled down to sleep when I thought I heard a whistling sound. I imagined at first it must be the whistling of the wind around the rocks. Then I was sure I was hearing the howling of wolves. *No,* I thought, *that's just the wind again. Don't worry about it,* I told myself. I curled myself up closer to Dorothy and fell fast asleep, which was when I dreamed a horrible dream. I dreamed I saw the Wicked Witch of the West, a warty old witch in a pointed hat and pointed shoes with one huge eye in the middle of her forehead. She was blowing on a silver whistle, and all around her the air thickened and swirled into clouds, gray clouds, that turned into howling wolves.

"I see strangers in my land," she was shrieking, "strangers lying asleep on my thrift in amongst my rocks. They are no good to me as slaves for one is made of tin, another of straw, one is a raggedy old lion, and the other a little bitty dog, and a slip of a girl, none of them any use to anyone. Go, my dears," she screeched, "go and tear them to pieces."

That was when I woke up. All around us was a pack of yellow-eyed, sharp-toothed wolves baying for our blood, and Tin Woodman was up on his feet, axe in hand. He whirled it round and round, and struck the first wolf, which was instantly turned to dust in the air.

"The Wicked Witch has sent them!" said Dorothy. "Just like the Guardian said!"

On and on the horrible wolves came, and all of us backed away, all of us apart from Tin Woodman. He kept swiping with his axe, spinning, and with every whirl he chopped off a wolf's head, then another and another and another, each one of them becoming nothing but a puff of dust when he had finished with them. All I could do was bark, which I did loudly, until Dorothy picked me up and held me tight. Lion had his paws over his eyes—he didn't want to watch— while Scarecrow clapped and cheered in wild excitement.

"Bravo, Tin Woodman! Bravo!" he was shouting.

"I'm awfully scared," said Lion.

And Dorothy was sobbing, her face buried in my neck. "Horrible! Horrible!" she cried. "The Wicked Witch of the West can make wolves out of dust."

Tin Woodman sat down, exhausted. "What a good axe!" he said. "Came in handy, didn't it? Sorry if I upset you, Dorothy. But it was either the wolves or us."

"This means she knows we are here," said Dorothy, looking around her. "The Guardian was right. She can see us with her all-seeing eye. She's seeing us now." And this was true, of course. I knew that much from my dream. All the next day we walked up hill and down dale, fording rivers and streams. So by sundown we were exhausted all over again, and I was hungry too, as I tried often to remind Dorothy with my pleading eyes, with my cold, cold nose. But she was too tired to care about anything, even me. Again we all lay down to sleep, arms around one another, me with my head on Dorothy's lap. I was asleep at once. I thought I heard a whistle blowing, and then the sound of crows cawing.

And then I dreamed a horrible dream again, but not the same dream. This time that warty old Wicked Witch of the West was up on the yellow ramparts of her yellow castle, and looking out toward us with her one huge, telescopic eye. And I could see what she was seeing. All her wolf guards were reduced to dust now, and all of us were lying there fast asleep, me too, my head on Dorothy's lap! I could see myself in my own dream!

Shaking with rage, she blew again on her silver whistle. "Those infernal strangers! They have defeated my wolves!" She pointed to the skies and shrieked a spell. Above her, crows gathered out of the darkening clouds.

"Find them, my darlings,"
she shrieked. "Find those strangers.
Go and peck out their eyes while they are sleeping,
tear them into little pieces for me."

That was when I woke up. All above us I saw the sky
filled with crows, dozens of them, all with black beady
eyes and cruel beaks, and they were cawing at us, diving
on us. Scarecrow was up on his feet, arms outstretched.
"Don't you worry, my friends," he cried. "It's what I'm for,
remember? I scare crows, don't I? I won't let them hurt
you." And for a while it seemed to be working.

The crows flew around and around us, cawing angrily,
and they didn't dare attack.

But then the biggest of them, the king crow, cawed out.
"He's not a real man at all! Look at him! He's just a straw
man! He can't harm us!" And he flew down and started
stabbing and pecking at Scarecrow, pulling out his straw.

That made Scarecrow mad, really mad. He reached up and took king crow by the neck, and shook him, until king crow cawed no more and was nothing but a puff of dust. That only angered the other crows even more, and they all came down to try to peck Scarecrow to pieces, and Scarecrow did the same to all of them. By the time he had finished, there were no crows left, not even a feather, just a lot of dust lying around.

"I'm awfully scared," said Lion. "I've never liked crows."

"Bravo, Scarecrow! Bravo!" cried Tin Woodman

"That's that then," said Scarecrow.

"The Wicked Witch of the West sent them," said Dorothy. "I know she did." And again I knew from my dream she was right.

All the next day we walked, wondering all the while what nasty wicked plans the Wicked Witch had in mind for us, and trying not to worry about it, which was impossible, of course. Dorothy was worried too, though she never said it. She just hummed a lot—a sure sign she was worried. She sang a bit too, to keep us all cheerful, I think.

Her singing never made me cheerful, if I'm honest. But the others seemed to like it. Lion and I found a rabbit or two to chase—and eat out of sight of the others—and that kept me a lot more cheerful. Dorothy seemed quite happy with the apples and pears she found, and Tin Woodman and Scarecrow didn't bother with food, so they were fine. None of us looked forward to the sunset though. Whatever the Wicked Witch had in store for us was going to happen after sunset, we knew that. And sunset comes, whether you want it to or not.

"Home is home, isn't it, Toto?" said Dorothy, sadly. "And home is best. Home is where I want to be, want to be so much."

Me too, me too, I was thinking. I gave her a lick on her hand to let her know. She patted my head. At least I had Dorothy, at least we had each other.

We cuddled tight together, but tired though we all were, I think I was the only one who fell asleep, and when I did, I dreamed a horrible dream once more. The Wicked Witch of the West was up on the yellow ramparts of her yellow castle again, her all-seeing eye spotting us at once, all of us asleep. She blew loud and long and shrilly on her silver whistle, pointed to the sky and screamed a spell. At once a great cloud of bees gathered about her, humming and roaring so loud it might have been thunder, swarming around the castle ramparts. "The strangers have destroyed my crows," she screeched. "Go, bees," she commanded. "Go at once, and sting them to death, that little bitty dog too, all of them."

That was the moment I woke up, and there above us was a huge swarm of black bees. Now we were done for, I thought, now there was no escape. Nothing could save us.

But Scarecrow and Tin Woodman were up on their feet, and Scarecrow was pulling out handfuls of straw from inside himself and shouting at Dorothy and me and Lion.

"Lie where you are, be still, and Tin Woodman and I will cover you completely with straw. None of the bees will sting you." So we did as Scarecrow told us, as he and Tin Woodman covered us all over with a thick blanket of straw, so when the bees flew down to attack, we were all safely hidden away and protected. There was only Tin

Woodman left to sting—and a rather thin and bedraggled Scarecrow—and bees, of course, can't sting straw any more than they can sting tin. In their fury they tried to sting Tin Woodman, though, and every time they tried, their stings broke against the tin, and of course everyone knows that once a bee has used his sting he dies. But these bees didn't die like real bees do, they just turned to dust, like the wolves had, like the crows had.

"Bravo!" Dorothy cried, and Lion roared, and I woofed, woofed like crazy I was so happy, so relieved. I really do not like bees—never have.

We soon stuffed all the straw back into Scarecrow, so that he looked much as he had before, even better I thought.

Bees, crows, wolves, whatever the Wicked Witch of the West sent out to attack us, we had defeated. It must have been Dorothy's magic red shoes, or that kiss from the Good Witch of the North, that had protected us, but I thought it was also because we looked after one another, that together we were strong, too strong for the Wicked Witch of the West.

She tried once more the next evening to destroy us, sending forty of her slaves, the yellow Winkies, to attack us with their bows and arrows, with their pointed spears and sharp swords. But Lion simply stood there and roared at them, and they dropped all their bows and arrows and spears and swords and ran away. When they had all gone we were so happy. We danced round and round, and sang and whooped and clanked and barked and roared, until we were quite giddy—and I chased my tail, which made me giddy too. We were all of us giddy with joy. We were all sure by now—surely we were sure—that the Wicked Witch of the West had done her best time and time again to get rid of us and had failed.

How wrong we were.

CHAPTER TWELVE

We Fall into
the Clutches of the
Wicked Witch of the West

I'm afraid things often get worse, my dear little puppies,
before they get better. It's like that, in real life as well
as in stories. And of course this story is real life as well as
a story. We thought the worst was over, that things could
only get better now. And that's how it looked. We walked
on day after day, always going westwards toward the
setting sun, finding enough to eat and drink on the way.
We had tired feet, or paws, but that didn't matter. We were

happy enough as we marched along. After all, we thought, we had overcome the worst the Wicked Witch of the West could do to us.

And then one night I had another horrible dream. I saw in my dream the warty Wicked Witch in her castle hall shouting and screaming at her yellow Winkie slaves. She was standing before them, hands on hips, a golden cap on her head. "You have failed me, you miserable slaves," she shrieked. "But now I have my magic golden cap on, which never fails me. Whoever owns this cap—and I own it—can command the terrible Winged Monkeys, but just three times. Once I commanded them and they gave me you, my yellow Winkies, my army of slaves, so that you could build me my yellow castle, so that I could rule over this country and make it mine. Then I commanded them to drive the Great and Terrible Wizard of Oz far away, to the Emerald City, so that his power could never harm me. And that they did. Now I shall speak the spell and they will do my bidding for the third and last time."

She stood on her left foot and wiggled her right. "Eppepeppekakki!" she cackled loudly. "Hillohollohello! Zizzyzuzzyzik!" The sky darkened, then lightning flashed, thunder roared, hailstones rained down. She looked up and pointed. "See, my Winkie slaves, they come!" she screeched. And out of the storm came a great rushing of wings. I thought at first in my dream that the sky above her must be full of ravens, cawing and chattering. Then all of a sudden the sun shone through, and all around the Wicked Witch I could see they were not ravens at all, but monkeys, flying monkeys! They sat around her now in the vaulted hall of her castle, a crowd of monkeys, huge monkeys with angry eyes and bared teeth.

"You called?" The voice I heard seemed to come from everywhere, from all of them, at the same time. "Remember, this is your last time, Witch. What do you wish us to do?"

"Go, Winged Monkeys, go to the strangers you will find sleeping out there in my country," shrieked the Wicked

Witch of the West. "I command you to kill them for me, all except for the lion. He may be useful. At least he is strong. He can be my slave. He can be harnessed like a horse and pull a cart. The rest are useless to me. Destroy them! Destroy!"

And at once the Winged Monkeys flapped their great wings, lifted off and flew out of the windows of the great hall, out over the ramparts and over the hills beyond; until they saw us lying there, curled up together on the ground, fast asleep. They were coming for us!

I woke then, woken by the fear of them in my dream, by the wind of wings and the chattering and hissing of monkeys. I wasn't sure whether I was still inside my dream or not. But Dorothy was screaming and clutching me to her. It wasn't a dream! Lion was roaring his anger and defiance, and the giant Winged Monkeys had already caught Scarecrow and were pulling the straw out of him, out of his clothes, out of his head. They made a bundle of his blue clothes and tossed them up into the top of a tree. Then they picked up Tin Woodman, flew him to a great height and dropped him down on to the rocks below where he shattered into pieces, nothing but a pile of twisted dented bits of tin. They dropped a net over Lion and caught him, and then, lifting him up into the air, they flew him away over the hills.

"Oh, Toto," cried Dorothy, her eyes full of tears. "Look what they have done. We have lost Scarecrow and Tin Woodman and Lion, and they were such good, kind friends."

I wanted to comfort her, but I was as sad as she was. Besides there was no time. The Winged Monkeys were coming for us now, landing all around us, and closing in, closer, closer, chattering and hissing menacingly. Well, I wouldn't stand for that, would I? They were attacking Dorothy!

I went for them, snarling and snapping at their feet, at their wings, but they just ignored me, and reached out their big hairy arms to grab Dorothy. I thought they were going to tear her to pieces. Suddenly, though, the chattering stopped, the hissing too, and they backed away, bowing their heads. "We can't touch her," said the tallest and hairiest of the Winged Monkeys. "Look, see her red shoes, and see on her forehead the mark where the Good Witch of the North has kissed her. This child cannot be harmed." He looked down at me—I was still snapping at him. "Is this creature a friend of yours?"

Dorothy nodded. "My best friend," she said, trying to hold back her tears. "My only friend in the world. You have killed the others."

"Then we shall not harm him." And before we knew it, the Winged Monkeys had picked us both up, and, gently cradling us in their arms, were flying us up through the clouds and over the hills toward a yellow castle in the distance. It all happened so fast, I had no time to be frightened. Soon we were landing on the ramparts of this great yellow castle, the one I had seen.

"Lion!" cried Dorothy. "Thank goodness! At least Lion survived."

The Winged Monkeys set us down, Dorothy and me, on our feet right in front of the Wicked Witch of the West.

"We have done as you commanded us," said the leader of the Winged Monkeys. "The tin woodman and the scarecrow we both destroyed." Hearing it said like that made us sadder still, Dorothy and me. But it made us angrier too. "And the lion, as you see, is now your slave to do with as you please. But this girl has the kiss of the Good Witch on her forehead, and she wears the red shoes. So we cannot harm her, even if we wanted to, which we don't. And the little bitty dog there is her best friend, so he is also protected. You have now used up your three commandments, Witch, so we will do no more for you. And we are glad of it. No witch was ever wickeder than you." And without another word, all the Winged Monkeys rose into the clouds above and were gone.

The Wicked Witch came up close to Dorothy, to look her in the face. She saw too, the mark of the Good Witch's kiss on her forehead, and she saw the red shoes on her feet. I could see she was frightened, and that she was pretending not to be. Dorothy couldn't see it, but I could. Dogs have a sixth sense, don't we? I could see the Wicked Witch was already concocting some cunning plan.

"I could kill you and I could kill your little dog too," the witch told Dorothy, "but I have decided, in the kindness of my heart, that I won't. Instead you will slave for me in the kitchen, do the washing-up, scrub the floors. You will polish, fetch water, keep the fire going. You will do as I wish or you and your little bitty dog will end up like that tin man and that scarecrow out there on the hillside, all in little bitty bits and pieces."

Dorothy didn't cry in front of the witch. She put a brave face on it. But over the days that followed, she cried quietly to herself as she slaved away for the Wicked Witch of the West, crying herself to sleep every night. "Oh, Toto, how I wish I was back home with Aunt Em and Uncle Henry," she'd often tell me. "Poor Lion is in his cage, and poor Scarecrow, poor Tin Woodman, when I think what has happened to them, I am so unhappy, Toto. But I shall work ever so hard, then the Wicked Witch will not harm you. To lose you as well would break my heart in two."

I touched my nose against her cheek so she knew I felt the same about her.

We were well guarded all the time by those yellow Winkies, the Wicked Witch's slaves. They weren't nasty to us exactly, but they weren't that kind to us either. They were always gruff with us, and always so sad and miserable. And being yellow I suppose, they smelled of custard too, which I didn't much like, still don't.

The Wicked Witch smelled strongly of vinegar, which suited her, because vinegar is the worst smelled in all the world. If ever I barked at her, which I did because I hated her, the Wicked Witch would beat me with her umbrella.

I managed to bite her more than once, but she did not bleed. All her blood had dried up long ago. She bled red dust. Not nice.

She was so cruel. Time and again, she would poke Lion through the bars of his cage with her umbrella, because he refused to be harnessed like a horse and would roar at her and tell her just what he thought of her. She starved him then, just to punish him. At night, when the Wicked Witch and all the Winkies were asleep, Dorothy and I would creep down into the courtyard to comfort him and to bring him food from the kitchen.

"We will get you out somehow, Lion," Dorothy told him. "I'll find a way."

And I knew she would too, somehow. But how, that was the question. I never saw Dorothy as unhappy as she was then. I did all I could to make her feel better. I never left her side all day, snuggled up close to her at night, touched her cheek with my cold, cold nose, licked her ear. I didn't really care where I was, in the Wicked Witch's castle, in the Land of Oz or back in Kansas, I just wanted her to be happy. And I knew she never would be, and neither would I, until we were home again.

Dogs have a sixth sense, one more than people do. I sensed, before Dorothy ever did, what the Wicked Witch of the West was up to. I could see her eyeing Dorothy's red shoes, and I guessed why. Dorothy loved

those shoes so much she never took them off, even in bed. Sometimes at night, when I was half awake, I would see the Wicked Witch stealing into our room, and would growl at her, baring my teeth. She did not like my teeth, not one bit. But I couldn't stay awake all the time. I tried to, but I couldn't. And early one morning when Dorothy and I were still both fast asleep, she crept in, and before I could wake up and bite her, she had reached down and snatched one of the red shoes.

"Aha!" she shrieked, waving the shoe triumphantly in the air. "Now you have only half your power. I have the rest." And she danced around the room cackling at us.

Well, that was too much for me. I went after her. I bit her hand and her leg, her ankle, and that made her hopping mad. The Wicked Witch lashed out at me then with her umbrella, again and again, and that made Dorothy really angry. She leaped out of the bed, shouting at her.

"First you kill Tin Woodman and Scarecrow, and imprison our friend Lion. Then you make a slave of me, then you steal one of my red shoes, and now you beat Toto. I have had enough."

She was as angry as I've ever seen her. She was looking around for something, anything she could use to fight off the Wicked Witch. Then I had an idea, which turned out to be a brilliant idea, just about the best one I ever had. There was a bucket in the corner full of rainwater that leaked from the roof—I'd had a drink from it earlier. I ran toward it, nudged it with my nose, woofed and woofed until Dorothy looked. She knew what to do now. She grabbed the bucket and threw freezing cold water all over the witch.

The witch was soaked through, dripping wet from her pointed hat to her pointed toes. She was capering all around the room, trying to brush the water off herself;

and she was shaking the red slipper at us, cursing at us loudly, screeching and shrieking. Then the strangest thing happened. The shrieking and the screeching became a wailing and a whimpering, and in front of our eyes this cruel Wicked Witch began to sob like a child. And then she began to shrink.

"Oh no," she cried pitifully, sinking to the ground. "Water may be life for everyone else. But water is death to me. It is melting me away! It is the end of me, the end of all my power, all my wickedness." Soon all that was left of her was the red shoe lying on the floor in a puddle of water, and a fading smell of vinegar.

Dorothy picked up the red shoe and slipped it on.

"Aunt Em said I should never lose my temper," she said, "but do you know, Toto, I'm very glad I did. Let's go, Toto. Let's rescue Lion from his cage, and then let's get out of here, back to the Wizard of Oz.

Then home, Toto, home. Home is home, and home is best, right, Toto?"

It was so good to hear her say that again. "You're so dog-gone right," I woofed. I woofed it and woofed it.

CHAPTER THIRTEEN

Promises, Promises

But it wasn't as simple as all that, little puppies, because these yellow Winkies, being the Wicked Witch's slaves, would not let us go that easily. We ran down to the courtyard to rescue Lion from his cage, and there we found hundreds of yellow Winkies, with their spears and their bows and arrows, and not looking at all friendly. "What have you done with the Wicked Witch of the West?" the chief of the Winkies demanded.

"We have put an end to her, washed her away, you might say," Dorothy told them. "And it was all thanks to Toto here."

I do love you, Dorothy, I was thinking.

She turned to the Winkies. "You are slaves no more, Winkies."

At this they gave us a great cheer, and after they had opened the cage and let Lion out, they insisted we stay for a party, to thank us and to celebrate their new-found freedom. But I could tell during the festivities that Dorothy was far from happy, despite all the dancing and singing and laughter that was going on all around us. I wasn't the only one who had noticed it.

"Why are you so sad, Dorothy?" the chief Winkie asked.

"I am thinking of poor Scarecrow and poor Tin Woodman," she replied sadly. "They should be here celebrating with us. I can't sing and dance knowing they are out there somewhere alone in the hills, our dear

Tin Woodman all battered and broken, and our dear Scarecrow all pulled apart and all unstuffed and not himself at all."

"You and your friends have done so much for us, Dorothy," said the chief Winkie. "So now we will help you. We will find Tin Woodman, and Scarecrow, and put them together again, you'll see."

And do you know, little puppies, those wonderful yellow Winkies did just that. They went out looking at once, and the very next day, a search party of yellow Winkies discovered Tin Woodman—or what was left of him—lying all in bits, broken and battered and dented in amongst the rocks. They gathered him up, and carried every last piece of him back to the castle.

Three Winkie tin-smiths soon knocked out the dents, put him together again, fixed him up, and oiled his joints and his axe, because, after all this time out in the wind and the rain, Tin Woodman had rusted up pretty bad. But even when they had finished, he still looked a bit battered, and not quite himself, and he couldn't move at all.

"He's still not himself," cried Dorothy. "What can we do?"

The Winkies all shook their heads. "We do not know," said one of them. "But perhaps if you do a little tap dance in your magic red shoes, and wish very hard… then maybe, maybe… Just an idea."

And so Dorothy did just that and at once Tin Woodman opened his eyes!

"I feel awfully stiff," he said, "but I think I'm fine." He waggled his arms, his legs, his head. "I'm fine! I'm fine!"

How I woofed! How Dorothy hugged him! How all the yellow Winkies clapped and cheered!

Then the yellow Winkies, who by now had come to like Tin Woodman very much, decided they would paint him yellow, bright yellow as they all were, so he would feel like one of them.

Tin Woodman loved his new look. "I look like the sun," he said, preening himself. "Thank you, Winkies, thank you so very much."

And meanwhile, another search party of yellow Winkies soon found Scarecrow's bundle of clothes up in a tall tree. They gathered some good clean fresh straw and stuffed him again so that Scarecrow was soon full of himself once more, if you understand my meaning. Again, he didn't come to life straight away, but when Dorothy did another tap dance in her red shoes, and wished hard, he was soon blinking in the light and marvelling at being there, in the castle, though he said he had far too little brains to work out why he was here, he was just glad that everyone was back together again and the Wicked Witch was gone.

I couldn't believe how kind these yellow Winkies turned out to be. When they were the Witch's slaves, they had been sullen and sad and not at all friendly, but now they were all smiles, and fun and laughter. "Just shows you," said Dorothy, "how powerful a thing is a little bit of freedom."

"I know how they feel, Dorothy," Lion agreed. "When you are behind bars, when you are not free, you have nothing to live for. To be free is everything. It makes them happy, look at them. And it makes me happy too—almost as happy as food!"

I woofed in agreement. The only thing missing for me was sausages.

They wanted us to stay, the yellow Winkies, but Dorothy told them we had to go, to get back as soon as we could to the Great and Terrible Wizard of Oz. "I so long to go back home to Kansas," she explained. "And Scarecrow longs for some brains, and Tin Woodman longs for a heart, and Lion so wants some courage. You see, the Wizard of Oz promised us all these things if we killed the Wicked Witch of the West. Well, now we have."

And those kind-hearted Winkies fed us like kings before we left, and gave us food for the journey. They gave each of us gifts too—Tin Woodman, a special silver oilcan full of oil because they thought it would come in handy in an emergency, and the Winkies told him, that now that he was yellow, he should come back to see them whenever he felt like it. To Scarecrow, they gave garlands of beautiful flowers; to Lion, some throat medicine because they thought his throat must get sore with all his roaring.

And as for me, I got a yellow bouncing ball that Dorothy could throw for me to chase. To Dorothy they gave

the Wicked Witch's magic golden cap, so that if she ever needed the Winged Monkeys, she could call on them for help three times. Dorothy thanked the yellow Winkies for all of us, and put on her new golden cap instead of her bonnet—it suited her much better, I thought; I never much liked her in that bonnet—and off we went out through the gates of the yellow castle, their cheering and well-wishing ringing in our ears.

But finding our way back to the Emerald City was a problem. We did not know the country at all. After all, if you remember, those Winged Monkeys had picked us up and flown us over hill and dale, stream and forest, to the Wicked Witch's yellow castle in the West. There was no yellow brick road to follow, and there was not even a path through the meadows.

"East," said Scarecrow, scratching his head. "We were going west to get here, right? So to get back we must go east. But the sun is right over our heads, isn't it? So we still can't tell east from west. Which way do we go?"

"Follow me," said Lion. So we did, but we soon found ourselves right back where we started. We'd just gone round in a circle.

"Follow me," said Tin Woodman. "I know the way." But he didn't.

"Follow me," said Dorothy, but we got lost again.

After a while wandering around getting lost in this unknown country, we all sat down in deep despair.

"Now we'll never get back to the Wizard of Oz, and I'll never get home," Dorothy said sadly.

"And I shall be brainless forever," sighed Scarecrow.

"And I shall be heartless forever," Tin Woodman cried.

"And I shall be a coward forever," Lion said, whimpering miserably. We were all tired, and sad as well. I was too tired even to chase rabbits and butterflies. But a squeaking little mouse that came skittering right past me was too much of a temptation. I was up and after it in a flash.

"That gives me an idea," said Scarecrow, scratching his head again. "Didn't the Queen of the field mice, who helped us once, say that if ever we needed her again we should call for her? We are lost, aren't we? We need her help. Let's ask her."

"Brilliant, Scarecrow!" cried Dorothy. "We'll all call for her." So we did, each in our own way. I barked, the lion roared. There was a long silence once the echoes had died away, and then we heard a squeaking and a rustling in the grass, and suddenly the little field mice were there, all around us, all over our feet and paws, and there was the Queen of the field mice herself, sitting at Dorothy's feet and looking up at her.

"You called?" she squeaked. Dorothy crouched down and explained everything to her, how we were lost, how the Wicked Witch of the West was dead, and how we had to get back as quick as possible to the Emerald City, to see the Great Wizard.

"Why are you asking me?" said the Queen of the field mice. "You have the answer on your head, girl, that golden cap. That is the magic golden cap of the Wicked Witch of the West, isn't it? It's easy. You just say the magic words to make the Winged Monkeys come, and then command them to take you there, to the Emerald City. Simple."

"What magic words?" Dorothy asked.

The Queen of the field mice thought for a bit. "I think I remember. Try: 'Eppepeppekakki. Hillohollohello. Zizzyzuzzyzik.' You're the owner of the golden cap. You're wearing it. The spell will work only for you. You have to get the words just right, mind." So Dorothy tried. She tried once, twice. We all looked up in the sky for the Winged Monkeys, and waited. There was no sign of them, no flapping of great wings, no chattering as they came.

It was no good. It seemed that nothing would ever get us home to Aunt Em and Uncle Henry.

"I don't like to correct you," said the Queen of the field mice, "but I think you said 'Zizzyzuzzyzuk.' It shouldn't be 'zuk' at the end, but 'zik'. It should be 'Zizzyzuzzyzik.' And I think for the spell to work you have to stand on your left foot only, and wiggle your right. Try again."

So Dorothy closed her eyes tight shut, concentrated very hard, and stood on one leg, and said the magic spell again.

At once they came.

Down through the clouds flew the
Winged Monkeys, chattering. I didn't
like them one bit, I never had, with
their hairy arms, their great flapping wings,
and their pointed ears—like huge, ugly chattering
bats. I barked at them ferociously, and couldn't wait to
have a go at them, give one of them a good bite when they
landed. Dorothy picked me up and held me tight as they
came down all around us.

"You called?" said the leader. "What is your command?"

"To take us to the Emerald City as fast as you can,"
Dorothy told him, clutching me tightly because she knew
very well it was biting I had in mind.

Before we knew it, those Winged Monkeys had picked
us up and we were being flown away, the little field mice
below waving goodbye to us and becoming littler with

every moment. I've never been so frightened in all my life. Up through the clouds we were flown, higher and higher. I closed my eyes, and just hoped my Winged Monkey would not drop me. I'd seen what they had once done to Tin Woodman, remember?

Then after a while, I forgot I was frightened, and the gentle rhythmic swish of their wings sent me to sleep. When I woke, I was being set down on my feet outside the great green gates of the Emerald City, and we were all standing there, looking in amazement at one another, the Winged Monkeys flying off up into the clouds above us.

"Well," said Tin Woodman, shaking himself, trying out all his joints to make sure they were all still working. "How was your flight, my friends?"

"First class," said Dorothy, patting her golden cap and looking up at the great green gates of the Emerald City. "This golden cap sure is useful. And I can still call on those Winged Monkeys twice more, if we need them. Just so long as I don't forget the spell. Isn't it wonderful? They brought us all the way back. Now, let's not waste any time. Let's go right in to see the Great and Terrible Wizard of Oz. We've done what he said, killed the Wicked Witch of the West, and this golden cap is the proof he said we had to bring. If he's a wizard of his word, he will grant us our wishes. He promised us, didn't he?"

"Promises, promises," Scarecrow mumbled doubtfully to himself as Dorothy was ringing the bell. The gates opened and there stood the same Guardian we had met before, dressed in his green uniform as usual, and with a green moustache, but now it was neatly trimmed. It was strange being in a green place again after all that yellow. "You've changed," said the Guardian, looking up at the tin man. "You're yellow."

"And you are green," replied Tin Woodman.

"You can't judge people by their color," said Scarecrow. "It's what goes on in our brains that matters."

"And in our hearts," Tin Woodman added.

"But weren't you going to visit the Wicked Witch of

the West?" the Guardian asked, handing us out those same glasses to wear again.

"That's where we've been," Dorothy replied.

"Well, I'm truly amazed she let you go," said the Guardian. "How brave you must have been! It's nice to have you back again."

"And believe me," Dorothy told him, "we are more than glad to be here. And you are much nicer than when we last saw you. I like your moustache much better, much nicer."

"Thank you," he said. "That is very kind."

I looked at Dorothy and she smiled. I could tell she was only being polite. My sixth sense again.

We were walking up the same street now where we had walked before. Everything was just as bright and sparkling as ever, just as green. And there were the same green sausages in the butcher's window. I licked my lips and Lion licked his! I couldn't resist. I dashed in.

No one was
looking. No one
saw me. Sometimes it is really
useful to be small. Lickety-split I
snatched the sausages and was out of there.

Lion and I shared them as we walked along. He had more than me, but that was only fair—as he was a bit bigger. Green sausages were the best, I decided, the best in the whole wide world, even better than in Kansas, though then I felt a little guilty for liking anyone's sausages better than Aunt Em's.

The others were walking on, they never even noticed. We licked our lips clean of course, and then ran and caught up with them.

"You look happy, Toto," said Dorothy, "which means you've been naughty. You're wagging your tail so hard it'll fall off."

"You may not believe this," Dorothy went on, turning to the Guardian, "but that warty old Wicked Witch of the

West didn't exactly just let us go. We melted her in water, freezing cold water."

"Melted her!" the Guardian cried in astonishment. "You melted her, all by yourself?"

"Sort of, you could say that," Dorothy replied, smiling at me. The Guardian was beside himself with joy. He was shouting the news out loud up and down the street, and soon there was a huge crowd following us along, toward the great Palace of Oz in the centre of the city.

"They've done away with the Wicked Witch of the West!" the Guardian was shouting it out. "They've melted her, done away with her once and for all! She's kicked the bucket, dropped off her perch. The Wicked Witch of the West is a goner!"

The bells began to ring all over the city, and everyone was cheering us, waving to us from windows, showering us with green petals and green roses.

Inside the Palace of Oz, everyone had heard the news and the whole place was a buzz of excitement.

"How happy the Great Wizard will be," they cried. To start with we were all a bit bemused by all this ruckus, but soon enough we began to enjoy it, to bask in the glory of it. Lion and I trotted along, our tails high, waving them proudly. Scarecrow and Tin Woodman and Dorothy waved their hands because they didn't have tails. We were all waving whatever we had to wave, loving every moment of it. We were all so happy.

"I shall soon have my heart," said Tin Woodman.

"And I shall soon have my brains," said Scarecrow.

"And I shall soon have courage," said Lion.

"And Toto and me shall soon be home in Kansas with Aunt Em and Uncle Henry," said Dorothy. "Home is…"

"…home," chorused the tin man, the scarecrow and the lion. "And home is best!"

"You're so dog-gone right," I woofed.

We thought we would be shown in at once to see the Great and Terrible Wizard of Oz, but the Guardian said that the wizard always slept in the afternoons and would be pleased to see us in the morning. The Guardian gave us a feast of food, and then showed us to a great bed chamber with a huge wide bed and a roaring log fire from which Scarecrow kept a safe distance.

"Sparks," he said, "aren't good for me." After we had eaten our fill, those of us that ate, we all lay down together on the bed, Scarecrow and Tin Woodman too. They all linked arms, and I lay with my head on Dorothy's lap. We were fast asleep before we knew it. And I dreamed of green sausages and the farmhouse in Kansas and rounding up the cows and chasing rats and rabbits.

In the morning, the Guardian led us down a long, long corridor to see the Great and Terrible Wizard.

We walked into his throne room, arms linked again, me at Dorothy's heel, all of us happy, all of us full of hope. But the room was strangely silent and empty. There was no one there. Then at last came the voice, his voice. It seemed to come from everywhere, from all around us. "I am Oz, the Great and Terrible," it boomed.

"We know who you are," Dorothy said, looking about her as we all were. "But where are you?"

"I am on my throne, I am invisible. You cannot see me," came the reply. "I hear you have done away with the Wicked Witch of the West."

"We have," replied Dorothy. "And look, I am wearing her magic golden cap to prove it. I melted her with a bucket of water. It was easy, really. And now you must keep your promises, to all of us."

"Promises, promises," came the voice. "Maybe, maybe I will, but I am a bit busy right now. I shall have to think about it. Come back tomorrow. Maybe tomorrow."

"Maybe?" cried Dorothy, stamping her foot angrily. "Now listen here, Mr Wizard, you made promises to us, faithful promises, and you are going to keep them, you hear me?" She was not just angry, she was furious. So I barked, because if Dorothy was furious, I was furious too. Tin Woodman stamped his feet clankily and whirled his axe about his head, and Scarecrow too was mad with

anger, shaking himself so hard that his straw began to fall out. And Lion roared. He let out a roar that shook the chandeliers and rattled the windows. He was standing right beside me.

I hadn't been expecting a roar like that. The shock of it made me jump half out of my skin. I turned and bolted. I was so frightened I ran smack right into a silk screen and sent it crashing to the ground.

And to our complete astonishment, we saw standing there, where the silk screen had been, a little old man, rather bald, with wispy hair, in a raggedy tweed suit, wearing a monocle and leaning on a cane. Dorothy cried out in her surprise, I barked, the lion roared, Tin Woodman raised his axe again, and Scarecrow was waving his arms and rustling his straw as he always did when he was agitated. No one said a word.

"You are the Wizard of Oz?" Dorothy breathed at last.

"Well, kind of," the old man replied. "Sort of, I guess. You could say that."

CHAPTER FOURTEEN

The Really Confusing Wizard of Oz

*A*s you can imagine, little puppies, after such a shock it took quite a while for all of us to calm down. Dorothy was the first to find her voice. "Who are you?" she said. "And where is the Wizard of Oz?"

"Oh dear," replied the old man, shaking his head sadly. "Oh dear, oh dear. I'm ashamed to have to say that you are looking at him. I am the Great and Terrible Wizard of Oz."

"But you looked like a sort of a huge Humpty Dumpty," said Dorothy.

"Then a beautiful lady," said Tin Woodman.

"Then a hideous beast a bit like a horrible, spidery rhino with cruel claws," said Lion. "Scared me stiff."

"And you were a great ball of fire too," said Scarecrow. "I remember you were, because I don't like fire. I don't like fire at all."

"They are right," said Dorothy. "You were all these things, one after the other. It was very confusing!"

"Oh, I do apologize," the old man cried, wringing his hands. "It was all nothing but make-believe. I am nothing but a humbug, a low-down trickster, a miserable fraudster."

"So you are not a great wizard at all," Dorothy said.

He put his finger to his lips. "Sshh," he whispered. "No one else must know. If I am found out, I am done for. Everyone in the Emerald City will hate me. And I can't bear being hated. I like to be liked and loved, to be admired. Doesn't everyone? Don't blame me too harshly, and please, please don't tell them."

"But," said Tin Woodman, "if you are not a wizard, you can't give me a heart, can you?"

"And you can't give me brains," said Scarecrow.

"And who else will give me courage?" said Lion.

"And, if you don't mind my asking, how will Toto and I get ourselves back to Kansas without the magic of the Wizard of Oz? You promised us, promised all of us. And we went and got rid of the Wicked Witch of the West like you said. It's not fair, it's not right, and it's not fair."

"You are right, Dorothy," said the old man, "but believe me I didn't do it on purpose. One thing just seemed to lead to another. I couldn't help myself. I mean, I didn't want to be here at all in the first place."

"Neither did I, nor Toto, nor any of us," Dorothy told him. "We want to go home, but we don't know where home is, nor how to get there even if we did. I mean, we know our farmhouse is in the land of the Munchkins, because that's where we landed after the twister that sucked us up into the air." And then Dorothy told the old man all that had happened to us since we landed, our meeting with Scarecrow and Tin Woodman, Lion, and all our adventures together. It took a while and was quite boring, because we knew the story already, of course. "And we never saw Aunt Em and Uncle Henry ever again, and now we never shall." And Dorothy cried then, sobbing her heart out.

"Don't cry, my dear," said the old man. He looked thoughtful. "Maybe there's a way I can still help you, help you all. 'Where there's a will, there's a way,' that's what I say."

"That's what my Aunt Em used to say too," Dorothy said, brightening a little as Tin Woodman wiped away her tears.

Scarecrow was scratching his head. "I don't understand.

Well, I wouldn't, would I? No brains, you see. But how come, if you're not a real wizard, you could change yourself just like that, be a baldy old egghead one moment, then a lovely lady, then that nasty beast, then a great ball of fire? I don't understand."

"It's a fair question, Scarecrow, that needs an honest answer. Perhaps I should tell you my story. I think I owe you some explanation after all the trouble I have been to you," said the old man, who always spoke very politely. "Follow me," he went on, "and I will show you everything, tell you everything."

We followed him through a curtain behind the throne and there on the floor lay the great pearly-white head we had last seen on the throne. "You see that wire up there above your head?" he said. "I just clip that Humpty Dumpty head, as you call it, on to the wire and hoist it up. Then I can pull the strings to make the mouth open

and shut. It's just a kind of puppet head, all made of wire and papier-mâché. That's all it is. And when I speak I can change my voice, become a man or woman or fearsome beast, and I can throw it too, make it seem as if it sounds very near or far away. You see, I am a ventriloquist and an actor, a showman."

He gave Dorothy a chair. "Sit down, my dear," he said. "This will take some time.

"I play many parts," he went on. "The young lady, the beautiful one, was me in a mask and a long green dress, and of course with a different voice; the nasty, spidery beast with the rhino's head—that was me too. There's the head on the chair over there." Somehow it did not look at all frightening on the chair. "Look at all my costumes hanging up, dozens of them, I made them all myself. And the great ball of fire? My *chef-d'oeuvre*, my masterpiece! It was simply a gigantic ball of cotton, soaked in oil and set on fire, then I just speak in a fiery sort of a voice. It's easy when you know how. If there is one thing I have learned in all my days as a traveling showman, it is that if I play my part well, people will always believe in who I am, in what I want them to believe; and this is mostly because they wish to believe what they want to believe."

"I only half understood that," said Scarecrow, scratching his head, "and I am not sure which half either."

"Do you come from these parts?" asked Tin Woodman.

"Oh no, not at all," the old man replied. "Do I look green or blue or yellow? No, I come from Omaha, which is—"

"In America!" cried Dorothy. "Where Kansas is, where we come from! How did you get here? Were you carried up by a twister like we were?"

"Well almost, you might say," he replied. "I travel to county fairs, rodeos and so on, doing quite well too. But I had taken my show on the road for years and years, and was becoming tired of it all. Then one day, I happened to be traveling along the road to my next county fair, when I saw an air-balloon flying overhead. I'd never seen one before. It landed at the very same county fair I was going to. I could not imagine anything more wonderful than to go up in such a balloon, to see the world from way up there. I had to pay to go up in it that first time, but it was worth it. It changed my whole life. When I came down, I at once got a job as a balloonist's assistant, then a year or two later as a real balloonist. There's no better job in the world, believe you me. You're up there with the birds, in your basket hanging from the balloon, and flying over mountains and rivers and meadows.

"But then one day it all went a bit wrong. I was up there alone, when the wind got up and the balloon started turning, whirling round and round, and soon the ropes that held the basket to the balloon became twisted. Up I went, up and up through the clouds, higher and higher, so high it was difficult to breathe, and I fell fast asleep. When I woke up, I found myself being carried through the streets of a green city, and the people were green too. Everything and everyone was green. I was the only one who wasn't. So to them I was a wonder of the world.

"And maybe because I had come down magically from the sky—from nowhere, it seemed to them—they thought I must be some kind of a wizard, with magical powers, and they treated me with such respect and honor, and I liked that. 'What's your name?' they asked me. 'Oz,' I told them, which was sort of true. 'The Great Ozzy Mandias' had been my stage name, my show business name back in Omaha. So they called me the Wizard of Oz, set me up in a great palace, built it especially for me.

"They were so good and kind to me, these people, as they have been ever since. I couldn't let them down, could I? I couldn't tell them that I was just an ordinary traveling showman from Omaha who had lost his way in a hot-air balloon, could I? So I pretended to be what they wanted me to be. I used all the tricks I had learned in show business, all my skills as a ventriloquist, hid behind my masks and my costumes and my voices, and I promised I would use all my powers, the powers they believed I had, to protect them from the Wicked Witch of the East and her horrible warty sister, the Wicked Witch of the West— she was the worst of all. They lived in fear and trembling of her especially, because she lived closer—which is why I tricked you into getting rid of her, which you did most successfully, surprisingly successfully. The real truth is that you, Dorothy—with the power of your red shoes, and the golden cap you are wearing, and the kiss from the Good Witch of the North I can see on your forehead— you are much more of a wizard than I am. I'm afraid I am just a selfish, vain and foolish old man who made you rash promises that I cannot keep."

He hung his head. "I am so sorry. I have no magic to offer you. I cannot get you home."

At this dreadful news, I thought Dorothy must lose heart, but she was up on her feet and wagging her finger at him—she reminded me greatly of Aunt Em when she did this!

"You are a bad man," she told him, "a very bad man."

The old man smiled sadly. "You are right, I suppose, but as you can see now, I am an even worse wizard, and I truly hate myself for being such a humbug. But don't give up on me yet. I'm not all bad. As I said, maybe there is a way I can still put things right. You will all like me if I can, won't you? I do so like to be liked. Let me think about it overnight. Meanwhile you will be my honored guests in the palace. Everyone will make sure you are warm and comfortable as can be, and you will have all you want to eat. But whatever you do, please don't tell anyone the truth about me. They would be so disappointed in me for being a humbug, if I turn out not to be the Great Wizard of Oz."

So we said goodnight to the Wizard of Oz—who wasn't a wizard at all, of course. All of us decided we liked him despite this, and all of us hoped that somehow, some way, he could make our wishes come true. I liked him because he tickled the top of my head in just the right place, and because he smelled of old clothes and pipe tobacco, just like Uncle Henry back home.

Dorothy said, as we all lay down on our great wide bed that night, that we should look out of the window, choose a star, and make a last wish before we went to sleep, and she told us we should wish the best, not just for each of ourselves, but more for each other, because we were all the best of friends. I nudged her cheek with my cold, cold nose just to remind her that I was her best friend, not the others. But I think she was fast asleep already.

CHAPTER FIFTEEN

The Wizardest Balloonist There Ever Was

*O*ne... two... three... four... five... six little puppies asleep. Just you left awake, Tiny Toto. You're my best listener, you always are. Come up here and snuggle a little closer. I can whisper then, so I won't wake your brothers and sisters up. Easy does it, you're treading all over them, getting your own back, I guess? Comfy now? Lay your head right there, just like I used to with Dorothy. Still do, come to think of it. Now, Tiny Toto, where was I? Oh yes, here we go.

After the most sumptuous breakfast the next morning—Lion had twenty green sausages, and I had six, which was quite enough for me—the Guardian with the green moustache came to fetch us. Still licking our lips, Lion and I padded along the corridor after the others toward the great throne room. The Guardian knocked on the door. "I'm warning you," he whispered, "he's feeling a bit ferocious this morning, as ferocious as any lion."

"Enter," came the reply, but strangely in a voice we all knew very well. It was Lion speaking, and he was right next to us. We looked at him amazed.

"Enter," came the voice again, a loud deep roar of a voice, a lion's voice, but Lion's lips weren't moving. He was shrugging his shoulders.

"Not me," he whispered, terrified. "I never said anything. Honest."

Well, we all knew that Lion never told a lie. "I don't like this," he said, backing away from the door. "It's too weird. I don't like weird. And it's scary too, I mean hearing your own voice when you're not saying anything. That's scary. I'm not going in there."

Dorothy put a comforting arm round his neck and ruffled his mane. "You'll be all right," she said.

"If you say so," said Lion, "if you say so." But he didn't sound at all convinced.

In we went, and there was a lion sitting on the throne, and not just any old lion, but just like our lion, and he was roaring at us. "Come along in," he was roaring. "I may roar, but I won't bite." He was beckoning us in with his paw. "Guardian, my friends and I have a lot to talk about. We do not wish to be disturbed."

"Your wish is my command, oh Great and Terrible Wizard," said the Guardian with the green moustache, bowing low and walking backwards out of the throne room. The lion on the throne waited until the door closed, and then stood up, taking off his head at once. The old man's face was wreathed in smiles, his eyes twinkling merrily.

"Well, what do you think?" he said, coming down the steps toward us, carrying his head with him. "I stayed up all night making the costume, and practicing my lion talk. How did I do, Lion?"

"Amazing," said Lion. "But I do wish you wouldn't roar quite so loud. Frightens me to death." The old man had taken off all his lion costume by now. He came over and stroked the top of my head.

"I had a dog like you once, Toto," he said, "just like you. My best friend in the world. I left him behind when I went up in the balloon that day—he never liked flying— and I never saw him again. Diddledeedoo, I called him. I still miss him every day."

"Just like I miss home, and Aunt Em and Uncle Henry," said Dorothy. "Now I'm sorry about you, and your Diddledeedoo dog, I really am, but my friends and I, we want some answers. We thank you most kindly for your hospitality—the green sausages were excellent— but you did say you would try to work something out for us. You promised."

"Yes, you promised," we all said, me too in my own barking way.

The old man nodded, but said nothing. Then he put his hands behind his back and began walking up and down in front of us. "You're right. I promised," he began. "All night while I was making my lion costume I was thinking. You know now that I have no magic powers, that I am simply Mr Ozzy Mandias, showman extraordinaire maybe, but not the Wizard of Oz. When you play many parts, as actors like me do, you have to understand not just about how people look and speak and feel, but about how people are, why they do what they do. Dorothy told me yesterday everything that has happened to you in all your adventures and what good friends you all are. She told it all so well, that I feel as if I have known you, each of you, forever."

He stopped in front of Scarecrow and looked up at him. "Dear Scarecrow," he said, "you think you want brains in that straw head of yours, because you think you are stupid. You want to be wise. To be wise you have to work things out, to ask questions, to think for yourself. You do all these things. I have heard of all you have done and said. So you are wise already, dear Scarecrow. You have all the brains you need. All you have to do is believe in yourself. You are perfect just as you are, a fine and wise Scarecrow. You do not need some wizard or magic to make you so."

He came to Tin Woodman next. "And dear Tin Woodman, you say you need a heart. Well, I have thought long and hard about you. I could indeed cut a hole in your tin chest and make you a pretty heart out of silk, and stuff it in you, and solder you together again. What clumsy and pointless magic that would be. The thing you need to know, dear Tin Woodman, is that you don't need a silken heart or any other kind of heart. I have heard of all you have done, so I know you have one already, a good and kind heart. Look around you. Think about it. You have friends you love, and they love you. Could they love a heartless person? Why do you think you are moved so easily to tears, why do you cry so much?" He knocked on the tin man's chest. "All you have to do, dear Tin Woodman, is believe that you already have a heart. Believe me, you have all the heart you need. But you don't have to believe me. Ask your friends, they will tell you."

And we did, all of us in our own way. Woofing is my way.

"As for you, dear Lion," he went on, stroking Lion's golden mane, "who says he has no courage; well, excuse me, but you really should know yourself better. Yes, you are fearful sometimes, but you conquer your fear. And this is true courage. A brave lion who knows no fear is not brave at all. What do you want, some magic green medicine I

could pour down your throat and fill you up with courage? You don't need it. I have heard of all the brave things you have done, so I know you already have all the courage you need to be a king of all beasts, king of the jungle."

"Really?" said the lion. "Are you sure?"

"Quite sure," replied the old man.

"But what about me and Toto?" Dorothy asked. "How are we ever going to get back to Kansas?"

"Well, this is a little more difficult, I'm afraid," he began, "but in a way, it was your little Toto here who gave me the idea that I might be able to help." I was trying to figure out what I had done, but could not think of anything. "You see," said the old man, "I have been here many years, and I would like to go home myself."

"Home is home," said Dorothy, quietly. "And home is best."

"Undeniable," said the old man.

"Woof," I woofed.

"I've been happy enough here in the Emerald City," the old man said. "The people are kind, I have all I need; but it isn't easy every day to pretend to be someone you are not. And seeing Toto reminded me of my dear little Diddledeedoo back home in Omaha, and how dreadfully I miss him. And if I'm honest, I'm a bit fed up with these spells and witches and all this magic stuff. So I was thinking that sometimes the best ideas are the upside-down ideas, don't you think? I was thinking last night: 'What comes down must go up.' Upside-down thinking, you see. You see, my balloon and I came down here in the Emerald City, so maybe it could go up again, with us in it. They keep the balloon in the Wizard of Oz Museum in the city. They repainted it after I arrived here, fixed it up. It's all in perfect working order. We could leave today, if we wanted to, just take it out into the square, light a fire under the balloon, fill it with hot air, and away we go."

"You mean we could go home today?" cried Dorothy, dancing around the room in her red shoes. "Do you hear that Toto? Do you hear that?" Well, I'd heard it, of course, but I could see the look on Tin Woodman's face, see the tears rolling down his cheeks, I could see Lion holding his paws up to his face and sobbing, and Scarecrow trying to comfort them both.

Then Dorothy noticed too, and ran over to them. "Oh, please don't be sad," she cried. "You could come with us to Kansas. I'm sure Aunt Em and Uncle Henry would like you to come with us, wouldn't they, Toto?" Now that was a grand idea, I thought, so I told them so, I barked them so. We would all of us be together forever!

But Scarecrow was shaking his head. "No," he said. "That's very kind of you, Dorothy, but I would rather go home to the land of the Munchkins where I come from. I liked it there. It's home for me."

"And I will go back to the land of the yellow Winkies," said Tin Woodman. "After all, they saved my life and painted me yellow so now I don't rust even when I cry. And anyway, I like being yellow as the sun like them. They will look after me and I will look after them. They told me to come back if ever I wanted to. I've always wanted a place to belong. It'll be home for me."

"And I will stay here, Dorothy," said Lion, "in this place where I found my courage, where I became who I

am, thanks to the Great and Terrible Wizard of Oz, or Mr Ozzy Mandias, whichever you are. I will be the only golden creature that lives here. I can hunt in the fields and forests nearby. Why would I ever want to live anywhere else? It'll be home for me."

"Better than that, Lion, my friend," said the old man excitedly, "when we leave I shall be able to tell them that the king of beasts himself will be looking after them instead of me."

"And can I have green sausages every day?" the Lion asked.

"You'll be king," replied the old man, "you will be able to have everything you want!"

"That'll do then," said Lion. "I'm happy."

And all the people were happy too, when they heard Lion would be staying on instead of the wizard—he'd been shut away in the palace all this time anyway, they hadn't seen much of him.

But it wouldn't be true to say that Scarecrow and Tin

Woodman and Lion were happy when the balloon was full of hot air and we were ready to leave. There were a lot of tears—in fact, not from me or Scarecrow or Lion, because none of us could cry, but from Dorothy. Dorothy can cry for Kansas! And she did. And so did all the people too, and Tin Woodman of course.

The balloon was tugging at its ropes. The time came for hurried goodbyes. I got a prickly cuddle from Scarecrow, a clanking cuddle from Tin Woodman, and a huge lion hug from Lion, and a mouthful of mane too!

Dorothy stood up on tiptoe and kissed Tin Woodman on his forehead tenderly. "I'm leaving you the kiss the Good Witch of the North gave me. It protected me and it will protect you. Goodbye, dear friend." To Scarecrow, she said, "I'm giving you my magic red shoes. They won't fit, but that doesn't matter. Keep them always, so you won't forget us, Toto and me, and all our wonderful adventures together. I hope they will protect you as they have protected me. Goodbye, dear friend." Then she turned to Lion and put the golden cap on his head. "If ever you need any help from those Winged Monkeys, put this on and wish. Remember you have only three wishes, so don't waste any. They will do as you command. Goodbye, dear friend."

Then to all of them, she said, "You make me think that friendship and kindness are the most important things in all the world."

They all nodded, but were too tearful to speak. Then the old man, Dorothy and I climbed inside the basket. Dorothy had her own basket still, of course, the one over her arm that she had carried all the time wherever she went, with Uncle Henry's hat still inside it. She was holding me close, and I could see her eyes were filling with tears again. "Goodbye, dear friends," she cried. "Be happy. I shall think of you often, dream of you every night. We will meet again in our dreams. We will always be the best of friends."

As the balloon rose slowly into the air, Dorothy was waving, the old man too. And everyone down there below us on the ground was waving back. The Guardian with the green moustache was saluting us, the tears running down his face. Up and up we rose, leaving the Emerald City sparkling below us. We could see the yellow brick road

winding its way through the green of the countryside, the road we knew so well, and then we were lost in the clouds.

"Excuse me, Ozzy, if I may call you that," Dorothy said, after a while, "I think we might have one small problem. We are up here, and that is fine, but how do we know which way to go? How do we find our way back to Kansas?"

"I suppose we go wherever the wind takes us," said the old man. "That's how I got here, after all. Isn't that what happens in life, Dorothy? It's what happens in balloons just the same. And don't you worry, I'm just about the wizardest balloonist there ever was. I'll get you back to Kansas, you'll see." He looked down at me and smiled. I believed him. But I was not enjoying this at all. I had discovered, after looking over the side for too long, that I didn't have a head for heights. I guess you can't exactly get seasick in a balloon, but I reckon that's what being seasick feels like. *Creep into a corner of the basket, curl up and go to sleep*, I told myself. Pretend it isn't happening; no nightmare could be as bad as this. Dorothy was so excited and she wouldn't come and lie down with me and cuddle me no matter how much I whined and I whimpered for her. So I sulked there on my own and pretty soon I was asleep. Sulking often helps me go to sleep, I find.

I woke up with a walloping bump and a crash. "Hang on," the old man was shouting. But I couldn't hang on. Fortunately, Dorothy grabbed me just in time, otherwise I would have been thrown out of the basket altogether as it toppled over. "You'd better get out," the old man was telling us, "this balloon is dragging along pretty fast. I reckon she wants to take off again at any moment. Out you jump, Dorothy!" So Dorothy jumped, clinging on to me as tightly as she could. We rolled over and over and over. Then we were lying there on our backs, all the breath bumped out of us, watching the balloon rising into the air above us, the old man waving.

"I hope you find your Diddledeedoo!" Dorothy was shouting up at him.

"And I hope you find your home!" cried the old man. "I reckon this is Kansas, by the look of it. Plenty of tumbleweed about. Trouble with Kansas is it's mighty big."

"We'll find it soon enough," Dorothy cried, waving back.

And so we did. Dorothy asked around, hitched a ride here and a ride there. Everyone was so friendly, just as friendly as anyone we had met in the land of Oz. And the food was a whole lot better. These folks understood what a dog likes to eat.

And then, after a week or so, we found ourselves walking up the track toward home, toward the farmhouse, which looked just about the same, but newer—the old one had blown away, if you remember. The cows were out there grazing away in the fields, the hens were all clucking about the yard, and the wind was blowing wild all across the plains, and there was plenty of tumbleweed rolling about and chasing itself.

We were home sure enough! And there was Uncle Henry plowing a field and Aunt Em hanging up the washing on the line. They both saw us at about the same time. At first they couldn't believe their eyes, then they came running as fast as their legs could carry them.

"Dorothy! Toto! Where have you been?" Aunt Em cried. So Dorothy told them, and went on telling them and telling them, but they wouldn't believe her, and they still don't believe her now, all these years later. People folk are like that, my little puppies. Haven't got no imagination, you see, that's their problem.

Anyways, Dorothy and I got home safe and sound, and boy were they glad to see us! Aunt Em gave us a good scolding for going off like we had and scaring the living daylights out of her. And Uncle Henry was happy, because he'd got his hat back.

None of it would have happened, of course, if the twister hadn't come and blowed away his hat. And none of it would have happened if I hadn't chased after it and brought it home. And that's the dog-gone truth!

—— ❖ ——

Well, That's
My Story Done

"Well, that's my story done."

That was how Papa Toto would always end his tale.

All the other little puppies were snoozing away, lost in their own dreams.

"You asleep too, Tiny Toto?" Papa Toto said. "That's good. I'm fairly tired out myself with all this storytelling. Still, it did its job, got you all to go to sleep. So now I'm going to have a bit of a sleep myself. Think I deserve it."

But I wasn't asleep, not really. I just had my eyes closed, that's all. I never once went to sleep during Papa Toto's tale, which is why I know it so well, I guess. I only ever went to sleep when he did, my head resting on his heart, so I could feel us breathing together.

I always loved that.

First published in hardback in Great Britain by HarperCollins *Children's Books* in 2017
HarperCollins Children's Books is a division of HarperCollins*Publishers* Ltd,
1 London Bridge Street, London, SE1 9GF

The HarperCollins website address is: www.harpercollins.co.uk

1

Text copyright © Michael Morpurgo 2017
Illustrations copyright © Emma Chichester Clark 2017

ISBN 978-0-00-825256-4

Michael Morpurgo and Emma Chichester Clark assert the moral right to be identified
as the author and illustrator of the work.

Printed and bound in China

RORY BLOCK

when a woman gets the blues

A *PDF* version of this boo'...images in color and
black and white plus 95 li...ic can be purchased at
www.ro...m

Sheep at Hazelwood House, S. Devon, England. By Rory Block

Credits

Cover photo: Sergio Kurhajec

Cover graphics: Mark Dutton- Cover layout: Bill Hurley

Design: Rob Davis

Copy editor: Jeff Stenzoski

All artwork by Rory Block

The title *When A Woman Gets The Blues* comes from a beautiful song written by Eric Kaz. I also have a CD by this name.

All photos have been credited where the photographer's name is known. Everything not credited was either taken by Rory Block, a family member, or has no information available. If you recognize an uncredited photo and have information, please contact us at <straybaby@mac.com>

Acknowledgements

Heartfelt thanks to the following people:

My husband Rob, who spent months scanning photographs and assembling this book in a digital format- all the things I would have been unwilling and unable to do by myself. But this is the nature of partnership, something we regularly celebrate...

Ron Cohen, for reading this book and offering support, encouragement and excellent advice- inlcuding urging me to call Pete Seeger ...

Holger Petersen of Stony Plain Records, who waited over a year for a new record- patiently putting his release schedule on hold while I digressed utterly to write this book...

Richard Pertz, for bringing a truly distinguished level of generosity and integrity to his chosen profession of law...

Guitar student and editor Jeffrey Stenzoski, who not only completed the first edit, but graciously allowed me to call him repeatedly and pick his brain regarding grammatical minutia...

Stefan Grossman, my first boyfriend and guitar duet partner who taught me much and helped immeasurably in the process of gathering information for this book.

Comments From Readers & Friends

"The most enjoyable biography I've read in years. Rory's phenomenal life story comes alive in a wonderfully woven tapestry of prose, photos and the poetry of the blues."
Steve Bryant- TV/Radio host, musican and author

"This is much more than just a book or life story. It's a collection of moving, gut-wrenching, soul cleansing prose artfully mixed with poetry, paintings, and stunning photographs. Rory proves to be a masterful, incredibly revealing writer. Just as she's a focused and intensely powerful performer, she demonstrates those same traits here. She takes the reader on a fascinating journey that ultimately proves that her strong will can conquer life's toughest challenges".
Jim Hynes, radio host and music writer

"A captivating narrative of a colorful life lived with uncommon courage and conviction. An intimate insight into the psyche of an iconic artist... a rich and distinctive voice... important... enriching...
JJ Stenzoski- lecturer, Indiana University/Purdue University

"Stunning... beautiful... the most honest book I've ever read..."
Jack Baker- guitar player and teacher

"Warm... real... captivating... important... courageous..."
Shari Kane- blues artist and teacher

"A WONDERFUL and VERY EMOTIONAL read. So much talent and what a roller coaster life.."
Stefan Grossman- blues guitarist, recording artist, teacher

"... a compelling, unflinching life story."
Sonja Gilligan- Documentary Filmmaker

"What a great book! I am proud to have been a small part of her grand story!"
Jim Gallagher- Audio Engineer, Producer and Educator

Pete's Blessing

1 wasn't certain that calling Pete Seeger directly was even possible, but a mutual acquaintance assured me that under the circumstances it would be fine. So I dialed the number and Toshi answered. "Rory," she said... "Let me get Pete." Then I heard a wonderful, musical voice saying "Rory Block- your father used to live in my house!" This was an astounding revelation which Pete soon expanded upon- but first I congratulated him on his 90th birthday and asked how he was doing. He responded that he is quite well, although according to him, starting to lose his memory a bit- however he immediately began relating vivid stories from as far back as the 1940s, explaining that his wife's parents lived in a three story brownstone on MacDougal Street in Greenwich Village where they rented out rooms on the upper floors. Pete, Toshi, and her parents ate dinner together every evening in the basement. William Steig, famous cartoonist for The New Yorker magazine, rented the top floor. "Your mother had an affair with Bill Steig!" Pete announced, and I burst out laughing, saying "I'm not surprised- my mother was an incorrigible flirt!" (I have since discovered that the affair was actually with my father's first wife- which could be why they parted- and thus my mother has been exonerated of this particular matter). Then Pete explained that my father had rented one of the rooms- this before my parents lived on Sullivan Street only a few blocks away. Toshi said that on Saturday nights they hosted informal music gatherings- friends getting together to play music- and that at one point this happened almost every weekend. My parents would return home from an evening out talking about singing with Burl Ives, Josh White, and Theodore Bikel the night before. It must have been at the Ohta's house.

Pete's voice was rich with wisdom, warmth, and humor. He explained that the emancipation of women had changed the course of history for the better, and I took this to be deeply supportive of the women in his life, but I also felt it as a wonderful encouragement to me and to all the women who have struggled to come out from under the yoke of servitude to play music, enter the business world, and to achieve anything that was once the sole domain of men. In fact everything he said was a gem falling on my ears. It was one of the most interesting conversations I have had in years. Pete went on to say "Whenever your name comes up I always say 'Rory Block- she's the best at what she does... but I just can't remember what it is that you *do*!" Nothing could have been a sweeter compliment rolled into a more wonderful little vignette. Then he said "When your memoirs are complete, make sure I get a bunch of copies so I can give them out and tell people about your book." This was a profound blessing to me. This legend, this father of folk music was touching me with the hand of encouragement.

Photo: Shonna Valeska

Preface

"Be not afraid, but speak and hold not thy peace."
Acts 18:9

*I*magine living every day believing that at any moment, everything will break wide open: the phone will ring, a check will arrive, and in an instant one will grasp overwhelming prosperity, opportunity and success. This has been my general state of mind my entire life. I can certainly say that my vision- and even greater- has manifested in every way satisfactorily. But it was not always so.

First, I must travel back to a childhood fraught with darkness and sorrow. It was my portion to be raised in a family that openly invited me to "go back where I came from" (which I might have considered had I known from whence I had originated). I tried once to leave, but my efforts failed. I have always been far too full of *the road ahead...*

While this book is a chronicle of my life in the music business, it is also a very personal diary. From bohemian beginnings on a hillside in New Jersey to countless stages across the USA, Canada, and Europe, I have persisted in my eclectic, counter-industry "stranger in a strange world" kind of journey. From my first recording at the age of twelve, to my adventures at the feet of the rediscovered blues masters when I was fifteen, I have loved and played blues against all odds for most of my life. Through experiences with record labels large and small, extensive touring that has worn out various roadworthy vehicles, dealing with naysayers, skeptics and detractors, I have somehow survived to earn a gold record in Europe and five Blues Music Awards. It's fair to say, "Been there, done that, and got the T-shirt." Over the span of sixty unusual and sometimes unbelievable years, I have gained perspective on a world which has undergone tumultuous change- from the music it listens to and creates, to the very essence of the lives we lead. Whether encountering a young Bob Dylan at my father's sandal shop in the sixties or working in the studio with Stevie Wonder, this book is about those unlikely adventures, and those noteworthy people, in the world of music of course, but also in my most personal experiences.

My sister urged me to write a disclaimer. As youngsters we competed, fought, and later, didn't speak for years... but as I told my siblings, there would be no book if it was edited by my family. Both of them had singularly different experiences from mine. There is no accounting for this other than the obvious outward differences- the oldest: my sister. The youngest and only boy: my brother. And me, the middle child- rebellious, highly driven, extremely outspoken, artistic and musical. My star was crossed from the beginning for a rockier road. But all is well with that now. I ask for their forgiveness as I unravel a more interesting tale that is only slightly edited to prevent lawsuits and the like.

Introduction

I always step on toes- it's a life long condition. My mother used to say, "Rory says things which cut to the bone and either make people laugh or cry." My father called me a "mutant" because of my unusually radical views. I'm told I am an enigma- I don't fit anyone's categories. I've been repeatedly questioned: "Why is a little white girl from up north singing the songs of old black men from down south?" There is no explaining this to people who think we should exist within our own "category." But I'm all about busting stereotypes, confounding assumptions, and defying labels. Sometimes I think I have become a goodwill ambassador, a bridge between elements many people mistakenly see as separate. Before I am white or black, male or female, old or young, I am human. I say to the detractors, "You're looking in the wrong place. It's not an outward thing, it's a spirit thing."

Credit Where Credit Is Due

From the beginning I have been meticulous about naming the original writers and celebrating the source of the music. That is not to be glossed over or hidden. No one can say I stole material as my own or devalued the artists who created the music. It has been a lifelong mission to honor them, play the music as written, and highlight the unique, historic, foundational quality of the art. But neither will I allow anyone to place rules, restrictions, or try to limit the spirit that inspires the family of humans. No one can control that, thank God. I will not apologize for loving blues.

About The Book

Writing this book brought up tremendous emotion- much joy and sorrow in the unearthing of long-forgotten memories. It strengthened an already vivid sense of purpose. Now I was able to see the shape and form of my life. I discovered photographs I had never seen before, many taken by professional and amateur photographers at shows, and others supplied by family. Some I assumed were lost, while others I simply hadn't cared about until now. During the recording session with Stevie Wonder, pictures were taken that disappeared. While searching through boxes, these photos seemingly appeared in my hand. "Oh my God," I shouted, "the Stevie Wonder photos... I found them!" Other pictures which I have lived with my entire life jumped out at me with renewed vigor, such as old family portraits. I came across hand-written notes detailing the names and relationships between the evocative faces. At last I saw the similarities in the features, and was moved to tears.

Each time the book was finished, another chapter would come to mind. A sense of the quilt design, as yet unfinished, began to emerge. Missing pieces were being placed into a puzzle that had been collecting dust in the back of an old closet labeled "Danger- Forgotten Memories." The fragments have been polished, carefully and lovingly slipped into their proper places, and now the image in the picture is visible. I feel I have been grafted onto a larger vine. The plant is fuller now, fed by a richer soil.

When faced with the task of recounting my life, I knew it would be almost impossible to manage if I had to sit down and start writing in chronological order. Far too many visions rushed in to make sense of it all, so I devised a method: vignettes, which began as notated head-lines- chapter headers, if you will. I made lists of notes with titles for each memory. When something occurred to me I didn't have to worry about its position in the lineup, I could simply write. This helped im-mensely, and soon I was assembling each in its proper order. In that respect this book was written the way a movie is made- the last scene could have been filmed first. Then it is arranged so it makes sense, and someone is hired to check inconsistencies such as hair length, outfits and so on. I have endeavored to do that, but the final result is really a mosaic, much like life. The chapters don't necessarily have only one correct order...

Dedication

*W*hen A Woman Gets The Blues is dedicated to the strongest source of my musical inspiration: my father- country fiddle player, poet and sandal maker Allan Block. Dad (now retired and living in New Hampshire), has been a popular and well-loved figure in the folk community; indeed a well deserved reputation. I adored him, and this book makes that obvious. But he was an imperfect person (as we all are), and that is illuminated through the experiences of my childhood and beyond. There is no slander here, nothing mean-spirited- just an honest view through the eyes of a daughter. This book is a gift to him as an important artist, writer and human being. If his fathering was less than perfect I can only point out that most of us- myself included- would love a second chance at many of the important events of our lives. In the end this book is about love, healing and forgiveness. I believe that the honest experiences detailed within are more likely to help someone with a similar experience than to hurt. As with the personal stories I tell from the stage, it is my profound conviction that many of us are healed by learning about other people's struggles.

A similar kind of dedication pertains to my mother. Not only could she have been a successful singer, she was easily as talented as my father- but her many fears drew her down a different path.

Mom had some kind of melancholy (whether she was bipolar, schizo-phrenic, manic depressive, or otherwise) that exerted seismic influenc-es on her personality. Those things had not yet been clearly defined in her day and time. As with my father, there was also great healing. But I know from stories I have revealed about her that at least one former-ly hurt and diminished young woman was encouraged. Coming up to me after a performance, she told me that what I said about alienation and healing with my mother had helped her to revisit her own dam-aged relationship. With her head tilted shyly to one side, she said she felt hopeful about reopening a dialogue with her mother. If I have been of use in the honest recounting of my life, I count it all joy.

Reflections

I know I'm not a great writer. On the positive side I am blunt and hate redundancies. On the negative, I tend to speak in rambling run-on sentences, so I go back frequently to edit myself down. I know that

less is more. My father loved words and gloried over their meanings. I got my respect for language from him. My mother was well-spoken and my grandmother was an editor, and that also helps.

Text messaging and email has all but destroyed grammar, spelling, and the art of written language, diminishing it to the lowest form of burps, grunts, and babblings. This book, though by no means brilliantly written (as I would wish), attempts to honor my dad's love of words, and recount some part of my life- a life driven by a total love of music which was clearly passed to me by my father.

During my early childhood, Dad was the more affectionate parent, which provoked bitter resentment from my mother. Although light years away from any traditional fathering role, he had a playful, child-like nature and was capable of being attentive and emotional- albeit briefly- in his own fleeting, quirky way. But for reasons I have never understood, the parental roles shifted as I got older. No doubt my father, being the eldest of two boys, had no training in raising women. By the time I reached my teens he was far more focused on having me arrested for skipping school than being supportive. He had become bitingly derisive and utterly rejecting, which led to an almost father-less adulthood. My mother, however, proved willing to step away from her "ice queen" facade and seize the opportunity to become friends. But by that time, both had inflicted serious damage, and the recovery would be life-long. When my mother died in 1992, I deeply regret-ted being unable to continue the growth we had started. Nonethe-less, through life's unexpected twists and turns, the process has been revived with my elderly father. In my mind, nothing is ever too late...

Dad is still alive but has some kind of Senile Dementia. He doesn't recognize people. He has little or no memory, but he is happy. When he hears music his mind is jolted and he makes lucid remarks. "That's the Block in you!" he observed when I played a song for him. I wish I could turn back the clock, restore his mind, and see him regain his faculties now that his heart is right and his dragons are slain.

I celebrate Dad's love of words, his enthusiasm for life and the natural world, and his incredible passion for music. In former days he was a purist who taught us to hate fraudulence, pretense, and insincerity. Even though he was a flawed father, I forgive him, as I understand how frail we all are and how impossible it is for humans to be perfect. What matters is remorse, honesty, and genuine restoration... a desire to make things right in the now. Dad recently made this entirely clear to me by expressing his love, his pride in my music, and his support for

14

my art in the clearest, strongest terms. The last time I saw him totally lucid he touched my hair and said, "I have a genius for a daughter." It may have taken eighty some-odd years of living for him to be able to say a thing like this- and for me to hear it- but no matter. It was said, and everything is healed as a result. When I arrived at the festival where our family was gathering, he wanted to hold my hand and walk together. He said, "Now I feel complete, because you are here." He said he loved me time and time again. I was fighting tears the entire time. My dad has always had the power to rock my world.

Many things have happened to me in my life that I haven't spoken about, and if revealed carelessly could implicate and offend others. I desire to be responsible in my recountings, as this needn't be a tattletale, tabloid style book. Lurid details are of little interest to me. While being mindful that simply being inflammatory doesn't serve any purpose, I still have to relate the journey, and at times I will not mention names for obvious reasons. But a name hardly matters... it's the experience that lingers. My stepmother once said (after reading the first draft of my life story that went onto my web site), "Now dear, you mustn't write about people until after they are gone." I pulled the story and edited it down about ten times as a result of her caution. Whether that would indicate another book at a later time I don't know, only that in this one I will probably relate as many facts as I can remember, minus a few names.

There is no way to cast certain things in a rosy glow. The fact that there was corporal punishment when I was growing up, that I was slapped in the face and hit fairly regularly by my mother, that there were spankings, once or twice with objects such as a board, and that my father beat me on a couple of occasions, once pretty badly- there's no way to sugarcoat that. To the world he was a mellow folkie, a poet, and a hippie, and it is shattering a certain image to reveal this. But that's what happened, and it formed me, and this is my story.

15

Pre-Memory

*T*he following was revealed to me years after the fact, having occurred when I was too young to remember, but not too young to be affected. For reasons that have never been fully explained, after my birth my mother had some kind of breakdown. Whatever it was- postpartum depression, bipolar disorder, or even some kind of psychosis- my father committed her to the horrible halls of Bellevue mental hospital. Next, he placed my sister and I into foster homes, frightening to contemplate. Were they thinking of giving us away? Is there some reason my father could not have taken care of us while our mother, for whatever hazy reasons she appeared to need hospitalization, was convalescing? These are thoughts that haunt me. With my mother now deceased and my father currently unable to remember, the matter will probably never be explained. What we did learn was mostly from Grandma, who said that for six months Mom was incarcerated in this hellhole. She wanted out- Grandma tried to get her out- but there was a doctor, eager to take advantage of an unusually beautiful young woman, who had blocked all efforts to release her. Grandma claimed there was sexual abuse, something which simply wasn't spoken of in those days. To think that my mother was labeled incompetent and placed into an institution where her hands (according to her own description years later), were tied behind her, and where her head was tilted back to force her to swallow medication- is totally unthinkable. In any case my sister and I were raised for six months in foster homes. Already a year old at the time, my sister was devastated and cried inconsolably. Then she stopped recognizing Grandma.

After my mother was released- the result of repeated letters and pressure- my parents went to pick us up. I learned that the woman caring for my sister and I wept when she had to part with us, and that she ran out into the road to beg my parents not to take us away. When we heard this story we cried, wondering if our fate would have been different had we stayed with the adoptive mother who had wanted us, and not the mother who made her dislike for *me*, at least, so clear from my earliest memories.

When I was in my twenties and thirties my mother and I had moments of deep communication in which her dark past began to reveal itself and my sense of indignation on her behalf grew. I understood that she had experienced much suffering, and when on occasion I found it possible to express compassion to her I would do so. In those moments when I could see the vulnerability and fear in her eyes- when there was no longer a veil- I felt I could look into her soul, and I felt that she needed my protection. I longed to prevent further injustice to her.

I cannot write a book detailing the many issues which created insecurity in my life without pointing out the obvious- the reason my parents had such an effect on me is that I loved them so much. I longed to please them and fulfill their expectations, but I just couldn't seem to manage. As a result I had a broken heart. It's how you feel when you've been dumped by a sweetheart for someone more clever, more beautiful, and more deserving.

Mom and Dad were very young when they married. I think there must have been incredible frustration for them both. Apparently mismatched, the resulting unhappiness created, at least in my mother, a kind of bitterness that caused her to vent at me. There was no way to understand this as a small child. It was terribly painful at the time- but I am able to understand and forgive it now.

After the bath. Photo: Hugh Bell

The Wilderness

Layer upon layer of leaves, green canopies arching overhead connected by endless veins drawing clear, perfect liquid from inside the earth. What is soil? Brown, lumpy, textured, with pebbles, sand, and organic material. It was once flesh, once decay. An old bird fell from the sky and lay on its infinitely comforting surface, then withered. Now it's loam, with the assistance of miniature monsters known as microbes. Perfect complexity, yet beautifully simple. Albert Einstein pointed out the inherent beauty of natural laws. If it's cluttered or complicated, it's not God. Only man could have taken something as beautiful as dirt and made it ugly. My father loved soil and felt happy when it covered his hands.

I was born in a small hospital, and was soon afterwards taken to live in an old cabin on a hillside. Another child, my sister, awaited my arrival. For a six-month window the Bellevue events occurred, after which we were all reunited in this peaceful place. An Artesian well stood in the grass where my father drew water. It had a pump handle which needed to be primed. The water was very cold and tasted incredibly clean. My mother boiled diapers on the stove and canned our food in glass jars. There was a view from the yard which faced a great valley- rolling farmland as far as the eye could see. A gnarled cherry tree stood off to one side where the woods and brambles wrapped around the little clearing. I climbed this tree countless times over the years when we returned to this pristine spot to visit. Within one year we left the wilds of New Jersey and moved to an apartment in New York City.

My Suicide Attempt

From the beginning I felt it. A deep, begrudging dislike- a plot to kill me. There I was, a small child reaching up to mother, when a shadow passed over me and cold predatory eyes looked down. This feeling of being hated attended my childhood. Standing on a trash can in front of the sink, it was my turn to wash dishes. Perhaps I was wearing a diaper, perhaps just training pants. I was small enough to have the chubby little cherub legs of a baby that appeared in photographs of me from that time. My sister, already well trained in the fine art of hating the younger, lurked nearby. Mother, hate masteress supreme, loomed above, radiating a cold and disapproving presence. My ways were wrong, and I knew it. Impulsively, older than my years, I grabbed a full glass of detergent and willfully swallowed it, knowing it would kill me. I remember every bitter mouthful, and the decision to keep swallowing. Suicide was a better idea, reasonable under the circumstances- a considered and mature choice. Surrounded by enemies who would love for me to be gone, I dipped the tall glass deep into the acrid bubbles, threw my curly head back, and drank deeply, thinking poison was my lot.

Photo: Hugh Bell

A Bigger House

God was my friend. Even though I didn't know his name, I always felt his vast presence. There was great love to be found in nature- in the sunlight, in my time alone. I never doubted that I was in larger arms and in a bigger house. This is what made continuing onwards possible.

I became wild. I was always a loner, always different. I accepted my insanity. I was not a "normal" child. People were mortal enemies. In their company I cowered, waiting for blows. Instinctively, I came to understand that all the dangers and conflicts in life emanated from humans, and all the comforts from God.

Cave Art

When I was a toddler my father took me into the bathroom and held my hand while he was peeing. I suppose that to him it was meant to be a kind of assurance that all this was natural. Perhaps he saw it as an educational moment. But to me it was about as unnatural and shocking as possible. He was peeing right over the top of my head just a few inches from my eyes.

Toting a holster of Crayolas and pencils, I covered the walls of my bedroom with drawings of boys peeing. Not unlike ancient art, everyone was in profile. Boys of different heights all had cowlicks and rows of thin pointed teeth. No one was wearing any pants- all were peeing. They didn't seem to think it was strange, but I on the other hand couldn't believe it. I contemplated the images. Later, humiliated by the flamboyant way my mother discussed this with her strange, bulky friends, I realized I had some kind of condition. I was sent to my room with a bucket of suds and told to scrub my cave art off the wall. I knew I was deranged, and words like "penis envy" were tossed about while I slipped as noiselessly as possible into the icy habitat which housed an uncomfortable bed- the cheerless place that was my room.

Adults

To me adults looked like grotesque, hideous caricatures. Distorted, misshapen and flabby, they were oblivious as they chatted away. I felt sorry for them. With hair pressed into unimaginably unattractive styles, shapeless dresses draped over swollen bodies- shiny pants, argyle socks, moles, flakes, wrinkles, wandering eyes, thick glasses and clusters of hair protruding from their nostrils- my school teachers exemplified this complete lack of awareness. All wore bunion shoes-large, lumpy, boat-like objects so common among educators they must have been legally required. "Do you wear Murray's Space shoes? *What*? You do *not*? I'm sorry, I'm afraid that will be necessary, Mrs. Binraddle." I created satirical drawings which brought gales of laughter and a sense of victorious joy. If I had to look at it, at least I should be able to draw it. I probably could have been a cartoonist.

Becoming A Tomboy

I tried to be a boy. Someone obviously felt it would have been better, most likely my father. Faced with two daughters, he had to make a decision. The first girl was welcomed- at that point it was still a novelty. The second was a sign of failure, and a more aggressive disapproval was necessary.

I was a "tomboy," what little girls became when no one was looking. We got a lot of exercise, we ran with the boys, and we could be tough. No one cared if we wandered into danger- after all, we could defend ourselves with our fists. As a result I was confronted with a dazzling array of life-and-death scrapes. I became unnaturally bold. I taunted death and believed myself invincible. Fueled by irrational curiosity, I experienced things so extraordinary that the likelihood of explaining them to anyone was remote, so the memories went deep into my subconscious and remained as disturbing images, only to surface in dreams- people with heads like hammers, flying animals, incessant wanderings. There was no rational way to express them.

My Dale Evans Costume

*O*nce I was asked what I wanted for Christmas. Ah, this was different... someone actually wanted to get me the gift of my choice! I requested a cowboy outfit: a holster, gun, boots, hat, and bandana. But when Christmas arrived and the box was torn open, it revealed a little fringed skirt and hat with rope designs on the edge. I was shattered.

This was not a cowboy outfit! Where was the shiny gun and holster? The message was strong: I would only be an ornamental second. I would be expected to stand about posing in my Dale Evans cowgirl costume. I never even tried it on.

Photo: Hugh Bell

The Night

I hated the night. That was when you were scared, sleepless, or sick. Getting sick made mother angry, so that was a hellish possibility. Sister didn't like it much either. "Mo-om!" she called loudly with obvious disapproval... "Rory got sick!" I stood aside as the sheets were resent-

23

fully torn off my bed. Best to grow up and leave home so as not to piss anyone off. Later I thought about it. Why was I, and no one else sick? Memories of the poison (which my mother taught me to fear) came to mind. I could hear my mother's voice echoing, "Why don't you go back where you came from?"

Stray Cats

$\mathcal{F}$illed with the rubble of some collapsed building, the open lot next door became a haven for feral cats- thin, ghostlike little creatures which slipped in and out of every dark, decrepit place. This was intolerable to me. I heard the chilling shrieks of battles in the night and shivers went up my spine- it sounded like death. I saw them lurking, haunted and hollow-eyed, in the daytime. I hated that they were hungry and fed them whenever I could- milk, tuna fish or sardines-whatever I could secret away to the alley. There were a few bowls already in place, put there by some kind soul. These poor creatures were starving, and once when I was sent to get milk, I snuck a bowl or two for my little friends. I lied and told my mother I had no idea how the carton got opened, so she sent me back to the store to return it. The proprietor had a sour look on his face. I couldn't tell my mother I had compassion for the cats- she wouldn't understand, I reasoned. It seemed that compassion was worth exactly nothing when I was growing up. Today experts pound us with the message: "self love, self love," as if it provides the solution to all our emotional problems- when instead it just might create them.

$\mathcal{F}$uzzy Sweaters

$\mathcal{M}$y mother wore long tweedy skirts and fuzzy sweaters which high-lighted her curved back. Her light brown hair was swept into some kind of bun. She was pretty, even beautiful. I later learned she had been referred to as "the most beautiful woman in the Village." When we were out she laughed a lot with various strangers. Obviously, some people thought she was funny.

Yelling at the carriage driver for mistreating the horse
Photo: Hugh Bell

The Exploding Radiator

*F*ather weeps while the radiator explodes. There is something about the angry steam, the pressure behind the water jet, and the teariness of the moment. A mini emergency- Dad wrestles the radiator off with a rag, then sits on the floor crying, saying his relationship with our mother has ended. Once again, we are totally aghast and confused.

The Grandfathers

One of my grandfathers died of a heart attack, and the other, who cooked holiday dinner at the family bungalow in Far Rockaway, died of self-starvation in a hospital years before I was born. The latter was my mother's father, and we understood that at the tender age of fifteen, she had never gotten over the shock.

I remember Dad crying on the occasion of his father's passing. I was five years old and had no memory of ever meeting this grandfather from the Midwest. Dad was wearing a red and black wool lumberjack shirt. He had gloves on and was nervously wringing his hands. I hated to see him cry. Both times it happened he fought visibly to prevent the emotion. It was so rare as to seem totally out of place, and I thought the world was coming to an end.

Grandpa Isadore Block with my sister

Dad's Better Nature

*T*hroughout childhood I had the deepest admiration for my father. I got my sense of humor from him- a unique, eccentric, joyful humor. Dad allowed me to be silly without condemnation. When shown my drawings, he would laugh gleefully. He closed his eyes when he drank a glass of water. "He must really love it," I thought. This somehow impressed me as an important sign that he enjoyed life. He allowed me to give him haircuts, which meant he either trusted me totally or had no vanity- perhaps both. More than once I gave him bald spots with my overzealous scissor technique, but he never seemed to notice. I was the official head scratcher- something I was apparently good at. He was incredibly appreciative and said I had "nimble fingers." When Dad approved, all was right with the world. I think I stored these precious compliments up for use at a later time- when the sheer volume of criticisms became heavy indeed.

Photo: Hugh Bell

Sullivan Street

We grew up in a neighborhood known at the time as "Little Italy," and now, in its greatly changed form, "Soho." My sister and I spent many afternoons zooming up and down the sidewalks on our tricycles- giggling, crashing into people's legs, and shaking our fists while pretending to be tough. We would clamp our lower teeth over our lips and say "Big boyz! Big boyz!" in unison, as well as one could with one's jaw locked. We sat in the second floor window with our legs dangling through the iron bars shouting and waving at bemused pedestrians. Our babysitter, at her wit's end, threatened to walk off the job if we didn't come in. We did not, though we later repented and begged her to come back. Long suffering and with a heart of gold, Rose returned. I remember her bright red hair which she wore in a bun, her diminutive stature, and her cooking, which was traditional Italian and always excellent.

The neighborhood boasted a tantalizing array of grocery stores and specialty shops as delightful as any you'd find in Italy. I lingered in the cheese store, soaking up the fabulous aromas and gazing up at the wax-covered globes which hung from the ceiling in every size. A cow bell jangled invitingly at the arrival of each new customer. The butcher shop displayed a veritable gallery of gourmet items, from the less-appealing lumpy things with claws that floated in jars, to ground meats covered with peppercorns, carefully sliced cutlets, roasts rolled neatly in string, and stacked chickens with beak and feet still intact. The bakeries had huge glass apothecary jars filled with brightly colored pastries and tiny striped cakes lined up like artwork in the windows. Could we eat them, or had they been there under shellac for years? I pondered this. There was a dry cleaner downstairs, and a watermelon truck which came up the street in summer preceded by cries of "Wa-ter-me-low! Water-me-low!" The same old man, seemingly shorter every year, appeared with a huge machete which he swung skillfully through the air to cut and serve slices. There was an immensely loud ice cream truck that broadcast a cheery melody which you could hear for miles. We jumped up and down screaming for Italian Ice, a super delicious frozen mixture drenched in a lemony syrup which I longed to eat all day long. I was allowed one, but often managed to sneak several. My friends told me the Boogie man would cut out my tongue if I used a swear word. I could rave on in a New York street accent if I wanted to, or speak in my elementary school dialect. I had a good ear and could pick up language nuances easily.

The rest of the years at Sullivan Street are mostly a blur. Now I realize that the sometimes frightening atmosphere around us was that of an intense Mafia presence- not the roving bands of angry young men we have today- but entrenched, mature, long-established crime organizations and the neighborhoods they controlled. Many of the faces I saw were menacing: impeccably dressed older men- bosses- some of the very same people featured in movies, and some of the wipe-outs depicted in famous films happened for real in this neighborhood- some right around the corner. A lot of the speaking was in a foreign language, which sounded angry to me even when it wasn't. There was a sense of secrecy, and a thinly veiled threat of unknown horrors. Every day I walked past darkened store fronts simply called "social clubs." I didn't want to know. I longed for safety. I wanted people to be reasonable.

When my parents fought (which they did frequently), I tried to patch things up. I remember clinging to my father's legs and begging them to stop. I suggested alternatives- no one listened. I developed the mind-set of a therapist.

I have never had a morbid curiosity about human intrigue. Horror movies are the last thing on earth I want to be subjected to. A child cannot understand the depth and intensity of adult society. It's a completely different world driven by forces as hard to relate to as life on Mars. Sex, marriage, couple-hood, betrayal, blind rage in voices... it was a beast that couldn't be soothed. I grew up with a strong desire to avoid these things. I can smell danger a mile away and always know before anyone else when it's time to split. If I see violence in front of me I cross the street. I have an incredibly accurate "shit detector." At the first sign of smoldering I'm outa' there.

New York In The Fifties

The City, my daily reality, was as dangerous, heartless, and impersonal as a phone book. All that was fun in daylight became depressing in darkness. My room had a view overlooking the bleakest of cityscapes. Sometimes at night, perched sleeplessly in the window, I would watch as an array of near-dead people dragged themselves down the sidewalk making scraping noises as they went. Old ladies with their swollen legs and stockings rolled to their ankles. Sagging eyes filled with moisture and redness- these were not happy lives.

The hallway of our building was tiled with tiny black and yellow squares that reeked of ammonia. There was someone called "the Super" who we never saw, but we knew he had recently been there from the smell of disinfectant. These same halls were often filled with the horrendous sounds of domestic violence. The woman across the way who looked like Marilyn Monroe was getting beaten up... again. Her husband was a skinny, twisted little man who lounged about in sleeveless T-shirts even in the dead of winter. When we passed in the hallway he always had a guilty grin on his face while one eye looked straight ahead and the other gazed off. His three daughters had an air of untimely sophistication- all looked like grown women at twelve- buxom, with long, blaze-orange hair, red lipstick, and painted toenails. This couldn't have been easy for them.

Beatniks

My father was a "beatnik," or so I was told. This meant he hung around in a striped shirt, wailed on a bongo, sported a scraggly beard, a tilted beret, and wore a large, unwieldy pair of sandals. In truth the only similarity was the sandals. Dad was the proprietor of a little place called The Allan Block Sandal Shop that began its existence in a tiny shop on MacDougal Street not much larger than a kitchen counter top. Having no room inside, he stretched his materials out across the sidewalk and made sandals in front of curious pedestrians, cutting each pair by hand with a curved knife. This must have been quite a sight as people stepped carefully over the array of cowhides. As for the rest, he was always clean-shaven, never played any percussion instruments, and only owned a few shirts, none of them striped.

All wearing Allan Block sandals- I'm on the right

Joan of Arc

My sister was better than I was in every way as per some ancient preference for the elder and hatred of the middle child (which I was soon to become), having been firmly established thousands of years prior. Born a year and one month before me, she was Joan of Arc and all that I aspired to be. She had a much better forehead. Hers was high and allowed her hair to be combed back. Mine was low and ape-like with a distinct widow's peak, which I was led to understand indicated a genetic connection to witches. She was older, braver, bigger, more experienced, and utterly arrogant. I knew I deserved the contempt, being smaller, wormier, and far less capable.

When we were not in public where it was important for her to lord over me, we shared much companionship and were at times great buddies. Being close in age was a blessing and a curse, competition being the worst of it- playmates in mischief being the best. Her dominance was a display for the parents which they seemingly relished, and both had an arsenal of belittling epithets they would use as they deemed necessary on a regular basis. My sister was chronically good- I, incessantly bad. She was by divine ordination truthful, while I, by some terrible judgment of nature, was apparently incapable of honesty. She was invariably worthy of praise, while I was the cause of consternation and conflict. But I was aware in our moments of friendship that she had a deep seated guilt about the entire dynamic. As much as she loved being favored, she also longed to escape the hot seat, as the burden of inadvertently causing harm to another by virtue of irrational biases becomes heavy indeed. She was the heir apparent, but she didn't always wish to be, and below the surface she harbored the same fears and insecurities that I did. She knew that any facade of being favored could fade away in a flash if the house of cards were to come tumbling down, and we both understood that when it happened (as we knew it would), we would have only each other to cling to in order to escape the ruins of the dangerous, precariously balanced world in which we lived and survived, hour by hour.

Dr. Lunginoti

As small children, my sister and I were taken to a doctor we both hated. To us he was a villain, a dangerous enemy cloaked in a white garment who hovered about surrounded by shelves of little bottles filled with horrible potions. He had thick glasses and an expressionless face with dry, pasty lips and those foamy strings of saliva that stretched across the corners of his mouth. As he pursed his lips absentmindedly it would make clicking sounds... "fish lips," we called them. It was the nurse's job to wrestle us into submissive poses with arms pinned behind our backs in order to stick us with needles of his evil concoctions. On this day my skin had been pierced with a series of little holes to protect me from a dreaded disease. After the shock of the pain abated I looked with curiosity at the interesting red dots. I carefully touched them and immediately a cry of alarm rang out. Before I knew it I had received another inoculation, and a new set of holes appeared that had to be touched. Now the entire office (which included the receptionist and a spare nurse they must have kept hidden for just such occasions) rallied against me as my arm was made ready for yet another injection. In an act of heroism, my sister, all of five years old and suddenly large and powerful, stepped between me and the doctor, waved her fist menacingly and shouted, "Leave her alone, you bastard!" We made a swift exit from the office, and I remember feeling that we had prevailed in our little uprising. That was our last visit to Dr. Lunginoti.

Death Threats

One understands how unimportant one's life is- and how extremely close to death- when one's caretakers (operating behind closed doors and without any safeguards whatsoever) continuously threaten your life. There is strangling, of course, neck breaking, the usual "I'm going to kill you!" the sinister "Why don't you go back where you came from?" and then the most devastating of all: "I wish you had never been born." These punishing words were hurled at me routinely by my mother and are still vivid today.

My father's unkindness took a more blunt, pointless form. As much as he was a man of depth with a keen appreciation for life and creativity, he also had a mean streak. As the first born son, he had clearly been the apple of his parent's eyes. He was incensed when his brother was born, feeling his kingdom was threatened, and his lifelong rivalry with our uncle was never a secret. "Danny stole the buggy," Dad said recently, a humorous but revealingly jealous statement regarding the usurping of his royal carriage (the stroller). Throughout his life, Dad retained this sense of indignant entitlement, and seemed compelled to make supremely insulting comments that hung heavily in the air, stung horribly, and were often so ridiculous as to seem like disturbed ramblings. I can hardly remember his remarks from my childhood, but as I got older I became more aware: accusations of mental disorders, and pronouncements regarding a person's innate dis-likability- even in regards to close family members. Behind my father's liberal facade lurked an incredibly conservative, judgemental mind that seemed determined to make others feel insecure and undeserving.

A therapist once said to me (while I sat clutching a pillow, crying, and feeling totally humiliated) that I was born into a very "dangerous" situation. Despite all the evidence, I simply could not believe this was true. I was so brainwashed I believed that all this fuss about rejection must have been my vivid imagination- or at the very least I richly deserved whatever I got and should confess to being guilty, and then go directly to jail- a jail where very bad children (who later became very confused adults) were incarcerated for the crime of irritating more virtuous people. By this time I had formed a very harsh opinion of myself. In my painfully shy nature, my lack of social graces, and my tendency to be a hermit, lies this rejected and hated child.

Most of the time, if we start our lives as abusers and bullies, we are eventually convicted- whether by our own conscience or by some unexpected suffering which drives us to enlightenment. Many people, by the time they are beginning to age and ponder their own mortality, mellow considerably- even apologize- and humbly recognize the errors in their ways. Senility is a great healer. As we unravel in the natural cycle of things, we become a vulnerable child again.

Little Red

My father's mother Valeria was known to us simply as "Nana." Our grandfather Isadore had been the owner of a "junk yard" (whatever that may have been- salvage, scrap metal, old appliances and the like), and had managed to stash away every penny until he had saved enough for his wife (after his death in 1955) to send her grandchildren to a school on Bleeker Street called Little Red School House. It was this school that was the center of my world. Known simply as "Little Red," school was a different universe. The halls were filled with light, and the front door was surrounded by large windows laced with some kind of thin metal chicken wire- perhaps to prevent shattering in the event of a flying brick. We knew we were a target in the neighborhood though we didn't know why. On a particular morning, "PIGS" was spray painted on the outside wall, but its meaning was unclear- except that someone apparently hated us. However, inside the thick walls we felt safe and optimistic.

The assembly room with its burnished wooden stage and fine theater style seating was a pleasant place that was daily filled with music and, on special occasions, dramatic presentations, musicals, plays, and recitals. Art classes provided a total respite from persecution. I gravitated towards the things I could disappear into. Later I discovered that this civilized world with its creative atmosphere was courtesy of Nana, who had arranged to pay for our education as well as summer camp and who knows what else. My father's chosen profession of sandal maker and Saturday afternoon fiddler was not known for generating great wealth. This could explain why we seemed to be fairly poor, yet at the same time enjoyed certain perks which were clearly beyond a sandal maker's budget.

The Velvet Horse

One afternoon we were on a rare family outing. Everyone was dressed awkwardly in their silly best- clothing stiff from storage, and in long-outdated styles. Dress up came from the yearly box of unimaginably ugly hand-me-downs sent by a cousin in the Midwest. Bright red gowns with gossamer plumage, green plaid button-up dresses, pedal pushers and felt skirts decorated with poodles would appear from the box, each more hideous than the last- who wore these things? To us they looked like costumes from the closet of a comic strip character. We were beatniks- these clothes had been worn by conservatives from Wisconsin. I hoped we wouldn't run into anyone we knew.

Gargantuan effort was required to herd us all, disgruntled and ready to mutiny, down the street. There was an utter lack of happiness in the air. I had a glum expression etched on my features which frequently caused people to admonish me- "Smile!" they would say, as if you could fake one. "What are they talking about?" I used to think, "That would be phony" (a word my mother regaled me with regularly). As I scraped joylessly along, there it was- a softly lit window, and in it a little velvet horse. It was a perfectly formed sprig of a unicorn, complete with a tiny saddle and bridle. I lingered at the window while the others drifted away. I longed for the little horse. Soon, irritated voices interrupted my reverie and called me to attention. I was taken home and deposited back into the cold cell I shared with my sister.

A day or two later my parents disappeared again for some event, and in the morning I awoke to find, perched quietly on the window sill, the little velvet horse. Perhaps it was the work of a good fairy and not the parents who had nothing good to say about me.

Soon afterwards I started a collection of miniature porcelain horses which I stored in the cubbies of my desk. These doubled perfectly as stalls, and eventually I filled them with every breed and color. How my mind raced with excitement when I looked at them! Someday, I thought, I would own a horse.

Stars From Heaven

One Christmas I was sent to my room in the middle of decorating the tree. Something I had done warranted early bed, and since Christmas lights represented love (and love, being God, was my only source of comfort), this was overwhelmingly sad. I lay in bed convulsing with sobs while my sister and mother finished decorating. Eventually I was allowed to come out and see the finished results. As I stood there shivering, I felt like the little match girl viewing a warmly lit room through frosted panes. I was an outsider and I knew it- a feeling I still have to a great extent. But the lovely colors shone as brightly as gemstones- like little dots of hope and happiness- and they comforted me.
It would be forces outside my family that would ultimately provide

the strength for me to survive. Comfort would never come in the form of a hug from my mother. I cannot recall ever being embraced by her, or ever receiving a kiss. I never heard her say, throughout the duration of my childhood, "I love you." I felt I was somehow dirty, perhaps smelly, and I felt ashamed- as if I exuded something that made people recoil.

My father, despite his known tendency to deride, was an innately passionate person, and his inclination to be more openly affectionate than my mother sometimes offset the frigid atmosphere. But whenever positive attention was expressed to me there was an immediate back-lash from his wife. It seemed that somehow she was determined that no one would be able to show me affection.

Call Me Jane

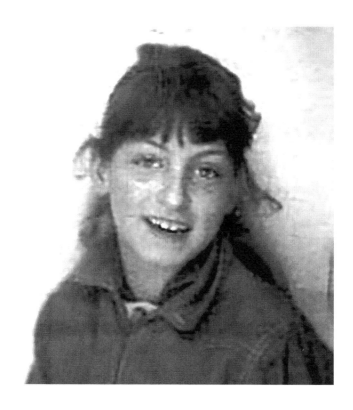

My friends had nannies and lived in majestic brownstones in neighborhoods where classical music wafted out of open windows and ivy climbed the red brick walls. These friends had lox and bagels, orange juice and cream cheese, and every overflowing delight from the best delicatessens in New York City. They had televisions, stuffed toys, and sleep-over dates. There were people who cleaned their houses and took them to the park. Somehow their parents (a completely different breed from mine) were friendly and warm, and showed a most solicitous concern for their children. They all seemed to get along perfectly with their spouses. Flat out, I always longed to be someone else- someone "normal." In my mind's eye was an image of me showing up at the door of one of these more privileged friends. It would be answered by a maid, of course. After explaining that I wanted to be a part of their family, I would be welcomed in, given a lovely room filled with sunlight, toys and pretty books, and my new life would begin. I would have a whole new set of parents that cherished me. Don't call me Rory, *call me Jane*.

Humanus Carnivorous

You couldn't go from a flute lesson to the dubious protection of a thinly walled apartment without passing through the powder keg atmosphere of violence. For reasons I was never able to comprehend, people were attacking and killing each other on a regular basis. Human beings, I observed (especially the male of the species, which in nature- just a power failure away- is without razor blades and comes complete with a shaggy mane akin to that of an adult lion), are predatory beasts taken to ambushing and dismembering prey following violent attack. What was the difference, I wondered, between our reality, with seedy back alleys where dead bodies decomposed, and the wild carnivores in the nature shows? Frankly, nothing... nothing, but perhaps the naive, misinformed vanity leading us to believe ourselves a superior species. Quite obviously, we're primates. But wait, primates are not as violent. We're a subspecies to the apes; *a distant, discontented, self-absorbed cousin*.

The Little Boy Who Screamed

Little brother was five years younger. There was a miscarriage before him which I was unaware of until many years later (although at three years old I created a drawing of a distressed pregnant woman which eerily mirrors what my mother must have experienced). My brother was a cherubic, mischievous little thing who got his way at all times by throwing his head back and screaming in a shrill, high-pitched

voice until no one could stand it anymore. It seems we all happily relented and didn't mind spoiling him. When he was still in diapers, we invented a game where my sister and I lay face down on a mattress while "Buppy" jumped up and down on our backs shrieking with delight. This was called "The Bigahini Man," and if he hadn't been so small, we wouldn't have survived. Miraculously, we thought it was funny.

A few years later my brother swallowed a whole bottle of baby aspirin. Teary eyed, he rode his tricycle until he was scooped up and taken to have his stomach pumped. My sister and I clung to each other and cried bitterly at the thought of losing him.

I had a special bond with my brother. Just about every photo of the three of us children shows him sitting on my lap. We spent incredible amounts of time together building what we called "setups"- mazes of marble shoots created from a huge block collection and entire towns with roadways for his many little Matchbox cars. I loved having someone to be silly with, and I would imagine I was the perfect babysitter. What could have interfered with such a close relationship? My mother. For reasons I cannot quite fathom she took an active interest in separating us and damaging the relationship. She relentlessly told me to find someone my own age to play with. She criticized so incessantly as to make me question my very sanity, and she certainly conveyed the message that at least in her mind there was something wrong with me for spending time with my little brother. It reached a crescendo at a friend's house in the suburbs.

Whenever I discovered a television at a friend's house, I would park myself down and watch old Westerns for hours on end. My brother and several of his friends sat on the floor in front of me playing with toys while I was draped on the couch engrossed in a shoot-em-up, ride'em-cowboy movie. Suddenly my mother appeared in the doorway glaring at me. "Zip up your fly!" she said in a horrible, accusative tone. Having no idea my fly was open, I became flustered- but whatever I may have answered, she swung her hand through the air and slapped my face violently. This was an awful, confusing, humiliating moment. My brother left the room at high speed. I must have cried out "Why did you do that!?" but the only answer was the back of my mother's frightening shadow leaving the room. The implication was clear- in her perverse mind I had been doing something unacceptable with my brother. Nothing could have been further from the truth. Somewhere after this point I learned to leave my brother alone, and this led to years of silence and alienation. This is the sad business that surrounded our lives, leaving us all with a sense of separation and anxiety about trying to get to know each other from scratch years later- with all this heavy baggage attached.

Nobody's Child

It was clear that a boy is what my father wanted when I was born. I had failed to be this boy, and no effort on my part could appease. No, I was the middle child, the second girl. I was nobody's child. There were photos of my father and brother rocking about in an old dingy holding up the prize catch, my brother's wide smile featuring his boyish buck teeth. There were nightly wrestling matches in the playroom, a wide selection of games and shared adventures. Being a girl meant doing your homework or suffer disapproval. My sister buckled down to her studies- I rebelled. I preferred sports, art, music and what would have been categorized as masculine pursuits. I had a competitive edge that was way outside the definition of feminine. The guitar would provide a way out of the dreary world of what seemed to be female submission.

My restlessness, my athleticism, my inclination to speak my mind all drew constant disapproval from my family, particularly my sister (who was being actively groomed to accept the outwardly submissive, inwardly subversive role which was the classic stereotype of female manipulation). Soon, she became the echo of my parents' rejection. By the time we were teenagers, she explained all my dislikable qualities in terms of astrology. In her eyes I was the evil Scorpio.

Boozer

The only unconditional love I received in childhood was from a cat. A magnificent creature with long, silky hair, Boozer was a Persian of mixed shades, mostly black, dark brown, and white. Boozer was always available when I needed affection. Boozer purred. Boozer slept on the bed with me. Countless times Boozer's reassuring presence and breathing brought me back to a state of peace after experiencing distress. On the downside Boozer clawed the living daylights out of the upholstered chairs, and there was nothing much to be done about it. We stopped noticing the dingy look of shredded fabric clinging to the furni-

ture. From time to time Boozer went into heat and howled, was allowed onto the roof, and at least once came back pregnant. Of course we set out a box for the birthing, but Boozer chose a cello case inside my sister's closet. I remember her brave little face as I swung open the doors and discovered her. I'm sure she was frightened as I shouted with surprise, but nonetheless she kept right on with her maternal duties and continued delivering her babies until all were born, cleaned, and nursed. I don't remember much about the babies but we obviously found homes for all of them.

I had never considered the possibility that Boozer might die. One day I came home from school to find my beloved Boozer in a cardboard box in the living room. My mother was quiet. She said Boozer had most likely died of hair balls from her long fur. My heart was gripped with sorrow, shock, and grief. As my fingers touched the still, lifeless form in the box I wept bitterly for the loss of my truest friend.

Candy

I had a terrible sweet tooth. With my miniature allowance I would stop by the local candy store and load up on every foul, tooth-destroying, sugared concoction and consume until I was full. I had striped straws packed with brightly colored granulated sugar, miniature wax soda bottles which had to be bitten apart and a horrible, thick syrup sucked out, and the usual array of nut-filled candy bars, including round things filled with caramel. I was clear on one account- I hated licorice and raisins- even raisins covered in chocolate, which I considered to be a poor excuse for candy. Despite all of this I had a ravenous appetite at dinnertime and appreciated the fact that my mother- when she wasn't having one of her "spells" as Grandma Keller used to call them- seemed to cook extremely well and put many interesting and good tasting meals on the table night after night. Apparently they taught her to cook in school (something which had gone out of style by the time I was a child and the shift towards more modern mores had begun to take hold). My enthusiasm for voracious eating- which started innocently enough- was probably the first indication of eating disorders to come which, rolled into a fabric of panic attacks of every kind, attended my childhood as one of the more frightening aspects.

Panic Attacks

It started with the pilot light. Entering the apartment after school one afternoon I noticed the smell of gas. As I processed this thought, I wandered into the kitchen to check the stove, where I discovered that the pilot light was out. In an instant I was consumed with a tidal wave of fear- fear so great and deep as to block out all else- fear so powerful it was as if my body had ceased to exist and only my head, large and exploding outward from pressure, remained. My vision blurred, there was a pounding in my ears, and I bolted for the door. I knew I was dying and could only hope to make it away, *away*, as far as possible to safety before being pulled into the dark world of death, alone in a hellish place. Struggling to breathe, fighting for consciousness, nothing was ever so gripping and all-consuming as this fear. The black hole was calling, the icy grave, the prison of eternal nothingness. I flew out the back door and down four flights without breathing. In the light and fresh air, I began to decompress. This was the time when the normalcy of other human beings was supremely comforting. My world seemed all swirling madness, but nannies with strollers, the gay neighbors on the ground floor, someone walking a dog, the noisy children returning from school- these people were normal- and if I tried hard enough, I could blend into their world and be spared certain destruction.

This fear ran its course over a year, but it was replaced by another, and then another. Fear of heart attacks gripped me in my bed. At first just a fleeting concept, then an accelerated beat, then a racing, pounding overwhelming torrent. My head felt light, sweat formed on my skin, and nothing I did could stop this runaway train. I don't remember exactly how it ended, but eventually, exhausted, I would fall asleep. Perhaps the most frightening thing of all was the nagging certainty that no one would care if I died.

Institutional Beets

The joys of voracious eating came to an abrupt end in the school cafeteria. I had already consumed the creamed corn I so loved, the institutional cubed beets, the meat loaf, and the mashed potatoes. I had already had "seconds." Full as usual, I sat at a round table with five or six others who were chatting away. Conversation turned to "Would'ja believe it" and "Guess what I heard" repartee, and before long someone was relating a true story: "Did you hear about the girl who ate so much that her *stomach burst*?" First, the familiar pounding in the head, then the dizziness and loss of vision followed by a melting sensation. I knew that my stomach had just exploded. But instead of bolting I sat consumed in a fire ball of terror, waiting to die while at the same time drawing comfort from the normalcy around me: the impassive, unconcerned faces of the students and teachers who did not seem to understand the danger that every meal and every bite had the power to destroy.

Over the space of several key years, poisoning, toxic gas, heart attacks, atomic bombs, radiation, and a host of other specialized fears dominated my inner life. Outwardly, I was precocious, artistically talented, and exceptionally athletic. But in that day and time such things were not valued much, and in the psychologically destructive environment in which I was raised, any abilities I displayed were beaten down with criticism and accusation. My musical talent was for the express purpose of "showing up" my sister (she, after all, who did not have a passion for a particular instrument, should not have to be discouraged by my obvious obsession). I was told that I was playing guitar to get back at her in some way- for being preferred? Certainly this was the message.

The Devastating Haircut

"Only take off a tiny bit" were the last words from my mouth. Assurances, assurances- "It will be perfect." Someone had decided my hair was too long, so I was taken to an official salon, now in retrospect more like a barbershop. My hair was my crowning glory, thus I anxiously sat down in the chair before the mirror with my mother's image in the glass to one side. Snip snip, snip snip snip. Soon I was saying "Stop, that's enough!" but the soothing words said it was just being evened out, snip snip, oh my God it was all gone! I reached for my hair. There was nothing there. I tried to pull on it but couldn't even get it over the back of my collar. I was horrified. This barber person was a criminal. Like Samson when Delilah stole his locks, my power was gone. I had been turned into a tennis ball. I would be the laughing stock of my class. Humiliated, grieved, and feeling ugly, I stepped out of the chair- never to trust anyone with scissors again.

Months rolled slowly by as I waited for my hair to grow out. Eventually there was enough for a ponytail. I pondered- what went wrong? My mother had been seated right there; she knew what I wanted, yet she watched my hair being removed. Why didn't she step in, why didn't she stop the barber? I wondered- did she want this to happen to me?

Today I cut my own hair, having never found anyone capable of understanding the concept of a trim. They see long and fantasize about trying out brand new styles on a new head. The temptation to practice their artistry is just too great.

The Bums

There is a particular deep throated growl typical of an incurable alcoholic. Loud, booming and harsh, this sound signaled the approach of a swaying, babbling drunk. There he was- I'd seen him often before. Maybe his name was "Omar." He had managed to get himself evicted from a doorway again. His life consisted of being yelled at and shoved from place to place. At times he protested with eyes half-rolled back in his head- incoherent, yet aware enough to know he was hated. On this occasion someone answered his deranged challenge and just a shove sent him sprawling. He landed on his large head and the cracking sound reverberated down the street. Dazed, he sat up. After a moment he managed to get back on his feet. I think there was blood. I recall a sickening feeling of sadness that a human being could fall so low, and that other humans could so totally lack compassion. Here were two very big problems, and clearly, the world wanted us to look the other way.

I felt tremendous sadness about these dispossessed people who walked aimlessly up and down the streets and asked no end of questions about them. Why did they have nowhere to go and why didn't anyone help them? Whenever I had change in my pocket I gave it to a bum. I have been easily conned in the past, but in my mind if someone is so desperate as to have to beg for a living, then no matter what their scam may be, their need is greater than mine. There but for the grace of God...

The Killing Fields Of Newark

It seems my father kept a car somewhere in the city which we used to escape whenever possible. We would pile into the back of the light blue wagon and wind our way interminably through Newark, New Jersey, and what might have been the most ghastly industrial area on earth. This burning hell was matched only by Gary, Indiana, when many years later, touring brought me through on the way to Chicago and points west. Past the endless sea of flaming stacks spewing orange-brown smoke that turned the stomach and burned our nostrils, we hid our faces in our clothing and tried not to breathe- to no avail. This was a dead zone which existed right on the other side of the river from the pleasant streets of the West Village, and although we were generally unaware of it, on windy days people would sometimes call the fire department, thinking a nearby building must be burning. There was an evil fluorescent glow around the place that clung to our skin and hair for hours afterwards. How, I wondered as a child, would we survive this scale of environmental destruction? Where was all that poison and filth going to go? No one else appeared to be at all concerned. The general attitude until only a few years ago was that space was endless, and resources unlimited. In this sense all my fears have proven rational and accurate lo these fifty- some years later. In the meantime, my father was a man who, although he thrived in nature, also had an acceptance of whatever was in front of him- perhaps seeing it as part of a flawed whole.

Poor Birdie's Dead

Some hours later, arriving at the old house on the hillside was like rediscovering Paradise. After opening the windows, priming the pump, sweeping away insect carcasses and fluffing the beds, it was out into the yard.

From time to time we would find a little bird, feathers forlornly disheveled- cold, stiff as a board, and lying in the grass where it had spent its last moments. I wondered at its life, so free diving through trees and sky. Perhaps it had a family, perhaps it was a mother. I wondered if it was frightened when it died- or sad? It seems my distress touched the gentler side of my father, and he organized a funeral. Leading us in a solemn procession with the bird cradled in a bed of moss, we marched down the winding driveway through the woods. As we made our way along, we sang in a tempo that matched the somber rhythm of our feet crunching through the leaves- "Poor birdie's dead, poor birdie's dead." Finding a suitable resting place, we dug the ceremonial hole which would be the eternal resting place of this once proud little creature. I was overcome with sorrow as I looked at its tiny head and tightly closed eyes. I never wanted anything to die.

Perry Street

In my eighth year we moved to the contrastingly quieter streets of the West Village: Perry Street, with its impassive brownstones. These so-called railroad apartments had once been housing (we were led to understand) for poor immigrants who had just arrived from Europe at a certain period in the history of the city. The Allan Block Sandal Shop relocated to its well-known address on West 4th Street at the head of

Jones Street where frequent sightings of Bob Dylan and John Lennon were all part of the incredible live atmosphere of the place. In those days, the West Village was a neighborhood where people knew each other by name. There were far fewer addicts or guns (at least that we were aware of) and only a handful of crazies.

The apartment in which we lived had a peculiar life of its own. It faced the street on one side, and then, room by room, all in a row, stretched back to the kitchen which overlooked the back yard gardens four floors below. This design meant you had to pass through each room to get to another, so with the exception of my parents' bedroom, which was at the far end, nothing was private... the place was one long hallway. The neighbors below, finding us noisy, talked my parents into going half and half on wall-to-wall carpeting. A duller than dull beige to begin with, it became the repository of the cast offs from every dusty, unsanitary shoe that ever walked a city street. In time it was covered with stains, burn holes and bald spots. No one talked of replacing it. Perhaps I remember it being shampooed a time or two. At least it wasn't *shag*.

After the move I walked everywhere in the West Village. At the time, the worst thing to contend with was an occasional drunk or a bizarre comment- but it was nothing one couldn't learn to ignore or avoid. Soon I grew more savvy and navigated the entire city alone. Although I understood the subway system well, I preferred to walk (perhaps a reflection of the country girl within who wanted the wind in her hair and rain on her skin). I never carried an umbrella and remember loving the sensation of being soaked in a downpour while the glum and disbelieving huddled in doorways as I strode proudly by, wet and happy. In fact I must have had a guardian angel with me, as I was certainly in grave danger many times- but I had developed a "no fear" attitude that seemed to work.

The Garden Apartments

I once threw a piece of dry banana bread out the kitchen window, something I would not have appreciated had I been the owner of one of the ground floor apartments. Knowing that any misguided or ill intentioned individual lurking above could despoil my little world, or worse, drop dangerously heavy objects on my head while I was sunning, would have been totally disquieting. Thank God this sort of folly never occurred to us (OK, so it did occur to us once).

At night, from our bunk beds one above the other (and later after they were moved to separate corners of the room), my sister and I communicated with each other through a kind of Morse code- knuckle taps on the bed frame. Tap tap, tap tap tap tap: "Mo- nie, are you a-wake?" Answered by tap tap tap: "Yes I am..." tap: "Good." This was a completely comforting memory. It's good to know, as you lie in darkness contemplating the confusion and sorrows of the day, that another person, similar in age (and possibly your only ally), is also awake and ready- for who knows what?

Shakespeare In The West Village

*T*here were many unique characters in the Village who we passed daily. My friend Marc Silber knew their names, though how he gathered such information was a mystery. I recall one incredibly pompous looking individual dressed in vibrant Shakespearian raiment who marched along with his huge arched mustache, skinny legs in brightly colored tights, pointed shoes with bells, and the striped, puffed sleeves of a Court Jester. He strode swiftly up and down the street with eyes trained in the distance as if with great purpose, completely oblivious to the possibility that anyone might consider him unusual. If there was anything truly interesting about the Village, it was this "anything goes" atmosphere. Here was a place where you could be and do whatever in the world you pleased- and no one would notice or care.

Summers On The Cape

Someone, quite likely Nana, seems to have provided funding for us
to rent a cottage in Truro every summer. The same place each year,
it was really like a second home. This is where my life became real.
The clean air and unbelievable beauty of the place- the Pamet River
with its fluctuating tides, the mud flats crawling with fiddler crabs
and rich with clams which we extracted while standing knee-deep in
muck, the pale green sea grass, wind twisted locusts, majestic willows
and sloping lawns. Whitewashed fences surrounded the loveliest of
weather-worn clapboard houses with landscapes graced by windmills
and lighthouses... I can never express the joy I felt standing barefoot
on Cape Cod sand. The clarity of light, the sense of peace- nothing
could equal being in Truro. From the moment we arrived I would kick
off my shoes and never put them on again until I stepped back onto the
filth encrusted pavement of New York City. My feet were so calloused
I could have run over shards of broken glass. This wild child is my
true self.

Psychiatrists

There were many professional people from nearby cities like Boston and New York who summered on the Cape, including a large number of psychiatrists- a group I felt entirely uncomfortable with. What did I have against them? It seemed you paid them year after year, and they made you feel sicker by the day. I often heard people quoting their therapists when referring to some incurable mental condition branding them as untouchables for a lifetime. No one seemed to be gaining anything but despair and shame. It was all about examining oneself under a microscope and finding fault. As a young person I was sent to a therapist a time or two and was regaled with various insulting labels which, like verbal abuse, seemed never to wear off.

There were also the less affluent painters, poets, and writers who were particularly attracted to the beauty of the place. My parents knew them all. Unlike in the city, on the Cape we appeared to be the only musicians.

Cocktail Parties

In summer life seemed to revolve around cocktail parties- the clinking of glasses and the crisp scent of vodka and lime. If you were tense when you walked in, you would soon be relaxed, charismatic, and holding court. You might even have a teaser before arriving to ensure a smooth entrance (as revealed to me once by my mother). Drunk driving was never spoken of. No one put two and two together. Mom was a chain-smoker, as were many people in those days, but nobody cared. As children we were glad to find our parents at ease, smiling, sparring, cackling over this and that and roaring over jokes. Our time was spent burrowing in and out of hiding places, scraping through brambles, or sharpening sticks for roasted marshmallows. I don't think we ever went inside. The campfire was the central focus of the evening- the crackling of sparks flying skyward, the rosy faces flushed with alcohol- our parents talked of wife swapping and other debaucheries. My father was the designated blacksmith and found natural authority in blowing the coals and poking the fire back to life with utensils. I don't

remember much of these nights after darkness fell, just the eventual quiet, the cessation of laughter, and tucking into a cold bed, followed by the pure redemption of a new day.

Ray's Skin Mags

One of my parents' friends was an artist by the name of Ray. At the time Ray was married to his first wife, though years later he married Alice, the woman whose name was made famous by Arlo Guthrie's classic song "Alice's Restaurant." Apparently Ray was a free spirit, but we knew nothing of that at the time. I recall going to their house when we were young and seeing various Playboy magazines draped about. There were centerfolds and pictures of naked women every- where around the room. I commented on this as a child might who was not used to seeing these kinds of photos- and Ray said, with an easy going smile that reached from ear to ear, that this was the "natural" state of affairs, that this was "the way we were born." I was used to artistic renderings of the human body especially through my mother's art- but this was different. I remember feeling uncomfortable about the whole thing.

As a youngster I detested these photos. The women didn't look real-certainly not like my mother, although she was widely considered to be beautiful. These women looked like over-stuffed sausages. Their bright pink bodies could have been made of compressed bubble gum. Their poses and expressions looked ridiculous to me- who were they trying to impress with those mock baby faces? Surely they should at least cover those huge, pillowy things with diapers. I was embarrassed that anyone, especially a grown human being, thought this was the way to portray themselves. In my eyes there was a certain end-of-the-road desperation to the whole thing. There were many nude paintings and photos that could be found in our house- mostly black and whites-artistic images portraying the shadows and shapes of the human form in a way that spoke of beauty, grace, and mystery. There were never stupid expressions- kneeling women with "O" shaped mouths or tongues circling their lips- but scenes of bathing, resting, walking, and thinking- things people did with dignity. I was always moved by the beauty of the human form as a child, but what I saw in girly mags utterly lacked that beauty.

Mom And Ray Make Out In The Car

My sister once discovered Mom and Ray necking in the back seat of a car. As we tried to piece together this memory, it seemed like it must have happened at one of the cocktail parties. Now I wonder how my father handled all of this. We did not see him with other women. But in fact his style was covert, while Mom's was far more conspicuous. We were never happy to have these doses of reality in our faces and wanted adults to walk the straight and narrow. My mother was an example of someone who tended to behave well outside the accepted parameters.

Recently, I called Alice. She laughed and said, "Oh yes, Ray was insatiable," and assured me that no one in his family would be either surprised or offended by these recollections. She said everyone knew the way he was, and she didn't seem at all upset. When talking to another friend I learned that Ray was a devoted artist who at one time incorporated the above photographic images into his work. Ray died back in the seventies around the age of fifty, said my friend. Now I'm a bit curious to see some of his work. I was told he would cut up the magazines and create collages and even sculptures from the body parts of different women. Could my mother's legs be part of one of his collages?

On A Chilly Night

One of the sweetest places to listen to music was from the warmth of my bed on a chilly Cape Cod night. Towards the end of the summer it was cool enough for Dad to light a fire, and as I lay in the dark listening to the comforting crackle of the logs, I was awash in the beauty and clarity of his frailing on the banjo- "Forked Deer," "Little Sadie," "Same Old Man Living At The Mill," "Yonder Stands Little Maggie-" the sweetest and finest of the old tunes made time stand still. *Precious memories, how they linger...* music was the life force sustaining me through everything. It was the greatest gift my father gave me- nonverbal, powerful, life-enhancing music. And this is what moved me, along with my mother's lyrical folk singing, and assured me that music was the single most powerful force for survival. Instantly everything was transformed- the belittling words, the disturbing realities, the feeling of being an unwanted child melted away and became irrelevant in an instant. Dreams, longings, and a kind of supernatural strength all took form. Were it not for music, I'd be long dead.

Falling In Love With The Neighbor

One summer I fell deeply in love with our next door neighbor. He was older, blond, and extremely good looking. I adored jumping all over him and making a nuisance of myself until late August, when he would go back to his home in New Jersey. After he left I lay in bed crying my eyes out with an overwhelming feeling of grief and loss. I can't imagine how someone so young could have been in love, but I was. I had a broken heart. Apparently my sobs woke everyone in the house. Dad and my sister came in and sat on the bed in the early morning light. They seemed sympathetic. Johnny came back for several more summers, and at some point we made a pilgrimage to East Orange to visit him. This was a random act of kindness no doubt

arranged by my father. When we got there I remember making a complete fool out of myself by dropping his prized Martin guitar on the pavement when it slipped off the strap. I was trying to show off my finger picking skills. We had to pay for the repairs to Johnny's guitar. This was not romantic.

The Rat In The Toilet

I've seen rats die three times. Each time I witnessed a soul leave their small bodies- a beautiful, intelligent, loving soul of one of God's own children. In an instant I realized that ALL living beings have souls, probably even bugs, and ALL are precious. Does this mean I *like* rats, or want them in my house? No, of course not- nothing could be more disgusting. Once years ago when a horse trailer was parked next door in the neighbor's yard, rats moved into the barn and had a real party. Since I don't believe in poisoning anything, we tried every other alternative, and absolutely nothing worked. They got bolder and bolder- and more and more aggressive. I couldn't believe it. They were not afraid of the dogs, they did not move when I came after them with a rake or pounded the ground with a heavy object. These critters have been friends with humans a long time and don't feel like changing that now. The only thing that eventually worked was cats, and now we keep a barn-load of 'em and a couple in the house too. Not a mouse, mole, rat, or other rodent has been seen since, except as a small offering on the floor from time to time just to prove a point: "Got it all under control." Love those cats.

One moonless night on the Cape I awoke to use the bathroom. The hallway was so dark I had to feel my way along the walls. Frightened, I must have gone towards the living room for a while, but finally, doubling back, my hand found the doorway. As I entered the bathroom I knew something was wrong. I turned on the light, and there in the bowl was a huge rodent looking up at me. The poor thing had apparently fallen in and could not climb out. So there he sat, lower half submerged in the cold water, terrified. I screamed loudly and my father soon appeared. It was a horrible death, squealing and screeching in a human-like fashion while my father pushed it down with a plunger until it drowned. I wished I had been able to save it, and felt guilty and grieved that I was the cause of its death. In a perfect world I would be able to convince certain creatures to live as far from humans as possible, mostly for their own safety- but nature draws them to food and water, and before you know it we are destroying them, and they are no match for our many devastating methods.

To underscore the point about even the tiniest critters having souls, I think of a friend who keeps a rat as a pet. He's a famous person whose name you would know, guaranteed, if I mentioned it, but there's no need. Despite his action-packed past, he has mellowed into a relaxed country person who eats lunch at the local restaurants. He is known and liked by everyone. If you happen to take a table with him you might become aware of something moving in the chest pocket of his shirt. Then you might see a tail poke out and wiggle around. Yes, he keeps a pet rat. They've become good friends, as this example illustrates. The little fellow feels comfortable in the sanctuary of his friend's pocket, and once in a while, crumbs are dropped down for his particular enjoyment. No doubt this little creature is as interesting to know as any of my cats, all of whom have extraordinary personalities. If they have so much character, why would the next size down have any less? It's something to think about.

Riptides

Cape Cod has spectacular beaches and imposing dunes. In those days we could race down the sides of the steep, powder-soft cliffs, skidding and slipping through the sand (now illegal to protect the dunes from erosion). We practically lived on the beach. We brought a cooler with sandwiches and cold drinks, a few towels, no sunscreen and no umbrella. Skin cancer didn't seem to exist. I got as brown as a chestnut, and noticed that the sun made bare skin, tinged with ocean air and salt, smell fantastic. It exuded a kind of pheromone. I used to stick my arm out the window as we were driving, rest my head in the crook of my elbow and breathe in the sun drenched smell.

One day my sister and I wandered into the water as always. We swam whenever we wanted to and no one ever paid particular attention. Lifeguards must have only been on the extremely busy beaches like Provincetown, because I never saw any. We ran out as far as possible across the flats when the tide went out. No one called or worried we'd get stuck in the swift, returning waters. Absolutely no one knew about Tsunamis. I remember several notable times when the tide went out a lot further than usual and we walked all the way out to the tip of the sand bar. On this particular day we had been playing about in the water when we noticed we were much further out than expected. We had been carried away from the shore and were swiftly disappearing from sight. We started to scream, but no one heard or responded though the beach was dotted with sunbathers. We struggled to swim forward but our efforts accomplished nothing. My sister shouted "Swim on your back!" I flipped over immediately. Having never been a decent swimmer, I was astonished to find I was light enough to float easily in this position. I put all my focus to the task, blotting out fears and distractions. With great determination, I kicked my legs steadily as we skimmed over the surface of the powerful tide, and gradually the beach drew nearer and nearer. When we climbed out of the water we were a substantial distance away from our starting point. That was a lesson in many things. We learned about riptides. Focus. Eliminate distractions, you can do it! Summon inner strength- it is there. Use it! Last, but not least, I observed that my sister had the answer. She was a hero to me that day. I have zero memory of anyone being surprised or concerned after we returned. No one even noticed we had been gone.

Searching For Grandpa

𝓘n the moments of communication my mother and I reached towards the end of her life, disturbing revelations regarding her own suffering convinced me that whatever she may have done to me was light in comparison to what she had endured. According to my mother, Grandma would wake her at odd hours of the night, place her in a taxi, and drive aimlessly through the city hoping to catch her husband in the act of some suspected adultery, using little Eleanor Jean as a witness. Of course they never did find him. Grandma, who apparently had the upper hand in the marriage, committed Grandpa to a mental institu

Uncle Bob, Grandpa Robert Keller and my mother

tion- the reasons being unclear. As a small girl, my mother was told to take her beloved father by the hand and lead him outside to the "loony van" which waited by the sidewalk. In front of all the neighbors, she led him out to what soon proved to be his death- self-imposed starvation in a hospital. Grandma had explained that according to some incomprehensible regulation, she herself was not able to commit him, and that Eleanor Jean must take her father out, present him to the authorities, and sign the papers. This my mother did against her will, and forever after, believed herself to be her father's killer. When they visited him, my mother recalled, he would turn his head to the wall and refuse the sandwiches they brought to him. In his death by starvation, my mother learned many hard lessons- that suicide is apparently a good option if father found it so. That starvation is a necessary evil to protect oneself from others who want to kill us- that food handed to us by loved ones is suspect. That those closest to us don't trust us, that we don't trust them, and so much more about futility, darkness and sorrow.

I certainly wonder if, in all this "committing" each other to institutions, there wasn't far more fear than reality. Indeed this must have been the ultimate weapon. Shame and uncertainty made addressing the issues all but impossible. Today, we'd have much simpler explanations for the innumerable variations and complexities of the human mind. Extended family members recall Robert as an incredibly likeable man of notable humor and warmth- a good cook, with a smile and a ready joke- more in-line with my mother's description of the father she loved.

The Grandma My Mother Knew

As a young teen my mother would come home each day to an empty apartment. One afternoon she heard a creaking sound and soon discovered an open window. Horrified, she looked around for signs of an intruder, but instead discovered Grandma hiding in a closet with a pair of scissors clenched in her fist. Apparently Grandma had noticed the same window and had taken cover. But my mother wondered how many other times (thinking herself alone while practicing guitar) Grandma had actually been there, silently listening. My mother would shake with fear at times while singing- I remember the quavering, fluttering sound of her voice. If I needed to find a source for the stage fright that bedeviled me for years, I didn't have to look very far.

My mother had a deep distrust for Grandma, who, mom explained, tried to turn her against her father. But that effort backfired as my mother had only loving memories of him and an unending wall of bitterness and suspicion towards Grandma. I never heard compliments, only critical words.

The Grandma We Knew

Grandma on the other hand was incredibly doting and affection-ate- far kinder to us than our mother. According to Grandma, she and Mom (who she referred to as her "little girl") had once been the best of friends... but then Mom changed and turned on her, blaming her for just about everything. Grandma said my mother was prone to "spells" which began at a certain age and were brought on by events in which she was "not herself." I never really knew what to think, but this did occur to me: Grandma was my protector, she brought us gifts, she complimented us, took us to museums, parks, concerts, and showed us off to her friends. Her treatment of us was a universe apart from our mother's. I wondered, had my mother's vindictive mind invented all this about Grandma? I will never know the answer.

Grandma's Bag As A Deadly Weapon

To the world they looked flabby, but we knew that beneath the jiggly surface of Grandma's arms lay the musculature of a wrestler. Grandma was nothing if not large and strong. She had a habit of throwing things that seemed to work well for her, but you didn't want to be in the way when an object was launched from the table to the sink. Once, a soggy washcloth whizzed past my cheek and wrapped itself flawlessly across the arm of the faucet. Grandma could put shoes and hats away from a distance. In fact we developed a name for this, and called it "Kellerizing." This referred to any overly aggressive, rough handling of objects: forcing- slamming- throwing- the sort of behavior often resulting from frustration. "Easy!" we'd say- "You're going to break that. Stop Kellerizing!"

Grandma carried a pocketbook which she used as a self-defense weapon, swinging it through the air with ferocity- explaining that she had defended herself from a pickpocket and had run him off with this very bag. Once, when we had gotten into a taxi with Grandma and the driver turned out to be incredibly rude, Grandma politely asked him to pull over. She paid him, and as we tumbled out onto the sidewalk

Grandma slammed the door with one of her powerful arms, and said "Good bye... forever!" He sped away, clearly the loser.

From An Earlier Age

Grandma wore pompadours and clunky-heeled shoes with open toes. She had a selection of flowered scarves that were either tied tightly over her thinning hair or wrapped around her neck, wore bright red lipstick and had numerous moles. Grandma believed in keeping out the cold and owned several large wool coats that were really more like tents. She had a friend who sang "I'm dreaming of a white Christmas" while leaning against a piano, arms folded, who sounded like Bing Crosby. Grandma enjoyed the Brooklyn Botanical Gardens and took us there frequently. She loved cats. She would laugh until she choked, slapping her knees and saying "Mercy!" when something struck her as funny. Grandma had attacks of "nerves" and cried easily. She had been raised on a farm in upstate New York among boarders taken in by her Uncle Preston. My great-great grandmother Theiss used to sit on the porch in her rocker, but in the end refused to go outside for fear that bats would land in her hair. Grandma's mother, Louisa Theiss, was an artistic, unconventional woman who ran away to be something or other- perhaps an actress. I have only one photo of her, standing temporarily still, surrounded by her daughter and grandchildren. Grandma's father, who she never knew, was shrouded in mystery. Various rumors drifted throughout my childhood regarding him, but now it appears from family research that he died four months before Grandma was born, leaving her fatherless, and her mother a widow. We speculate that Louisa Theiss gave her daughter to her brother and wife to raise at this time and went off to live the life of a single woman. As a result Grandma had free rein of Uncle Preston's farm- the apple orchards, woods and fields. In the photos she looked like a wild little sprite. Who can say- perhaps I became a free spirited tomboy through some gene passed on to me by Grandma Keller.

Grandma had an olive complexion and ample figure- what today is called "plus sized," yet she always had a shape- a distinct waistline- and carried herself proudly so as to make her weight an asset. Society had not yet placed a value on anorexia, and "buxom" was very much in style. She knew how to attract men and had an array of suitors, one of which we met- a tall, razor thin, silver-haired man who fought over her. Grandma was considered quite the prize.

Grandma was a proof reader by trade, but she also wrote poetry. Although it seemed like a childish, rhyming kind of verse to me at the time, it actually indicated a fascination with words which I have inherited from both sides of the family. I am also obsessed with correcting spelling and grammatical errors. At least I come by it honestly.

Grandma Keller as a child with boarders on Uncle Preston's Farm

Great-great Grandma Theiss seated, holding my mother's hand. Uncle Bob on left, Grandma Keller and Great-grandma Louise standing-1936

*My grandfather Robert Henry Keller (Grandma Keller's husband),
in center of back row, surrounded by his six brothers and one sister
Gertrude Keller, with my great-grandfather Louis Edward Keller and
my great-grandmother Ida Estelle Rogers Keller.*

Great-great-grandfather James Calbraith with his children. One of the boys is Grandma Keller's father John- perhaps with the banjo. Grandma Keller's uncle, Uncle Preston, may be the one seated on far left.

Great-grandmother Fannie Block with Grandpa Isadore

Great-great-grandfather James Finch Calbraith from Scotland. He was said to have changed the spelling at a later time to Callbreath.

Uncle Bob

$\mathcal{T}$ he name "Robert" was a family tradition on the Keller side, and so many male offspring had the name you could barely distinguish one from the other. Uncle Bob looked a bit like Dave Van Ronk- tall, with very straight brown hair that swung incessantly across his eyes. He had a cigarette dangling from his mouth at all times, wore glasses, and looked intellectual. Once he brought over a girlfriend who was almost as tall as he was- her hair was in a pony tail and she was dressed in extremely tight clothing that highlighted her huge breasts.

Uncle Bob managed a coffee shop in the Village called The Cafe Figaro which had become pretty famous. Writers, musicians, artists, and hip people went there to have coffee, whipped cream, assorted pastries, and hang around smoking and gabbing. Downstairs you could watch classic movies. Once we even ate Thanksgiving dinner there. Uncle Bob, an occasional chef like his long deceased father of the same name (the one who made the holiday meals at the family Bungalow), did the cooking. It seemed an interesting change, sitting in the dark, mysterious room with espresso machines gleaming, waiters calling out orders and clanging in and out of swinging doors. The place looked like it had been there forever with its deeply burnished wood interior and round, dark tables. An array of multi-paned windows provided a view of all the activity on the street- the atmosphere was very old world European.

It was the dangling cigarette that killed him. I remember my father grabbing my mother in a "Get a'hold of yourself!" kind of way, and my mother looking downward and folding inwards- in, in- until her face was almost gone- and I knew in a flash that something awful had happened. Uncle Bob had died in a fire. They said he fell asleep while smoking in bed, and his MacDougal Street apartment went up in flames. I learned recently that my mother's cousin Frances (who I didn't know existed at the time) happened to be watching the evening news and was horrified to see Bob's lifeless body being carried out of the burning building. The next day the blackened mattress and charred belongings were piled out in the street, and Uncle Bob was gone forever. I hated death. I have heard it called "the last enemy"... truly, death is an enemy.

With terrible finality the Figaro closed. It reopened as an utterly soulless modern restaurant. The fast food joint that occupied the old space brought with it a complete and total end to the historic charm of the corner. With glaring lights, stainless steel and a boringly modern design, its sterile facade became a stark reminder of Uncle Bob's absence. Nothing could ever replace the Figaro.

At the funeral I fell apart. My mother said I should not go... I wouldn't be able to handle it. They thought I was a baby, but I would prove them wrong. So I went, but the moment I saw the casket and Grandma seated in the front row (Grandma, without a husband, Grandma, without a son), my eyes filled with tears and I couldn't stop crying.

I hated coming unglued, hated to seem weak in front of people. I think I'm stronger than I really am. But when crying takes you, it grabs you with complete power, and you are putty in the hands of grief. Staring out of gushing eyes, I look around and desperately wish for control- but it's not there. I have come to understand that this pain is about how deeply connected we are, and that without it, nothing has any meaning.

Girls And Sports

Had athletic endeavors not been frowned upon for the female sex, I would have been an Olympian. I had boundless reservoirs of strength and energy, good balance, speed and agility. It would be impossible to explain the complete lack of support for physical fitness for girls when I was growing up. My childhood was attended by unending ridicule of my athletic prowess. I was a "tomboy." I was a freak. I had no interest in dolls and wanted to play baseball. My pitching arm was lightning fast- I scared even myself. I would stand about pitching at ferocious speeds to anyone brave enough to play with me... I always prayed they would not miss and take a hardball to the face.

I was small, but I could outrun every boy in my class, including the tallest. When I beat him in a race he cried foul- an untied shoelace- so we raced again, and I beat him again. I felt strong, powerful, and swift.

I was on top of the world. There is no doubt that I had the heart of an athlete.

At the onset of puberty sports became a "no-no." Was I going to be a girl, or not? I would see a group of boys setting up for a baseball game and ask if I could play. Disbelieving stares would penetrate through the playground fence. Clearly they thought something was wrong with me. The undeniable message was that sports were unfeminine. I felt withered by the disapproval. I decided to slow down- I had no choice- I had to buckle down to the task of gaining weight, developing some kind of bust line (of which I was quite apparently devoid as a rail-thin stick figure). I was crushed, disappointed, and saddened. I began eating copious amounts of ice cream in an attempt to gain weight.

A Journey In Time

Once, on our way to the little house on the hillside, we pulled off the road to stretch. An old farmer spotted us and walked over slowly, legs stiff with age, and addressed my father. Through my youthful eyes the man looked to be a hundred years old. When he asked our business, his straightforward manner impressed me as the essence of simple honesty. My father's answer must have satisfied him, and they began talking about encroachment, buildup, and loss of open land. The man squinted angrily, saying that people from the city drove around on his fields and threw trash out the window. Men like this old farmer were visionaries in their day, as the wholesale destruction of farmland hadn't quite begun- but these are things that can be sensed- and he knew, with a terrible certainty, that his way of life was ending. All that was sacred and beautiful was being destroyed.

Years later we made an emotional pilgrimage, just my dad and I. As we got closer, I looked for the familiar landmarks- the field where we had seen the old farmer. But where was it? Suddenly I realized, as I stared at a sea of condominiums, that I was looking at the same spot. Gone forever. No one will ever drink from that stream again. I wondered where the old man was buried. Then we came to the crossroads. Zion Church, made of stones, still standing in the speckled light.

Across the road I looked for the tangled barbed wire fence and the black and white cows. Can't remember what was there now. I couldn't see all that well as my eyes were filled with tears.

Up the winding dirt road my heart was racing. Why must I be so emotional? Once again I tried not to lose control in front of someone who could humiliate me. We reached the old house and I sat in the grass by the well and the cherry tree, completely overcome. Dad left me alone for a while- perhaps my tears were not something he could handle- perhaps he thought I was being a baby.

Great Big Guitar, Tiny Little Voice

There was something clearly detestable about my desire to play the guitar, and my mother never let me forget it. She made no end of discouraging remarks. There were the usual accusations that I played to make my sister feel bad. Then, it was loud and ostentatious- I only did it because I "wanted attention" (the worst criticism of all). Calling attention to oneself was something to be ashamed of. Many times my mother said that I was the girl with the "great big guitar and the tiny little voice," whatever that meant. I suppose in retrospect it meant I was a small child holding a large instrument, and my shy voice was just starting to manifest. Of course she could have been proud instead of unkind... it was certainly an option. It's no wonder that I lost valuable years in starting a professional career as a singer- I had these withering deterrents ringing in my head.

Getting Beaten Up By Dad

I once got a massive slap in the face from a bullying teacher. It was a complete shock, and utterly humiliating. The man was a gym instructor and carried himself with the certainty that he was a very important person. Incredibly hairy, with a deeply lined face, he had a fuzzy layer covering his arms, hands, back, and chest. There was a kind of Burt Reynolds masculinity about him, but over the hill and without the humor. Imagine my dismay when I discovered that he had somehow become a counselor at my summer camp.

One day a group of us were in a rowboat, joking and laughing. Lou, who had been rowing and acting altogether friendlier than back at school, chimed in with an incredibly silly joke, to which I happily responded "Oh Lou, you're such a jerk!" I grant you this was not polite sounding, but having grown up with a lack of formal distance between adults and children, I had mistakenly assumed he was one of the gang. Both at school and camp our elders were all called by their first names- someone had decided to dispense with "sir" and "madam" for whatever reason they deemed it unnecessary. Lou dropped his oars, swung around at high speed, and slammed into my face with the flat of his hand, which was larger than my head. He was beet red and every vein stood out on his neck. If I hadn't been so shocked, if it hadn't been so painful, and if my hand hadn't been cupped hard against my stinging face, I would have felt sorry for him. In my experience when people lose control they are always ashamed. I was not the first student he had slapped, and shortly afterwards, he was dismissed.

But my father could not be dismissed. There were simply no checks and balances. There were no "800" numbers, no hotlines, web sites, or children suing parents. I got wailed on a bunch of times by both of my parents- spankings, a board, numerous face slappings, and then, the beating. I don't remember what I said. I was a teenager, and no doubt said something rude. My father was playing with my little brother and holding a football. Suddenly he launched it at me, and this started a complete knockdown. Fists, feet, flailing, kicking- I went down, and was so shocked I peed in my pants. I was utterly humiliated. Even though I thought I deserved it for some unknown crime, in another way I knew it was all-out ugly, inappropriate abuse. I knew it was wrong, but it still hurt horribly. The particular kind of humiliation that comes from physical violence is almost impossible to explain and can only really be understood by those who have experienced it. Perpetrators are so pathetic you can't help pitying them, while at the same time hating them- and worse yet, holding yourself responsible.

The Huge Hug

I remember a brief moment in early childhood when I felt bathed in loving affection. I was small- six or seven. We were in the dingy living room with the claw-torn, frazzled chair legs and the well-worn carpeting. For no reason that I can recall my father sat me on his lap and affectionately rubbed my back. It was not a sexual moment, nor was it perverse. His gentle touch was entirely fatherly and reassuring. I felt pure happiness. I felt loved. I think this sort of thing is experienced routinely by many children in "normal" families. It does not qualify as abuse on any level, just gentle affection.

Several times as a teenager Dad grabbed me suddenly and hugged me. Confused and startled, I wondered, "Does this mean he really *does* love me? Is this his way of saying he's sorry for all the other unkindness?" But I was left with a whirlwind of conflicted feelings. How could someone who bubbled with enthusiasm and happiness when we played music together be the same person with an acerbic tongue filled with withering criticism and annihilating insults? How could the same man who knocked me around violently and stood over me with fists clenched like a deranged prize fighter also wish to grasp me in a long and almost suffocating embrace? I didn't have the answer. If I did I'd have unlocked some of the greatest mysteries plaguing mankind, and perhaps would have found a solution to human dysfunction.

This is where greater insight into the natural laws of the flesh would be helpful. Are we all just a gesture away from incest? Is it crouching menacingly behind every moment of existence waiting to be released to pervert and destroy lives? Or is there such a thing as true and devoted parental love, warm, physical in its way, without sexual overtones? I know that lack of touch and embracing is almost more debilitating. I recall the study of monkeys raised by wire mothers in cages, and those with terry cloth mothers to cling to. The ones with wire mothers died.

Was Dad's embrace perverse in some way? After much consideration, I don't think so. Is this an accusation of abuse? No. Perhaps in some way it was Dad's indication to me that I had reached an important milestone, and that he approved, even wished me well in his own nonverbal way. This was the only physical sign of affection I received after the age of twelve. There was nothing to follow that would qualify as memorable other than a notable lack of demonstrable warmth.

The Acid-Tongued Ancestors

1 had heard that Dad's acid tongue was a family trait. Various sarcastic uncles and aunts were legendary. One of Dad's poems was about his great aunt Bertha and her "peevish tongue." There was apparently some kind of attitude of superiority. If so, in a political sense, I perceived this as an acquired skill needed for survival in a world which was obsessed with hating and killing Jews for most of recorded history. It seemed society had led us to believe that Jews (from which I had inherited fifty percent of my genetic makeup, the other half being entirely "WASP") taught their children to excel at arts, at music, and at every intellectual and professional pursuit. I saw this as a great quality: when oppressed beyond measure, fight back- not with bitterness, or by fighting fire with fire, but by excelling. Success is the best revenge. It seems that no one would rest until their children were doctors, lawyers, or rabbis. It was unclear at the time how girls fit into this profile.

My father's ancestors seemed to have developed, along with high intelligence, an attitude. Of course they were by no means the only people on earth who had one. At times it must have made the difference between success and failure- and in the past, life or death on the battlefield- if not hand-to-hand combat, then a battle of wits. If you think you know more than your opponent and are confident, it's hard to defeat you. This could be how the Block family, seemingly competent in so many ways over the years, prevailed. Concert violinists, poets, writers, valedictorians, and businessmen who prospered and saved. Dad won a literature prize in college and went on to become a master craftsman- of leather, of music, of words- and then came little old me, obsessed with guitar and blues- and now, trying to explain myself. In my case, I have no particular inflated self-regard. But when I look around I see a great many people who have labored hard to do well instead of buckle under.

Dad harnessed his acid tongue putting down every human being we met. He used to express the rather vulgar opinion that everyone was "a walking shit" until proven otherwise. I know there was humor there, but there was also a terrible truth in his words. Everyone got cut down to size (behind their backs), and it has taken most of my life to recognize how skillfully he divided and conquered by taking each person into his confidence while verbally slaying everyone else. The result was to make each person feel (briefly) favored, and all others hated. It caused us to see each other as competition. But no matter, if he once meant to harm, age and time has changed him. I believe when I see the sweetness in his demeanor now that he has lost his taste for manipulation and moved beyond pettiness. Perhaps he doesn't remember how to be unkind.

The Most Beautiful Woman In The Village

People used to tell me my mother was "the most beautiful woman in the Village." Indeed she could be charismatic and alluring- but the flip side was a distant, brooding, stranger with glazed eyes and a vacant

expression. In an instant the outgoing person disappeared and Mom became blank. This was the face she often wore when we were alone. I remember thinking "Maybe Mom is resting her eyes..." but it made me feel sad, as if my presence brought her no joy. At times it was even frightening. Reality had faded and some unpleasant world taken hold. This must have been where demons roamed and despair thrived.

"WASP" was an unkind term I heard often in childhood meaning, among other things, that one was apparently "repressed." It was all a mystery to us as children. Mom's generation had been raised to believe you must never bother other people with your problems. She was undoubtedly attracted to the things she was taught to avoid, yet could not abide those things either. This could also be said for my father, who never went out with anyone but supremely Protestant, Anglican, and Lutheran women. I think in retrospect my parents' rebellious personalities drew them to the people and things they thought would have most displeased their relatives. Mom ran off and married my father at the age of eighteen- it must have felt independent and powerful- yet it seemed she hated the little girl who looked so much like her husband, and on some level, didn't want to recognize me as her own. It was as if World War II played itself out in our household. I felt, having a Jewish father and an Anglo-Saxon mother, distinctly biracial. Who would claim me? Which culture would I relate to? My mother loved Christmas and instilled an enormous appreciation of the holiday through her traditions- the most delicious homemade eggnog, beautifully decorated trees, gifts, festivities and trimmings. My father sullenly hated it and eventually refused to participate. In his critical, judgmental way he made us feel awful about many of the things we most cherished.

My Mother's Keeper

The more my mother rejected me, the more I loved her- the more I longed to please her, take care of her, and make her like me. I could see she was unhappy and wanted to make it better. I became in a sense a kind of nurse. When at times she allowed me to fuss over her, I would be utterly solicitous. At other times she would be cold and unreceptive. If I learned anything, it was to expect an emotional seesaw-

friendly one moment, defensive and distant the next. In a strange way it helped when I figured this out.

In later years the awful stigma regarding my mother's supposed "mental illness" began to wear off. The possibility that she had never been "schizophrenic" (a term far too carelessly tossed about), occurred to me more and more. Yes, I could live with the idea that her chem

istry went from high to low rapidly, as did mine to a lesser degree- but I perceived that this was probably not the kind of condition that required hospitalization, strong prescriptions, and hopelessness. It seemed likely that my father had over-reacted when he committed her, and that once she was incarcerated, the sense of degradation became self-perpetuating. For my mother, believing herself to be anything other than damaged goods after experiencing Bellevue was going to be almost impossible. The true diagnosis could have been much tamer: the precarious chemistry of the artist's temperament which runs in our family on both sides. The low side, which qualifies as depression, can seem oppressively heavy. The high side, which produces great energy, artistic and musical activity, is not ordinary- no- but not mentally ill. Later, when my mother was *not* on medication, she seemed virtually normal. How could someone once supposedly in need of a straitjacket ever become such a low-keyed, gardening, flower-painting, condo-owning middle aged adult?

Music Lessons

At eight I started playing recorder, one of the choices presented to me in school. Cello never called to me- piano was interesting. But at the time the little wooden instrument seemed like a good idea. It

was then that my teachers began to comment on a particular kind of aptitude, though it came in the form of a criticism. Apparently I refused to read music. This also happened with the written word; I was the last one in my class to learn as I either found it uninteresting or intimidating, can't remember which. The teacher claimed I lacked the discipline to follow the notes, that I "anticipated" the music and played it intuitively. She thought this was bad, but I knew (somehow it seemed obvious to me) that this was good. I smiled secretly. Did my mother realize what was being said? I have no way of knowing as she made no comment. For my entire life I have had the strange ability to anticipate music. I routinely sing harmony to songs I have never heard before. I can't always get the melody right, but I can almost always sing harmony immediately. I don't know how this works, but when I am singing I have total awareness of where the next note will go. I surprise even myself.

Songs At Bedtime

Mom had a large repertoire of child ballads, folk, classical, and spirituals which she seemed to draw from various music books we had lying about. She read the music and picked out the notes in a clear, meticulous style and sang to us at bedtime, one of the sweetest gifts she could have given. Her beautiful voice sent chills up my spine and the vivid images of human drama brought tears to my eyes. Perhaps she favored sad songs, or maybe many of these old ballads featured tragedy: "Here I sit on Buttermilk Hill, who could blame me cry my fill, and every tear could turn a mill, Johnny has gone for a soldier"- "Make my bed soon for I'm sick at the heart, and I feign would lie doon." "The Water Is Wide," "Pretty Polly," "The Golden Vanity"- there were countless songs of murder, betrayal, lost love, and death. Ancient songs- heartbreaking, sad stories that filled me with sorrow... yet it was a moving, sweet kind of sorrow that was about the deep connection between souls. When my mother sang, I quietly wept. I always felt ashamed of my weakness- but now I recognize that she had the power to move with her singing. Through her poignant performances I understood that although she might not always have known how to express her tender side, it was there in the sweetness of her voice.

I like to tell audiences to sing to their children at bedtime. Even if you can't carry a tune, nothing could be more wonderful and soothing for a child. It sends the sweetest message that all is well with the world, and ignites a flame of inspiration. It gave me the belief that I could sing.

Mom And The Weavers

We grew up with a rumor that before I was born, my mother had auditioned for the Weavers and had been accepted. If true, this would have explained how my parents knew Pete Seeger and others, estab-

lishing their early connection to some of the most important folk figures of the century. Toshi Seeger once said, "I've known you since you were just a gleam in your father's eye" and I was intrigued, though I knew nothing of the details until much later. The rumor about my mother and the Weavers was reinforced recently by family friend Penny Caccavo, who attended one of my shows in Pennsylvania.

Penny is still bright, clear, and energetic enough to sit through the entire performance. In the back room she gave me more information. Yes, she said, it was true- my mother had auditioned for the Weavers and was accepted, but pulled out at the last minute because she would have been required to travel- adding that my mother was pregnant with my sister at the time. Afterwards when I called Pete he did not recall my mother auditioning- however I later realized he may have been thinking of my father's first wife (the one who'd had the affair with Bill Steig and who was not a singer). In any case these events would have occurred almost seventy years ago in the 1940s, and one of the first things Pete said is that many people were coming and going from the group in its formative days.

Penny spoke of the exciting music scene next door to her parents house when she was growing up. The Caccavos were neighbors of Toshi's parents during the time they hosted the music parties in the basement of their MacDougal street brownstone where Woody Guthrie, Pete Seeger, Leadbelly and other luminaries gathered. I was surprised to think that my mother chose raising us to a career- but this was what society required, and to leave us alone with my father would have necessitated his commitment as well- who knows if he would have given her support. Years later, when I had become an established singer, I felt I was carrying the torch for my mother. She gave up a career to raise us, yet she clearly could have made a name for herself. In retrospect I wish that for her sake she had chosen the career. It would have made her feel like somebody instead of the anonymous house-wife who grew more and more depressed.

If my mother had decided to travel, I'm sure we would have survived being raised by Dad despite his notably earthy ways. At the dinner table, for instance, "Please pass the string beans" meant Dad's hand directly in the beans- lifting, carrying, swinging like a construction crane, and dropping them on your plate. We would have had a few more germs to contend with, no doubt, but Dad's theory was always that we needed a little dirt in our diet lest we become weak.

My First Recording

Mom accompanied herself with a soft arpeggio style of finger picking and sang with a rich, clear vibrato which was often compared favorably to Joan Baez (a vibrant new talent who had recently burst onto the folk scene). This was how people expected me to sound simply by looking at me... and that was stereotyping of course, no more appropriate than any other. In fact my mother did it exceptionally well and her voice was pure information to me as a singer. As an adult I discovered an absolutely ancient recording of her wailing away like Bessie Smith- but that wasn't until I had been singing blues and soul for an eternity, so it was all the more revelational to hear her and to feel this uncanny connection to early blues. Apparently Grandma, feeling she had a talented daughter, brought my mother to a studio to record this amazing song. Mom did the same for my sister and I when we were about ten or eleven. This LP, no doubt heavily scratched and languishing away in a paper sleeve somewhere, revealed the raspy, quavering, self-conscious voices of two children who had only one chance to seal their offering on vinyl.

In those days the engineer pressed the start button, shouted "Go!" and you began abruptly, knowing, with fear in your heart, that you had this single opportunity, mistakes or no. This is the way the old blues records were made, resulting in unbelievably interesting recordings with sudden stops, completely off-the-cuff beginnings (which many times included the engineer's voice), and the anything-can-happen atmosphere which was an intense part of the beauty and realness of those incredible recordings. Today's ridiculously high-tech capabilities leave the element of spontaneous music entirely in the dust, but that would make another chapter- a boring, complaining one which I will purposely try to avoid, except to say that if you have a computer, and any inkling that you might make it big as a recording star, you've probably already sampled someone else's cool song and played your own voice over it with a keyboard, and maybe posted it on your web site or some music site in the hopes of getting billions of hits- no, suspend all that for the moment and time travel to the past when it was "one time through" and you were handed the results. Of course there were a couple clunkers on our little record, but overall I heard the voice that later became my familiar style. I suppose the fact that my mother took the trouble to do this indicated a kind of support that in many ways offset the unkind words and undercutting I was so devastated by. Despite her worst and most negative attitudes towards me which filled me with terrible insecurity (and caused me to lose valuable years in terms of a career)- the memory of this recording alone makes me realize that somehow she knew I could sing, and in her own nonverbal way introduced me to the music business.

For The Sake Of The Children

My parents continued to live together for years after their marriage appeared to be over. They slept in separate beds, and my mother (from the time I was quite young) was seeing someone else openly. I found this totally disturbing... there's no way to marginalize my hatred of our family falling apart. Yet throughout my childhood, despite this overt relationship with another man, certain elements of normalcy continued- perhaps some kind of charade my parents mistakenly thought would be helpful. My father once said they stayed together "For the sake of the children." But given the atmosphere of unhappiness and hostility, I can't imagine what good they really thought would come of it. In their own misguided way they tried to balance what they thought was right and wrong: parting would apparently be wrong- loving whoever they wanted to was apparently right. So it was confusing, upsetting, and not at all common at the time. In my mother's defense she later explained that my father had betrayed her early on by seeing an old flame right after they got married, and given human nature mixed with various unknown factors, she obviously felt this was her "right." Kids are pretty pure in their observations, however, and from a child's perception, I simply saw two out-of-control, self-interested people living in a completely hypocritical way. In retrospect, if they had parted and I had been transported between two households as so many children are today, that would probably have seemed just as unacceptable.

My parents were almost always a source of embarrassment to me. At summer camp my friends seemed comfortable when their families arrived. I on the other hand cringed and couldn't wait for mine to go away. They were ridiculous, I thought- particularly my father, who, in my view, resembled a skinny, birdlike creature. He invariably dressed in some odd way that only served to call attention to himself. Then there was my mother who acted loud and inappropriate or distant and depressed. I wanted "normal" parents, but it was not to be.

My Mother's Boyfriend Will

No wonder I hated my mother's boyfriend. For one thing, he wore Murray's Space shoes. For another, they were both married, and worse yet, one of them was married to my father. I didn't think this was OK, but they did, fumbling and kissing awkwardly in front of me to my total consternation. Even I, at the tender age of eight or nine, had the sense to know they should do this in secret, if at all. When I confronted my mother later, she said something that rang in my brain as the height of entitled arrogance (at the expense of everyone else on earth). "When I love someone, I *kiss* them!" she announced. I was flabbergasted. Did she not realize that this was the blatant destruction of what I had come to count on as my damaged, dysfunctional, entirely unusual family- and this was not a part of that at all?

Around this time Will used to come over in his woody station wagon dragging along a beat up old duffle bag filled with various recreational items such as soccer, basket, and footballs- bats, mitts, and assorted items. There were often several glum children in the back seat whose parents wanted them entertained for the day. There was some vague notion about "fresh air," and this seemed to fulfill their expectations. We would pile into the wagon and drive, until what seemed like a half day later, we would arrive at the Staten Island Ferry. I should have loved this, but I was horribly uncomfortable with Will. In some sadly perverse way, I discovered that pretending to like him seemed to please my mother, so (there being almost nothing else that had ever worked to impress her) tolerating Will seemed acceptable, if revolting. Notably, my sister never pretended to like him. He had a detestable habit of asking us to kiss him, saying "Give me something *sweet*." My stomach would turn when I gave him a peck on the cheek, but my sister would run away screaming "I hate you! I hate you!" Of all the times I had the greatest contempt for my sister's out of control, tantrum prone personality, this was not one of those times. Hating Will openly made her a hero.

Will was anything but attractive. Paunchy, bald, with transparent pink rimmed glasses, he had wrinkled eyes surrounded with something slippery and shiny that was apparently Vaseline. I never saw him wearing anything but the same faded, stained sweatshirt. He was the vision of repugnance to me.

On one unbearable ferry ride to Staten Island I remained in the car, having decided I was too cold to stand around in the sharp wind of the upper decks. Upstairs assorted travelers milled about pointing, taking photos, and wandering from one side of the boat to the other while stuffing themselves with hot dogs, sodas and candy. I had seen the Statue of Liberty many times before on class trips. I can't recall why, but Will stayed in the car with me. When he asked why I hadn't gone upstairs, I responded that I was cold. Then he announced that he would warm my hands. Frozen between the desire to get away from him or somehow tolerate him for my mother's sake, I weakly surrendered my hand, which he immediately put into his crotch and began rubbing it over whatever lumpy portion of something was in his pants. He was explaining that this was the warmest part of the body and that this was the best way to keep one's hands warm. Disgusted and horrified, I jumped out of the car and raced for the stairs and the safety of the windy decks. I never mentioned this to anyone but my sister until I was a teenager, when, in the heat of an argument with my mother, I broke the news that Will was a "pervert." Nothing had ever had such a dramatic effect on someone so incessantly impervious. She was visibly shaken- who knows what was in her mind- confusion, jealousy, anger... she was transformed into a person who groveled for details. The balance of power immediately shifted and she was no longer in control. I had the information, and she must have known it was true... and who knows who said what to whom after that. In any case they didn't break up. He probably convinced her I had lied. I'm used to that by now (dealing with other people's deceit). I believe there are very few truly honest people on the planet. After I left home they married. At that point my hatred of Will was no longer a secret.

When Will died none of us grieved- in fact I can say we openly celebrated. I got a phone call from my mother and I heard a haunted voice say "The worst has happened." I had a strange feeling of peace, followed by a sense of relief. I felt that now, somehow, I might be able to reach my mother. When she opened the door of the Perry Street apartment, she had a look in her eyes I had never seen before. Completely transparent, with nothing hidden, she radiated unguarded emotion. It was a moment when our souls connected, when neither age nor experience meant a thing. If we know each other from other lifetimes, if we have connectedness on deeper levels, this was such a moment of recognition. It's as if our lives had played out in darkness, and now, at this predetermined juncture, we said, "This is it, we have reached this point in the story." It's as if we both knew this moment would come, and whatever mysterious forces bring us together as souls, this was a profound intersection in that journey. As I stepped into the long dark hallway of the apartment which held so many bad memories for me, I felt strangely empowered. I walked into the living room where Will lay on the floor under a sheet. I have no idea why this didn't bother me. I stepped right over him. I thought "You can't hurt me anymore."

Years later my brother sent me a photo of an elderly man whose spongy face sagged off to one side like a tilted bowl of oatmeal. Bald on top with only a few wisps of hair around the ears, the man grimaced in response to some medical procedure, perhaps an injection. My brother scrawled something irreverent across the page, something to the effect that Will was apparently still alive, and indicated that there might be no escape from the man someone once aptly called a "bag of worms." This description struck me as quite brilliant. Entirely perceptive, it was graphic, clear, and accurate.

Sister's Closet

My sister had a closet full of stolen dresses. She realized that hiding things potentially drew more attention to them, so she hung them neatly on layered hangers in the front. They were the first thing you'd see, in all their illegal glory, when you opened the door. Once, fatigued by my father's endless praise of my sister's virtues ("honesty" being mentioned frequently), and wearied by his insistence that I was terminally dishonest (despite much evidence to the contrary), I told him about my sister's closet of stolen dresses. Squirming, my father declined to listen. No, he was not interested, and no, he would not look at the dresses- this despite the fact that many of them still had the tags attached- and no one had taken my sister shopping. He clung irrationally to an imaginary vision of my sister's purity.

Shoplifting

Convinced my image was toast with my parents, I decided to live on the wild side. "If you can't beat 'em, join 'em," I must have thought. My sister got away with it and still got admired- maybe there was something to this. At thirteen, I walked into May's Bargain Basement on east 14th Street carrying a large pocketbook. Apparently, I needed to discover for myself that theft feels bad.

Rummaging through the overstuffed racks, I hurriedly shoved some items into my bag, confident I hadn't been seen. Hidden cameras didn't exist (at least not in public locations), and there were just burly security guards posted in doorways. As I walked towards the exit I began feeling anxious, and the feeling increased to a high level of fear as I neared the guard. This is where criminals and non-criminals part ways. Apparently this kind of high emotion makes some people feel exhilarated- I just felt terrified. Some people crave this sensation like a drug, while others wither away. I didn't get caught, but it felt so horrible I never did it again. I was clear about something immediately. I said "This isn't worth it." Instinctively I understood that stolen goods would always feel tainted, and there would be no way to enjoy them or have a quality life. No one really benefits by taking advantage- it just doesn't happen- some day the bill comes due with a high finance charge added. I understood that peace of mind was worth more than money.

I became the antitheft superhero- not by monitoring others, but by being obsessively honest. I developed the compulsive need to point out if I had been *undercharged*. Perhaps someone else would smile and think it their lucky day. I go back into the store and explain that I discovered an error in my favor while examining the receipt.

Mom's Suicide Attempt

One day my mother tried to kill herself. It was brutal. I walked in to find her white as a sheet and unable to move. My father attempted to lift her but she was like a sack of potatoes with her head drooped forward onto her chest like a dead person. She had taken sleeping pills, and if I had known more, I would have realized that she was close to death. If shouting at her and dragging her around didn't wake her, she wasn't far from it. This is all I remember. I don't know if an ambulance came, I don't know if she went to a hospital, I don't know anything. I couldn't believe it was real. It was a dream, a very shocking dream. The aftermath was horrified silence. There was no explanation. Not a word was spoken. It was impossible to understand. Why did my mother- my only mother- wish to leave her children and this beautiful world, abandoning us like useless trash on the side of the road, to go somewhere else- perhaps to oblivion? What was this- our lives together here- garbage? This was a horrible, horrible message. Finally, after all the insults and put-downs, I got it. I was of no value to her. In a better world she would have been so happy and proud to have three beautiful children.

I have since discovered more about this awful event. I learned that my mother had been visited by a series of personal tragedies in the space of only a few months. Feeling she had failed as a mother, failed as a wife, and that her life and all she had once dreamed of was crashing down around her, this kind of despair and hopelessness (coupled with depression and potentially even prescription drugs which could have increased the risk of suicidal tendencies), most likely led her to think that her children and the world would have been better off without her. How sad it is to think of her feeling this way.

While on the one hand many good things existed around me- from music to school, friends, camp, summer vacation, sports, and art- there were these horrifying realities going on continually behind the scenes. Frankly no one would have believed me if I had explained it. I wonder now as I write this how I stayed sane.

Pills In The Trash

Medication was out. Although I was quite sick on certain notable occasions in childhood, the pills went first to the center of my fevered palm, and then directly into the trash at the first opportunity (the moment the killer nurse left the room). Evil nurses wafted in and out of my childhood- can't remember one who wanted me alive. Take the pills handed to me? I think not. I remember feeling such a sweet sense of relief that I had not ingested whatever strange chemical they had chosen for me. No doubt they wanted me sedated and helpless. In those days death was so ordinary no one ever investigated anything. I would imagine a nurse or doctor could make short work of someone who simply bothered them, and most likely no one would even question.

In 2004 I saw an article featured on the cover of Forbes- a hand outstretched over a trash can with an array of multicolored pills flying towards the garbage. I had to laugh, having been aware of this from earliest childhood. Hopefully I have never given support to an industry that has "overdosed the King's Legions" (from a novel by George Elliot) for profit.

Organic Music

Music, all things natural, and a love for words and poetry- these were things I could cling to which laid a foundation firm enough to walk on. I wasn't Daddy's little girl, though I longed to be. My friends had those kinds of doting fathers- I did not. Mine was the "Call me Allan" type and the "Leave me alone- raise yourself" kind. But still, I was his protégé, the only one of his children who could match him note for note, and he often revealed (in the things he said about me to others) that he was proud of me.

Dad introduced me to the love of early American music, though his field was Appalachian and mine was to become rural blues. Most people probably have no idea how the two forms are related. If you wandered into a tiny rural church in Appalachia or a black Baptist church in the South- the experience and style of worship is almost identical. Wailing, singing, stomping, shouting, weeping, open and fervent prayer, the din of many voices, and worshipers moved by the Spirit to speak in tongues or roll in the aisles... I know, I've been in both, and I see the direct connection. Sadly, there have been forces and circumstances which have separated these groups at times, yet the family relationship is obvious. Healing is what is needed, and a realization that we are all one seed, and all well-loved children of God.

Environmental Awareness

As I was writing this chapter the oil spill of epic proportions was spreading ominously across the waters of the Gulf of Mexico. Now supposedly sealed, I wonder- can it ever really be cleaned up? Will there even be a home called "Earth" in the near future (teeming with diverse life forms which evolved in a magnificently fragile, perfectly balanced ecosystem over billions of years), or will it simply be a superheated dead zone like Venus, with scorching or subzero temperatures, deadly winds and clouds of sulfuric acid, left rotating lifelessly in space? Could another civilization, equally clueless, have used and abused that place as well, until it became a floating casket? Do we not yet comprehend how completely irreplaceable, how miraculous, and how utterly unlikely the combination of elements which came to support the birth of life really are? Note: thus far no other place like planet Earth has been discovered in the known universe. This could easily be the last, fading chance for the life experiment to succeed.

But I leave this thought for the moment to visit the past. Come, and step into the time machine with me.

My parents were basically green before anyone had any inkling that "green" would ever become a category. I am grateful for this, and count it among the hidden blessings of my upbringing. I knew when I was very young that the planet was being destroyed by misuse, over-development and pollution. In biology class, when the teacher was explaining how plants breathe in carbon dioxide and breathe out oxygen (and how we do the opposite, thus supporting each other)- I raised my hand and asked, "What will happen when we cut down all the trees?" The teacher dismissed my question with prophetic abandon. His ridiculous answer was "That will never happen." But I had seen the hellish smoke stacks which stretched as far as the eye could see, breathed the choking fumes of the chemical plants across the river, and witnessed the endless sea of asphalt jungle, junkyards, landfills, filth, trash piled into vast mountains, and the utter waste which stretched almost to eternity. I knew Armageddon was coming, and no biology teacher was going to convince me that what was perfectly obvious was fantasy. As a species, one of our greatest skills is hiding from reality.

My Uniform

My eyes were very green, and I had a round baby face that made me look younger. Every morning I donned my kneesocks, an earth brown wraparound corduroy skirt, a burgundy cotton turtleneck and last, a vintage jacket in a faded green color which tucked in at the waist and had soft, rounded lapels. This was my uniform. In those days "new" was of no interest to me. I loved weather-beaten, old, broken-in, and worn. I had ONE favorite item, and that was it. Later, after the green jacket disappeared, it was an old suede jacket with little pull tabs at the sides to give it shape. Stonewashed had not yet been conceived, but this jacket epitomized the look. The world hadn't yet introduced credit cards or the shop-til-you-drop mentality. Old was good- it had character, it made a statement. I favored vintage, organic, and natural materials. There is no doubt this preference was passed to me via my artistic parents.

Summers in Vermont

Is there a sweeter, greener place? Do cows long to be somewhere other than Vermont? If I could go back to the fifties and settle into an old clapboard house on a quiet lane, I would gladly let my hair turn white and embrace age without fear of scorn. I would use my gnarled hands to bake pies. I would pin my thinning hair into a standard bun, wear spectacles, plant flowers in window boxes, and sit quietly in church on Sunday. I would say "God willin'" frequently. I would favor a comfy chair and exclaim "Mercy!" like Grandma Keller whenever I laughed. I would be a comfort to family members, and one of the generation who dutifully performed their chores without complaint, who never knew technology, nor ever would have cared had it been invented. When we rented the cottage on the Cape in the fifties, Mrs. Slade, the landlord's wife, was just such a woman. On the night we arrived, there would be a fresh-baked loaf on the kitchen counter, miraculously, still warm. Women like Mrs. Slade are precious. Having reached an age where vanity becomes meaningless, grace takes over. Dear, loving grannies, with parchment faces, freckled skin, and large, comforting bodies softly draped in granny dresses- this world calls to me- a world without guile, without harsh edges or greed as its central driving force.

Killooleet

It didn't seem surprising at the time that we went to a summer camp run by Pete Seeger's brother John, that there was a tremendous amount of music there, or that Pete and Toshi's daughter Mica was a camper. Many of the counselors were accomplished musicians, and nothing was more memorable than assembling on blankets around a roaring campfire on a summer's evening while talented staff members like George Ward or Rusty Simonds serenaded us. Pete stopped in more than once while I was a camper and I recall the wandering tale of an adventurous frog "Way down yonder on a hollow log," a beautiful African folk melody, "Weemaway," an incredible guitar instrumental evoking bells, and a song that sounded like it was from the Islands. Guy Davis, son of Ossie Davis and Ruby Dee, was a fellow camper.

He was younger than me, and although we knew each other, no one ever hung out with anyone but their own age group- just like at school. If a seventh grader ran with a sixth grader everyone would think you were weird. So I simply knew this extremely cute, energetic little person who raced around and probably got into his share of mischief. As young adults we met at a camp reunion and had a proper chance to say hello. He asked me about the Robert Johnson stuff I had just performed. He wanted to learn it, so we knelt down in the back room and I showed him some of the "Walkin' Blues" licks I had just played. "That's cool," he said.

Many of our friends were musicians, and many of them were famous. This was normal. We owned a Belafonte album that pictured Harry on the cover wearing a belt made for him by Dad, which meant that at the very least he had come into the sandal shop. My parents often spoke of famous names in a familiar sounding way. I understood it to mean that everyone knew each other from the Village- from parties, concerts, Washington Square, the grocery store- wherever folk singers and music lovers gathered (in the Ohta's basement, as I later learned). A number of the children went to school or summer camp together.

Artistic Endeavors

$\mathcal{M}$y fascination with art started long before I was able to play an instrument. Although I was athletic and leaned heavily towards outdoor recreation, my indoor hours were spent in creative activities which consisted mostly of drawing. I would immerse myself in the minutia of the most detailed projects- things that would later seem daunting. I wrote and illustrated books, produced an endless stream of long stories laid out in boxes like comics, drew cartoons and caricatures, and created ornate, decorative mazes and labyrinths in addition to a continual stream of renderings of the things I saw around me. No handwritten note was ever without extensive borders and doodles. Of course we had no television when I was growing up, but there was always a wealth of art material. Frankly it was a major blessing that I did not spend my time parked in front of a glowing box but turned my attention entirely to creative pastimes as no alternative existed for me.

My mother's college experience had been as an artist at Cooper

Union, thus her love of both art and music were inspiring to me. At various times, particularly in the latter portion of her life, she returned to painting, with nature as the focus. Her lovely watercolor renderings of flowers covered the walls of the condo she purchased after leaving New York, and now make up a large body of work which cries out to be exhibited.

Although I would later be accepted to Music & Art High School as an art student and have on several occasions devoted full attention to drawing and painting, my energy would soon go almost entirely to music. Currently my artwork, mostly landscapes, is displayed in my home. I had a show in my twenties and sold a number of pieces, but the reason I haven't done this more often is because I hate to part with my paintings. They are like old friends.

Early American Music

Our house was always filled with music. First it was classical, then, Old Timey. Roscoe Holcomb's *High Lonesome Sound* was one of the most powerful records I had ever heard. There were Charlie Poole records, Gid Tanner and the Skillet Lickers, and Depression era songs with words like "The blue eagle it is ailing, the little writer said, and when he finished writing, the eagle he was dead. There is a man in Washington, Roosevelt is his name, and how he's mourning for the bird it is an awful shame." I still throw my head back and sing "My Home's Across The Smokey Mountains!" which I learned at that time from one of these old records. There was also folk, the clear soprano of Richard Dyer Bennet singing English ballads, and Dave Van Ronk growling "Come back baby, mama please don't go!" My parents had early Muddy Waters records in the house recorded when his name was McKinley Morganfield. He played acoustic slide guitar in a percussive style clearly reminiscent of Robert Johnson, Son House and the great Delta players. I remember the words "Lord I'm troubled," but haven't figured out exactly which song it was as many of the old melodies intertwine. This is what I listened to in the '50s and '60s. I was raised on early American music and in my way of thinking it was the best and most soulful music on earth.

Froggy Went A Courtin'

When I was ten I decided to teach myself guitar. No one suggested it, it was simply my choice. I sat down with my mother's classical guitar and began picking out the melody to "Froggy Went A Courtin'." Almost immediately my parents decided I should take classical guitar lessons, and although I fought them tooth and nail and utterly refused to practice, the foundation that was laid has served me well. I learned respect for clean notes, and for the power of repetition in gaining mastery. Classical is a discipline, and sometimes with folk we try to get a little sloppy. I can't allow myself to rush into a song without being able to play it slowly, in large part due to my training, but also because my father pounded the following message into my head throughout my life: "It's harder to play slowly than to play fast." What a message, and how deep the wisdom that can be applied to more than just music!

Grandma's Tears

Although it could not have been easy for Grandma to get around, she insisted on being active and independent, traveling constantly via subway, bus and taxi. Once, when I encountered her walking down the street on the way to our house, I was alarmed to discover that she was crying. When she noticed me, she made every effort to hide her emotion and put on a happy face. This was extremely upsetting as it indicated a much heavier reality than the one Grandma projected. The sense I got is that her daughter's constant rejection hurt her, but whether that was the problem I will never know. It could have been some romantic issue we were totally unaware of, it could have been a memory of her deceased son, Uncle Bob- it could have been anything. Grandma kept those things to herself.

On another occasion my sister found Grandma in the same condition. We both speculated on the cause and wondered why this perpetually jolly person would actually be so sad. It seemed like there was unspoken tragedy, trauma and sorrow in her past- and in our mother's as well- but it was a box we could never unlock.

Two Ways Of Thinking, Two Ways Of Seeing

I'm about to describe something I have never heard mentioned in my entire life. It is apparently some kind of mental phenomenon. It occurs when I am walking along a familiar street, a place I have seen a thousand times before, and suddenly, it looks completely unfamiliar. It's scary in that I will become lost. It happens rarely and goes away quickly. But it happens, and I recognize it immediately. "Oh no," I think, "Not *this*." So I wait, sometimes using willpower to help regain the familiar way of seeing, and in a minute things are back to normal. Perhaps this is a sign of some unusual mental condition, some kind of disorientation. Perhaps it is even a sign of faculty loss yet to come.

I have developed a theory after observing this over the years... I wonder, is this alternate vision, in its *lack of familiarity*, a mirror of *the very first time I saw that particular place*? Is it possible that it is an imprinted memory of the initial viewing? It appears to be a recollected image, a repeat vision emitted by the brain which temporarily overrides the present. What's odd of course is that this alternate image is familiar in itself- and now I am able to gain some control over it- to revert to the familiar- and more recently as an experiment, to revert to the *unfamiliar*. I can look at an intersection and "will" myself to see it this *other* way, just for fun. Perhaps some expert in the workings of the brain will read this, and will be able to shine some light on this, or perhaps even want to do some research on the subject.

I have always felt I was exceedingly different than most people- not in my soul, but mentally and emotionally. I am far more vulnerable to a myriad of feelings which don't seem to affect others. I always attributed this to being an artist- however maybe there is more to it.

The Farmer And The Corn

When I was twelve Dad walked in the door exclaiming that he had just met an old farmer in he street who was selling corn. Of course this made no sense, but none-the-less Dad unrolled a piece of newspaper that revealed four fat ears of farm fresh corn. He wouldn't be playing "violin" anymore, he said, but a new style called "Old Timey" which he learned about from this farmer. He took the instrument from its case and announced that from now on this was a "Fiddle." He dem-

onstrated the style, which was scratchy and bouncy. We already knew about the music from the old records, but my father invariably found ways to embellish reality with unlikely stories, mostly made up on the spot. None of us ever knew what was truth and what was fiction.

One thing my father couldn't help but give me was his music, and it was a powerful gift that could never be taken away- not by denial, or by any other method. He conveyed this incredible drive and passion, particularly for traditional American music, to me- as his heir. When I was younger this was the primary way in which we shared closeness, and it was completely nonverbal. I saw that music brought him joy, and that his face lit up when I played. No one else had this connection with him, and though he later went on to use just about everyone but me to record and perform with, I always knew that in a way he was running from the connection, as it was so strong it probably unnerved him.

Art Lessons:
The Arrival of Our Beloved Fleur

1 cannot explain why we hated Will so much, yet loved Fleur. It might have been because he was obnoxious while she was wonderful- or it might have been because Will was seen as an intruder, injecting himself into our family when it was still technically a unit. Maybe my parents could have survived had Will not come along, who knows? Or maybe, as my mother once said towards the end of her life when our communication was vastly improved, we might have come to like Will if he had lived. People do change and mellow, so she had a point. But Fleur came along well after Mom and Will were an item, thus Fleur was seen as a gift, and not an enemy. It seemed only fair that Dad should have someone too. Up until the arrival of Fleur, our parents still cohabited, though awkwardly. There were the separate beds, ostensibly because Dad was not able to get any sleep with someone else tossing and turning next to him, but we knew this was pathologically rejecting. Both his wife and his sweetheart got the same cold shoulder.

One day I was taken to art classes on Barrow Street. The moment I walked in I felt happy. I was standing in the middle of an artists' paradise. The walls were decorated with paintings and photographs, there were flower-filled vases everywhere and cozy furniture draped in soft fabrics- this was Fleur's apartment. Fleur had a joyous, bell-like laugh which made me feel comfortable. She was beautiful, with a clear, bright demeanor, long dark hair, and incredibly friendly brown eyes.

During art class she gave us complete freedom- brushes, colors, and different mediums were laid out for us to choose. She never interfered or criticized, and loved everything I created. I looked forward to these lessons as I felt so encouraged in her presence.

We did not think she was Dad's sweetheart at first, and perhaps she was not. But whenever it happened, we were completely accepting. She was more of a mother to me than my own at that point, and I am certain that her kindness provided the emotional support that had been missing, allowing me to gain the confidence I needed to face adolescence.

I know now that in the beginning Fleur believed Dad was long-parted from our mother. Who knows how he represented it to her, but when she found out he was still living with his wife, she disappeared for some time in protest. Fleur was too ethical a person to have anything to do with an existing marriage. Eventually they must have come to an understanding- that my mother was with Will- and that things were really over between my parents... I was a witness to that.

Dad took my sister and I to the Cape several times in early spring to plant the garden. We'd stay for a week and then go back to the City, so that when we returned for the summer the plants would be well established. We had just arrived and dropped our suitcases into our rooms, when we heard the sound of someone entering the kitchen. We came around the corner to find Dad and Fleur wrapped in a loving embrace. It filled my heart with the most wonderful sense of happiness and conveyed so much nonverbal information about the sweetness of love. I had a feeling of hope, as if there was a more positive future ahead. It taught me that love was wonderful, where my mother's relationship with Will taught me that love was obscene. I'm sure they were embarrassed and no doubt pulled away when they saw me, but the positive message had already been delivered.

I was surprised to learn, years later, that my sister found the hug distressing, and I marveled at how two people could have such different reactions to the same thing. Perhaps she didn't want to share her father- perhaps she was afraid of losing him. We've always had very different perceptions of Dad. From my point of view the relationship with Fleur was going to make him a better father. In the case of my mother and Will, the only time Mom paid positive attention to me was in front of Will. If Dad was happy, the same could apply to him.

The Silly Letters

*F*leur and I gave each other the giggles. The only people I've ever gotten along with are people who were not afraid to act completely silly. I'm a generally silly person who loves to laugh, and I get along with other silly people. I have always been eccentric and Fleur seemed to delight in this. We drew funny pictures for each other with spiraling words circling the pages so that the only way to read them was by turning the paper around and around. We invented wild characters and wrote stories about them, roaring with laughter and out-doing each other with each new letter. You can survive almost anything if you can find a way to really laugh.

Elizabeth Irwin

Little Red and Elizabeth Irwin were sister schools. Little Red was "the fours" through the sixth grade. EI was the seventh through eleventh grades. It was an excellent education light years ahead of public school. I know, I experienced both. I'm guessing that Little Red and EI were the choice schools for the children of liberals, beatniks, artists and progressive thinkers of the day. Two of Woody Guthrie's three children went to school there- Nora, a year older and in my sister's class, and Jody, who was in my class. He was a sweet, thoughtful young man who looked almost exactly like his father.

We had a fellow student whose parents had been framed by the government in a very public trial about some kind of top secret something or other. It all seemed like science fiction to us- we knew there was just no way they could have been spies, nuclear scientists or anything else they might have been accused of. I mean come on, we were all from these nice, hip, progressive, intellectual households. Everyone was reasonable and friendly- good people- not spies, not enemies of the state. Their son was a wonderful kid and we all understood that horrible things could happen to people and we realized that somehow, it had happened to his parents. So we silently rallied around him knowing it was unfair that his mother and father were somewhere else- maybe even in jail- for something they didn't do. When we went to our friends houses they had such pleasant families. The parents were kind and soft spoken- the mothers slaved away in the kitchen making wonderful food and the fathers were professional people. We imagined the FBI knocking on the door during dinner and arresting these two nice people. They would be asking continually why they were being taken away... it seemed like World War II, and not the relatively peaceful fifties.

That's How To Read A Poem

In the seventh grade I had a homeroom teacher whose name escapes me. However she became the prototype for many of my cartoons of elderly female authority figures. Rotund, draped in a bosom dress speckled with little eyewearying dots that cascaded over a closet-sized bustline, she was the picture of the intimidating matron. She had a storage area somewhere in her bodice which housed pens, glasses, tissues, and other items which she summarily retrieved as necessary. Her large, quivering arms hung well below her sleeves, her pale, freckled face was able to go from white to crimson when angered, and her transparent blue eyes could drill holes through the back of your head. She was the perfect homeroom teacher as she was able to maintain a strict law and order in her classroom. Ruler-whacking had just gone out of style, or we would all have received the stick sooner or later.

One day we were studying poetry. Most children hated this class, but I, having a father who was somewhat of a poet, had a liking for words. She was calling on us randomly to stand and read passages. My classmates responded with mumbling, almost inaudible monotone voices. Suddenly I was called. There was no time to think. I began, determined at least to speak louder than the others- I hated having to strain to hear and detested whiny, boring speaking. When I finished I looked up, and to my horror, the teacher sat motionless at her desk with her head resting in her hands. Fear shot through every fiber of my being. She hated me! I was going to be expelled from school! Various scenarios raced through my mind as I watched and waited. Slowly, slowly, she lifted her head. Her face was rosy, and there was a look of emotion in her eyes I had never seen before. With a passionate, shaking, contralto voice she said, "Class, that's how to read a poem!"

Dad's Authority

For all his skinny, reed-like appearance most closely resembling Woody Allen without the humor, my father wielded incredible natural authority over everyone around him. He was a charismatic personality who others automatically acquiesced to. This authority made him the High Priest of the jam sessions at the Sandal Shop. Even Bob Dylan paid his respects, and no one wanted to be scolded by him.

Dylan At The Sandal Shop

I remember the hat, the round, youthful face, and the long nails. He was not yet famous, so at that point he was just another interesting person stopping by. He may have recently been signed to a label, but I don't think his first album had come out yet. When I walked in he was sitting there talking to my dad, and I remember thinking that he had a very unique presence. After he left Dad told me something about the conversation. He said that Bob was a poet first and foremost who really didn't care for the "business" side of things. His priorities lay in being true to his art. Right away I resonated with the message. I understood it to mean that Dylan had integrity that he would not compromise. I also understood from this that it was OK to buck the system, to reject the shiny, glossy world of business in exchange for artistic honesty, a lesson which stood me in good stead many times over the years. It was an inspiration and the way I was raised to feel about music. People like Bob Dylan served to reinforce this important, grounding piece of information.

I recently learned that Dylan and his girlfriend Suze had lived only a few doors away from Dad's sandal shop. The store's address was 171 West 4th Street, and Dylan lived at 161. In addition, I read that Suze had once stayed with her sister on Perry Street, no doubt only a block or two from where I grew up. How small a world it really is...

Positively Jones and West Fourth

*L*ater when Dylan's records came out I remember loving his references to my beloved Fourth Street- my home turf, and where Dad's store was located. There were photos of him walking down what appeared to be Jones Street with Suze. Dad had an apartment on Jones which he later shared with Fleur after my parents parted. Jones Street was only one block long and intersected Fourth Street directly at the Sandal Shop. For its extremely limited size it must have been a great place to get an apartment as John Lennon, Ralph Lee Smith, my sister and a number of other friends and acquaintances also had apartments there.

In my view it was probably one of the best locations in the Village.

My father knew and visited with many of the interesting people who passed through town in the sixties, so this sort of thing felt like an everyday experience. As a result I developed a sense of ease with famous people. In Dad's store everyone was just "one of the folks," and no one pulled rank on anybody. Some had records, some books, some were known everywhere and some not... many became famous later, like Dylan, but it hardly mattered. We were all in this together. The list of luminaries that came through the door was so long and spectacular I simply can't remember them all now. There was a very exciting energy, and to me this was normal.

Photo: David Gahr - © The Estate of David Gahr

If I hadn't been so distracted with a terrible feeling of rejection and worthlessness, I might have blossomed into some kind of activist early on, but instead my attentions focused on music and the guitar which carried me far away from unkind words and transported me into the timeless joy of creativity. Music, art, words- these uplifted my soul to a place of power.

It matters not the mood to begin with- whether a performance, a recording, or just sitting alone writing a song- one can start with the flu and be transformed into a completely healthy person in the time it takes to sing and play the first few notes. For me, music was, and is, nothing short of miraculous.

Gatherings and Parties

It wasn't that long before I was being included in the jam sessions. I was only about twelve, but I had figured out how to play a sort of Carter Family style of guitar that approximated flat picking with bare fingers, and soon I began backing up Dad's fiddle playing. People immediately took notice. John Herald, a brilliant singer and songwriter in the great country style (and at that time a member of the Greenbriar Boys), asked Dad if he had forced me to practice. John was laughing when he said it, so this was his way of complimenting. He was by no means the only one to inquire or remark at the unusual nature of my ferocious devotion to the guitar.

Bralph

One of Dad's best friends was an exceptionally intelligent, energetic man named Ralph Lee Smith. Ralph was primarily a dulcimer player, though he also loved guitar and banjo, and as such he and my dad became musical cronies who sang and played frequently in the Sandal Shop. Ralph had an incredibly shrill voice which we always giggled about as children, but he made no pretense at changing it. This was in fact quite authentic in that the old players never sang out of vanity but simply from pure emotion, and often had a similarly edgy, almost nasal style. It really doesn't matter whether one is schooled sounding or not- true singers lift their voices in song for the joy of it. There was no question that Ralph loved the music.

Some years later after my son Thiele was born, Ralph was still a presence in the neighborhood and at the Shop. In his particularly cute way, Thiele referred to Ralph as "Bralph," and the name stuck. Forty years later he is still Bralph to me.

The White Horse Tavern And Dylan Thomas's Ghost

*D*ad and Fleur now lived in an apartment on West 11th Street only yards from where the famous Welsh poet Dylan Thomas once passed untold hours drinking himself into oblivion. The White Horse Tavern had a soul lingering about its darkened windows and burnished counters which one could sense passing by. On Perry Street we had often listened to Thomas's powerful, uniquely lilting voice on LP. His dark, fascinating poems taught me much about the possibility and beauty of language.

At this time my mother wanted me out and I was handed over to my father as the unruly and rebellious daughter. Dad (most likely as a result of Fleur's kind influence) agreed to let me live with them briefly at their pleasant apartment. I had my own room facing the street. Every morning with Dad gone, Fleur and I had breakfast together. This was fabulous. We laughed, shared deep conversations, and ate onion byalis with orange marmalade. I don't remember how long I stayed- perhaps only a matter of months- but when I left I was a little better prepared for the various trials that lay ahead.

Maria, Herself

*O*ne of our neighbors on 4th Street was a strikingly beautiful young woman with a long black braid, alabaster complexion and Madonna smile. She was everything I thought a woman should be- sweet, intelligent and gorgeous- and all in a wholesome, folkie kind of way that Dad thoroughly approved of. He had very specific requirements, and

NATURAL was one of the biggest (I'm still unable to wear makeup because he made his disdain for it so clear). Maria D'Amato had large, almond-shaped eyes that made everyone melt. She moved like a

Maria, Bobby Neuwirth, Tex Isley, and Dad's knee. Photo: John Cooke

dancer and exuded a sensual, magnetic charm. No doubt my dad had a crush on her (despite the fact that she was just a few years older than his daughters), and soon she was playing fiddle, scratching out the first tentative notes and bouncing to the music in a decidedly alluring way. She ordered the most flamboyant pair of sandals in the store that laced all the way up the leg, and looked so terrific in these she could have drawn in countless customers and sold a thousand pairs. Fiddle was an entirely unusual instrument for a woman, and she later explained that my dad had been her mentor. Maria joined the Even Dozen Jug Band, which included Stefan Grossman, Bob Gurland, John Sebastian, Steve Katz (later in Blood Sweat and Tears), and David Grisman, who would make a name for himself playing alongside the bluegrass masters and founding his own innovative "New Grass" style. Soon, Maria was the central attraction of the Jim Kweskin Jug Band, married Geoff Muldaur, and became Maria Muldaur. She recorded "Midnight At The Oasis" and suddenly had a hit record.

Maria is my favorite of today's traditional female singers. Her style is totally unique and heartfelt, and she can sing an old song like nobody's business. She's closer to Bessie Smith and Ma Rainey in spirit than anyone since. She's outspoken, more so even than I, and always hits the nail squarely on the head with observations that invariably change my life. She's a sister to me, and a role model.

Rumor And Reality

It was my understanding (and many of these early impressions have since been proven to be correct)- that my mother and father were among the first musicians to sing and play music in Washington Square Park. Someone even told me my parents actually started the entire tradition. There is an old photo, which may or may not be located by the time this is released, showing the two of them singing together with just a few interested onlookers nearby- exactly what you'd expect for the beginning. They both looked very young, so this was probably in the late forties given that my sister was born in 1948 when my mother was only nineteen.

Music In Washington Square

*B*y the early sixties an extraordinarily vital music scene had taken hold in Greenwich Village. Who can say exactly why- perhaps its residents, brought there by fate, chance, and a shared notion of freedom, were somehow ready to love acoustic music, perhaps as a way to underscore their individuality. Certainly my parents fit this scenario.

The fountain in Washington Square where musicians once gathered-the World Trade Center still standing in the background.

Washington Square Park was home soil. Its kindly, gnarled old trees and scrubby little grass islands nurtured me. It was a companion, a babysitter, and a protector. Other than the interminable hours spent confined in classrooms, and the unhappy nights enduring fear and loneliness on Sullivan Street or at the Perry Street apartment, the park was where freedom and living occurred.

Every Sunday crowds gathered around the fountain, a large circular structure resembling a giant brick bird bath. In summer this was a cooling off place for children, a survival area for homeless people, and of course beatniks, hippies, and intellectuals also gathered there. It was no great surprise that musicians loved the square, and at some point it became the favorite hangout for poets and talented performers of almost every style. People stood around in clusters, pressing together to watch incredible musicians playing styles at one time largely unheard of up North. Frank Wakefield, Mike Seeger, Jodie Stecker, John Herald, Roger Sprung, John Cohen of The New Lost City Ramblers, Ralph Rinzler, Bob Yellin, Steve Arkin, and Winnie Winston, in addition to Eric Weissberg and Steve Mandell (who recorded the Deliverance sound track), were among the bluegrass and country players. John Sebastian, Maria Muldaur, Stefan Grossman, Marc Silber, Jack Baker and others were playing ragtime, blues, swing, and early barrelhouse jazz. Then there was John Fahey in Washington DC and Taj Mahal and Ry Cooder on the West Coast.

Stefan Grossman: From Ragtime To Blues

On a sunny afternoon, wandering from one group of onlookers to the next, I happened upon a throng of people surrounding a guitar player. The intriguing notes of ragtime guitar wafted through the crowd. Somewhere between jazz, blues and classical, it sounded utterly appealing. Squeezing my way through the press, I saw a young man with a large Gibson J200 Sunburst slung over his shoulder. With finger picks and a slight smile, he plucked out the notes of the most alluring music on the planet. Ragtime played on strings instead of piano, a novel and refreshing idea. Stefan Grossman and I started talking and struck up an immediate friendship. He handed me my first Country Blues compilation, an Origin of Jazz release called *Really the Country Blues*, and another collection comprised of short snippets from various tunes- no doubt to squeeze in as much as possible into a limited space. Of course it was annoying in that each song came to a swift end with a sudden fade just as you were starting to enjoy it. If nothing else, it led to an immediate desire to hear the complete song.

Stefan and I fell in love. It was the tender, completely vulnerable, enraptured love of young people experiencing everything for the first time. We drove everyone around us crazy by constantly kissing and hugging. Stefan ushered me into adulthood, and I was ready, being all too happy to leave a debilitatingly painful past behind me. I was prepared to take the reins of my life into my own hands. I don't think I could have picked a better person than Stefan. In retrospect his good qualities shine more brightly in a world filled with less-than-noble

people. Inexperienced and eager to escape my family, I could have picked a bad seed. But there wasn't a mean bone in his body. He was level headed, responsible, kind, and devoted.

Of all the harsh realities, broken relationships and betrayals to come, Stefan wasn't one of them. Despite whatever rumors I heard about him becoming a tough and irascible businessman, he never showed me this tougher side. In a perfect world I would have simply stayed with him.

Saturday Afternoon Jam Sessions

Dad eventually became the reigning impresario of the incredibly vital folk revival scene in the West Village, hosting regular Saturday afternoon jam sessions in his Sandal Shop after music in the park was banned (something about a "no loitering" law). Bursting with enthusiastic musicians and fans, the players and spectators literally spilled out onto the sidewalk while the center of the room steamed up from the intensity of the music as my father held court and directed. Everyone knew his thing was "holding down the beat," and from time to time an excited musician would receive a gruff reprimand as my father snapped, "Speeding up!" while casting a grave eye at the offender. One then had to pay sharper attention to his stomping foot, which pounded out the beat like Big Ben, seemingly setting the standard for worldwide time. I have often been asked about my own pounding foot- videos have been done of my boot in motion, and bass drums have been triggered in the studio from the sound of my foot. Let the question be forever put to rest- clearly, it is hereditary. This small inconvenience aside, these Village sessions were frequented by some of the most phenomenal musicians, famous and otherwise, and this exciting atmosphere formed the core of my musical life. If my father was a bit imposing with his fiddle and his watchful eye, he was also a catalyst for those eager to share in a truly historic musical transformation that was to be part of the wider phenomenon of renewed interest in American roots music.

Dad later moved to the remote reaches of the backwoods of New Hampshire and quietly continued his leather work and music until age and memory loss made it all but impossible. Over the years he has published several wonderful books of poetry. In his imagination I think he is still searching for that old farmer with the corn- or perhaps he has truly become that farmer.

The Folklore Center and Izzy Young

The Folklore Center was another hub for music lovers. It started on MacDougal Street and later moved to Sixth Avenue right where Third Street came to an end. The burnished wood paneling was dripping with one-of-a-kind guitars that hung from pegs on the walls. There were racks of fascinating books and cases of finger picks and capos. The repair shop was in the back and someone like Eddie Deal, Marc Silber, or Fred Weiss would be there to look over your guitar: hold it up to the light, squint down the neck, pluck a few strings, tap a few struts, and make some kind of diagnosis. You could leave it there, but one of the unwritten laws of instrument repair is that it is never, never ready on schedule. By the time you get the call that it's finished, you might have moved to another state.

Izzy was the owner of the Folklore Center. He was a large, imposing looking man with big teeth and thick glasses. He was very brainy, and one would imagine an expert at whatever he did. We had no idea how much influence he really had- to us he was just Izzy. Once at a party someone asked him to demonstrate "Morris dancing." Everyone clapped and shouted while Izzy, with scarves clutched in his hands and tied around his ankles, bounced up and down with such violence that I feared the entire building would collapse.

Much later, after he left the Folklore Center and I had moved upstate, my mother and Izzy came to the house for Christmas. They must have had a crush on each other from way back. My mother was sitting on Izzy's lap when I walked into the kitchen. Clearly they had a lovely few days together in the country. Izzy was probably as radical as anyone in the Village... maybe he was the King. After he moved to Sweden his absence left a noticeable feeling that something was missing.

Marc Silber and Fretted Instruments

*E*veryone was madly in love with Marc. Originally from Ann Arbor, he was tall, had wavy black hair, blue eyes, and was totally gorgeous. It was tough being a teenager around him because he was what we really wanted, but we were just too young. Still, we swooned over Marc.

Photo: David Gahr - © The Estate of David Gahr

We hung on his every word. Marc had tons of natural charisma, and everyone admired him. He was an accomplished guitar player, and an expert builder. He sat behind the counter at The Folklore Center and later was the proprietor of Fretted Instruments. If you needed a Marc hit you just had to walk in, and there he was, in all his glory. Stefan and Marc were good friends and we all hung around a lot. There were other great musicians, too numerous to recall, who sat for hours playing music, jamming, and just relaxing at this beautiful store, knowing that any guitar question they might come up with could be answered by Marc.

Marc has always been a repository of information. Not only does he know the names of just about every Country Blues artist who ever recorded, he can also play their songs with authority. He can tell you the story of everyone you pass on the street in Berkeley and everywhere else between the two coasts. Marc is a born raconteur and historian. Someone should follow him around taking notes to gather some of the information that only he is carrying. He is a hippie for life and manages not to have a care in the world, so it's all the more important that someone write about his life before he drifts to another country and becomes impossible to find.

The Drug Score

Despite the fact that I knew drugs were not for me, I had an occasional longing to be "normal" (and normal at that point was drugs). I wanted to share in the experience my contemporaries were having... if only I wasn't so scared! My friend Suzanne and I decided to walk down MacDougal Street and score some amphetamine, a drug we had heard of that seemed like a reasonable choice. Knowing it was incredibly stupid, we decided to do it anyway, and walked up to a well-known dealer- a teetering, greasy haired man whose eyes were always half-closed in a painful squint. Every time we saw him we couldn't believe he was still alive. We didn't think anyone could get skinnier and still exist. We handed over a few dollars which we had somehow acquired, and reached out to take the pills. Suddenly I felt a strong hand on the back of my shirt. In an instant Suzanne and I were lifted up by our collars and transported down the street to safety. It was Marc rescuing us from incredible stupidity and danger. I don't remember what he said- it might have been "Oh no you don't!" I know we felt unbelievably foolish. Marc was a hero in the truest sense, and his strong protection momentarily filled a terrible void in my life.

One of the features of freedom is the ability to destroy one's life and make dreadful choices- and there would be many other bad choices to come. But this is essentially what freedom is all about: the good with the bad.

Artie Traum

I was in elementary school when I met Artie. At Little Red, "Assembly" consisted of everyone sitting on the floor in a big room listening to announcements and presentations. Things promised to drone on in their usual way when out of nowhere a bluegrass band was introduced. Four young men calling themselves "The B Flat Stompers" were going to play for us. Artie stood in front holding a banjo. He was a handsome, rosy-cheeked teenager who played lightning fast Scruggs licks. I was impressed and amazed- he knew about the secret music! He had this appealingly shy look with a slight smile. I introduced myself immediately- I knew Artie was a kindred spirit and a brother. His face had a kind of transparency and he wore his emotions in a completely honest way. Artie had no guile. He was one of the straightest arrows I have ever known- honest, moral- a truly good person. We almost have to ask what that means today. "Good" seems like a gimmick. If at times we can't really remember, think about people like Artie.

Seamlessly, Artie became a familiar presence at the Sandal Shop. He was family. At the time Artie had a girlfriend named Susie who was petite, blond, and beautiful. They seemed like the perfect couple. Artie and Susie came up to the Cape one summer to visit. Susie, who had a slender little figure with a tiny waist, wandered about unself-consciously in her bikini. I on the other hand felt horribly shy as a slightly chubby teenager. Hiding in the bathroom in my two-piece suit, I was convinced I was unsightly. Susie came in and showed me in the mirror where my waist actually went in, something I had missed altogether. In her kindhearted, sisterly sort of way, she helped me feel better about my looks as only a tender-hearted older sister could. Over time Artie and Susie drifted apart.

Eventually Artie moved to Woodstock where he spent some time in Bob Dylan's large home, a housesitting arrangement. I visited him there a couple of times and we went skinny-dipping in a lovely little landscaped pool off to one side of the house. We were not boyfriend and girlfriend, just pals, but everybody did things like that in those days- it was normal. I was extremely shy and was used to being called "uptight," so I always tried to push myself to *relax* and *go with the*

Photo: David Gahr - © The Estate of David Gahr

flow. In this way I was a total failure as a "Sixties Child." But Artie would never have been the source of pressure, that wasn't in him. He was a sweet, respectful, gentle person. Over the years if I needed a sympathetic ear I would call Artie. He always understood, and he always took my side.

Artie's instrument changed to guitar and his bluegrass morphed to modern and jazz. He married Beverly, and there were never two people more compatible. His talent just kept expanding and his knowledge of the guitar and growing prowess produced some of the sweetest music I had ever heard. He was a shy singer but pushed himself continuously as he felt it a necessary element to showcase his very personal material. Artie's songs were honest, revealing, and would pierce to the core.

We loved and admired each other but always knowing we were sister and brother. Our deep affection was family and our connection, spiritual. When he died of cancer in 2008 a vacuum was created in the world which started a tiny black hole. In a nightmare this hole is drawing good and soulful people away, away, until the earth is filled only with recorded voices regurgitating automated options and radioactive web sites filled with distorted little figures screaming helplessly to pass as reality. Hell, hell on earth. Give me a little festival in the Southern hills with local boys singing under the lights on a makeshift stage made of barn wood. Give me an old Church with voices rising to the Heavens and hands lifted. Give me people who sing for the joy of it, not for the glory.

Did I mention humor? Ask anyone who knew Artie. He had an unending stream of witticisms which revealed the world in all its artifice with a most charming sarcasm.

Doc and Merle Watson
Union Grove North Carolina
Fiddler's Convention

In 1964 Dad, my sister and I, Stefan and Artie packed into the station wagon and drove to the Union Grove North Carolina fiddler's Convention. The ride down was memorable in that it was the tentative start of my affection for Stefan. In youthful stages I was able to consider the emotion that was growing. I rested with my head on his lap in the back seat, one part of me a child, the other part a woman. It was innocent enough and the sort of thing young children do, but at the same time it allowed me to become close to him. On the way down we drove through Nashville and stopped for the night in the darkest, quietest part of town. There was no avenue of lights, no flashing signs, and no traffic- just an old hotel on a dimly lit street.

We visited the home of country musician Tex Isley and sat outside with Tex and Clarence Ashley playing music and talking about how the Old Timey players and Country Blues musicians knew each other and traded licks. Clarence said they swapped songs all the time and learned each other's tunings.

This led me to understand that there was far less separation than supposed and that these two great styles shared influences and evolved together in ways few people understood. We're so wedded to the idea of separation that we can't see the forest for the trees.

Tex and Clarence were country gentlemen, neatly dressed with stylish hats. My heart was filled with joy knowing this was the real deal, water flowing straight from "the musical fountain."

When we got to Union Grove, Doc and Merle Watson were sitting there playing music. Merle was a young teenager and very shy. Doc was the greatest flat picker in the universe, and I was already familiar with his incredible playing. Fred Price was there along with a host of other fabulous players. I was totally inspired. This was worth living for.

On a recent tour we left the highway looking for diesel. The road got smaller and smaller until we found ourselves weaving down a country lane with no place for a bus to turn around. The GPS, which often goes crazy, directed us here and there on every little farm road, and suddenly, there it was- the sign read "Union Grove" and the plaque indicated the entrance to the festival grounds. My heart stopped. Part of me wanted to pull over and make my way down memory lane. Another part of me felt it was sacred ground- I was frozen. No, I would not dig up that peaceful resting place. I would leave it as a precious memory for now. As we drove away my mind immediately placed it into a dream status and I rejoiced, thinking, "I had a dream I drove right past the entrance to the Union Grove North Carolina Fiddlers Convention- it was still there just as it was in 1964!"

I have opened for Doc and Merle (and after Merle died, for Doc)- on a number of occasions over the years. Once, after my opening set at a theater in Ann Arbor, Michigan, Doc said something kind about my music from the stage. When I greeted him with a hug afterwards he said "Don't ever cut your hair."

Enthusiasts And Historians

As luck would have it, Stefan knew everybody. He was friends with an amazing array of record collectors, musicians, historians, instrument builders, and adventurers who went searching the Southland for surviving blues masters. Son House, Mississippi John Hurt, Skip James, Bukka White, and a number of others were located and brought out of retirement to perform and record. In a recent conversation, Stefan listed some of the names, and it was boggling. I remembered every one, having heard all of them frequently in the sixties, but I wouldn't have been able to recall the details.

There was Dick Waterman, who later went on to manage Son House and other noted artists including Bonnie Raitt. Dick drove to Mississippi with Phil Spiro and Nick Perls (founder of Yazoo and Blue Goose Records), only to discover that Son House had moved to Rochester, New York. Tom Hoskins, known simply as "Fang," discovered Mississippi John Hurt living in Avalon, Mississippi. Hurt soon moved to Washington DC, according to Stefan, to be available for concerts and recordings. John Fahey located Skip James in a hospital in Mississippi and also sent a wire to General Delivery in Aberdeen Mississippi addressed to "Bukka White old blues singer" which eventually led to his rediscovery. We didn't have to go far to see Reverend Gary Davis- he lived in the Bronx. All this was going on around me- I was just lucky enough to be in the right place at the right time.

Waterman's recent book *Between Midnight & Day* is a very interesting read, chronicling his experiences with many fascinating artists and featuring his one-of-a-kind, behind the scenes photos. Dick would give me a helping hand in the "rock'n'roll major label days" that were soon to come, speaking to the biz people on my behalf and offering good advice- this during the time he was managing Bonnie. Dick knew and loved real music and had demonstrated excellent taste by working with artists like House and Raitt. He might have been one of the only successful roots music managers on the scene at that time.

The Blues Mafia

Stefan reminded me that the crowd who hung in the DC area were known as "The Blues Mafia." This group consisted of people like John Fahey, Ed Denson (originally from Tacoma, Washington), Mike Stewart, aka "Firk," and Tom Hoskins, otherwise known as "Fang." Together, Denson and Fahey founded Tacoma Records. Nick Perls was a part of the scene in both states, living with his parents in New York and also keeping an apartment in DC where we used to visit him.

The Record Collectors

Then there were the record collectors who were no less active in searching out old music. One of the incredible perks of knowing these devoted people was that as records were located, I got to listen. At that time the songs would be compiled onto reel-to-reel tapes. It was like unwrapping a package from the past straight from some archeological dig. Stefan lent me a tape recorder which I planted next to my bed. Clasping the headphones, I'd fall asleep with the latest rediscovered Country Blues gems running through my brain all night long.

According to Stefan, Bill Givens founded the "Origin of Jazz" library with collector Pete Whelan, and it was the one existing reissue label when we first started listening. Chris Strachwitz had a house in Berkeley and his specialty was Memphis Minnie, Sonny Boy Williamson and others. Strachwitz founded Arhoolie Records sometime in the 1960's. Pete Whelan of the drug store dynasty collected old Paramounts of Charlie Patton. He later sold his collection to an accountant and collector named Bernie Klatzko. Stefan says Whelan had the best collection which included a number of Gennett and Black Patti Records, among them recordings blues artist Sam Collins had made for Gennett, and a number of Charlie Patton and Son House records which were eventually sold to Nick Perls. Gayle Wardlow went to Mississippi with Klatzko and found Charlie Patton's wife Bertha Lee. Richard Nevins later bought Yazoo and Nick's collection in addition to doing field research in Kentucky and founding Shanachie Records. Pete Kaufman collected old Reverend Gary Davis 78s. Dave Freeman's specialty was Old Timey Appalachian music.

Reverend Gary Davis

Stefan and I used to take the subway to Reverend Gary Davis's house in the Bronx. Stefan was among a handful of individuals who got face-to-face instruction from the Reverend. While never considering myself an expert in Davis's style, I took in the fantastic atmosphere of the place. My area of focus was the Delta styles from day one, but I was only too happy to listen to Stefan and Davis joking mercilessly and pounding away on their two guitars. The great Reverend, whose music was sacred to me, playing, singing, and quipping with Stefan. When teaching, he never slowed down to explain, he simply played it at you with lightning speed and had a lot to say if you couldn't catch on. His

formidable little wife entered the room from time to time to remind him that playing blues was not acceptable in God's sight, and instructed him to play only gospel for the salvation of his mortal soul. I did two drawings of the Reverend- the one above done from a photograph taken at a festival, and another sketched while he was sitting in our living room.

At some point someone contacted me to ask about my experiences with Reverend Gary Davis. Perhaps they were writing a book or creating a web site. I sent the following which describes my memories, whether accurate to the detail I can't be sure:

Bronx, New York 1964

First, the long subway ride. Then, the stares from the locals- what were city folk doing venturing so far out of town? This was "rural" Bronx, with little wood and brick houses on scrubby lots, trees and beat-up sidewalks. This was a pilgrimage to a sacred land. Inside there was the element of soft lighting- a warm glow from a small lamp with a tilted shade which lent a beautiful, burnished bronze cast to the room- the flavor of an old house from another era, walls adorned with framed plaques reading "God Bless This Home," doilies gracing the arms of threadbare easy chairs, the grayish haze from a cigar, and a room filled with too many salvaged and cherished things to fit into one small space- cozier and more wonderful than ever- filled with sweetness and profound meaning to a fifteen year old girl who had already dedicated her life to playing and living inside this absolutely mystical, overwhelmingly meaningful music. Blues- one guitar, one voice, one thumping heart and a soul so powerful it could speak straight to God...

Holding court was the magnificent Reverend. With his Jumbo in hand, he danced across the strings with a smile so sly that his mocked irritation was like a ritual blessing. On the one hand were the jokes- the flood of wisecracks that always brought a chuckle or a belly laugh- then came the reprimands, and your fingers turned to jelly before the master. He growled, he cajoled, he sang with his throaty, raw voice: gospel tinged with blues, blues coated with gospel, till his wife entered the room, dish towel in hand, to remind him that he was not to digress into the devil's music. This was Reverend Gary Davis's house, this was everything that mattered, this was blues to me in 1964.

Son House

Son House was not just any genius. The following excerpts are taken from the liner notes of my 2008 release *Blues Walkin' Like A Man*, which was a tribute to this astounding man I met when I was fifteen.

"Son House is one of the foremost founding musical giants. Where

Robert Johnson is the celestial notes wafting from the highest tower, Son House is the boulders upon which the Cathedral was built. He was so stark, so intense, driving and raw, that to do his music faithfully you must be shrill, edgy, harsh, and always slamming, snapping, and torturing the guitar."

I had an instant crush on Son House. He was supernaturally gorgeous. Our first meeting was at a club in New York City where he sat in the back room and played music prior to his performance. His expression was worth a million words and entirely evocative of the day and time in which the music evolved. He was a living envoy, a true ambassador, and a gift to all who met him and valued the history of blues. He was Robert Johnson's teacher.

Son had a legendary drinking problem. Dick Waterman, who accompanied him everywhere, was the keeper of the bottle and tried to somehow balance Son's continual requests with an effort to keep him sober enough for his next performance. This didn't always work out, as Son was vigilant and would search around until he found the hiding place. Some of the recording sessions demonstrate a gradual descent into alcohol. There is a video out there where Howling Wolf confronts Son about his addiction to liquor. For all of this, and his advancing age, Son House was still one of the most brilliant and passionate players in the world of blues- even after his rediscovery when the health issues had become more pronounced. His earth-shattering attack on the guitar taught me more about technique, presentation, and passion than any other artist. His influence is with me every single performance.

The liner notes go on to say: "This record was recorded in a tiled room where various background noises (a nearby freight train, the pinging of an ice storm, the clamor of five dogs, two cats, and an occasional dripping faucet) are all discernible somewhere on the tracks. But no matter, the soul of the blues never worried itself about clinical perfection. There is nothing sanitary about Son House's music. The early masters were all spitfire and engine grease, whiskey and locomotives. Smoky juke joints ruled the night. The music is a wave, and when you are swept up there is no sense of time. Leave the cat fight on the tracks- and a passing tractor hauling a trailer overstuffed with hay bales. When I listen I hear bells- phones ringing- we stop the tracks to answer... it's Son House calling from 1930.

Cut to 1965. I am fifteen and Son is sixty three. Dick Waterman and Stefan Grossman talk in hushed tones in the background. Dick is trying to hide Son's whiskey bottle, Son is inquiring as to its whereabouts, I am playing a Willie Brown song and Son is asking 'Where did she learn to play like this?' Son House is thin and handsome. His eyes shine with the pain of someone who has recently been crying, or maybe coughing. There is a wildness in his demeanor- you have no idea all the places he has been and the things he's seen. You'll never know it all even if the interview was never ending. It's too late now. Books will be written, speculations raised, even careers and movies made. It's in his music now. Watch his videos, listen to his recordings. He hung out with Willie and Charlie- he'll tell you that he taught Robert Johnson how to play guitar. This is the man Robert Johnson idolized."

If I had understood the precariousness, the fragility, and the pure luck of being in the right place at the right time to be sitting in a room with someone like Son House- hanging out, playing music, talking, discussing other blues giants like Robert Johnson- perhaps I would have been more uneasy... nervous that I should pinch myself before the vision disappeared. Very few people were filming or recording such moments in those days. What we take for granted now, making movies on our cell phones, didn't exist. So I look back and think, if only I had asked more questions, dug deeper, and picked his brain for more information which is now gone forever. If only I had understood how fleeting that moment really would become...

Mississippi John Hurt

In December of 1963 I met Mississippi John Hurt at a concert in New York which also featured the great Old Timey musician Doc Boggs. We went back stage as we always did. Stefan was part of the accepted insiders group and we never needed special passes. Hurt's presence was shy and gentle. His face was beautifully weather beaten, he wore a signature hat, and always had a mellow smile. I loved the way he rocked around when he played... it was a bounce that started slow and built up to a strong pace that carried the music. He had his own way of doing this- I never saw anyone else with this exact style of moving and playing. A couple times when I was performing I felt this energy come over me: the Mississippi John Hurt bounce energy- but my style is usually more like the painting of Robert Johnson seated from above- two feet on the ground and a guitar locked against the leg. It's about feet more than the upper body weave.

Stefan and I traveled to Washington DC to stay with Nick Perls. Mississippi John Hurt was now living in the area so we went to his home. I remember this unpainted wooden house- it was very quiet, and beautifully bare inside. Hurt sat on a chair in the middle of the room while we talked and played music. Later some small children tumbled across the floor. "Frankie and Albert" was my favorite Hurt song and I would imagine I played it for him. He offered us coffee, but neither Stefan nor I were coffee drinkers. I never felt the urge to pepper him with questions or pry for information- I was not a filmmaker and left that to the historians. When in the presence of great blues masters I always felt a sense of joy and purpose. This was where I wanted to be.

Photo: John Cooke

Skip James

According to Stefan, we once sat in a room with Skip James and played music together. Apparently Steve Calt wrote about Stefan and I walking in on this occasion. Other than a recollected vision of Skip's wide brimmed hat and melancholy expression, I don't really remember this meeting.

What I do remember is the hospital. It's sad that by this time Skip was already dying of cancer, an unusual disease in his day. I had been playing Skip James songs and listening to his haunting music for some

Multi-media portrait of Skip James- Rory Block 2010

time- he was one of the best and most powerful, certainly one of my favorites. But surrounded by grief, Skip had gone way inside. A hospital is no place to see a man this great. He wandered about in a bathrobe. I think he smoked a cigarette. He never met our eyes but gazed downwards. I could feel his despair.

Bukka White

*T*he only time I spent with Bukka White was simply sitting next to him in a back room somewhere in the City. He had an impressive aura, formidable in every way- his voice, his guitar style, even his appearance- everything about him was very powerful. I don't particularly recall conversing with him, but his presence alone was an inspiration, another window into the historic atmosphere in which blues was born.

Nick Perls

Nick, for all his reputation as a cantankerous roots music aficionado, was a pivotal and important presence in the early blues revival. He founded two labels, Blue Goose and Yazoo records, both largely devoted to reissues, but occasionally strayed to record various contemporary blues musicians like me, noted illustrator R. Crumb, and others.

Nick was one of the first people I knew who was openly gay and spoke to me about his issues and concerns before anyone seemed to know or care. He was the first to tell me of the coming epidemics of diseases, when AIDS didn't yet have a name but was making its way into the population, and he talked a lot about his lifestyle. He had a sense of humor and portrayed everything graphically. He told me his pushed-back hair style and leather jacket were part of "the uniform." When his friends started dying of AIDS, we knew his time couldn't be very long.

When Nick was younger he lived at his parents' gorgeous brownstone on Madison Avenue. Nick's father founded the successful Perls Gallery, and there were gigantic Alexander Calder mobiles which filled entire rooms on several floors. We had free roam of this extraordinary place, and on a number of occasions had dinner with his family in their elegant dining room. They had hired help, and it was like a wonderland there.

One of Nick's friends was blues enthusiast Al Wilson. Al was a Country Blues freak like I was, and he sat in the basement with old records trying to decipher them just like I did. Al and I compared notes and were on the same page. He later went on to form the band Canned Heat named after Tommy Johnson's heart wrenchingly beautiful song by that name. Al died years ago after only injecting a song or two into the mainstream which carried a powerful message of the old music into the ears of the unsuspecting public. At that point almost no one knew the source of the music but a handful of people, most of them my friends in New York and Washington DC.

Over time early American blues continued to slip into the pop market virtually unnoticed through bands like The Beatles, The Rolling

Stones, and Cream, whose version of "Crossroads" made it obvious to me that Eric Clapton admired Robert Johnson- but I doubt very many people had any idea who Johnson was at that time. I heard the Country Blues influences in some of The Stones' material immediately, influences such as Reverend Robert Wilkins. Had it not been for this gradual introduction, it might be that the mainstream market would still be unaware, and had it not been for Eric Clapton and Keith Richards writing liner notes for the Robert Johnson reissue, that recording *might* not have become a gold record.

Jo Ann Kelly

The only other woman I knew in the sixties who was playing Country Blues was British artist Jo Ann Kelly. I met her at Nick's house, and the two of us (though with a different style and approach) were kindred spirits. Jo Ann had a deep, raspy voice which was perfect for Charlie Patton, Blind Willie Johnson, Willie Brown and Bukka White songs. She was a slide player light years before I was. There was never competition between us, only a shared sense of purpose and mutual respect, particularly since we covered different bases. I had no idea how she was able to get so much grit into her vocals.

Jo Ann and I met again years later when I was touring in Europe and we had a moment to catch up in the back room. She told me about her cancer and was in low spirits. I wasn't sure what it all meant as brain tumors hadn't become as common as they seem to be today, and I was hopeful she would survive. The next time I saw her we were co-billed at a show in Germany (which was later released on CD: *Women In Emotion*, I think it was called), and she was so ill she had to take a break in the middle of her set just to breathe. It was distressing to see her this way, but you've got to hand it to her- typical of a blues singer, she sang to the last. The next thing I heard was that she had died. She was the female Charlie Patton in the flesh.

The Kettle of Fish, The Dug Out & Gerdes Folk City

You took the stairway down into the basement. The Dug Out was a hole-in-the-ground Coffee House where established names and up-and-comers performed. I saw Mississippi John Hurt there, as well as people like Richie Havens, David Cohen (later David Blue), Patrick Sky, John Sebastian, David Bromberg, Dave Van Ronk, and others. My sister and I watched John Sebastian play harmonica with John Hurt, giggling and whispering because he was so good looking with his holster of harps and easy smile.

A few doors down was the Kettle of Fish Bar where many of the musicians gathered after playing the local clubs. It was bursting with artistic energy. Some of these folks moved on to fame, while others faded from sight or became just plain dissipated. My sister and I were too young to enter at the time. I'm told that on a given night you'd find people like Dylan, Phil Ochs, Tom Paxton, Paul Siebel, Eric Anderson, David Blue, Dave Van Ronk, and Barry Cornfeld sitting around a table. Jack Baker told me that even Linda Ronstadt, and Emmy Lou Harris (who Jack said once went out with Sieble) would stop in on occasion. Eric Frandsen, who would come to see me play years later at the Speakeasy across the street, was another Village regular. A talented singer and performer, Eric had an endless stream of hilarious jokes at his fingertips. Later he worked at Matty Umanov's guitar shop where he continued to be a source of laughs and one of my favorites there. Gerdes Folk City was a bigger venue where rising stars and established luminaries played. You could see Peter Paul and Mary, Buffy Saint Marie, Dylan, and Joni Mitchell, as well as some of the more old time musicians such as Lonnie Johnson, Reverend Gary Davis, and piano player Roosevelt Sykes. We all went down to Gerdes to hear great music at one time or another.

Don't Call Me Dad

My relationship with my dad began deteriorating into complete alienation. He announced one day when I was about thirteen that we should not call him "Dad" anymore, but "Allan." I was horrified as the message was clear. "Hi, my name is Allan, and I don't want to be your father. Deal with it." Somehow my sister seemed to like the idea and started calling him "Allan" immediately, but I never acclimated.

The Bad Trip

I was predestined not to be a pothead- my mindset having always been wired against drugs. Yes there was the occasional, fleeting temptation to experiment (such as the fiasco on MacDougal Street)- but even that was more of a pretense than the real deal. We wanted to hold the pills, not ingest them. Unfortunately almost everyone I knew in those days (except for Stefan, Jack Baker, and the super-straight guys like Izzy) were sucking on joints and sometimes doing the big one: LSD. We went to a psychedelic movie and I tried to groove with all the flashing images. Freaked out hallucinations and melting visions were meaningful to a lot of people in those days. As I sat there I thought it was artistic- but I would never have had the courage to swallow LSD myself. I read about it, even idolized the concept: wandering about in another dimension of intensified experience accompanied by high powered perceptions- able to view the inner workings of life, or so it was rumored. It was probably very cool. But you had to be extremely brave to take it, or extremely stupid- and I was neither.

Timothy Leary led the drug culture and had worshipful followers. In the end, with the world waiting for him to commit suicide on mass media, I am not surprised that the final phantasmagoric experience of living with drugs would lead to a brick wall like suicide. When you've reached the pinnacle of drug-induced states, and sober life has long ago lost its appeal, the only experience left to crave is the slamming door. I find that sad and depressing.

I tried to experiment with pot but on the two or three occasions when I actually inhaled, I immediately had a horrible experience. It was pretty scary for a person who likes reality. I found myself losing touch with all that was familiar and on one notable occasion seemed to actually go mad. I thought I was dying. I had just had an argument with my mother where she approached me with the swinging, face-slapping palms that had always worked in the past. I leaped up onto one of the beds and waved my clenched fists in her face. I was ready for battle. I had never done this before, and it felt empowering. My mother backed away, startled. I raced to the bathroom, angrily smoked a wrinkled old joint I had been carrying around in a pocket for just such an emergency, and raced out into the street. Then it hit me. My head floated off my body. I was looking down at myself from above. I went numb and couldn't feel my legs. This was it, I was dying. I began to ask people for help. They looked at me with saucer eyes and scurried away. I started to slap myself in the face repeatedly. The feeling of panic was beyond out of control. I leaped into a cab and went racing to the east side to the apartment of a pot head I knew who I somehow decided would know what to do to "bring me down." When I arrived he was shuffling around his pad and gave me a drink of orange juice. He calmly asked me what I had taken, and when I said it was pot, he said, in a quiet voice, "You'll be OK." He told me to relax and let it wear off.

So it looked like I was going to have to get my kicks with the safer things like waking up in the morning, walking out into the sunshine, breathing the fresh air, viewing the majestic landscape in God's magnificent world... and then of course love, sweet love... and music, music, music! These things filled my soul from the highest mountain to the deepest ocean and left nothing more wonderful to be desired. This is probably why drugs held no appeal.

Playing Hooky

Every morning I rode the subway to 125th Street, walked in the front door of the imposing stone fortress known as "Music and Art High School" and out the back door into Harlem, where I marched alone (the only white person for miles, a solitary teenager in my corduroy outfit and long brown hair)- all the way to the Village. People looked at me, and I waved. I was sick and tired of heartless adults whose only purpose was to herd me into jail cells called classrooms and force-feed me stuff even they wouldn't eat. To me it was the height of hypocrisy and the moment I was able to escape those bonds I left, and good riddance. At fourteen I found a complete description of myself meant for the police lying out on the counter in my Dad's store. I was a runaway and for a brief period of time, retrieving me and putting me back into the jailhouse of school must have seemed like a concept. But no one really wanted me back- I would be like a stray dog captured and sent to a shelter. I would die if I stayed there, so I escaped to starve in the streets (how often have I stopped our bus to try and coax some suffering animal over to a bowl of kibbles and water, and every time the desperation and hunger in their faces is overruled by fear of humans. Only once has one of these poor creatures ever come to the food). Had I not found Stefan and his kind parents to "adopt me" I might not be writing this today. I might have been in that cold black box of nothingness that to me was death. I might have been a stray running from the warden whose job it was to capture and kill me. Escaping to the freedom of the pavement (where no food, water, shelter, or kindness existed), was most likely a better death.

After I left Music and Art High School there was a brief effort to have me continue my schooling. At that point I had not yet finished the tenth grade, so for the eleventh, I would have to repeat the tenth. I was transferred to the unbelievably ghastly halls of an area public school. This place was clearly a juvenile detention center, the closest thing to jail I hope to ever witness up close. In no time I officially quit, thus ending my formal education. I left behind girls who looked like prizefighters dressed in ugly uniforms, brawling and swinging their fists at each other daily. No one was studying anything. In retrospect it was lucky that I had gone to the Little Red School House. When I entered public school I immediately noticed that the courses for the tenth grade were far below the level of what I had already studied in the fourth and fifth grades at Little Red. I just couldn't believe the low quality of the education that was out there. At Little Red I couldn't wait to go to school- it was actually fun. These public schools felt like Alcatraz.

Runaway- Hitchhiking to California

At this time I realized the only alternative was to run away. There's no great excuse to remain around people who don't like you if you don't have to. The description for the police was not a deterrent- I knew it was just a concept. No one was going to bother to drag this distraught, angry teenager back into custody. I think the plan was to forget I ever existed. My father and mother both set the example of living entirely for "number one." I believe my sister bought the package on some level, however I was forever turned against the concept. Selfishness has such diminishing returns.

When Stefan and I left New York we started out with a couple of friends as designated drivers. Being city kids, we had never learned to drive and were at the mercy of those who did. By the time we reached Ann Arbor I was in a trance. It was as if someone had given me a sedative. My body was still bouncing around from the movement of the car. It was a no escape feeling, and I hated it. Years later, after getting off an endless flight to Australia where we had flown directly through a massive storm with lightning striking the wings attended by huge free fall drops in altitude, I had this same horrible feeling- that I was still in the air. I could barely walk and my legs felt like rubber.

Along the way we connected with different drivers, often times unknown to me. I can't remember how this particular character managed to be at the wheel (he later stole some money and split), but I awoke after we left the road. I saw wet grass spinning past the windshield and felt us striking a wooden fence which split and flew away from us. Eventually we came to rest in a cow pasture. It was all in slow motion. No one wore seat belts in those days. In the wee hours of the morning it was miserable out- dark and rainy. The police said our driver had gone straight off the road, having fallen asleep at the wheel. It's more miraculous than ever that we were not hurt- not a scratch- no one's head hit the windshield or worse. It seems that guardian angels were watching out for us. Later we were walking around a brightly lit police station at two thirty in the morning like nothing had happened. There was a vague fear that somehow we might get in trouble for something- any number of imagined offenses. Although drugs would never be the issue for either of us, I was in fact legally too young to be crossing state lines in this way. I learned in a recent conversation with Stefan that Marc had warned him to get a note of permission from my father. I never knew that Stefan was carrying such a note for the unlikely event we were ever questioned.

Pawn Shops and Old Guitars

In certain areas of the country pawn shops lined the streets, sometimes several per block. These intriguing places often held a treasure trove of old instruments. It's hard to believe that Stefan was only a teenager at the time, but he was totally savvy about guitars and equally talented at unearthing valuable ones. We would walk in and he would say something like, "Got any old Martin guitars?" The proprietor would rummage around in the back and come out dusting off some priceless old pearl inlay that needed a neck reset. Stefan would say "How much do you want for that *old* guitar?" He had a way of putting it so that it seemed like something they'd practically want to give away. But who knew? In those days "old" was bad. People hadn't really started collecting early Martins yet and Stefan was ahead of the curve. I used to hear things like "Gotta have fifty bucks!" and Stefan would say "Forty bucks." The pawn shop owner probably thought Stefan was some whacky kid who was going to sling the guitar over his shoulder and play Yankee Doodle Dandy for his girlfriend at the drive-in. Stefan would buy these things for a song, and when we came back from our trip he had amassed a large number of incredible (soon to become ever-so-valuable) prewar Martins of every description.

That was my earliest experience with really beautiful instruments. Afterwards I knew I could never be happy with anything less. In my eyes Martin guitars were the gold standard. Now I have four, but then I only had my humble little antique Galliano, a gem in its own right, but not really a blues guitar. It had nylon strings and was perfect for classical and folk, but I was trying to bend and snap strings, and this just didn't work on gut strings. I switched to silk and steel, but that was causing the delicate wood to crack and warp. From that point until Martin presented me with my first herringbone- a road warrior of a beautiful instrument which I still take on tour- I used to borrow guitars from my friends to make albums.

Stefan Answers The Door In His Underwear

We stayed for a time in the Colorado Rockies with Laurie and Bob, a young couple with two children who were living the mountain existence in a newly built cabin a fair distance from anywhere. Laurie showed me that water boils at a different temperature in thin air. I also discovered that I don't like extreme altitudes and feel a kind of panic rising while crossing high peaks.

Later we discovered a tiny cabin yet further out in the expanse. Stefan started up an old wood stove to the best of his city boy abilities, but smoke immediately began back-drafting into the room. Escaping to the bedroom, we were fooling around when we heard a loud knock at the door. Who on earth would be coming to call at this isolated hunter's retreat in the woods? Stefan went to the door in his underwear, swung it open, and there stood a policeman. I cowered under the covers- this was it, Stefan was going to be arrested for statutory rape. I was fifteen and looked twelve. This was a bad situation. Of course I had no idea about any signed permission (not that anyone would have believed it). I covered my head and waited. Soon Stefan came back. It seems that someone had reported smoke and the cop had come by to check. Convinced everything was under control, he left. I'm not sure why we didn't encounter any bears or deranged mountain men. We were too young to be fully aware of the dangers.

Boulder and Denver

We stopped for a couple weeks to stay with Harry Tuft, proprietor of the Denver Folklore Center. We visited some of Stefan's friends in Boulder, then an open expanse of gorgeous vistas stretching into eternity. It hadn't yet been turned into an endless sprawl and these were the first few houses in what would later become out-of-control development. Years later I learned that Chief Niwot, who had been betrayed and driven from this spectacular homeland, put a curse on the valley as he turned to go, essentially saying, "You will never be able to leave this place..." in other words: "Take it, destroy it, and it will eat you alive." This pretty much sums up all of our environmental indiscretions. Of course this is not the only place of extreme natural beauty which settlers have wantonly abused over time.

However I loved the painted deserts and was totally drawn to the Badlands and the canyons of Colorado... the empty spaces of the western frontier were utterly beautiful to me. I could still feel the Native American presence in those areas and loved the fact that no modern buildings rose up to mar the landscape.

The West Coast-
Berkeley and Ed Denson's House

I found out immediately that I was not a West Coast person. When we came to the brown hills of California, nothing ever looked so much like the moon. I didn't resonate with the landscape and had the nagging feeling that something vital was missing- perhaps the full green of the Northeast that I was so used to. I think the fact that I was depressed and lost must have created this sense of sadness, as I don't feel it anymore when I'm in California. In addition I have long since discovered the extreme beauty of Northern California- the Redwood forests, Mendocino, and the lush valleys of the San Fernando farmland. But a dispossessed fifteen year old was seeing things through the saddest of eyes.

In Berkeley we stayed with Ed Denson, hippie businessman and founder of Kicking Mule Records. He had a little pad on some side street surrounded by the kind of dry grass typical of that part of California. Ed was gruff, and I was awkward, so the combination was like oil and water. I had zero people skills and was basically a scared, wild animal. I only came out of hiding for a few people, and to the rest of the world I was basically a biter. I'm sure I was totally unbearable. Pot smokers always hated me instantly as I was on the opposite side of the spectrum. I clung to reality while they clung to hallucination- that was the whole point in those days. When I look back I don't know how I survived the drug years with so many people going down all around me. Perhaps total abstinence was my secret.

Ed was all about a new style of guitar playing. John Fahey was making records and had set the standard for writing totally different music. Ed was against the exact arrangement thing I was wedded to- my mission was playing and transcribing the music note for note. Ed disapproved of this entirely. Once, just to call his bluff, I played "Old Country Rock" for him one fret up. Nothing could have been more dissonant. I did this as a joke, and it sounded dreadful. Ed loved it. He never knew I was spoofing him.

Fred McDowell Grabs My Breast

One day Mississippi Fred McDowell showed up. We all went down to the Jabberwocky Cafe to watch him perform. He was so tight- a short, thin guy with a huge presence and the Mississippi mystique all around him. I was fascinated. This is when I felt really comfortable- when I was with Fred, Son, Mississippi John and the other blues players. It was familiar territory to me- like we were speaking the same language. I loved the intensity, the fire, the rebelliousness and quiet passion that surrounded these amazing musicians. It was a feeling of being among kin.

At some point we all got up to play. When it was my turn I started with Tommy Johnson's "Big Road Blues," or maybe "Statesboro Blues" by Blind Willie McTell. Someone jumped out of his seat and shouted "She plays like a man!" I wondered what that really meant. Were women only expected to play the feather-light arpeggios my mother had played? Was there something masculine about my playing? Was I once again out of step- was I flawed, or perhaps even damaged goods? I never figured out why women were not expected to

play with hard driving intensity, and why this seemed to be the exclusive territory of men. I did not see myself as male or female, black or white, old or young, from the north or from the south. These distinctions were meaningless to me. I am human, and that's what matters. If there's one thing I just don't enjoy, it's dividing people up according to categories and assigning expectations to them as a result. This is crazy, and I want no part of it. As stated I always give credit where credit is due. I have never tried to cop someone else's song, to steal music- and have always made it a point to mention the original writers. But I also don't expect people to assign all passionate playing to men and all fluffy playing to women. That's just too limiting for me.

Back at Ed's place I was wandering around in tight little T-shirts. I never wore a bra in those days, no doubt a form of rebellion. I was a free spirit and wrote my own rules. When I walked down the street men were constantly calling out and making appreciative comments, and I enjoyed this as opposed to being outraged by it. Don't get me wrong, it doesn't give anyone a reason to assault or take advantage- far from it. It was simply a statement I chose to make, and I liked being physical- it was a powerful feeling. I guess Fred noticed this. He came up behind me one day when I was washing a huge sink of soapy dishes. All of a sudden I felt a hand grab my breast- it was just a quick squeeze, and pretty firm. I was startled and spun around to see him, but he turned away to avoid my eyes. For a moment I could tell that to him I was a perfectly acceptable choice for a little girlfriend. I took this as a compliment. He was letting me know he thought I was sexy, and to me at the time it was confirmation of my new found woman-hood.

And here I make a point. In Fred's day and time this was not the crime it is today. This doesn't make it less than a crime today. I applaud awareness regarding abuse and its prevention. But it's also impossible to apply our standards to another period of history. We have to be careful lest we start rewriting the past and demonizing people who led important lives that were in step with the morality of their day. Fred's well known version of "Good Morning Little School Girl" may be gritty, but it's not evil. It embodies a different time, and it has to be respected as a result.

Old Folk Singers In Hats

One day Stefan and I went to a festival at the university. We walked up the wide stone steps carrying our guitars and made our way to a small room where a number of artists were performing, one after the other, throughout the day. Stefan and I played our favorite duets by Willie Brown, Charlie Patton, and Tommy Johnson. Another performer, in his signature hat, sat off to one side. I was holding one of Stefan's beautiful Martin guitars, which immediately drew attention and comment. I proudly related the tale of our pawn shop adventures, and at that point the guitar was already worth four figures. When I stated the current value, which was something like $1,200 (today of course, immeasurably more), our colleague in the hat laughed contemptuously. But I knew this was the correct value as the instrument had been appraised by the experts- John Lundberg and Marc Silber- who both worked at Lundberg's Guitar Shop on Dwight Way- and they had given it a number. I continued to insist that this was the correct information, but he refused to believe me. He acted like I was nuts. I guess he looked at this fifteen year old kid and assumed she couldn't possibly know what she was talking about. It was demeaning, and eventually I stopped talking to him. He was undoubtedly thinking about the top dollar a quality guitar used to bring (something in the low three figures no doubt), and didn't realize that values were starting to soar. A lot of people must have been surprised by this interesting turn of events. This is probably what makes some people try to anticipate trends and buy stock.

Country Joe & The Fish

As we left we passed a group of musicians in the courtyard. They were seated with crossed legs on the pavement and there was a lively debate going on about musical styles. An unusual looking young man with sandy colored wavy hair (who had some similarities to Al Wilson) was prominent in the conversation. We joined in for a while, passing the guitar around and voicing various opposing opinions. At that point things were being discovered at a mile a minute and just about every day there was a new piece of information- a new record discovered, a new fact regarding the life and death of another player, a new photo of someone revealing what kind of guitar they played, a surviving relative that shined new light on the known facts, that sort of thing. After we walked away Stefan said that the sandy haired guy was Country Joe McDonald from a band called Country Joe and The Fish. We probably saw him again somewhere, and were soon aware that his band was making a name for itself.

We ate dinner at Lunberg's house, hung around with various friends from back east who had recently relocated, and saw a number of people who looked a lot like Charles Manson wandering the streets. There was pot and paisley everywhere. It just never felt like home to me.

Return To The East

After a while Stefan and I got burnt out on the West Coast. We were drifting and we knew it. Marc stayed, being a west coast person by nature, but we journeyed home. I don't recall much about the trip back, only that life resumed one day in New York. I think there is actually a different temperament for each coast.

We got an apartment on Saint Mark's Place in the East Village, a fourth floor walk-up that got hotter than a tinder box in summer. The neighborhood had not yet been renovated and was a pretty scary place, though there were some fairly good areas nearby- Second Avenue, home to Ratner's Deli and The Filmore East (where I saw Eric Clapton perform back in the Cream days)- but there were also very bad areas: needle Park, the Bowery, and other sad, dangerous realities.

One day Stefan brought Gary Davis over to the apartment. No doubt the stairs were an immense chore for an old man, but he never complained and made it to the top, clutching Stefan's arm and joking the entire way. He sat there smoking a giant cigar and playing his big Gibson J200. Stefan used to reach over and flick the ash off the end from time to time so it wouldn't burn down the house. I did a pen and ink drawing of the Reverend which attempted to capture some part of his fabulous, imposing demeanor.*

How To Play Blues Guitar
Peter Siegel and The Elektra Days

When I was twelve, Dad and I played two tracks on an album called The Elektra String Band Project which featured numerous talented folk musicians of the day. Four years later Stefan and I went to Peter Siegel's apartment and recorded an entire album in his bedroom on a Nagra tape recorder with a couple of mics. That album, called *How To Play Blues Guitar* was released briefly on Elektra, then on Transatlantic, and eventually on Stefan's own label, Kicking Mule Records. I had a somewhat skewed perception that there was compromise involved in presenting the music in a "how to" format, and as a compulsive purist trained by the best (my father), I decided to use a fictitious name as a kind of pointless protest. At the time I felt that the musical offering stood on its own and didn't need any "gimmicks." I rejected anything that could be construed as an adulteration or dilution of the direct message of the old music. So that's how I came to be called "Sunshine Kate." Incredibly, there have been people at my shows- particularly in England- who knew all about this ancient record. However it no longer bothers me that it was an instructional album, and now I have numerous teaching resources out and have come to enjoy passing on whatever I know.

Recently Stefan informed me that there are still more of our old recordings sitting in boxes that have never seen the light of day. A few years ago we mastered a collection from as far back as the 1960s and released it on his label as a duet album called *Country Blues Guitar- Rory Block & Stefan Grossman- Rare archival recordings 1963-1971*. I hear my familiar voice on tracks such as "Canned Heat" (which I still sing today), but I sound like such a baby: an incredibly young, high-pitched version of myself.

*This drawing is available in the online version of the book.

Don Thiele

Some time around the end of 1965 Stefan and I began to drift apart. I was working at the sandal shop and had a whole new crowd to relate to. One of my favorite people was an artist named Don Thiele. Black-haired and dashing, Don was a lady's man and modern day swash-buckler. He looked like a pirate with his flashing eyes and full beard. He was outgoing, dramatic, charismatic, and sexy. Don was probably ten years older and I viewed him (as I did Marc Silber) from the per-spective of a young girl mooning over the unattainable. His girlfriend Linda was a sweet, patient person- good looking and intelligent. She was the brains of the operation and held down a straight job while Don cavorted around. Her money must have paid for their lifestyle. I'm sure Don put her through the wringer, but she always forgave him.

For some reason Don came to work for my father. Leather probably appealed to his artistic side and seeing him with a custom-made knife sheath on his belt or the large leather bag he made for himself fit his image. After hours we would go to Don and Linda's and sit around as they smoked pot and set the stage for how this kind of life was to meant be lived. Even though I was accepted and loved, I was still an outsider in that I was the "uptight" one who needed training... training in the art of living the drug life. Don popped LSD fairly regularly and extolled its virtues. His colorful paintings embodied the wildly chaotic world of psychedelic images.

Of course Don eventually put the make on me and at sixteen, it's an honor to have a gorgeous older man consider you desirable. So we had a one-time fling. But in the end it was clear we were simply meant to have a long-term friendship. He later told me that Linda used to refer to me angrily as his "second wife," so I realized I was more important than I thought. On the occasion of this "fling" Don did a nude draw-ing of me which he gave me after we reconnected on one of my many European tours. He had moved to Holland and had become a full-time painter, and by then his work had taken on some of the unique beauty of the impressionist styles which were all around him. I think he burned out on the harder drugs and probably just liked the un-oppres-sive, freewheeling atmosphere of the European lifestyle.

Don died of heart failure several years ago. I'm deeply saddened that he is not still here, but extremely glad I had the opportunity to reconnect with him.

Every time a dear friend leaves, I have an increasing sense of isolation, and often a feeling of not being able to comprehend the reality of death.

Faye Dunaway

My sister and I shared ownership of the Sandal Shop for some years after Dad moved to New Hampshire. One day Faye Dunaway knocked on the door after we had closed for the day. Someone refused to let her in and she walked away shaking her head in disgust. I couldn't blame her a bit. At the time we were perpetually swamped with customers and had developed a policy (as a result of endless after-hour requests which made it almost impossible to leave for the day), to be firm in not letting customers in after the doors had closed. But sometimes that resolve ended up making us feel downright mean- and some customers really knew how to beg and lay it on thick. I saw people weeping and clutching their sandals. "I've had these for twenty years!" one lady sobbed, "They're the only things I can wear on my feet. You have to fix them! I came all the way from Long Island!" Everyone had a good reason and a compelling need. Dunaway was just part of the amazing clientele we were lucky enough to have (I once made a tooled saxophone strap for Sonny Rollins), and even though I was not the one who turned her away, I apologize to her for the unfortunate aggravation since it happened at my family's store. In fact I was walking up to the front door right as she was leaving and witnessed her exasperated exit. As she passed me I recognized her. I asked if they realized who they had just turned away. Someone ran back out into the street and called to her but she was gone.

Babies Having Babies

In 1966 I began going out with a young man who worked at the shop. He was a close friend of Don Thiele's and shared Don's enthusiasm for pot smoking. In retrospect I probably chose him because he reminded me in many ways of my father, but of course seeking mysterious, distant men was ultimately not going to be anything but punishment. I would say that choosing a man who reminds you of Dad works

if Dad is an attentive, loving father who sets an example as a good husband. If Dad is any other kind, it's probably not the way to go. Best to choose someone for the opposite reasons- someone totally unlike Father in looks and temperament- for better results.

We were young and idealistic. We got married and started a family way ahead of schedule. I was only sixteen and needed written permission from a parent or guardian, which (at the end of an incredibly awkward visit with my mother where I sat on the couch nervously clutching a pillow and fidgeting), she provided. However, for the first time I felt her advice and concern was of a more tangible nature, and her questions to me made a lot of sense. She asked if I was truly in love. I thought I was, but I would have a different answer today simply knowing the huge implications of these decisions. She tried to get me to think long-term, but I was not capable of that at the time.

In a nasty twist of fate, my new husband decided he was "not ready" to be a father, and, being heavily wedded to his hand-rolled joints, expected me to carry the baby and give it up for adoption. When I think about the life this would have created for me, choosing pot smoking and dragging around New York while his parents paid our rent- instead of keeping my baby- I'm just glad I chose my child over this other pointless option. We parted, came back together, and so on, until he ran off with some totally silly girl, and that put a full end to our relationship. Of course his other fling was brief, but these are things we are not wise enough to realize at the time... if I destroy my marriage and family to go off with this person I just can't resist, what will I have after the fling is over? Most likely a wrecked marriage which might not ever be restored, and a child that lacks a parent.

Thiele was born in Florida where my husband's parents lived. It was a shocking experience which no one had prepared me for. As I gripped the bars on the hospital bed and writhed in unimaginable pain, I wondered why there was this complete dropout in the support systems for such essential life skills. Not only did I know nothing about relationships, pregnancy, birth, cooking, making money, paying bills (or any other skill required for survival in the world)- but I wondered: when had we become so separated from the nuclear family that females of the tribe no longer attended the birth, washed the baby, or helped with infant and child care? My generation seemed to be stumbling around without the lights and doing everything in a vacuum.

My mother had nursed all three of her children and I fully intended to nurse. The notion of boiling bottles and wrestling with gadgetry that required washing, sterilizing, and all kinds of maintenance was totally unappealing when we had been designed with a completely simple, natural arrangement. But when they handed me my perfect little baby boy, I noticed there was no milk. Distraught, I asked one of the nurses what the problem might be. "Oh," she said, "they gave you shots to dry up your milk in the delivery room," as if this was as natural as breathing. I was shattered. I couldn't believe they would make such a critically important decision for me without asking first. They just went ahead and shut down my body's natural processes with chemicals. I began to cry. I was in this state of despair when an incredibly kind nurse discovered me and inquired about my obvious grief. I explained, and she said, "Don't worry- just put the baby on the breast and within three days you'll have milk. Nothing is strong enough to stop the nursing reflex." She was right, and to me it was as if she had saved my life, and in a way my baby's life too with her simple, cheerful reassurance. Within three days I was nursing. I later discovered that according to the hospital, hardly anyone nursed- and that the hormone shot to dry up a mother's milk was just routine!

I recently found a hand-written diary from that exact period of time. I have no idea why I hadn't seen it for forty years- it was as if it had been buried in the sand and was suddenly pitched upwards into my hand by some earthquake. There it was, a worn, little blue book, and I opened it. My God how it took me back- the details of my breakup with Thiele's father, his affair, how I felt, what I did. This took courage. It was almost unbearably painful. As I read these despair-streaked pages it took me back to how it feels when there seems to be no way out, nothing to look forward to, and no improvement possible. Many people feel this way, and some don't make it. If only there could be a crystal ball nearby to bring us hope- a picture of a rosy day in the future when all that will be past, and will no longer have power over us. When you're broke, when you have no way to make a living, have no family connections, and no hope that you will ever be *somebody*- that's a dangerous kind of despair. At that point I had no idea I'd ever play music again much less make a career of it. It was part of the distant past. The world was against me.

The Paradox And The Orgy Master

Back in New York, I soon discovered health foods and macrobiotic eating. It was a "no brainer" for me as I had always valued everything natural and this made perfect sense. I read macrobiotic cook books. I

shopped only at health food stores, and ate at a restaurant on the lower
east side called "The Paradox." It was there I learned about buckwheat
groats, miso, udon noodles, aduki beans, hiziki seaweed, umboshi
plum, tahini, sesame oil and so on. Thiele's father, who paid us an
occasional visit, would sometimes accompany us there. One afternoon
we became aware of an ostentatious individual with a goatee, a rugged
face, and an aggressive attitude. He was flanked by two submissive
women (both with dark, waist-length hair and incredibly full figures) who followed him about and obeyed his every command. They
stood next to him as he went from table to table introducing himself.
His name was Stanley, and he was searching for men and women
interested in having orgies with him and his two lady friends. I can't
remember how he referred to them, but clearly they were like sexual
slaves in his mind. He resembled a Centaur, and I fully expected him
to pull out a harp or a flute and begin some sort of minstrel show. His
technique was intimidation. The more you shooed him away the more
persistent he became. He had a method of asking probing questions
until he was deconstructing you and eventually pinned you down as
"sexually uptight." Thiele's father, who was generally a passive type,
faded away like a wallflower, but I got drawn into the challenge.
Somehow, I managed to have an adventure with them. Not only was
it an awful experience which I utterly regretted, but I was able to discover that neither of his accomplices were at all happy. As the disguise
was stripped away, Stanley was revealed as a compulsive seducer who
manipulated and browbeat women into servicing his insatiable appe-
tites. With psychological weaponry that overwhelmed his victims, he
was the ultimate sexual predator- but there was no name for that sort
of thing in those days- so he got away with it. I was drawn into a few
other less-than-wonderful experiences at the time, but it didn't take
me long to realize that what I called "recreational sex" was pointless,
joyless, and even dangerous. In the name of being "cool and groovy"
we ended up degraded and demoralized. There was a little thing called
"the clap" which people seemed to be coming down with regularly
that made the whole idea yet more unappealing.

The Despair Years

"Behold, I am vile... "
Job 40:4

*F*or years and years my feeling of being pathetic cannot be properly described. I was worse than nobody. As I wandered about pushing a baby stroller, the gloom in my life was palpable. My parents were not interested, thus my child had no grandparents. No one ever contacted me. My family didn't exist. I was still the little match girl out in the snow looking in at the bright lights and the warm rooms where happy people celebrated. I was an untouchable. I don't know how I survived these times, only that if suicide was ever a thought, I nixed it instantly as I knew that quitting was not an option- don't know how I knew this, but I did. The closest I ever came to harming myself was after Thiele's father walked out to see his new girlfriend. I went to the bathroom mirror and pulled out large chunks of hair, as much as I could grasp. Then I banged my head against the wall. Afterwards it seemed stupid and pointless, and I knew it did no good. Something always drew me right back and straightened out my thinking. Despite times of deep suffering I have always valued life above all else. I knew instinctively that somewhere, somehow, it was still OK. Why couldn't I just try suicide or go mad like my mother? I contemplated it, but couldn't seem to get a handle on it. One of my classmates from Little Red had jumped out of a window during an argument with his parents. His father was a psychiatrist and his mother a glamorous woman with lots of jewelry. We thought they were the picture-perfect family. Their son was an artistic, talented child: witty, intelligent- the funniest kid in the class. Imagine his parents' horror and grief as they looked down to see their son's lifeless body on the sidewalk below. I wondered, was suicide cool? Was it for the bravest of the brave? Was I too weak and scared? Everybody else was falling apart and dying from overdoses, but I had only taken a drag or two on a joint- and hated it. Why couldn't I get it? What was wrong with me? So I thought about suicide, but it always ended up feeling crazy to me. I wanted to take drugs, but I was just too scared. I was square, that was obvious. I loved reality. That made me weird, as everyone else seemingly loved LSD. For me, nothing could be more terrifying than completely losing control. *"Relax!"* was one of the most frequently repeated criticisms from people around me. I was barely a child of the sixties. My father was forever calling me "a mutant" (whatever *that* meant). He thought it was an interesting thing to say, but I thought it was a slap in the face. It meant I was not a real member of the family. My genetic code was from *outer space*.

Gabriel

At nineteen, despite appropriate measures, I became pregnant. I later learned that statistically, the most popular medically accepted method of birth control was not a 100% guarantee, and in addition the doctor told me that I was "unusually fertile." But when I switched to the pill, it almost killed me. I blew up like a balloon and turned white as a

Photo: Bill Knight

sheet with dark circles under my eyes. I guess I was one of the people who would get the horrible side effects listed in the fine print. Pills- not something I should have been messing with anyway.

166

Believing this pregnancy to be an insurmountable problem, I traveled to Puerto Rico where one could somehow manage to have an abortion quietly despite laws against it. The experience turned out to be a horror show. Holed up in a fleabag motel on the beach with a confused and frightened two and a half year-old in tow, a nightmarish scenario played out where I was refused the operation due to a shortage of funds. I remember sitting in an office listening to a merciless nurse repeat "Bring the money" about a hundred times. In addition they wanted me to take antibiotics for two weeks as a precaution, but by then I was too far along anyway. Thiele was able to pass some of the time pondering several poor monkeys incarcerated in a cage behind the hotel, and we must have gone to the beach, although I hardly remember.

I called my friend Jack Baker collect from a phone booth and told him my desperate story. I remember asking for forty dollars (which seemed like a thousand) to help me get home. Jack sent the money promptly, bless his heart. To this day I can't relax when I am overseas as this low grade fear of not being able to get back and getting stuck on the other side of the ocean attends my every waking hour. In certain lovely places I fantasize about which house or location would suit me if it came to that- a global war, some kind of lock-down, the inability to board a plane. I comfort myself with this thought each time, and choose an elegant, antique home to hold in my imagination.

The Welfare Department: Hell On Earth

All the connections with my childhood had been severed- the good and the bad. I existed in a small apartment I couldn't afford, raising a child I didn't know how to raise. It was painfully obvious I needed help, but there was nowhere to turn. Someone must have told me I could get welfare. Depressed and pregnant, I hiked Thiele onto my hip and took the subway to one of the world's bleakest places, the Welfare Department. There we sat for hours with some of the most frighteningly lost people on earth. Many were clearly deranged, and many belonged in hospitals. Some were outright dangerous and should have been incarcerated for the safety of those around them. This was a totally distressing, demoralizing place. I waited my turn to fill out papers. They grilled me. They wanted me to move. Apparently a one-room apartment on Mercer Street with cockroaches was not low enough- and they refused to pay my rent. I was given a tiny allowance for food. I had to come back every week in person to get my check. That was one of the lowest times of my life, entering this hellish place every week and sitting for hours.

One day a man who clearly should have been under supervision began raving loudly, ranting and swinging his arms. A policeman who had been standing nearby exploded violently into motion. A briefcase flew through the air directly over my head and caught the man on the temple- there was a flurry of lightning-fast tumbling and smashing sounds followed by the most haunting cries of an injured human being. Thiele and I had barely missed getting hit and sucked into the fray. Hyperventilating, I grabbed my child and ran. I never went back. I have no idea how I survived after that but I knew I wasn't risking my life and sanity to go back to that place.

The Facts

The term "the facts" was actually an amusing comment an x-boyfriend often made when referring to feminine attributes. I use it here in the more familiar way: I had to face facts. I was going to be raising two children on my own. In those days 800 help lines, incentives, funding, and assistance of any kind was almost unheard of. Those were the "leave the baby at the Nunnery" days. I was totally broke and without prospects. There were no child care options whatsoever, and unless you could pay a babysitter you were stuck. Leaving a child alone would be a desperate measure bordering on madness. There was simply no way to go out to do anything. The father had turned out to be a volatile personality who I knew I had to escape from for reasons of safety. Fear consumed me day and night that I would never be able to find a man who would want me with two children if I couldn't even find a man to want me with one. At that point it seemed men were these creatures who impregnated women and then wandered off to the next encounter. Those were "the good old sex days," to quote a friend, and those of us who couldn't roll with it seemed like oddballs. I had a strong desire to be in a committed relationship. I didn't want to share my partner. I wanted to be married- I wanted it to be forever. I was really out of step.

I used to think that if I found the right man everything would be OK. I turned out to be wrong of course, as there is no perfect relationship, but I used to contemplate different men and wonder if they might be the right partner: devoted, honest, loving, tender, and understanding. I remember the feeling of tremendous hope in starting a new relationship. This was *the one*. But what a bubble that was- relationships are a revolving door and unfinished business with the last one is recycled directly to the new one, and sooner than later it's the "same old same old." Now I know that we can't be made whole by others. Wholeness comes from within, from a certainty of who we are and what we value. At a particular moment in my life I realized, while listening to someone screaming insults at me and blaming me for the ills of the world, that their unkind words meant nothing to me. I had finally developed duck feathers, and the words just rolled off. I felt clear inside. No one could destroy me if I did not let them. The unkind person left. I survived. Later I realized he had betrayed me, and to cover his shame he attacked. But it didn't matter. He had harmed himself far more than me, and ultimately I felt only compassion. We have to sleep with ourselves at night, and memories of wrong words and deeds bother me more than anything else.

So I bided my time for several lonely years until someone I thought would be a stable father came along. In retrospect we were both too arrogant and confused to do the job long term. I believe that if we had the right support and information we might have understood that each time we "tear it up and throw it in the trash" it's harder to piece it back together. I believe I probably could have made it work with my very first love had I fully understood the triviality of thinking that some great world awaits out there... and the confusion of believing we need something new to satisfy our curiosity. From my point of view we haven't gained a thing but regret and remorse. But this is not to say it is all for naught, or that things are not as they should be. I think they are, and there is a reason for everything.

The Hand-Crocheted Coat

Stefan, who moved overseas for a time and married a European wife, took pity on me one day. We went to an artsy, handmade clothing-from-around-the-world kind of store, and he allowed me to pick out a winter coat. He had noticed that his first girlfriend had become a lonely waif with a huge belly and no food, so he bought me this lovely hand-crocheted coat to wear during my pregnancy which I still own-can't throw it away, can't wear it, can't quite offer it to anyone. But I also cannot look at it without tremendous pain. So there it hangs, heavily stretched in the middle, forlorn, like a relic from an ancient civilization. As if in a museum, we imagine some person, long dead, wandering about in another life with this garment, and it now seems a part of history. But despite the sorrow there is also great gratitude for the kindness and generosity of a friend who was there to help me through.

After the pregnancy was well underway and the reality of my situation sank in, I found some kind of inner strength to move forward. I think I "made a plan," something I have always managed to do at the lowest times. But I don't really think this makes me "strong," as people have often pointed out (almost by way of accusation- as a way of saying I don't need help)- I'm simply reality based.

In the doctor's office I was counseled repeatedly to give the baby up for adoption. This was something I hadn't contemplated. I always thought I could somehow find a way, but it was deeply discouraging to hear about how much better off the baby would be in a "real" home. It was hard to deny that a stable environment was better than what I could offer, so once again, insecure and easily diminished, I became convinced that this was "the right thing to do."

The first part of the plan was to survive the pregnancy. At the airport in Puerto Rico I had discovered a book called *Have Your Baby, Keep Your Figure*. It became my Bible, as I was determined not to become a stretched-out old woman following two pregnancies. Every night before bed I maintained a strict regimen of exercises and began to feel the results almost immediately. I started to feel stronger- even attrac-tive- and I remember strutting about like a real babe with men whistling at me regularly. I always knew how to walk (so I've been told), and confidence mixed with sensuality seems to have an instant visual effect. One time a man followed me down the street making admiring remarks behind me- then he passed me, saw the belly, and apologized profusely as if his lewd comments would have been acceptable had I not been pregnant.

Then I made a simple nutritional plan based on no money whatsoever. Cottage cheese, orange juice, milk. This was my shopping list. Next, I contacted an adoption agency in the city thinking this was my only alternative. I thought it would be something I could face. Little did I know just how unbearable it would actually be, but at the time I was optimistic and needed something to cling to. I once carried around a quote scribbled on a wrinkled piece of paper which read "The path of love is like a bridge of hair across a chasm of fire" and there were many times when I felt the full meaning of these words. I thought the best way to love this baby was to surrender it to more qualified parents.

Life After Adoption

Empty, sad, gray. A nagging sense of loss and the disturbing realization that this was not an acceptable outcome. It took me six months of internal struggle to sign the papers. Birth had been the easy part, with many compliments from the doctor about how I was strong, young, and a proud producer of boys. It was surreal- birth, alone in a hospital, without a husband or friend to share in the experience. I knew that poverty awaited me along with the grief of returning home empty handed. I had to be strong for Thiele, but I cringed, as I knew the message to him was beyond painful- my brother is gone- but where? My mother is bereft- am I next? These were terrible, unimaginable realities. I had no answers, but checking out was not an alternative- moving forward was the only possible choice.

Little Gabriel, as I named him after the angel, had long, slender legs, was perfectly made, and utterly beautiful. I tried to change my mind when I saw him, but they said I had already signed the commitment papers (under tremendous pressure and duress), and they whisked him away from me immediately to go where babies go when this sort of thing happens.

Photo: David Gahr - © The Estate of David Gahr

In the coming weeks I couldn't finalize that last required signature and held on to the dream that I would meet a wonderful man who would say "Absolutely, bring the baby home, I'll be the daddy!" (remember that amazing song which came out a few years too late: "If your child needs a daddy I can help")? But that man never materialized. I spotted one I thought would be a safe choice, but he reacted negatively when I asked if I could bring home the baby. He was willing to take Thiele, but not a second child. I had no idea what else would ever work for me, and I went with this alternative. I remember making the decision one day. "Go and do this," I said to myself, "You'll be better off. You can move forward, and your child will be raised by a family in the suburbs with two cars." This was all they would tell me, and it was repeated to me mercilessly. I felt so inadequate words cannot express. I would never be that rich. So I made the call, boarded the bus, walked into the agency and signed the papers. My cheeks were bright red, and I was flushing and changing temperatures repeatedly. My heart was palpitating. I was panicked. This was one of the lowest points in my life, and it haunted me continually afterwards like a wound that would never heal. Years later I hired someone to find this child, which I did, but apologies will never change the facts. This wound is felt from both sides.

As I relate this it is unbearably painful. I can almost not write for fighting back sorrow. I don't really know how I survived. I couldn't handle anything like it now. I'd simply die. My heart would cease to beat. Lord knows I didn't even have my music then. It would be a long, slow climb.

Often, I pray that the damage I have done to others will be healed- that the effects of my stupidity will be eased in their lives. This is among the greatest of offenses despite whatever reasoning I can find to justify my actions at the time. In the Bible it says that the laws of God are written on the hearts of human beings, so that they are without ex- cuse. I doubt there is any sin ever committed without the deep internal knowledge that it is wrong. There is always a little voice screaming in the background that our choices are flawed- but we manage to sup- press it with some arrogant notion about being unaccountable. This is always wrong as we must later review our lives- without the help of any judgmental outsider. I always end up being my own worst critic.

Alone In The City With Thiele

Nineteen, no money, and raising a baby alone. There are few things more difficult and discouraging. You know you should have a little help- you know the baby's father should be at your side and not running around with a new girlfriend somewhere. You know your parents should be involved. You know a lot of things, but as you sit there trying to sort out how to survive, how to be good to your child, how to eat... there is no other answer than the one that has come to me again and again throughout my life: just keep going.

We managed to spend time at the park everyday, but as I sat on a solitary bench watching the kids play, it was hard to sit motionless for so long. It was lonely and boring for a teenager who longed to have a life. What is now so easy for me- sitting in the grass with my cats, spending quiet time- this was just not where I was at when I was nineteen.

We know it takes a village to raise a child- that is the natural order of things. Aunts, uncles, grandparents, extended family- these are the greatest resources. But I lacked them. What I had was a huge heartache. I was longing for a man who would care, and wondering where the next meal was going to come from.

Sing A Happy Tune

I sing constantly- fantasy-based, rambunctious, kooky little melodies. I am easily fascinated, delighted and surprised. I make up nicknames, secret languages, and words. Children like this about me and recognize a kindred spirit. When I held Thiele I was one thousand percent attentive. I used to get very close to his ear and make little noises: clickings, rollings, and melodies with rhythms. The only thing I can compare it to might be Bobby McFerron and his throat sounds: vocal percussion. Of course I hadn't heard of him at the time, but this shows that the human voice loves to experiment in this way. I have since discovered that there are certain languages which have these kinds of sounds, and that comes the closest to what I am describing.

Thiele loved it and would become quiet and attentive. He would keep his little body very still while listening to the rhythms I created. He later told me this was very inspiring to him.

Jack Baker

And there I was with my little boy and the four walls. I had no money for food. A couple times a week Jack would appear with a takeout dinner, and bless his heart, he would play with Thiele. And play they did! Jack was tall and lanky, and Thiele a small cherubic three-year-old. There would be the most wonderful ruckus of scuffling and laughter as

Jack wearing a leather vest I made for him at the Sandal Shop
Photo: Ellen Pehek.

Thiele pounced on Jack. I doubt I can convey the joy this brought us

both for a while, when my lonely world was interrupted, and Thiele's lack of a father was temporarily healed. "You'll not get me this time you little curtain climber, you crumb snatcher, you!" Jack played with Thiele for hours, wrestling and always losing, begging loudly for mercy while Thiele shrieked with laughter, twisting Jack's arm while Jack writhed in mock pain. It's amazing how much meaning these brief moments in life can have.

Jack was also a talented and inspired musician. He had devoted most of his focus to Chet Atkins and could play just about everything Atkins had ever recorded- but he also loved and understood Country Blues and provided nonstop appreciation and support for me to play the old music. Jack ran the Fretted Instruments School of Folk Music where he established a solid career as a well respected teacher. Over the years he has been plagued by tendon problems in his hands and endured numerous operations to regain the freedom of movement required to play his beloved music. It caused him incredible amounts of pain and discomfort- but Jack never let this or anything get him down.

We used to meet for breakfast practically every day at the Bagel, conveniently located across the street from the shop. Casey was the reliable, hard working chef who flipped omelets in the window, while Frances and Gloria took orders. Occasionally owner Phyllis would make an appearance. I always had a swiss cheese omelet "soft" with rye toast- Jack was a coffee hound. I think he liked pancakes. Jack and I are still close, though now it's more about an occasional phone call since we've all moved away. For years, when visiting the city, I'd stay at Jack's little apartment. He'd leave the keys somewhere so I'd have a place to put my feet up.

Howard Vogel

Howard was an incredibly kind man with a cheerful demeanor, an infectious laugh, and a heart of gold. A superb classical musician and teacher, he lived in the city but eventually relocated to Woodstock. Howard married an old school friend of mine named Jodie, also an accomplished musician. I used to run into them on occasion in New

York, later on Cape Cod, and finally, in upstate. Howard adored Thiele and never failed to focus on him. I recall Thiele, at three or four years old, donning Howard's T-shirt (which touched the floor), running about wildly, and acting silly with Howard. Howard would walk around on his knees to be the same height as Thiele and they would have no end of laughter and games.

As the years roll by and we lose touch with old friends, it's always a shock to get the news of someone's death. I had heard that Howard was ailing, but of course I never expected it to be fatal. It's so hard to believe bad news when you don't want to. Before he died Howard called me out of the blue to tell me of a vivid dream he had about Thiele (dear reader, I jump to the future: this was some years after Thiele's death). He thought I would want to know. Now I wrack my brains to remember what he told me. I know he had seen Thiele, and Thiele may have given him a message for me. But when you're grieving you're not always as clear, so I took in the feeling of his words but forgot the content. Howard died shortly after that. Thank you, Howard.

John Lennon On Jones Street

At some point I became aware of a man who looked a lot like John Lennon coming and going from a building on Jones Street. Eventually I realized it had to be him, and again marveled that Jones Street, only one block long, had been the lodging place of so many extraordinary people.

One day a friend pulled up a few doors away from the shop and managed to squeeze into a parking space. As I watched him opening the door, two figures lurched towards us, one struggling to support the other who was obviously drunk. My friend was wearing a pair of round frames in a retro style and had an angular, pleasant face. As he stepped out of the car, the inebriated man walked up to him. John Lennon looked him in the eye and said "Peter Fonda or what... fuck you!" and then staggered away down the street. My friend was thoroughly amused and thrilled to be thus addressed by such a star, and immediately began proclaiming to the world what had just happened.

The Man In The Rumpled Suit

"Would you care for some paid companionship?"came the voice. I turned to see a dumpy middle-aged man in a rumpled suit. In those days I used to walk around in revealing outfits- nothing by today's standards, mind you- no enhanced breasts in push-up bras sticking out of sleeveless tops or bare midriffs- our big thing was miniskirts and heels. At the time it felt like looking sexy was tapping directly into the life force. I knew I had good legs and got enthusiastic attention for showing them off. So here was this incredibly unattractive guy offering me money. I felt sorry for him immediately. Because I was anything but normal in my approach, I went in a completely different direction, one that knocked him totally off base and swung the balance of power. I looked at him, sized him up, and made a plan. I would befriend him, walk around with him, offer to buy him an ice cream cone, eventually discover his motives and ultimately enlighten him. He was shocked but accepted my offer. We walked and talked. I endeavored to find out more about him, once again taking him by surprise. We must have walked across the entire island of Manhattan and ended up on a park bench in the East Village. By this time I had discovered that he was married with four kids, and I urged him to go home to his wife. His head was spinning. This was not his idea of his perverse plan playing out. At that point he just wanted to get away from me- he probably thought I was an undercover cop.

It could have turned out much worse, but I was wise enough to know that all our conversations had to take place in a public arena. I never would have disappeared with him into any room- that could have led to my becoming a statistic, and I was too aware to let that happen.

Music In The Middle of the Night: "When You've Got A Friend"

During the toughest times, I developed certain tricks to get by. Of course I was not a candidate for medication. Overdose was the most common cause of death among our contemporaries in those days. What other way could a young person die in a city in the sixties? We didn't have drive-by shootings. Crack hadn't yet been invented. We didn't have cars, so death in a wreck was remote. There were maniacs, but we could spot them a mile away and avoid them. It was drugs. My escape was music. I slept with the radio on by my head and listened through the night. If a song was powerful and spoke to me I would wake instantly. In the twilight of sleep I heard a familiar sounding voice. It had the vulnerable, quaking tones of an insecure girl- like me, I thought. It was a beautiful song with a simple, touching refrain... Carole King was singing "When You Got A Friend." "I can do this," I reasoned. Carole's honest voice and beautiful song was the catalyst.

Bonnie At Max's Kansas City

Bonnie Raitt has been an icon to me since I discovered her moving, heartfelt singing and awesome playing in what must have been the early 1970s. Here was a woman who managed to get signed, record, and do well all without compromising her art. She opened the door for other blues artists, particularly females, bringing traditional sounds and unique artistic integrity to the stage. Even today, her voice, along with Joni Mitchell, is the most imitated female singing style in pop and country music.

One night, single, and toting Thiele on my hip, I managed to make my way into Max's Kansas City, a chic little venue somewhere downtown. I couldn't believe it. Bonnie was on stage with Freebo, who followed her every move with his intuitive playing. She laid down the coolest songs one right after the other. Her presence was fabulous. She was it, and I was nothing. I left there thinking there would never be a need for another female blues artist since Bonnie had covered that base like nobody's business. My pathetic attempt at music was never going to make it.

My Six-Stringed Friend

Somehow I picked up the guitar after what seemed like an eternity. I had assigned music to the past along with many other things. Perhaps I thought I was living in a new world now, the world of "adults" (whatever bland, boring life that was supposed to be). The guitar felt awkward in my hands. It used to be my best friend, but now it was bulky. I stumbled along trying to remember the notes I used to play. I thought it was like learning to walk again after a debilitating disease.

The Peace Church

My comeback concert was at the Peace Church on west Fourth Street right off Washington Square park. Nothing could have underscored the meaning of stage fright more vividly than that performance. I was completely terrified. Not only was I trying to sing in public for what felt like the first time, but I was playing again after a long absence. Nonetheless I ended up taking the stage. Somehow there were people there, though I didn't know who they were or how they knew about the concert. I closed my eyes and kept them tightly shut the entire time. I sang, played, and shook. When the show was over I opened my eyes. There I saw a long line of friends- even my dad had come- and they were smiling. They kept stepping up to hug me. I couldn't believe it. I thought they would hate me or just feel sorry for me.

Then, a miracle. John S. Wilson, who I never dreamed was in the house, wrote a fabulous review in *The New York Times*. Can't find it of course, but I know that somewhere, at the bottom of a vast pile of reviews and articles I have amassed over the years, is this wonderful review. It is this sort of thing- a completely unexpected ray of sunlight- that has sustained me through the years of difficulty and discouragement.

Heading North

In 1970 the city was becoming too dangerous. There had been numerous close calls with gun-toting, knife-wielding, freaked-out crazy people, and I finally said "This is not the place to raise a child." So we began driving. From Nova Scotia to southern Pennsylvania, I have no idea how many properties we visited. One day we wandered into a little real estate office situated on the Hudson River and saw a photo of a grand old house well beyond the humble budget. With a ceiling of forty thousand dollars, the houses we had seen did not speak to me- most looked like bunkers surrounded by cyclone fencing. Then I spotted it- a black and white photo of a center hall colonial of grand proportions. "I'd like to see this one," I announced. "That's a lot more than forty thousand," came the skeptical retort. No matter, I wanted to see it. I had a feeling.

This house, whose exceptional historic beauty spoke to me loud and clear, ended up being my beloved home for almost ten years. The process of buying it was a learning experience. After visiting the property I wandered about in a daze. I had to have it- despite an obvious lack of financial resources. A friend who was a successful businessman counseled us to offer a far lower price, one I thought could have seemed insulting- but I knew nothing about negotiating. So we took the savvy advice and offered less than half the asking price. They responded immediately with a deeply discounted number. I realized that this was for real, and countered again. It happened fast. They came down even more- and wham, sold!

The House In Ghent

Nobody could believe that a couple of kids from New York City were living in this mansion. It was a bold move, irrational by most standards- and way beyond the original price range. However it often happens that surprising leaps and accomplishments take place in unexpected ways.

The house had an extraordinary past. We learned that several children had survived an Indian attack by climbing down a rope into the very same well that stood outside the kitchen door. Built by one of the original Dutch settlers, the building had been occupied by some very colorful people for more than two hundred years. One of the early residents was a lady named Belle Flannigan who sold it for a dollar to pay off her debts. Another was a violent husband whose booming voice curdled the blood of those who overheard his rages from the bottom of the hill. Numerous babies belonging to the Hoogeboom family that had lived and died in the house were buried in a long, jagged line of gravestones in a cemetery just up the road. It was hard to believe this poor family kept losing all their children. Six months, two years, three days, and so on... I guess there must have been incredible hardship and disease- how did they cope, I wondered? It was clear this house had many souls who had marched through its halls- people who had lived, loved, suffered, and died there. Thiele was always uneasy in the house, as if it was haunted.

By now I had two children, and raising them occupied all my time. Once again it seemed that music would become a part of my past, but ultimately I began to feel that familiar sense of emptiness, as if something vital was missing. After my youngest son Jordan was three or four, I started to write songs and again dream of recording contracts. I spent endless hours at an old grand piano banging out rambling melodies while the kids tumbled about, played, fought, got into mischief, and needed my attention. This is when I came up with idea that the oldest needed to help take care of the youngest (a time-honored tradition), while Mommy was writing. It worked out rather well and Thiele became Jordan's best pal despite their five-year difference. But there was never much time to pursue a career... that would come later.

Jordan

Having been born after we moved to Ghent, Jordan was considered a native of upstate New York. He was a happy little guy with many toddler friends in the area. Thiele on the other hand continually pined about moving to "the middle of nowhere." He missed Manhattan and his former haunts. After it became apparent that he was having an unhappy experience in the local school, I knew I had to find something different. One day my eye fell on a little brochure which featured children sprawled on the floor with paints and crayons. I drove out to see what this alternative school was all about and enrolled both kids

immediately. The Mountain Road Children's School became the best thing to happen to them for a number of years. Thiele began to thrive and feel accepted in the small class of artistic students. Jordan loved school as well, and every day I drove seventeen and a half miles one way (just beyond the fifteen mile school bus limit), to take them to this special place. There were split shifts, and the younger classes let out early. I calculated this meant I was driving round trip three times- one hundred and five miles per day- but I didn't mind.

Jordan was academically inclined. I noticed he enjoyed his math workbook and actually advanced a year beyond grade level in his spare time. This got my attention as I had hated math, but I knew it was possible to be very intelligent and simply direct your mental energy elsewhere. Thiele's interests leaned towards music and art, while Jordan's (though he was also extremely artistic) focused at that time on chemistry and computers, which were just being introduced on the market as these clunky, heavy plastic things in big boxes. He raced around in overalls and had a pretty carefree existence until the day his father and I announced our separation- and then it was clear he was shattered.

Moving On

After a protracted divorce I had to leave the old house, unable to come up with the buy-out price. Crafty lawyers framed a deal that was just beyond my reach, and some outside money appeared which outbid me. But because the income from the Sandal Shop (during that time owned and operated by my sister and I) had purchased and almost entirely paid for the house, it made no sense that I would now have to be the one to vacate (as if my decision to buy it, along with the continued financial resources from the Shop, hadn't made it all possible). However those were the days when women and their annoying opinions meant very little to many lawyers and judges, and everyone kept saying (when I indicated my desire to continue living there with my two children), "You can't keep a man from his equity." What about a woman's equity? For some reason this didn't compute much in those days.

I have no idea why this house had so much power over me. Someone once said I was one of the former owners who had come back again- maybe Belle herself trying to grasp at it once more. But as with Belle it was torn away. The day I left I walked from room to room crying and kissing the walls. I stretched my arms open and hugged it- I loved that place so. Of course, I had to leave just so it could be sold on the open market, and someone bought my beautiful house right away. It was over.

But the house continued to haunt me. It called to me in dreams. It looked different each time- sometimes it was terribly rundown, other times beautifully appointed and elegant. Once or twice it was endlessly rambling and huge, more like a state building. I would wander about discovering new rooms and pondering "Where did this room come from? I never saw this before!" It seemed to mirror some inner growth I was experiencing, alive with new possibilities and unfolding options. Some nights I was the owner again and filled with joy to be moving back in. Then the house would be crumbling: the stucco covered with huge cracks, plaster peeling from the walls, and the building sinking into the foundation. I despaired of having the resources to do all the repairs. Whether overwhelmed or overjoyed, I would wake with a terrible feeling of loss. This went on for years and years. The house was alive- it ran in my veins. Songs began to materialize... "All My Life" and "Silver Wings" are the two most prominent tributes that come to mind. I decided that someday, some way, I would buy it back again. I knew I'd have to be a millionaire to make it happen.

Today there is peace and forgiveness with my ex. As young people we both could have used much better training in life skills, but our generation was totally on our own- one of the first to be cut so completely loose- and not always to great effect. A couple years ago the house in Ghent appeared on the market again, and in a truly great gesture of reconciliation, my ex tried to help me buy it back again. I considered it, he urged me to, but it would have been just out of reach, having been allowed to deteriorate by the interim owners (recalling my recurring dreams where the house appeared to be crumbling and in need of vast amounts of repair). I didn't buy it, and now the Ghent house is owned by people who have put great effort into restoration, and once again it looks lived in and well loved.

The Little Green House

After losing the Ghent house I searched extensively for a suitable replacement. Eventually I found another Colonial situated in a small hamlet. Compared to the Ghent house, the new place seemed tiny. Ghent had twenty two acres, a good chunk of land for upstate. This house was on half an acre. There it stood on a corner, an empty shell. But I loved the center hall design, the dentil molding, and the rippled glass windows. When I walked in, the old wood floors were warm and beautiful in the sun. The light shone appealingly through the windows. I decided to buy it.

In the beginning it was tough. There was no kitchen, no stove, refrigerator or cabinetry. I had two children to raise, no child support, no money, and no place to cook or keep perishables. A kind guitar student brought me an old apartment-sized stove. Someone else brought over a used refrigerator. I built shelves out of bricks and old boards I found in the barn. There were tools, wagon hitches and bridles, antique doors, and magazines from the 1930s. I found an advertisement claiming that a certain brand of cigarettes was actually "recommended by doctors" to be "therapeutically soothing." It stated that doctors "prescribed" this brand of cigarettes to help with throat problems! There was a fabulous old privy in the barn with ancient clippings pasted on the walls, an old check to a local bank nailed on a board, and sepia-colored photos with curled edges... you name it, it was in there.

After one despair-filled night I awoke and came downstairs. Through tear-stained eyes I looked around at this empty shell. I had lost everything. The beautiful house of my dreams was gone, and here I was with the booby prize. I clenched my fists in sorrow. Then something came over me- a spark of hope. "Wait," I thought. "I could fix this place up." I don't know where the motivation came from, but it began with some stenciling- poor person's wall paper, I remember thinking. The Ghent house had plaster walls covered in every elegant style of period paper and ornate trim- this place had bare sheet rock. Nonetheless I started in the dining room and the effect was lovely.

Soon I would begin to focus more attention on music. As my career gradually became established and touring increased, I started to fill the house with every beautiful thing. I painted the entire outside myself, teetering on a ladder. I built stone walls and had stockade fences erected, and finally surrounded the property with perennial gardens. I sat in the dirt and installed a walkway by hand, brick by brick. It was great fun, like making mud pies. Now the house draws many admiring comments. Funny how I didn't realize what an elegant place it was at first. Through devotion and TLC it has come back to life again in a major way.

Nathalie

Around this time some friends and I decided to start a women's group. The goal was to share our stories, create an environment where we could be completely honest, and offer each other support. But the group did not flourish as it soon became apparent that not everyone was interested in this level of communication- which ultimately defeated the whole purpose. But no matter, I met Nathalie. Dressed in a most unusual outfit- a handmade dress which might have been crafted in South America along with a pair of very interesting tall boots- she was clearly an outstanding, artistic kind of person. Blond, with a peaches-and-cream complexion, she was what most people would call beautiful, even stunning. I knew the moment I started talking to her that we would be friends. We were both outspoken, had a sarcastic sense of humor, and didn't suffer fools. We were able to confide in each other instantly, and I learned that she had just met an amazing man, but was convinced he was a "womanizer."

She became my best friend, and we went about as two women do when they are confidantes- taking walks, going here and there together, and laughing about men. At some point she married the womanizer, and things were not to be simple for her after that. We both had man troubles and once when she was pregnant she knocked on my door needing to camp out overnight. I didn't ask the details- I knew there had been a fight and that she wanted to make herself scarce. So I put her up on a couch with a blanket, her specific request. Once she started having kids we drifted apart. There was no time for leisure now that we both had families. However, after years of living separate but in some ways parallel lives, we came back together again for renewed friendship at the end of her life. More on that later.

David Bromberg & The Philly Festival

My life was becoming a whirlwind of showing up and playing- invited or uninvited- wherever and whenever- pay or no pay. Renowned guitar wizard David Bromberg (one of the "anointed few" who studied in person with Reverend Gary Davis), was well-established by this time. David always managed to be where I wanted to be, and at various times I would throw myself at his mercy. Hearing that he was at a particular venue, I'd go down and make a pest of myself. Finding my way into the back room, I'd ask to sit in or just to be allowed onto the stage. I could sing harmonies... I could make myself useful. I remember the feeling of exploding from within watching my friends perform. I had an irrepressible desire to get up there, and unless they invited me, I would very likely run up screaming. David took pity on me whenever possible and arranged various opening spots- but I knew there were times I was pushing him to the limit of endurance. On one such occasion he gave me the phone number for the agent who booked the Philadelphia Folk Festival (my idea of the ultimate, prestigious gig) but they turned me down. I was shattered. In a fit of defiance I decided (as I have on numerous occasions) that I would single hand-edly make this thing happen. I drove the five hours to Philadelphia and found David backstage. I hurled myself at his feet. He agreed (despite the fact that the festival said no) and put me on the main stage while the crew was tearing down for the next act. I played "Mississippi Blues" by Willie Brown, and when I had finished, a roar of approval went up from the crowd. David signaled me to do another, and I don't recall which song I chose. A few days later he called to say I had got-ten a fabulous review in the *Village Voice* which basically said I was the highlight of the festival. The headline read "Foot Stomping Be-tween Yawns." The reviewer said something like (and I paraphrase): But it came between acts as the stage crew was setting up that a young woman blues singer came up and played two songs... it went on to say that it was moments of this kind that made the festival memorable. It seemed surreal, but it was an example of what hard work and determi-nation could accomplish. It was a big payoff for getting crazy and not giving up.

Bad Advice From The Experts

Some of the people I trusted most were giving me discouraging advice. This is one of the names I won't mention as there is no need. This person, who had credibility in the business, told me in no un-certain terms that I would never make it doing blues. He granted that I did it well, but said it was a "curiosity" that could never be taken seriously. It was an art form whose time had passed, he explained, and said it wasn't "commercial." But I have survived to prove him wrong. And there were many others in the business, mostly record company people, who pounded this same dreary drum. All I ever heard was how I'd have to give up acoustic blues, go electric, and start writing songs-something I had never tried. This was going to be like swimming the ocean. I had no idea where to start and felt totally overwhelmed. It was sad to think that blues was viewed as so unimportant by the music business.

Songwriting: A Homework Assignment

$\mathcal{P}$rior to this point I had never even considered writing a song. However, given that I was seeking a recording contract, I had to deal with the industry's apathy towards blues and their belief in the apparent urgent need to become a songwriter. I was led to understand that there wasn't going to be much motivation for a label to sign me unless I started writing. I wondered why no one in the biz saw the inherent beauty in early blues the way I did? I would have purchased an all-blues release of an artist like, say, Jo Ann Kelly- so I couldn't comprehend the lack of enthusiasm- but I did understand the mandate to write.

Resentfully, I decided to try. As a person who had always hated homework, my first efforts felt far too similar to this dreary task to be enjoyable. In addition I was determined to be one hundred percent original. I had noticed that the great majority of songs used the same chord changes incessantly, and as a result, in my mind, originality was sorely lacking. So I determined to put chords together in a completely unique way that would not mirror any other song in existence... an insurmountable task. The result was random and strange sounding combinations- not very listener friendly.

Eventually I found a kind of formulaic method based on pop music, and my first efforts are now totally embarrassing, even ridiculous sounding to me. However, I suspect this comes with the territory- and if you've got tenacity, your talent eventually finds a path. The sound of a novice songwriter is often distinguished by self-absorbed subject material such as the "You did me wrong, poor me, I'm so heart broken, and you're so at fault" themes. In order to work, it must step outside the box descriptively, such as "Nobody answers when I call your name." The song is about heartbreak, but it's set in a completely evocative narrative about coming home from work and walking into an empty house. We can hear this man calling his wife's name and having it echo through the eerily vacant rooms.

Songs usually tell a story, and the more originality combined with familiarity the better. "He stopped loving her today... they placed a wreath upon his stone..." is another example of a totally unique way of telling the same tale- heartbreak and sorrow- but placed in a powerfully different package.

Ultimately, there really is no formula that I know of other than honesty. I never did think of myself as a songwriter anyway, but despite any shortcomings, I think I've managed to hit the nail on the head a few times. I believe that a good song needs words that can stand alone without the music- as poetry. If you separate the words and they sound stupid or one dimensional, this tells you to make them better. Music alone can't hold up weak words... well, OK, on pop radio sometimes it can- but so what? I want to reach a little higher.

After pounding away I amassed a collection of odd and rambling songs which I collected on reel-to-reel tape and later offered to a name producer who made off with them. There were big promises, followed by months of delay, and ultimately, he lost my only copy of the tape. At that point I was getting nowhere.

David Gahr

Strangely enough it was photographer David Gahr who got me my first record deal. He was tops in his field with published hardcover books of his work. His clients were the stars, folk and rock. He photographed just about everyone- Bob Dylan, Joan Baez, Bruce Springstein, Billy Joel, Carly Simon and countless others. David walked right up to me at the Folklore Center saying he wanted to take my picture. I was fifteen at the time and wearing a revealing knit dress which I later realized was coming open across the front- and David spotted it. He posed me in the doorway and gave me copies of his beautiful black and white 8 x 10 prints. He had a signature enthusiasm for which he was well known, shouting compliments in his boisterous, irreverent, humorous style. Over the years David photographed me with Thiele, did record covers for me, took my picture at festivals... anywhere at all that we happened to cross paths. We did countless sessions at his Park Slope studio. I have no idea how many photos he actually took of me. His incredible book "The Face of Folk Music" which includes a picture of me as a teenager holding Thiele, is on my coffee table as I write this, but you might not know it because there was a misprint of my name- I am listed as "Roy"- and it used Thiele's father's name, which was Biehusen. Thus it says "Roy Biehusen and Thiele" in the index. Who on earth is that? The same book also features a beautiful photo of Maria Muldaur with her infant daughter, Jenny. This goes back to the '60s.

David may have been outwardly tough, but he had a heart of gold, and he never failed to be concerned about me. Once (when I was totally broke and pregnant with Gabriel) he photographed me for a women's magazine just so I could make some money. The pay was seventy five dollars, which was more than one month's rent at the time. David knew all the music biz people from artists to managers, record company moguls to booking agents. One day he announced that he had spoken about me to someone at RCA, and recommended that I contact them. I got signed immediately and went to Toronto to make an album with a band.

Photo: Carla Gahr

RCA Records

My first major label experience brought with it all the expectations of greatly heightened career visibility and the potential for stardom. The stakes were much higher, the budgets in those days were huge, and there were attitudes to match. I choose not to dwell excessively on this first adventure except to say that all the hallmarks of most major label deals were present: arrangers, producers, string sections, bands, expensive studios, hotel rooms, travel, dinner with company executives- plus complete and utter lack of artistic control. All the decisions, financial to musical, were made by others. This caused me no end of distress from day one. How can an artist who has grown up with some of the most deeply personal music on earth- folk, country, and blues- be expected to hand over the reigns entirely to others? So it was a painful experience which went from the rosy glow of joy and anticipation to a despairing sense of disillusionment very quickly. There was the usual insane breakdown of communication in the studio leading to alienation, and soon after, exhausted, I returned home.

Trashy Opportunities

When I was on the major label circuit I learned up close and personal that being asked to do favors to get ahead was for real. The first awkward situation came when I was dropped at a radio station. The DJ had been playing my record and the label had taken me there to thank him in person. Some joints were included with the drop-off and I could see that I was expected to hang with a man I had never met, smoke grass, and no doubt act provocative. I just couldn't handle it. I was a loser, I thought- I didn't know how to be cool at all. I never even took a toke. The DJ ended up puffing and choking all by himself.

One night at a biz convention there were two knocks on the door. The first visitor came in and made his intentions clear, and the second one arrived to find the first one already there. The whole thing didn't work for me. I wasn't into doing "favors" for anyone.

The next thing I remember was being taken to the distribution department. A heavyset man with a few hairs combed sideways across his bald head was seated in an office chair under fluorescent lights. I was instructed to "Go sit on that man's lap and run your fingers through his hair." I froze. I looked at the man. "Go!" I said to myself, but my body didn't move. I thought about the other female singers of the day. Did they have to do this too? Was I so uptight that I just couldn't get with the groovy program? Was there something wrong with me? Would I ever get ahead? Is this what was required? I ran various female singers through my mind trying to envision them sitting on this man's lap and wriggling around. Finally it hit me like a ton of bricks. I was too square. I couldn't do this at all. It was not for me. I'd rather fail, or get nowhere than try to "dig" something I didn't dig. That was the end of that.

Blue Goose Records

After my discouraging experience with RCA, Nick Perls scooped me up for a recording called *I'm In Love* which was half acoustic Country Blues and the other half a drastically under produced R&B style- one side for each. Nick was also a big fan of soul music and was totally open to the idea of me recording it even though RCA had been opposed, saying people would expect me to do rock'n'roll, not R&B, and that they wouldn't be able to market me as "a white person singing black music." They said white radio wouldn't play me because I sounded black, and black stations wouldn't play me because I was white. Like it or not, this is what they told me. But I was there before Vicki Sue Robinson- before time, before trend. I won't whine and say this has been the story of my life: being there so far in advance that no one was ready... but there is truth to this. I doubt I opened any doors, but I can tell you many doors were shut to me. How times have changed in the business since then!

As humble as it was, my little release (which cost a whopping $1,900 to make at a day and time when people routinely spent half a million) got a terrific review from the venerable Peter Guralnick, who compared the vocals favorably to Curtis Mayfield, someone I deeply admired. Nothing could have been a bigger surprise.

From RCA to Chrysalis

After Blue Goose Records I continued to search for another major label. I fully believed there would be a better experience out there and had no thought of slowing down. Eventually I caught the eye of someone at Chrysalis Records and Terry Ellis, one of the two owners, flew in from LA to see me perform. He arrived at a tiny Massachusetts airport in an executive jet, and as I stood on the tarmac waiting for him to step out, my heart fluttered in anticipation. In those days I had zero sense of how to dress, having been raised in hippie clothing, and I tended to think I was supposed to wear a skirt or a dress for the occasion. In retrospect this looked totally out of character, but that was the way I approached it nonetheless. Terry was a thoughtful, good looking man with a mellow demeanor. We climbed into the required limo to drive to the middle of nowhere for my concert. I have always been hopeless at small talk.

Everything that could go wrong went wrong that night. The sound system shut down, the mic ceased to work, and I was standing there with a band pounding away behind me with no vocal in the house. It could have been a disaster to end all disasters, but suddenly something clicked inside me and I thought "Forget the record deal. Forget who's in the house. Forget hopes and dreams, and just do a good show. Roll with it!" That freed me up to get creative, and somehow I must have become entertaining, perhaps even funny. I made the situation work, but I don't remember how. It was a miniature triumph on some level, and all I know is that the sound came back on mid-song, and at the conclusion of the evening Terry jumped up and applauded, leading the house in a standing ovation. I got signed, and went to LA to record.

There were the usual hotels, producers, bands, big budgets, arrangers and lack of artistic control. There were billboards everywhere with the plastic-looking faces of stars that left me feeling like a nobody. There were "Big Bad Agent Men" (as per the song on one of my later albums) everywhere. And there was the worst air I had ever breathed, New York included. I developed a chronic headache and felt totally poisoned the whole time I was there.

Women And The "B" Word

If you were female, and you tried to get your hands into the mix as I did, you were swiftly defamed across the industry as a "bitch." This was such a big problem that I heard other female singers, some famous, referred to in this way by some of the band members who worked with them. On one such occasion I stood up for this other artist, who was hugely famous, and I asked the person making the accusation what proof he had? Was this just some male bias, I asked him? Is it that she didn't want to get pushed around in the studio? He went silent. I explained that I believed this was the plight of strong women in the business, to get tarred with this brush, but he didn't seem to care about what I was saying. Women were Diva's and "bitches" to him. In the meantime men were ruling the sessions, the studios, and the companies, and no one complained much when other men trashed hotel rooms, threw tantrums, and made irrational demands. People went running around gathering up all the "pink elephants" (as a European booking agent once called them) that the band desired. Didn't anyone notice the double standard?

Little Feat: Sam Clayton and Billy Payne

On the plus side, someone came up with the idea that I should record with Little Feat. First we went to a premier club in LA and watched Lowell George playing his screamin' slide and performing with his monstrously funky band. I was blown away. George would be somewhere else at the time of the session but most of the other guys were available.

In the studio they were like brothers- mellow, welcoming, and charming. Again I found the companionship of great musicians totally rewarding. Never an attitude, always a helping hand. It was the business side of things which seemed to be the problem, and I took courage remembering my father's words regarding Bob Dylan's integrity and his general rejection of the business state of mind in favor of his art. Musicians wordlessly understand each other's dreams- we all know what it means to struggle, bounce back from personal rejection and attacks, and keep on keeping on. We understand the love of music and how it sometimes makes us different.

Billy Payne was there along with Freddie Tackett and Sam Clayton. I clicked with Sam immediately, and we ended up hanging out after the sessions were over. He took me to his house in the hills where I had my first breath of fresh air since arriving in LA, and it revived my spirits greatly. There were other friends from back East who also took pity on me. I was all too happy to escape the stale air of the hotel and go shopping at the health food store, eat a bit of home-cooked food, and look at a few trees. Someone took me to a party somewhere to the north of LA where Joni Mitchel, someone I admired greatly, was walking around from room to room acting completely shy, much as I was. It seemed that songwriters, musicians and artists were cut from a different cloth, and were, like Robert Johnson, shy by nature. My songs are so personal that anyone who listens to my music knows everything about me. So in this sense we are somewhat naked in the world- and it's no wonder some are self-conscious.

Sigma Sound

The second Chrysalis album was done in Philly. This made sense to me. We'd use a great soul producer, Bobby Eli, who had done Major Harris singing the unbelievably sexy, soulful hit tune "Love Won't Let Me Wait." Walking through the halls of Sigma sound was like touching musical history, not unlike performing at The Apollo Theater in New York as I did years later. It's probably impossible to comprehend how much earth shaking R&B came out of that building. Suffice it to say it was an honor to work there. But the majors were still exerting overwhelming influence, and the style (which the execs decided had to be disco in order to be in step with the day) was chosen for me, along with material, musicians, arrangements- everything. Once again I found myself trying to fit into someone else's plan, something I've never done very well.

I have taken more heat for this record. How could I have made a disco album? But "disco" is only a word, and in retrospect that album was almost identical to what is on the radio today. The term "disco" was replaced by other names. What I hear, on brief attempts to listen to pop radio, is the same exact stuff we were doing in the seventies. Only now it's just plain automated. At least we sang it. Today there are sampled vocals played on keyboards- not every artist of course, but enough to have the host on Entertainment Tonight explain this as a normal procedure in the studio along with "pitch control," programs which grab your voice and move each note to the nearest in-pitch frequency, and keyboards which create ornate flourishes in your vocals that you yourself couldn't sing. That was a totally new invention in those days. We don't use those devices ever. If I can't sing it live, you won't hear it on my records.

A Million Ways To Pass

There were always a million crazy explanations for kicking a musician in the pants and trashing their dreams. You name it, I've heard it. There are more ways to "pass" in the music industry than almost any other rejecting business on earth, and I think there are more twisted, frustrated, sadists writhing around in leather mogul chairs at record companies than anywhere else (but that's just my educated opinion). There was the "I forgot your tapes on the West Coast" excuse used by the hotsy-totsy producer, and the ridiculous "We've already got a 'chick' singer on the label." No one even dreamed that someday that would be considered "sexism." I heard every withering put-down imaginable and every lame excuse, always delivered with a contemptuous edge or dripping with cruelty. Who cares if I spent half a year assembling every tune I ever wrote on reel-to-reel and lovingly hand delivered it to their gleaming office, just to hear, eons later after a series of avoided calls, that they lost the tape- or they were too busy- as if they hadn't been leading me on with all kinds of carrots and assurances in the first place- as if this didn't mean everything on earth to me. Artie once told me that he and Robbie Dupree used to say "it's not the music, and it's not personal." That about covers it. We knew it was some other perverse reason having nothing to do with talent. We hardly wanted to imagine what it was. So we understood that whatever gimmicks these strange beings in charge of signing people at labels were seeking (whether extremely scanty outfits, physical attributes, outlandish behavior, or some other attention-getting trick they somehow deemed salable)- whatever it was- we recognized that we just didn't want to go there. We were about music, not ripping our clothes off in videos. Sorry guys, we're just old fashioned. Yep, we're square. We're songwriters, singers and players who think music is about *music*, not about slithering dancers flexing their gluteus maximus muscles for the camera. Maybe I'm weird, but I haven't yet seen anything I can stand to watch in that regard. It just looks like the cheapest porno to me. Give me an old record without a video any day and let me hear them singing in sweet harmony. That's what rocks my world.

It was horrifying to learn that another artist on the same label had committed suicide after being dropped. Wordlessly, we understood the man's pain. But for the grace of God, it could have been one of us struggling musicians- the huddling survivors. No one wanted to admit just how much was at stake, and how deep it cut when our art was rejected.

A fellow singer once described their agent to me in vivid terms. After almost dying of laughter I wrote and recorded a song called "Big Bad Agent Man." Inspired by my friend's ranting description, it pretty much says it all. Ok, there are some nice, quality folks out there in the business. Ken Irwin at Rounder Records is one of them. Holger Petersen at Stony Plain is another. Good people who love the music and have spent their lives trying to make it possible for talented artists to record.

I don't know if there's a crueler industry than music. Maybe modeling, or perhaps acting. But of course the world has changed and people are spared the pain of rejection as they simply make their own recordings and post them on the internet, perhaps using shock value to grab what can now become worldwide attention overnight. We didn't have any of those methods. But who really cares now, I suppose. Soon, few will remember how we slaved away for years to get signed and established. Oh, but this is bitter you say. If not bitter, at least aggravated.

The Marketing Dilemma

Two albums later we were still faced with the white/black marketing dilemma. If only people had been more open-minded this would not have held me back, but in retrospect it led to starting a career with Rounder Records which allowed me to return to my roots, and this was where my destiny lay.

The phone call reached me one evening at home. I was in the middle of dinner and totally unprepared. One of the upstarts at the label was calling to drop the bomb- an annoying young man who felt himself altogether cool to be hanging with "the big boys," the smart alecks who went to venues on the company expense account and scouted for talent. They must have enlisted him to make the call, and he was feeling important. "We're letting you go..." he was saying. "You're a disco artist, and we're looking for R&B." This is the same man who prepped me for the disco album by saying "We need you to make a disco record. You're an R&B artist and that just isn't selling right now." This was a surreal moment. "Oh, that's just great," I said. "First, I get forced to make a disco album because according to you R&B is out of style... then you call to say I'm being dropped because I'm a disco artist?" The last thing I said to him was: "Thanks a lot. You guys really *raped* me."

Courage For Discouragement

Launching a career takes persistence. Sometimes you have to take what you can get, crumbs, breaks, setbacks- it all works together. Courage is a huge element. Even after the major label experiences I had not yet become a touring artist. Going back to being a solo artist again was going to point me in the right direction.

One of the first solid gigs I had was at a little venue in Pittsfield, Massachusetts called The Brewery. It was run by Michael and Sue Pierce, two of the nicest people I had ever met. Pittsfield is a small "city in the country" which has been experiencing a gradual return from a depressed economy that must have rolled in some time after the 1930s. A few businesses were popping up again on Main Street, and this little cafe was among the first signs of urban renewal. I would drive out there on weekends, rain or snow, and the cheery little place was usually packed. I'd sit there in my spiked heels and sparkly bracelets

Photo Carla Gahr

and play old Country Blues songs I had learned when I was sixteen. People went for it in a big way, and Sue and Michael brought me an endless supply of mocha drinks and hot cider, whatever I needed.

I met some extraordinary people there, poets and intellectuals. In particular I remember a sweet man who would now be called "mentally challenged." In his simple and direct way he was one of my most devoted fans, and once, after endless encores where the place had gone ballistic, he shouted out "No, you rest!" It struck me that he was more grounded and intelligent than anyone realized- that his handicap- whatever it may have been that caused his speech to be choppy and slurred- was only superficial, and that he had the same high intelligence as the average person- we just short-changed him and people like him on a regular basis.

At this time I was trying to push through my overwhelming shyness, and there would be a few crutches I would lean on along the way. Somehow, in a fit of bad judgment, I decided that dirty jokes would be just the ticket. I would sit there telling the worst ones I had ever heard. This was usually just going to be fun for a rowdy audience buzzed on good beer. But I took it to the max, which is where I take most things, and it went beyond the realm of fun to the arena of bad taste. But I didn't know that some day down the road I would look back in embarrassment. It seemed it had its place at the time- it was an icebreaker and a confidence builder. It made me feel bold. I'm just glad that phase didn't last forever. Now, when I hear people swearing openly, it sort of burns my ears. It's not that I'm a prude- far from it- it's just that it starts to sound like a brainless excuse for lack of communication. And it's also too aggressive, and that's something I don't want to be. But I remember, when I hear people who try to provoke with foul language, that I once did the same without a thought. So I don't judge others, I just know it's not for me. Tried it... got burnt out.

Rounder Records

After the disillusionment with the major labels and their iron fisted dominance, I approached Rounder Records. They not only loved what I was doing, they gave me support and encouragement to be artistically honest. When asked if I should give Rounder a "radio friendly record," Ken Irwin responded "Don't worry about that, we don't do singles anyway. Just give us a record you think is beautiful." I couldn't believe my ears- this was too good to be true. A number of albums later, Marian Leighton, one of the three owners, said to me, "Don't change, the charts are coming to you." Man, what a message. The words "Thank you Rounder" come to mind. They allowed me, with fourteen records on their label, to completely establish myself on my own terms.

For my very first Rounder recording my old friend John Sebastian and I went into Bearsville Studios in Woodstock where the greatest of the greats had recorded, and in the cavernous rooms built for live bands, we recorded the humblest record called *High Heeled Blues*- a nice little title suggested by John. In those days my image was faded jeans, silky blouses with jangly jewelry, and the highest of spiky heels. I have run the gamut from long dresses, business suits to ball gowns, but have long since returned to my roots: jeans, bling and heels.

I can hardly tell you what a good person John is, and how much support and time he gives to the people around him. For all his hit records with The Lovin' Spoonful, John has never had an attitude. He's a rock star, but is also one of the humblest people I know. So John gave his production as a gift to help my career. *Rolling Stone* returned the favor by saying "Some of the most singular and affecting Country Blues anyone, male or female, black or white, old or young, has cut in recent years." This record launched my life as a touring artist.

Filled with the desire to make acoustic blues "commercial," I have stripped down my productions to the bare bones and presented the starkest music, sometimes so stark as to make people squirm. At first I did this due to total lack of budget money, but now I do it to make a point. The guitar is a multifaceted instrument, and if played the way the old masters did it, there is no limit to its versatility.

Whiskey With Dave Van Ronk

Dave Van Ronk and I did shows together from time to time, and one night in Connecticut I told the story of a new song I had written called "Since You Been Gone (Some Things Have Changed)". It was an unbelievably winding tale of betrayal and payback which had the house in stitches, and afterwards Dave complained that he didn't want me opening for him anymore. With his face screwed into one of his amazingly evocative expressions, and his voice dripping with sarcastic emphasis, he said "I don't want to have to work *that* hard!" and then he let out an exasperated breath. This was a high compliment, of course. Even though Dave could hold his own after Godzilla, I know the feeling of having to follow an act that was somehow received extremely well that particular evening, and how it can interfere with your energy. It all depends on a million factors and is different every night.

With Bob Brozeman, Dave Van Ronk, Artie Traum, George Gritzbach, Roy Bookbinder. Photo: David Gahr - © The Estate of David Gahr

One day I decided to stop in on Dave at his Waverly Place apartment. Surrounded by the chic intellectual and artistic clutter of a Greenwich Village musician, Dave announced that I was acting far too sober and said I needed a little whiskey to warm me up and slow me down. Knowing that I was indeed an intense, high-strung personality, I humbly agreed. Dave handed me a glass of amber liquid and we sat on the couch getting medicated. I think he put his head on my shoulder, and I don't remember much after that. We probably just sat there and forgot what we were talking about. Maybe we fell asleep. Maybe I left feeling a little worried about my friend Dave. I probably barely sipped my drink, not trusting it much more than I had ever trusted pills.

They say that after an alcoholic stops drinking, sometimes the beleaguered partner picks up the bottle- an odd contradiction. The person who suffered so greatly at the hands of an angry drunk waits until after the drink is cast away and healing begins. Then it's as if they are so shocked by the experience they somehow feel they should just check out this booze thing- just to see what the fuss is all about- now that the pressure is off. How strange we are as beings. Only God could love such unaccountable, confused behavior. I had a brief stint with alcohol, but it didn't last long, as my usual reality based personality overruled the possibility of self-destruction.

Vodka And Cleavage- Opening for Taj

I first heard Taj Mahal in the late '60s when I was staying at Happy and Jane Traum's house in Woodstock. I discovered an album called *The Natch'l Blues* and played it until it couldn't be played anymore. "She took the Katie, and left me a mule to ride." What a fabulous album! Here was this gritty, dynamic man singing unadorned, old style blues. This was good. It was also paving the way and opening doors for other blues artists. The more people found out about blues from artists like Taj, the less they would stare at me as if I was from outer space when I said "I play blues" in response to the incessant "What do you do?" question.

After the early years of banging around on the tour circuit playing for suppers, pass the hat, and two people audiences, I started to get better gigs. I was opening for Taj Mahal at a beautiful theater in Brooklyn. Taj radiated power and charisma- I felt small and utterly insignificant in his presence. Imagine my surprise when he sat down at the table with me in the back room, spotted the bottle of booze I was working on, and said "Vodka and cleavage... my, my, my!" He raised his eyebrows in a friendly kind of concern, I think.

I have now opened for Taj many times- and he has since dubbed me "Rorita." We recorded together on one of my early Rounder releases, and although I am still shy with his powerful, magnetic self, I can say he is a friend. Taj is a man who has put in a lifetime of hard work and has earned well-deserved recognition as a great American blues and soul artist. At one point he gave me a quote for my press kit which read "I love it. I love it. She's simply the best there is!"

From Grapes To Grains

Those were still the stage fright days and at some point I had discovered (along with a number of others on the planet) that alcohol was the perfect drug for confidence. I went from a sip or two of wine to a whole bottle fairly quickly, and a taste of hard liquor turned into a "had to have it" state of mind that created a real problem for me one night at a theater in Arlington, Massachusetts where the promoter came in and read the riot act about there being no liquor allowed because it was a "dry" town. I had to sneak outside with another blues artist and gulp whiskey in the car. He was the first person who called it "medication." I felt like a real criminal. I knew everyone in the place could smell it on my breath.

One night I had a crisis. Here I was- the little natural foods, macrobiotic, organic vegetarian food freak from the time I was a teenager- getting wasted on alcohol. That night my head was spinning so badly I couldn't sleep, so I got up and took a hot bath in the cheap hotel room. I sat there assessing my life. Did I want to feel this way? Did this fit into my healthy life style? The answer was a resounding "NO," so I decided to do something about it. Luckily, I was not an addict at that point. I don't think I have an addictive personality because logic and reason always win out.

I managed to find an interesting "Doctor to the stars" type while I was on the road. Some of the biggest names in the industry were his patients. I can't recall who recommended him or how I ended up there, but as I sat in his office he showed me a pressure point to relieve stage fright. He said, "if you press this point for three minutes before you go on stage you will never need alcohol again," and he was right, I never did. I have long since stopped pressing the nerve, but the confidence this gave me is beyond words. The first night I tried it I threw my head back and sang with my whole heart- I thought, "I am free!" That was some time in the eighties. Now my biggest drug problem is coffee.

Acting Like A Star

Bonnie Raitt once said something that explained so much... she said there's your name with a capital letter- "Bonnie with a big B" she called it. Then there's your name with a small letter- that's us to the people who've known us all our lives and think we're still eight years old- or it could be the cashier at the chain store who couldn't care less who you are and treats you like a worm. There's a vast difference between the disrespectful level and the worshipful level. We have to know who we are to weather this and not get confused by it.

Many years ago in Stone City, Iowa, there was an ice storm and severe fog at the same time. Two people made it to the show that night. I was already a trooper, but some things are harder than others. I had a little talk with myself before I went on stage- something to the effect that those two devoted, dedicated people had braved the elements because they wanted to see a show, and it was my job to give it to them. It was not their fault that they were the only two people there, and it was not my fault either. It wasn't even the venue's fault. So something changed in me that night. I went to another level because I decided to think big even though things looked small. I decided to feel like a star when there was no evidence to support it. I believe in the power of ideas, and I made up my mind to do several things: to reach open my arms as wide as I could at the end of the show like a rock star, to tell everyone that blues was experiencing a major revival, and to give my all to each and every fan who was good enough to come out to the show. If I was feeling great, the audience just might feel great too. It worked. This is always my policy now: I love every show and every audience. I'm just so glad to be wherever I may be. No room is too small, and no room is too big. It's all great.

Opening For Jerry

1 opened for Jerry Garcia twice- the first time was at a theater in New Jersey. Thiele was just turning sixteen, and on his birthday, I promised to introduce him to Jerry. After my performance (during which I was treated to the "Jerry! Jerry! Jerry!" experience), I brought Thiele into the back room and Jerry graciously shook his hand. I will never forget how Thiele's face filled with disbelief and wonder. I could see this meant more to him than words could express.

The next show was at a venue in Chicago. I was wearing a baseball shirt, my signature jeans with high heels, and was feeling totally giddy. At the last song the audience went crazy. I was walking off through the back curtain when one of Jerry's entourage smiled and pointed back at the stage. It seemed I was being encored, something of a miracle under the circumstances. Jerry's people were all down to earth- great folks- which shouldn't have been much of a surprise since Jerry's music was so real and down to earth.

I was invited to follow the band to Denver- a great honor as someone must have felt I was a good opening act. The following memory is vague, but I think it played out like this: a ticket was supplied which had to be picked up somewhere or other the following morning- at an office I think. When I got there the ticket had gone with someone else and I was now to pick it up at the airport. I must have arrived just after the passengers had boarded, and the ticket ended up with the road manager on the plane. Despite the fact that this was way before to-day's extreme security, I couldn't board without first sending someone to get the ticket. As I gesticulated wildly and repeated that my ticket was on the plane with one of the passengers, I was met with blank stares. Freaked-out sweaty people with unlikely stories at airports are never a welcome sight- long and short of it was that I was at the gate but missed the flight. In a crescendo of untoward events (isn't that a prominent Murphy's law?) the next flight was canceled. Suddenly there were zero options. I remember making frantic phone calls from a pay phone to inform the agent. This unfortunate situation led to another series of disastrous mishaps trying to get back to a festival in the northeast and inspired a desperate, long song- but not as desper-ate and long as the real life adventure. In addition I was a pathetically nervous flyer, and panic probably added substantially to the mix-up. I had been invited to continue on the road with Jerry and who knows but that I could have done a number of dates with them were it not for this fiasco. My spirits were dashed, and I was now in a panic to find alternate transportation to the next important gig- a festival headlined by Bonnie Raitt. Carrying a heavy guitar and some luggage, I dragged myself into the streets of Chicago while someone pointed the way to the bus station. If anyone ever questions why I now have my own tour bus, this is the number one reason.

I seem to recall it was one of the big holiday weekends, perhaps Independence Day, and there was an unprecedented volume of traffic. I managed to push and pull my stuff down some scary looking back streets until I found the station. When I arrived the lines were to the back of the place and my bus was about to depart. Some kind person let me step in front of them, but of course an angry cry went up from the line of ticket holders. I couldn't blame them and tried to explain, but nobody cared... everyone's bus was about to leave. I finally bought the ticket and raced to my gate. Out of breath and relieved that the bus was still there, I handed the ticket to the driver. In a calm voice he said "This ticket is not to Albany. This ticket is to Toledo." They had given me the wrong ticket- and some weary traveler who needed to go to Toledo had a ticket to Albany.

I don't know how I survived the chaos that ensued. I was running and carrying a heavy guitar which felt so weightless from my adrenaline I thought someone must have stolen it from the case. Light as a feather, it flew through the air next to me. Finally, I ended up taking a later bus, which- incredibly- broke down en route. We just pulled over and stopped in the dark. Sitting helplessly at the side of the road, I realized things couldn't possibly become more surreal. Then there was an announcement and we all had to get off. We were in the middle of nowhere. From a phone booth I called a friend on the East Coast who coaxed me into taking a taxi to the nearest airport. I flew on some wildly bouncing mini-plane to Buffalo, New York, while my friend drove six hours through the night to meet me. He scooped me up and we sped off to Massachusetts. By the time we reached the festival it was an hour late for my set. I wandered about, gig-less (a new word), feeling like a worm. Welcome to life on the road.

Carla Gahr

Me and Carla in the rain- Cambridge, Massachusetts.
Photo: Paolo Galassi

𝒟avid's daughter Carla is as bubbly and enthusiastic as her father. A terrific photographer in her own right, she learned the craft at her father's feet. We struck up a wonderful, giggly, girly sort of friendship and soon Carla began taking my picture. Our sessions were always about fun- screaming, spinning, laughing, and making a spectacle of ourselves wherever we went. She was the first photographer with whom I felt completely at ease. For the first time in my life I didn't feel ugly, flawed, or self conscious. She became my exclusive photographer- with David's resounding approval- he said we brought out the best in each other. Carla and I were "Sweetie" and "Honey." She liked the way I looked, approved of everything I wore, and never criticized. Having been an incredibly shy, insecure person, this was an immense help. She taught me how to be freewheeling and happy in front of the lens. David used to say "one moment... one moment" in a mumbly sort of way as he was changing film. Carla inherited the same style and mannerisms- she was so much like her father it was scary.

At some point Rounder asked me to try a new photographer. This was painful to me as I felt it was tearing an important bond- but Rounder was firm. They wanted variety and different energy despite what had become numerous successful years of collaboration with Carla. Her wonderful photos are displayed throughout this book and on many of my albums.

Carla and I are still in touch whenever possible and it only takes a split second for us to go right back into our old friendship. David's passing has been a terrible loss. He was in every way the perfect father.

The Alternative

Whenever I felt overwhelmed or just wanted to consider a more peaceful existence, art would loom to the foreground. Up until a certain point I had used mostly crayons, craypas, ink, pencil, and watercolors. One day it occurred to me that I had never tried oils. Living in the country made the idea of landscapes very appealing, so I set out to learn how to use a new medium, one which I felt was the choice of the masters. But it was not going to be easy. There was much to be learned about application, mixing, transparency, technique, and even cleanup. But I applied myself and began to get a feel for it. Soon I was driving around searching for beautiful locations. Finding a lovely view, I'd set up my easel, open the box of paints, and work.

It doesn't take long to get covered in paint from head to toe. None of my clothing was spared- I developed piles of stuff forever consigned to the "painting clothing" box, which no one would ever wear again- but at the time I didn't care at all. The work came first- concern with being tidy didn't exist. There would be paint on my skin, paint in my hair, even paint on the car door- that was just the nature of it. In addition the entire house took on the somewhat evocative smell of turpentine, paint thinner, and all the chemicals required for the task. However, being uncomfortable with the thought that these materials were toxic, I began to search for less poisonous substitutes. Soon I switched to acrylics, a much more fast drying, "plastic-y" kind of medium, but even that I worried was not biodegradable. Bottom line, much of our artistic pursuits, from painting to photography (with its array of deadly chemicals), are horribly polluting. I suppose this is what leads some people to be environmental artists who use only natural materials.

Nathalie and her son John at my art show in Old Chatham.

I have never found anything more peaceful than painting. Untold hours would pass without my realizing, and soon it would be dark. The following day I would place the painting on the back porch and continue working, and once again I found this quiet pastime made time stand still. There was much joy to be found there.

Eventually I built up enough material for a show, and after looking around, found a local gallery at the Shaker Museum in Old Chatham, New York that would host the exhibit. It was my first show, a multimedia display spanning works past and present. The weather was lovely and sunny. Looking at the photos I note that my mother and sister, aunt and uncle, Nathalie, her husband, and numerous close friends

213

were there- along with quite a few people I had never met. It was a success in that I sold a number of pieces, mostly oils- but this is when I discovered that it was difficult to part with my work. I had a deeply personal connection to each piece and actually missed them when they were gone. The music business presented no such quandary, as duplicable mediums such as LPs, tapes, and CDs made the issue of permanent physical separation from your work a moot point. The only other show I ever had was at the Spencertown Academy in Spencer-town, New York, and once again, after selling various pieces, I felt I would be better off keeping my professional focus in music, at least for the time being.

A Grain Of Mustard Seed

1 met Steven at a little venue in Greene County. He was a keyboard player and part of a band that had been hired by someone to sit in with me for several shows. He had jet black hair which he wore in a ponytail, and as he stepped off the stage something possessed me to walk up to him (a man I barely knew), and remove the elastic band that held his hair- which immediately fell around his shoulders. Although it startled him, it was obvious that he liked it. Tall, and with chiseled features, Steven was gorgeous to begin with- but now he was glorious. His skin had a burnished kind of glow as if he might have been part Native American, although he turned out to be English. We became friends immediately. He was the most peaceful, gentle soul I had ever met- kind, and endlessly helpful. Soon I discovered he was a Christian, a fact I specifically chose to ignore. But over time Steven began to urge me to read the Bible. I thought he was a wonderful hu-man being, but in this sense I considered him naive and deluded, my upbringing having been strictly atheist. People around me had always dripped with contempt at the very idea that there might be a God. It seemed like a childish fantasy: let's invent a Santa Claus in the sky and we'll all be happy... that was the general attitude. However he eventually got to me, and one day, telling myself I wanted to see what all the "fuss" was about, I picked up the Bible. Here was this huge book with miniature print. Reading- something I'd always avoided! I once finished *Shogun*- but this was bigger by far. So I flipped through the pages until I saw something that said "The New Testament" and started to read. At first it was just interesting. I noticed that it was filled with many familiar phrases which had apparently made their way into our language and culture but were no longer associated with the Bible. Then it got deep, profoundly deep. I was amazed. There was no doubt that this man Jesus was way beyond anything we had going on down here on earth. He confronted people with the highest truths: Love your enemies. Turn the other cheek. Pray for those who use you. Give to everyone who asks. Sell all you have, give to the poor and follow me... had anyone considered the profundity of this teaching? Was anyone willing to live like this? Then I got to the end of the first gospel. As Jesus- this incredible man whose existence had become so real to me on these pages, was being murdered- I started to cry. It was horribly unjust. He went gently and willingly to his death. He continued to say earth shatteringly beautiful, simple and truthful things to the last. He forgave his murderers. He had compassion on those who were being cruel to him. Grief washed over my soul. This was the saddest story I had ever read. Here was this brilliant, beautiful, loving, man who was innocent of all charges, and people were killing him. I couldn't believe it. My heart was broken for Jesus, and for everyone who had ever loved and lost.

As time went on I continued to read this book. My initial responses were similar to those of others who had only read bits and pieces. Jesus was a great guy, they reasoned, but he lived in another age. His teachings were relevant to the day and time, but now we're ever so much more enlightened and modern. We can pick and choose from his cool words, and continue on in our "taking care of number one" sort of way. We can even think of ourselves as Gods and Goddesses, because the Jesus spirit can be applied as necessary. In this way of thinking it's not really about him- it's more about us. As a friend said to me recently "Take my advice: stick with the New Testament." This is often the understanding of the casual reader. I used to say that the Old Testament was filled with violence, incest, and domination of women- but that when Jesus showed up it all got better- so I understood the root of this idea. But as I continued I found something very different. Next I read the entire book pretty much cover to cover, skipping some of the incredibly complex details in Leviticus, and some of the Proverbs. But a pattern of continuity began to emerge which I had initially missed. I started listening to recordings of the Bible while driving. I ended up absorbing and recalling a fair amount of the text. Suddenly Scripture would pop into my head at surprisingly appropriate moments.

Bob Dylan, James Taylor, Elvis Costello and countless country artists use biblical words in their songs. People are deeply moved (without ever knowing that what they're listening to comes from the Bible) because the words are filled with power. It's possible for a songwriter who doesn't believe in God to skillfully use these words- they work because they are beautiful and moving. "Chariots of fire" comes from 2 Kings 6:17, "East of Eden" from Genesis. Shakespeare used "O death where is thy sting?" from 2nd Corinthians. "My brother's keeper" is yet another familiar figure of speech from the Bible. Remember the Byrds song "To every thing, turn, turn, turn, there is a season, turn, turn, turn"? This comes from Ecclesiastes chapter 3. Rock fans who loved these powerful lyrics may have had no idea that they were written by King Solomon and were from the Bible. They just thought the Byrds wrote GREAT words.

Thiele's Death

"The Lord giveth and the Lord taketh away"
Job 1:21

It's almost impossible to write about something as horrible as the death of a child. It happened in 1986, but it still seems like yesterday. It's something you never get over. There will always be an empty chair at the table, and there will never be a simple answer to the happy question "How many children do you have?"

Artie Traum reminded me once that I used to fret a lot about Thiele's safety. As he entered his teen years Thiele began pushing the envelope. He was angry. He started to let me know he could do whatever he wanted whenever he wanted, and that included drugs, booze... whatever. I hardly knew what to say, but my heart froze with fear watching him provocatively guzzle a beer in front of me for effect, as if to say, "Do something about it if you can!" knowing there was nothing I could do. Telling him to stop made it worse. It was an untenable situation, and I used to wrack my brains for some male role model who might have influence, as it was clear that as "mom" mine was fading.

I felt, from personal experience, that women begin to have a lot less influence with boys when they reach puberty. Robert Bly, who wrote *A Gathering Of Men*, used to say that men needed older men to initiate them into manhood. He said gangs were young men trying to initiate themselves, and that, he said, didn't work. He stated that young men need older men who care about their souls. He pointed out King Arthur and the Knights of the Round Table as a mythical example. Strangely enough, I felt he was 100% correct. His theories did not make me feel defensive as a woman. I did not rail against them as ignorant, biased, or one-dimensional. To the contrary, I felt they were

"For in much wisdom is much grief;
and he that increaseth knowledge increaseth sorrow."
Ecclesiastes 1:18

spot on. I got goose pimples when he told a room full of men to stand up. He asked all the men over fifty to come forward and sit in the front rows. Then he had all the men under fifty stand and applaud the older men. To me this was fabulous. It did not un-empower women, it filled the missing gap. This was what Thiele needed, and I looked around-but there was no one to fill those shoes at the time. It was heartbreaking. What had gone wrong?

So Thiele continued to bang about, lost, angry, and immensely talented- a high risk group of the most extreme kind. His guitar playing skills had taken on massive proportions. I am qualified, as a guitar player, to note that his abilities exceeded mine from the time he was eight, when he stood on the corner of Jones and West Fourth Street across from the Sandal Shop with his electric guitar, a tiny Pignose amplifier, and an open case where onlookers could drop donations. He played every song Jimmy Hendrix ever recorded- note for note. With a bandana around his forehead and a rock star quality which eclipsed any I have seen before or after, he made eighty dollars in just a few hours, a fortune for an eight-year-old. As a teenager with an electric guitar he became popular at school- the auditorium filled with fellow students and parents went wild as he streaked across the stage with his instrument flying, falling to his knees, plucking the strings with his teeth, and playing the guitar behind his head. I couldn't believe it- this was my son! The girls acted like he was one of the Beatles.

Thiele was also deeply skeptical- and I could see why. His life had been attended by many traumas, including the constant presence of unstable adults making bad decisions. How could I be a better parent? I worried myself awake at night. I had acted too much like my own parents, had somehow become a distant "hands off" mother like my own, had stood at a distance acting like children just raised themselves- like my father. All the things that my parents had done to make me bitter- I was doing the same things. True, I had been the world's most attentive, storytelling, doting mother to Thiele as a small child; this despite poverty, despair, lack of a stable father figure, and so on. Through all I had done my best, kissed him often, held him close to my heart, and sung into his ear. I shared his feelings of wonder and told him endless happy stories of little made up characters and their adventures. But the moment he became a preteen, I stood back. I had no idea how to steer that boat alone, so I let school and society step in- and let's face it, that is a recipe for disaster. There's no warmth in something as vast and impersonal as "Society," and that's who I was handing my child over to without realizing it.

I'll tell you what else had gone wrong. I was too damn busy trying to "take care of number one." There was support for that everywhere around us. But that way of thinking was not doing the trick either. I was running around looking like a babe, turning heads and attracting the wrong kind of men while desperately looking for Mr. Right... and failing my child. It was all so pathetic when I thought about it. I decided in the middle of the night to reach out to Thiele in the way I used to when he was little. I needed to tell him I loved him.

A car turned the corner, pulled in front of the house, and out stepped Thiele. He was a brand new driver. I was impressed but worried. I held my breath. Then I remembered- don't stand back, reach out! I put my arms around him and said "Thiele, I love you." He pushed me away- "don't start that again!" he said. This was not going to be easy.

In the following months I kept up this approach, and in not very long Thiele's defenses began to break down. We took a long ride together and talked about life, music, God, relationships, parents, the world... I felt good about this progress.

I was never a conventional mom. When the kids were in elementary school I would drop in from time to time- a forgotten lunch, a note- whatever parents bring to school- and Thiele said his friends would see me as this young, foxy looking woman and say "That's your mother?" This was probably more embarrassing to him than a source of pride. Mothers were supposed to look like nurturers, not babes. Mind you I was simply a slender person in well fitting clothing, not provocatively dressed- but the other mothers looked very different at the time. To make matters more complicated, his lunches were health foods- yogurt, peanut butter, whole wheat bread, juice, and not soda. The other students had bologna on Wonderbread. Once someone asked what was in his little lunch cup. Thiele answered that it was yogurt. The other student spit on the ground. Thiele came home saying he wanted normal lunches from then on.

When Thiele was eighteen he was visiting family on an island off the coast of Maine. One evening an up and coming band called Los Lobos was performing at a private party. Someone informed them that there was a kid in the house who was an awesome player and urged them to let him sit in. No one really wants to hear this sort of thing when they're trying to get through a tough gig, but someone must have convinced them- so they called Thiele up to the stage. The story I heard from his girlfriend Martha was that when Thiele started to play,

one by one the band stopped to listen. Eventually everyone stood there with their mouths open as he soloed for a half hour straight.

I met Martha crossing Sixth Avenue. Suddenly, there was Thiele with this sophisticated, dark-haired lady. She was dressed in a fluffy gray faux fur jacket and looked entirely rock'n'roll. He introduced me, and later I learned that she asked the usual: "*That's* your mother?!" and then said "She looks younger than I do!" This same Martha, who was over thirty when she met Thiele, was at the party with Los Lobos. Someone had set her up with Thiele's stepfather, but according to her, there was no attraction. When Thiele started to play guitar she was mesmerized. "*Who* is that?" she asked. Immediately they became an item, even though she had been on a blind date with someone else. She made a good choice, I must say.

The day Thiele died I had a gig in Massachusetts. After the show someone confronted me outside the venue. The original album cover of *I've Got A Rock In My Sock* was a silly concept. The song was a tongue-in-cheek, risqué little number like many of the old Bessie Smith songs- and I decided on a comic book approach for the graphics. I was photographed seated on a doctor's table with Ron Levy, my friend from Roomful Of Blues wearing a white coat and examining my boot. My idea would have been to have an artist retouch it to look like a hand-painted page from a comic book- an R. Crumb kind of thing. But no, they printed the photo clean and straight, making it look like a serious attempt to present some misguided concept. So this woman was saying that it exploited women. "Wait a minute" I said, "are you sure? Who does it really exploit- the man or the woman? Look at the photo. Isn't the man in a subservient pose removing the woman's boot?" It was a pointless argument, and a stupid choice for a cover. Rounder later gave me the opportunity to redesign the artwork when my records were released on CD, and I was only too happy to accommodate. That was the first one I changed. But this confrontation only added to my feeling of distress that night.

After the show I pulled into a train station outside of town to rest. My marriage was on the rocks and I was meeting a friend, a potential relationship, at the train. For reasons I will never quite understand I had a terrible, ominous feeling all night. I couldn't sleep. I kept tossing and turning and felt that life was filled with sorrow and despair. There were dark shadows moving through my mind- frightening images, and a deep sense of loneliness. After we left New York City for upstate, Thiele used to say "something's missing." This comment, usually spoken while I was tucking him in to bed, gave me a terrible feeling of fear... what was missing, a sense of peace? The train arrived at two in the morning. Awful things often happen in the wee hours. My friend stepped out onto a dimly lit platform. I walked up to him and said "something terrible has just happened." Little did I know that on a winding road in upstate New York only an hour or so away, my son had just slammed into a tree and died. It was a week before his nineteenth birthday- November 2nd, 1986.

The next day, still unaware of the tragic events, we had parked at a rest area on the way to a show in Vermont. The following series of events are surreal and seemed to happen in slow motion. I saw a car approaching. My estranged husband got out. His mother was in the front seat, his brother in the back. I stood there with my friend- like a criminal caught in the act. I wanted to shrink into the earth. What were they doing there? Was I being arrested? My mind was spinning. Then I heard the words "Thiele is dead!" I collapsed. I was making strange howling noises. My fists were clenched. I was convulsing with sobs, but there were no tears. I was put in the front seat of my car, my friend was quickly removed to the other car and taken somewhere, perhaps back to the train. I have never felt such terrible grief. It's almost impossible to breathe, and the air vibrates before your eyes. My baby, my baby was dead! This had to be a dream! In shock I began to say I had to go to the gig. Someone said it had been canceled and I was going home.

Later in a fitful sleep I saw Thiele. He was dressed in a long, white robe. He was being received into Heaven by many beautiful looking men with flowing beards and radiant faces. Thiele's face was glowing, his cheeks were rosy, his outstretched hands were being grasped as he was being led into this magnificent place- a beloved friend being welcomed home after a long journey. Throughout the unspeakably horrible aftermath of his death, there were many powerful dreams in which I saw him- in person- not a figment- not a facsimile- but the real personage of Thiele- his vital, ever-present soul- and it was comforting. If you have lost someone, God forbid a child, ask your mind to bring you dreams. You will see that the deceased are well and out of all danger. Nothing could comfort a mother's heart more than knowing her child is safe. In a strange way, this was another kind of safety. I no longer had to worry about him dying. This is the ultimate lesson in acceptance, and love.

At the service I was dressed in a white coat that came almost to the ground- this to honor the dream of Thiele in his long white robe. I was dazed. As I received the line of mourners, friends I hadn't seen in many years were stepping up to take me into their arms. I couldn't believe the outpouring of tenderness. Although I was beyond devastated, I was still aware of this immensely loving feeling. My mother got up to speak and began to faint. Thiele's other grandmother compared him to a crazy quilt, a mosaic of artistic elements lovingly sewn together. His teacher said we had all had "The Thiele Experience," which elicited a ripple of knowing laughter from his friends. Young person after young person got up and testified that Thiele had been the single most important person in their lives- sensitive, caring, encouraging, and several even said that they played music because of his support. I never knew how many people loved him.

"Three Trees In Paradise"- this is the place where Thiele died

And then I went back on the road. I thought that my survival depended on forging ahead with what was most familiar. I didn't know what else to do. Sitting at home would not have been better.

The first show was in Arkansas, and it was probably the most difficult show of my life. No one had any idea what was wrong with me. I felt like I was caving inwards- my eyes were swollen, my voice was faint. Thiele's death was something I never could have spoken about on stage... that came later.

My new road manager Suzanne and I plowed down the road, acted wacky, drank too much coffee, spoke in crazy accents and took on different personalities- anything to get by. I felt like I was being squeezed to death in a vice. I went off by myself as much as possible, searching for some connection to my child.

A New Age State Of Mind

Somewhere on the road we stopped at a gift shop. As I walked in there were little bells chiming. Soft music was playing and crystals shimmered in the display cases. A book titled *Life After Death* jumped out at me. My heart leaped. I would find Thiele! I would search and search, and would find him in the sky, in a book, in a crystal, a dream, through channeling... any way possible, but I would find him. If I had to join him, I would find him. Death no longer seemed like a bad idea. We would get to be with our loved ones.

But I continued on somehow. I had many dreams, wrote poems, read books, carried crystals- anything that was comforting. I recorded an album for Thiele called *House Of Hearts*, and while we were working I filled the control room with photos. Everyone was able to see who the record was dedicated to. Livingston Taylor (who sang a duet with me) was incredibly kind, looking at the pictures and expressing sympathy. All of this helped me to carry on, step by step- and on some days that meant one step forward and two steps back. It's all about "one day at a time." No one should ever try to rush you, or hint that you should "get a grip," get back to living, or whatever else well meaning people might say. If you want to grieve for the rest of your life, I say go ahead. It would dishonor the dead to slowly forget about them.

I used to get letters from a dear fan who had lost her sister, and later her husband. She quoted from the songs on the record one by one and told me how they had carried her through the hardest times and had given her hope. This is one of the things that makes my life worthwhile- being useful in this way.

Channeling

My heart also bled for Jordan. He had lost his best friend, and had watched his parents lose a child- inconceivable suffering for a fourteen-year-old. He began a series of heartwrenching drawings of Thiele in the spirit world- it was as if he was able to directly interpret Thiele's experiences in the afterlife- traveling in strange galaxies, flying, fighting with demons- clearly Jordan could see into another dimension. These images were gripping, powerful, and unbelievably sad. I couldn't breathe looking at them- pain would tear at my heart. Jordan seemingly traveled through the realm of grief by creating these intense images as a road map.

One day we were sitting in an upstairs bedroom talking about Thiele when we both felt a presence. Turning his head, Jordan said, "Thiele just came into the room." We had goose pimples. It was a physical sensation, not a thought- the air was tingling. We could feel energy, electrical in nature, in our hands and feet. Shortly afterwards we decided to try channeling. Jordan lay down with his eyes closed. I took notes, and later made recordings. Eventually Jordan felt Thiele had arrived, and we began to talk. I filled a couple of books with all the information from these sessions- some handwritten, some transcribed from tape- but I can tell you this: I have no doubt that Thiele spoke through Jordan. The first book, titled *I want to tell you that I love you* is not only filled with abundant information Jordan simply couldn't have known, it was clearly not the voice or thoughts of a fourteen year old. Thiele addressed certain issues directly to me, answering specific concerns of mine. He also spoke of how it feels to die, explaining that it's more difficult for the soul to separate from the body when you are young, that it is more bonded to a youthful body- but that when an older person dies, the soul separates more easily. This made sense. There were countless things like this- brilliant, insightful, surprising- things Jordan never could have imagined on his own. It was eye-opening, comforting, even educational. Thiele talked about other dimensions, and how the physical plane is limited to certain perceptions. To some extent it was a lesson in physics. He shined light on mysteries from earlier years, things which answered unresolved questions. It was beyond amazing, but that's a whole other book.

A Way Out Of No Way

I was the walking wounded after Thiele died- but life had to go on, tours had to continue, and records had to be made. I constantly nursed a broken heart, but through some great mercy I was ultimately able to use the grief to create. I had the distinct feeling that Thiele was watching, guiding, and urging me on to new heights, and that he had added his musical energy to my war chest- so eventually, instead of stopping, I felt more motivated. I had to make this work, for all of us- Thiele, Mom, Grandma- my whole family, living and deceased, here or on the other side. I felt I was not alone, and frequently heard Thiele giving me advice and urging me onwards. It gave me hope to think he wanted this for me.

I wrote a song called "Spiderboy" about Thiele's death. It is difficult to sing live, and even harder to explain without falling apart. But every time I do people come up to me after the show to tell me that they too lost a child. It's the most terrible bond to share, but it helps us to know we are not alone in our suffering.

FOR THIELE :

" YET IS NOT DEATH THE GREAT ADVENTURE STILL,
AND IS IT ALL LOSS TO SET SHIP CLEAN ANEW,
WHEN HEART IS YOUNG AND LIFE AN EAGLE POISED ? "

JAMES ELROY FLECKER

In The Studio With Stevie Wonder

Photo: Jim Gallagher

Gypsie Boy

Gypsie ran away, to an island in the south,
My love, sweet love, with berries in his mouth,
Somewhere in the wind, he smells a sweet perfume,
My love, sweet love, whistling a tune...

Chorus (humming)

Gypsie Boy, said you own my heart,
You hold it in your lovin' hand,
And you carry it beside you, in your sweet and lonesome land,
And it's all that I can do to make it through...

228

Chorus (humming)

Notes upon the strings, so lovely while he sings,
His song, his song, if only I had wings,
I would fly away to his island cabaret,
My love, sweet love, love to hear him play...

Chorus (humming)

Words and music by Rory Block

*I*t's been said: "Be careful what you wish for, because it might come
true." Then it follows to wish for what you want. I have always believed in the power of thought, and when I look back on my life and
list all the things I have envisioned that have manifested, it's obvious
there is a direct connection. I also felt at times that Thiele was watching, and somehow helping. Perhaps he had God's ear and had asked
for a small favor for his mother...

I had recorded a very simple piece of music- a ballad called "Gypsie
Boy". It had good words, but it lacked something. Stevie Wonder,
that's what it lacked! At that point it was irrational to think a huge star
would agree to play on my record. I wasn't well known and had only
three releases on Rounder. I was small, my recordings were small-
but I decided to think big. This crazy streak has been one of my most
unlikely assets. How else could someone playing acoustic music that
had gone out of style some fifty years earlier expect to get anywhere
in an industry which favored electric, extreme flash, and ostentatious,
flamboyant style? I was none of these things. I didn't even know how
to apply makeup.

I decided to call a friend of mine who worked with Stevie Wonder
in LA. Jim Gallagher and I had done several projects together in the
past. I had stayed in touch with him and knew he was working at
Wonderland. When I called him he said "well it's worth a shot" so I
sent a cassette for Jim to hand deliver to Stevie. About a week later
the phone rang at one in the morning and it was Jim. I heard this voice
saying "guess what, Stevie said yes." I leaped out of bed and booked a
train to LA.

We found a beautiful studio with an opening in their schedule- but let's face it, who wouldn't find an opening for Stevie Wonder? While we were waiting we started discussing the status of the track, and a mild debate ensued- should we play it for him with or without drums? My position was, as usual, keep it simple, leave it wide open. Let him get the full flavor and mood of the song with nothing in the way. As we sat there someone pointed out that we might have gone too far in assuming he would show up. What assurance did we have? We got nervous, so Jim called and spoke to someone at Wonderland. They said that Stevie was on his way.

Then the door opened and Stevie walked in. The man is beautiful. He has a golden glow around him, an aura you can literally see. After recovering from my shock, I got supernaturally brave and explained about how I hadn't included the drum track so he could hear the unencumbered song. He responded "whatever you want, you're the artist." This rocked my world and changed *everything*. Not only was it an incredibly respectful and considerate thing for a huge star to say to a struggling unknown artist, but it forever laid to rest the question of who should be in charge of the music. I could always quote Stevie Wonder from that point forward, and no one would be able to refute this.

Nothing could have been more profound and deeply moving to me than the fact that Stevie Wonder showed up to play on my album. When he went into the studio I knew I had to be there, and he didn't object. *Stevie Wonder* was standing next to me. I could feel the vibration of every note passing through me as he played three solos in a row, each one more perfect and beautiful than the last. As I stood there feeling overwhelmed, my eyes filled with tears. I was overcome with emotion and kept thinking "If I die tomorrow it's OK because I'm standing on the mountain top. It just doesn't get better than this." All my struggling, all my discouragement, all the unkind voices, the detractors, the vile music business types with their put downs- it was all gone. I felt certain: no one could hurt me now. And no one could take this from me! I can't recall how many times (mid-song anywhere on earth) this thought has rippled through me and strengthened me: Stevie Wonder played on my record!

I tried to control the tears of joy but they just kept pushing on my lids. I looked at the faces through the glass and hoped I wouldn't lose control. Then I remembered seeing Stevie on television receiving a huge award- maybe for lifetime achievement- and I remembered that there were tears rolling down his face. Then I thought "what a beautiful man... he's not afraid to cry"... and my tears started to flow. I was drowning in them, but I didn't care. I asked him if he minded that I was crying. Of course he didn't.

When it was over we tried to pay him, but he wouldn't let us. This was very touching to me. He knew I was a starving artist. We had gotten him a gift, a leather carry bag with an alarm on it that beeped when you clapped your hands. He seemed intrigued by this and clapped until the alarm went off. So Stevie took the bag and went back to Wonderland, and "Gypsie Boy" went on the *Best Blues and Originals* CD. Jim took some photos which I hope to find some day, perhaps in time for this book. Found 'em!

There have been certain landmarks in my career (this being a huge one) which filled my heart with a sense of joy and accomplishment and gave me the courage to continue.

With Stevie and co-producer Carey Williams. Photo: Jim Gallagher

Mom Leaves This World

As my mother got older she got smaller and smaller. She had scolio-
sis, a curvature of the spine which got continually worse over time.
Her back became "S" shaped, compressing her internal organs. She
complained often of pain, though I had some slight suspicion that she

might be crying wolf or choosing life as a victim instead of thinking
positively and putting up a fight. For much of her life she viewed
things in the worst light. I wanted her to be strong, but it seemed she
often gave up in advance. This might be why I am such a fighter. I
have the desire to prevail, and can't stand to be the victim.

After Will died, Mom had a series of ridiculous affairs with completely bizarre men. The first was a con man she met on an exotic island
vacation. He was an "entertainer" at a resort who spotted bereaved
middle-aged women, put the moves on them, inveigled himself into
their lives, proposed, and then funded his life by wheedling money
for his supposed dream projects. He was a professional whiner who
played on the tender hearts of lonely women who craved to be caretakers. He got them to "believe in him." My mother and this man came
back to New York together, Mom all aglow. As soon as we met him
we knew something was terribly wrong. In no time he made off with
a good amount of money and a guitar. Then she started getting phone
calls from other women who claimed to be his wife. Everyone had
the same story. Turns out he was marrying and ripping off inheritance
money all over the place. This guy was a pro. I can't remember what
became of him, but Mom finally got wise. She sold her apartment and
moved to a condo on Cape Cod.

It was then that Mom and I became much closer and had many
wonderful, deep conversations. She openly confessed to feelings of
remorse, and acknowledged that she felt she hadn't been a good mom.
She said "No one taught me how to be a mother." I thought this was
an astoundingly honest confession, and I had compassion. No one
taught me either. I learned the details of her horrible experiences at
Bellevue. She explained that after she was released from the hospital
she was told she was being watched, and that if there were any signs
of deterioration she would be sent back. I can imagine the anxiety this
must have caused her. She said she felt totally intimidated all the time,
and that Dad constantly held this over her head.

If she hadn't fallen back into despair and stopped eating (which led to
her death from starvation at sixty), she would be alive today to be a
much needed mother and grandmother. I'm angry at her for giving up
and pulling out, but I understand that this fluctuating confidence runs
in our family: the bipolar, manic-depressive, artistic whatever-it-may-
be. Sad, very sad. I'm glad there is awareness of these things now and
that people can get help.

It started with her not eating. Bulimia and fear of poisoning was at the
root. I began to realize that this was always present in the past and had
influenced me without my conscious knowledge. We were well aware

of Grandpa Robert's story- death by starvation- so this pattern started to reveal itself and become clearer over time. This was a generational, genetic, physical problem, one that cannot be separated from the psychological. She found things to be afraid of. She said her caretaker, who had moved in with her shortly after she left New York, prepared food in glass bowls, cutting and mashing with sharp implements. She showed me these bowls. They were heavily scored and grooved. It was glass and the shards had to go somewhere, most likely into the food. She thought this could be the source of her stomach aches- that she might be ingesting small bits of broken glass. Of course the caretaker was eating the same food, so I suppose he was either stronger, had a greater reserve of blood, or perhaps these bits of glass were not affecting either of them, I'll never know. In any case he was not doing anything purposely, but it was cause for concern.

Then I stopped hearing from her. The caretaker didn't return phone calls either- apparently a lifelong habit. I became worried and called her church. The Minister sounded relieved. "Rory, thank God you called," he said. Some of the parishioners, along with the Pastor and his wife, had become concerned that no one had seen her or been able to get in touch. They went to her house and knocked on the door. The caretaker answered but wouldn't let them in, saying my mother didn't want any visitors. They became much more worried after that. The Minister tried to reach me but couldn't locate my number. At that time I went to the Cape and found my mother lying in her bed, all the shades drawn so that the room was dark at noon. She was just a shadow, weak and thin. To me it was clear she was committing suicide, finishing what she had started forty years earlier. I played "Walk In Jerusalem" for her, one of the most powerful songs I had ever recorded. When I sang it, I felt this divine spirit in every cell of my body. It wasn't me singing- it came from somewhere else. All of a sudden she raised a thin little arm and waved it gently in the air as if to worship along with the music. *I want to be ready, I want to be ready, to walk in Jerusalem just like John!* It was touching, but also heartbreaking. It was as if she was at her own funeral.

I called the doctor who had treated her in the recent past for stomach complaints. He was clear in stating that he could find nothing organically wrong with her. This thing had to be psychological in his estimation. They had cared for her and released her on several medications which I can't now recall, though I grilled him on the names and uses and wrote everything down. A feeling of panic rose up in me. I had to prevent her death- it was suicide, I was sure, and she was staging it gradually, using the caretaker as the unwitting enabler.

Mom died on the way to the hospital. Her heart stopped in the ambulance. The caretaker explained that the evening began with her experiencing strong feelings of dread, as if something was terribly wrong. There were other symptoms-numbness in limbs- things which precede a heart attack. She became worse over the night hours, but didn't want to go to the hospital. In the caretaker's defense, he was trying to honor her wishes, but in my estimation she was well past rational, and this would have required intervention. I believe swift action could have saved her. But eight hours later, by the time the ambulance arrived, she was probably in the final stages of heart failure, most likely exacerbated by the devastating effects of long term poor nutrition. So when the ambulance pulled over to the side of the road, it was clear something was very wrong.

My sister went to identify the body. She was badly shaken. She said Mom's eyes were open, frozen in an expression of fear- and she closed them. At the funeral I was a mess, as usual, crying the whole time. I was angry, very angry that this had happened. All of this was as confusing as my family had always been. Nothing was ever done out in the open- shadow surrounded everything. I have automatically steered my ship into the light as a result. I can't stand darkness and secrecy.

I don't doubt that the caretaker and I feel differently about this, and that there was tremendous pressure on him to accommodate her, rational or not. Even I had received a phone call from her a month or two earlier in which she described a fantastic out-of-body experience which had shown her that death was something beautiful that was not to be feared. She wanted me to promise that if she declined suddenly, I was not to try to save her life. I found this very upsetting, as she was asking me to assist in her suicide (no matter how beautifully she described the feelings). Because the doctor had assured me he found no further physical reason for her to be ill, this just confirmed that her death was willful. It needs to be pointed out that she was only sixty, the age I am as I write this, and that she had no particular life-threatening illness at the time. Therefore I could not have agreed with her request *not* to try and save her. I often miss her and see no reason why she could not still be with us today, an eighty-year-old mother and grandmother- which is certainly my own goal- indeed to make it to a hundred and ten. I can't find any good reason why my mother continually wanted to check out before her given time was rightfully over.

Eating Disorders

"My heart is smitten, and withered like grass;
so that I forget to eat my bread."
Ps 102:4

Regarding my mother's manner of death- the same as my grandfather- I see the pattern clearly in myself. I know that it is a power that can grab you and not let go. First, you have nagging stomach aches, in retrospect most likely caused by anxiety, or perhaps allergies. We know there is some cause, but that's a gray area that might be different for each person. Then you think you feel much better when you stop eating. How easy! The less you eat, the better you feel. Then you start to look like a model. Everyone thinks you're gorgeous, and the photographs look better and better. One day, standing on a scale, you see you've dropped to one hundred and four pounds. Rob is saying "I really don't want you to lose any more weight." So yes, I have an eating disorder. I am not bulimic, but I do have a problem eating. It has been a struggle for the last fifteen or more years to build up my diet to something resembling balance- me, a person with a fairly deep knowledge of natural foods and good nutrition since I was sixteen. It is a battle that I must win, because the alternative is death.

Thanking My Mother

Before mom died she came to many of my shows, giving me the most loving kind of support. Once, I went to her church on Cape Cod and invariably was asked to perform. When I stood up the first thing I said was "I'd like to thank my mother for inspiring me to sing." I looked over at her and she was crying. This is another time when I could see right into her soul. It was the most vulnerable, telling kind of emotion. After all, she had been a Weaver! This was a person who had set aside personal ambition to raise children, had ended up in a failed marriage, felt in retrospect that she had done a bad job as a mother, often spoke of feeling regret about her life, and had experienced such deep discouragement that she had tried to kill herself. Now, publicly, in front of a large number of kind people, she was being recognized and given credit for something that might never have been acknowledged. Then I started crying. I could barely sing.

After she died I had the distinct feeling that there was a front row of balcony seats filled with my family- Mom, Thiele, Grandma Keller

After my parents parted in the sixties I almost never saw them together. This rare photo of the two of them side by side was taken at a graduation. To me, there is something compellingly sweet about this picture. In their easygoing smiles I can see why they were once drawn together.

and other relatives cheering me on. Sometimes they would give me a standing ovation. At the last vibration of the strings I could hear my mother's voice exclaiming in a sigh of delight. She loved the show! She was there!

Despite many setbacks and challenges, there have always been the things I cling to for strength: music, art, poetry, nature, love... these things gave me comfort. I continued to tour and make records as always, with the added encouragement of feeling that I was moving forward with the blessings of those who had gone on ahead.

The Anti-Grandfather

At some point my father decided he was no longer going to be a family man. Perhaps it happened when my parents parted, or around the time he told us to call him "Allan" instead of "Dad." But whenever it happened, and for whatever reason, he went from what might have appeared to the world as a caring father- posing proudly with his children for family photos- to a man who seemingly wanted no attachments to his former life. This meant that someone already trying to sever his ties as a father was completely absent as a grandfather.

One of the last times I went into the Sandal Shop to see him, he looked at me (all of fourteen years old and missing him after he had moved out) and he said in the cruelest way, "you *need* me!" Nothing could have cut more deeply. It seemed like there must have been something disgusting about me, something which made him want me to keep my distance. I was being accused of being "needy." Needing someone you love must be very bad, I thought. But what I didn't know at the time was that needing your father was normal and healthy. The message he conveyed was that I was repulsive, annoying, and perhaps even disturbed. Because of the many frightening words regarding psychological illness which had been hurled about during my childhood, it was easy to reopen those wounds. I walked away with my heart bleeding and my mind reeling, thinking the worst of myself. I had gone in to see my dad. I was leaving feeling creepy crawly. No one in this world would ever like me...

It continued to hurt that I almost never saw Dad. He was not there for family events- marriage, birth, or holidays. I have photos of only one visit where Thiele saw his grandfather, and only one visit with Jordan at our house. Perhaps there were others- maybe one or two ever. Dad attended my sister's son's graduation but not Jordan's graduation. His reasons were never made clear but sat there like a continual slap in the face. Every time I invited him he had excuses which bordered on ridiculous. It seemed like my father and I were just going to be like oil and water... but I didn't know why. I had followed in his footsteps. I was his protégé. Were we too similar? Did I remind him of someone he hated? I wracked my brains for years.

The oddest thing of all was that when he did visit, he locked in with each child like he'd been there from day one. Games, laughter, silly languages- the whole shebang. My dad obviously had a little child in him which was ready to play- a quality I value immensely. I only wish that whatever issues led him to disappear afterwards could have been addressed. Dad had a bad habit of becoming a distant memory almost immediately.

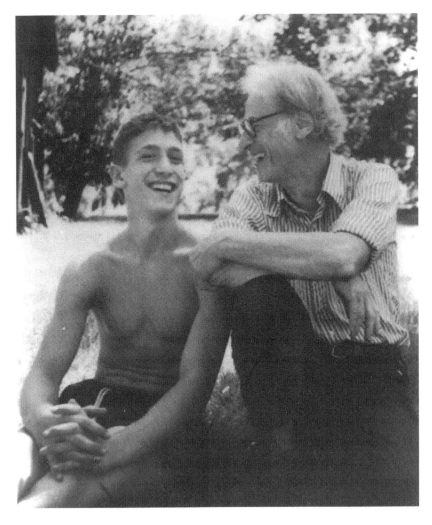

The worst offense came when Thiele died, and Dad didn't come to the service. Something in me clicked, and I called him and insisted he come over. I had to say repeatedly, "Dad, your grandson has died!" but he hardly heard me. Eventually I must have said something that made him feel obligated as he finally arrived at my house after the service was over. But he was like a ghost. I was trying to teach him how to be a father and grandfather, and it was just too much. At some point I gave up and looked elsewhere for family. I think he sensed when that happened.

There was one particular phone call which made it final. I was in my late thirties when I reached the saturation point. I screamed at him that he was a nonexistent father and hung up. I was boiling mad, which felt like a relief at the time. He called back- a total surprise. "Leave me alone!" I screamed, and hung up again. He even called again, but it was too late for me. I heard him say something like "you're giving me the blues..." but I had already spent most of my life waiting for him to get involved, and now that I was releasing him, suddenly he was objecting. It was time for me to bury my old life and make a new start- with people who wanted me, not with people who didn't. And this is the strangest paradox of all. Music, the gift my father gave me, is what saved my life. On a far grander scale there is a method to this mad- ness. Through the music, through the passion for the art form and its inherent life force, comes a mutual understanding and closeness. Per- haps it's again about souls touching souls, and much deeper levels of reality. Towards the end of her life my mother used to say that she was getting closer to her long deceased father through recurring dreams. Forty five years after his death, he told her to go back to school.

Now, Dad is sometimes only able to remember *me*, no doubt because of this musical connection. None of us really know what is going on in his mind, but I have noticed that when I come around he starts calling me by name and wanting to play music. My brother has related touch- ing stories about Dad's awareness of me and my career at a time when he is forgetting everyone and everything else.

I'd hate to prove his cavalier remarks correct- that his rejection caused me to work harder. He used to allude to the idea that he had done me a favor by swatting me out of the nest like a mother bear with her cubs. Like Alex Haley in Roots, his rejecting father finally claims him at an airport. "That's my son!" he shouts enthusiastically to a stranger as Alex walks away carrying his best seller.

My Florida Parents

I have always loved the name Virgil. It was straight out of the Civil War days, and had a spiritual ring to it. The Band used it in "The Night They Drove Old Dixie Down"- it gave me goose pimples then as it does now. I met Virgil at a difficult period in my life when I knew I needed some grounding advice. He was a Minister and a therapist who was highly recommended by a trusted friend, so I made the drive to Great Barrington to meet this humble, sweetspirited man whose words of wisdom and support changed my life. Every time I was at a low ebb I would drive out to see Virgil, and he would, in his clear, often amusing way, put his finger directly on the problem. He was not afraid to be real. Once, after a distressing breakup followed by a new girlfriend being rubbed in my face, Virgil responded with the wisdom that lifted the pain. After careful consideration he said: "You know, it doesn't take long for the shit to hit the fan," and indeed within six months the two lovebirds had broken up. Invariably, I left his office laughing. His words were always uplifting. I felt better, stronger and happier than when I walked in.

The patient/therapist relationship morphed to a family friendship after Thiele died. I brought Jordan to see Virgil and it was incredibly helpful to us both. Virgil demonstrated something about souls on the other side. He said, "look, the only difference is this." He walked over to his coffee cup, picked it up and moved it to a new location. A departed soul was no longer in the physical, he said, and moving a coffee cup would no longer be something they would be likely to do. But in every other way they were still present, he explained. Virgil knew- he too had lost a grown son.

At some point Virgil became entangled in a law suit. Something had occurred between him and a patient, and the word-for-word transcripts of the trial were printed in the newspaper daily, turning the entire thing into a lurid dog and pony show. I was outraged and refused to read about it. I was not going to glory in the misfortune of my friend. I heard that his gentle wife Marie sat in the courtroom crying as Virgil was forced to recount every word that passed between him and this other woman. I see this as one of the true ills of today's society. We obsess with other people's sexual experiences, eagerly searching for ways to entrap and shame them, while at the same time no doubt hiding our own indiscretions. This is true hypocrisy. A wise man once said that it is a shame to even speak of the things others do in private. Talking about it is worse than the act. Leave it alone, I say. If a president, a politician or any other public person does their job well, let it be. The question in my mind will always be: do they do a good job? I am not interested in the details of anyone else's sex life. Society is entirely confused about this. We glorify women in naked photos in magazines, then defrock them and remove their jobs as a result. We love celebrities who wander about almost naked and who have graphic sex before the world in movies, then punish people for some old photos, discovered by some creep who revels in hurting others, and we revile them for their immorality. But which will it be? Is it to be good, or is it bad?

So Virgil was banned from the ministry and for some time his life unraveled. He asked me with a quaking voice if I had read the papers. I said no, I had not and would not. I told him those things were private and none of my business. I told him we remained steadfast and dedicated friends to him and Marie, and nothing would change that. Virgil later explained what had happened, in person and in his own words. It was clear that it had been a weak moment and was something he deeply regretted. It did not change his devotion to his wife. It was over, and I appreciated his candid desire to clarify things with me directly. It was never mentioned again.

Virgil and Marie moved to Florida where they rebuilt their lives. We always went out of our way to visit them whenever the tour took us to Florida. There would be shared meals, board games, laughter and deep conversations. They attended several of my shows over the years and expressed tremendous pride in all that I had accomplished. Spending this family time with them became some of the best memories of my life, and I let them know in no uncertain terms that I considered them to be my other parents- my "Florida parents." It is often acquired family, manifesting at exactly the right moment, that makes surviving a dysfunctional family possible.

After their own son died, Marie felt she received messages from him in the spirit world. She did not consider this to be at odds with her Christian beliefs. Once when we were at their house, Marie got a message from Thiele. I was having a problem with my eyes and swelling around the lids. Thiele told her that I was to put thin slices of potatoes on my lids. Anyone who knows naturopathic medicine knows that potato plasters are used to draw out toxins, so this was an accurate prescription which I tried to excellent effect. She told me Thiele had explained my eye problems were related to grief.

It was a travesty that Virgil, a man filled with great talent, knowledge and compassion, could no longer preach or counsel. However he continued to supply me with gems of insight that rocked my world. Both he and Marie are gone now, but they lived full, wonderful lives and were a comfort and a joy to all those who knew and loved them, myself in particular.

Survival On The Road

High Heeled Blues, my first album for Rounder Records, was released in 1982. This is when I started traveling for real, but getting out the door for the first tour was a completely traumatic experience. At the last second I changed my mind, afraid to leave the sanctuary of my home in the country. Overcome with emotion, I started to cry.

If anyone had looked into a crystal ball and said "Dry your tears and get used to it. You're going to be doing this nonstop for the next 28 years!" I would have run in the opposite direction. Accordingly I was dragged kicking and screaming to the over-stuffed station wagon and the tour began. Miraculously, we never had any incidents with that car which later became famous for spontaneous combustion.

Eventually I graduated to a minivan, a palace on wheels in comparison. Over time I developed a strategy to survive the rigors of life on the road, which eventually became an advanced science. I had seen the

My old blue minivan with the ridiculous clam shell carrier

obvious- fast food, living out of a suitcase and sitting motionless in a cramped vehicle for weeks took a major toll on your health. I had to do something drastic or face an early death.

The back of the van was opened into one large bed with storage underneath. I began carrying a cooler which I filled to the brim with healthy foods. I had a box of dishes, utensils, a cutting board, and some cooking pots- enough to double as a mini kitchen. I had an electric burner for use in hotel rooms, and even a plug-in hot water heater for making soup and beverages in the car. We located all the health food stores we

245

could find across this great land and drove miles out of our way to get supplies- all this without cell phones or a GPS. This was about reading the dag nabbin' map (remember those)?

Once there were very few health food stores. What you found was often a dusty little cubby of a store with crooked shelves of dry, stale groceries, the kind of stuff that gave health foods a bad name. But eventually I saw the birth of the Whole Foods Markets which seemingly started out west. We noticed them first in Texas and Colorado. I used to describe them to people like they were paradise on earth... "You wouldn't believe it," I would say, "out west there are supermarkets filled with health foods!" But gradually they spread to the east coast cities and then everywhere- and we now take it for granted that every town has at least one or two. So we'd find these places somehow, shop, and then drag my "kitchen" into the hotel. There weren't many smoke detectors in those days and I was able to make rice and vegetables in the room. In the car I made salads, miso soup with scallions and fresh ginger, and also coffee and tea. It's amazing what you can do if you're determined.

The Vast Highway

The road traveled became vast- up, down, north, south, east, west, back and forth, coast-to-coast, island-hopping and border-crossing ad infinitum. I've seen thoroughly amusing exit names in out-of-the-way places. "Toad Suck Park" is a real place. "Bumble Bee" and "Crown King" are towns on a single exit sign somewhere in California. We try to photograph them all but some go by too quickly- and you know how those digital cameras sometimes decide to wait- gathering battery power- while the moment passes. So we decided to use these names as aliases. I'm Bumble Bee, the bejeweled barrelhouse singer. My husband Rob is Crown King, the cantankerous manager with a huge cigar, heavily oiled hair, and shiny silver suit... well perhaps not all the time...

My first minivan had almost two hundred thousand miles on it when I traded it in. I owned it for less than two years. The sales people at the dealership came out en masse just to see what one of these vehicles looked like after all those miles. I maintained it meticulously, enriching car washes all across the country, and you could hardly tell a thing by looking. Minivans were a recent invention and I had one of the first. We drove the next one just as far, and that was only the domestic tours- I have never clocked all the European miles. Wherever the tour ended we would simply drive home nonstop- Sante Fe to New York in fifty two hours- crazy stuff like that. We left Colorado two days before Christmas and arrived home in time to plug in the lights and celebrate. We did this sort of thing all the time. It helps to hook up with people who love to drive. I'm good for about four hours with two strong cups of coffee- but that's it for me. I've known drivers who get into the seat and go for days. It's a mental thing, and the energy comes from a wandering spirit. I've asked, and that's what all the driving freaks say. They love to see the scenery pass by, it gives them energy.

I can't remember all the times I've crossed the most extreme mountain passes in winter, winding endlessly around "S" curves on icy roads with eight and nine percent grades and no guard rails. We've driven through every kind of blinding storm and dangerous conditions, all in the name of the tour. I've shown up plenty of times when the venue was shut down from foul weather. We were there, holed up in a nearby parking lot, ready to play. For years we did all the ski areas from Vail to Aspen, Jackson Hole and Crested Butte. Driving through the mountains was an every day event... Wolf Creek pass at two in the morning in freezing rain with twelve feet of snow piled on either side of the highway, clutching hot cups of coffee for comfort and praying we didn't lose traction and end up in an icy grave thousands of feet below in some canyon. I've been funneled off Route 80 multiple times when the highway was shut down due to blizzard conditions across the state. I've stayed at just about every rest area on just about every road from here to Timbuktu. I've crossed the country on 90, 80, 70, 40, 10, you name it.

Going Nuts In Tucson

One night we pulled up to a venue in the desert. There out front stood a sandwich board with a giant sign reading "Cold Beer"- and I knew we had a problem. Not surprisingly, the evening was a real nightmare. The audience was in no mood for a solo performer, and since ninety percent of the place was inebriated, it didn't take long for someone to start shouting during an a capella song: "Sing You're The Reason God Made Oklahoma!" Here I am reminded of another show at a bar off the coast of Massachusetts where a drunk patron walked right onto the stage, threw a ten dollar bill at me and passed out across the monitors- but back to "Cold Beer" night. Between the amateur photographer sitting on the floor in front of me snapping incessantly and the mani-acs raging in the back, I walked off and almost no one noticed. In the back room (which of course had no amenities and was in fact a locker room with rows of metal cabinets), I lost it. I am not an out-of-control Diva who lives to have tantrums. No, it takes a lot. But that threshold had been reached and I screamed "I hate this place, I hate this fuckin' place!" and I kicked my patent leather shoe repeatedly into the side of a metal locker. I was so mad I didn't even notice that I had injured myself and broken the heel off the shoe. I limped out, one pump with a high heel, the other a flat shoe, and performed the second set to half a house. I thought grimly, "I'll never play again. This is the last show of my life." But miraculously, at the end of the night I found there were a number of die-hard fans who had traveled a great distance to see me and were incredibly kind and understanding, even outraged on my behalf. They couldn't believe I had come all that way just to appear at this awful place. They apologized for the rude behavior of the other patrons.

I'll never be able to recall all the places I've been and all the experi-ences I've had- but I can say I've become a road warrior as a result- a kind of Green Beret of touring. You either fold or push through, and I have somehow managed to do the latter. Jorma Kaukonen calls the worst venues the "vomit-through-the-nose bars." Those are the places with filthy black walls and bras hanging from the rafters. Been there, done that. The venues I play have evolved into listening rooms over time, thank God. Even the occasional bar pulls out all the stops and sets up shop for a concert... and the audiences are all about that.

The South Rules The Airwaves

Big rigs roll down this nation's roadways twenty four-seven, three hundred and sixty five days a year. Come what may- ice, snow, wind, or rain, they stop at nothing. They don't even slow down. I once knew a trucker who explained that the drivers speed up in inclement weather because the four wheelers are finally out of the way. Fearless, sleepless, focused, and in a hurry, it takes a special breed to drive these behemoths.

Trucking is a universe unto itself, a vital sub-culture. Cowboys never really disappeared, they just became semi drivers and bikers. The highways revolve around them, from truck stops to rest areas, restaurants and repair shops. Whenever there is an emergency, you better hope you can find a trucker for a friend.

Long before the cell phone was invented, it was a CB world out there. Recently we got grounded during a wind storm and confirmed that the CB is still very much in use. Fact is, if you were born north of the Mason Dixon line, there's not much point in you using one. You won't get an answer. The deep southern drawl rules the airwaves. When, on rare occasion, a timid northern voice pops on the line (sounding anemic and insecure in comparison to the authoritative boom of a Confederate growl), the radios go silent. Like a field full of prairie dogs that disappear down their holes when a coyote comes sniffing, the truckers wait in silence for the intruder to give up and go away. Soon the chatter begins again, and things are back to normal.

Stage Fright

*F*or years stage fright was a monster I couldn't control. The break-through for me came via identifying the irrational basis of my fear. One day it hit me- I was like a little child clinging to my mother's aprons; I feared being hated. Children who meet new people are almost always shy- and if there is too much activity or even enthusiasm, they cry. We have this primal feeling built into us and have to get past it- but I hadn't. So I realized it was time, just like that. I said "Look at all the people who go to work every day without being paralyzed with fear- the stage is my office- now get a grip!" This realization helped immensely, along with the thought that the audience members were my friends. After all, people who can't stand your music aren't going to come out to see you perform, so this is already a comfortable atmosphere. I'm not saying there isn't excitement and energy before a show- if there wasn't it would be dreary. But fear is a negative kind of energy that you don't need.

When I first started touring my abilities were less than solid. I believe that the fans forgave me many times. Over the years I've learned a great deal about performing and today it's hard for anything to distract me. However, here is a scenario which can rattle me: knowing that a celebrity or someone important I haven't seen in many years is in the house. I never want to be told beforehand- only afterwards, as I end up being preoccupied and anxious the entire time. Anything that can cause a sudden lack of focus is probably the culprit. I was stepping on stage with one foot in the air when someone said "Leo Kottke is in the audience." I tripped and fell. Ladysmith Black Mambazo came to hear me play in Holland. Bonnie Raitt visited the show in Utrecht- and because I knew it, it was scary. Linda Barnes, successful author of many mystery novels, is a fan and has written me into her books. One night I was told she was at the show, and I did the worst performance of my life. She probably eliminated me immediately from any further adventures. Having label people, reviewers, friends or family in the house makes it harder. Receptions, meeting people beforehand- not a good idea for me. My best bet is a quiet space and uninterrupted focus at show time- then, meeting people afterwards is easy.

Foot-In-Mouth Disease

Got this from Dad- only he's not held responsible and I am. People think he's cute when he rambles on and says wacky things. I fear I will be run out of town. Blurting things is part of my dad's nature. It's about making provocative, rude remarks which are almost always inappropriate. I see people who start and then can't stop, like a windup toy. It's sad, because they always feel sorry later, but you can't withdraw the damage of ugly words.

Of course I do it too, but over time I have endeavored to weed out the personal and the unkind- to choose support, not criticism, acceptance, and not judgment. After all, I have been damaged by careless, insulting words, and as a result I understand the power of the tongue. Some of my less than brilliant remarks were not as hostile as stupid, and I became determined to do this less and less over time. However I still hold views that are radical. I'm still a solo agent, and under the circumstances will probably always make startling remarks. But now I strive to have them be useful, not harmful. I believe that having a platform like a stage brings with it a solemn responsibility. I'd rather make a fool of myself than hurt someone else.

Aftershock

I can't count the nights I have spent tossing and turning after a show feeling embarrassed and ominous, thinking that whatever I said was totally out there- that I had made a complete jerk out of myself. By morning the feeling would ease and I would get on with my life. But over time I became much more careful not to go off the deep end- to be sure my ramblings and babblings had some kind of direction to them. It has taken a great deal of practice, trial and error to get a handle on this. Because I'm relatively vocal, I can't help surprising- if not outraging- someone sooner or later. This just seems to come with the territory. A wise friend once said "Nobody ever got in trouble for saying nothing." Of course he's right. However I don't think I'm ever going to be the picture of discretion. I've never known how to act the part of casual observer- I've never been laid back about anything. Perhaps this is why I resonated so totally with blues. Blues is not about mild-mannered feelings. It is not about polite people sitting together with their legs crossed taking tea.

Vanishing Habitat

1 probably know more than a developer about which areas of the country have gone from wilderness to malls and condos in the last twenty five years. The only way to know more is by using satellite imagery. Every time we come through a beautiful wooded area (with a few wild creatures still clinging beyond hope to their habitat), it's possible to predict with an ominous certainty that the next time through we'll be looking at a new exit with the exhaustingly familiar group of mega stores scarring the landscape. At some point there will simply not be enough people with credit cards to keep shopping at all these stores- some will have to fold, abandoned and crumbling into the ground- but tragically, the wilderness will be gone forever. I heard recently that in one particular state, 130 acres of wilderness disappear every day to development. Has anyone considered: is the supposed increase in the quality of life created for human beings by building another place to shop (and go into debt) worth the dwindling wilderness and displacement of countless animals from their last best hope for existence? The infinite ribbon of roadways which now encircle the globe have severely impacted the migration patterns of animals. This is having devastating effects on species, not to mention the tragic numbers of animals left crushed and rotting on roadways. We saw a story on the news about a fox who showed up in a coffee shop in Chicago- everyone was so surprised. Hello... he used to live there. I have seen the polluted little strips of grass surrounding malls and gas stations- and in amongst the litter and plastic bags, a bunny clinging to his meager existence. Now the remaining grass areas are covered in pesticides. I wonder, is there any limit to our power to destroy?

Reflections On A Dream

Last night I had a horrifyingly vivid dream. All the trees on earth came crashing down at the same time. There was not one tree left standing, and earth was a wasteland. Something happened globally that killed them all simultaneously. It was as if they were saying to us "The earth is no longer a fit place for us to live." So they all collapsed and died. It was only a matter of time until we joined them in extinction. This was the end of the world. Make no mistake... this is prophetic...

Rory Block

Softball At The Rest Areas

For several years road manager Suzanne and I traveled together. She was a fantastic lady with supernatural endurance and patience who wanted nothing to do with the idea that there might be any limitation to being female, so she jumped into the driver's seat- carted everything from instruments, wardrobe, kitchen equipment, and product into hotels and venues- and never let me lift the guitar. She lived on strong coffee. One thing Suzanne didn't love was my obsession with stopping at rest areas to play softball. I had decided at a certain point that this was the perfect way to get exercise, and it worked like a charm. Drive, then take a break to pull out the ball and

mitts, throw and run. Work up a sweat, get back into the car, and voila, you could stay in shape. But Suzanne hated softball, so it was torture for her. But even with all this- the improvement to my health etc, came the realization that a minivan was just too cramped.

Back Rooms
And Other Horrible Realities:
Or Why I Invested In A Tour Bus

I've seen some of the most disgusting back rooms on the planet, the kinds of places that make a weary tour survivor downright depressed. When you've just crossed the country jammed into a cramped car, nothing could be more demoralizing. We know about the graffiti-covered hole-in-the-wall places with the bare bulb on a wire and the crumbling plaster- those are part of the deal when you're getting established. Every freaked-out-no-name band since the dawn of time has scribbled something lewd on the walls. But I would have expected better at a particularly nice folk venue in the Midwest. The back room was a heavily trafficked public bathroom by day. I almost died when they opened the door and ushered me in. It looked like a bomb had gone off, or maybe a football team had just had a party there. I dropped a few paper towels on the floor (the only islands in a sea of filth), and balanced on them with my bare feet. Carefully, one leg at a time, I stepped into my pants, keeping the fabric off the floor at all times. I was tempted to spend a few minutes straightening up the place. No, this was too big a problem for one touring artist- which begs the point- how hard would it be to get a little soap and water and clean up the Green Room? Get a dag nabbin' broom and sweep, bring in a little table, a nice lamp, a full-length mirror, a place to hang clothing... put a light above the mirror so a person can see their face. Then, put out a little bowl of fruit, some healthy snacks, and a vase of fresh flowers. How hard could this be? I have often vowed that if I ever owned a venue, the first thing I would do would be to create a lovely back room, a haven for exhausted musicians. I can't tell you how many perfectly nice places have deplorable, revolting back rooms. It sends a really bad message and makes life on the road so much harder. In fairness I should mention that there are nicely appointed back rooms out there, but for now, we look at the worst. And I can say, that within a certain circuit (and this does not include the theaters which always have beautiful back rooms), an appalling number fit the former description. This is why I couldn't do it without my bus.

The First RV

One night in the Detroit area I had a vivid dream and woke up with the realization that we had to get an RV. Coincidentally this was motor home heaven as many of the major manufacturers are located there, and the search began. The first one I looked at was a cab-over known as a "Class C"- a van with a wider body welded on top. It wobbled a bit, but it was the cutest thing I had ever seen with a dining table, wallpaper, curtains in the windows, a bed, bathroom, kitchen, and closets. This was fun. We spent the entire day looking, but came back

to the first one as the nicest of all. I made the wild and crazy decision to get it. We sat down in the office with someone who looked like a music business mogul. He filled two chairs, was covered in jewelry, and had an aggressive, pushy attitude. He said "Do you want it or NOT? There's a line of people sitting outside who'll grab it if you don't." I knew this was stupid, but I wanted it. The Gulf War had just started and gas guzzling vehicles were practically being given away. With a huge reduction in price and five thousand dollars in tour cash plunked onto the table for a deposit, we drove away with this house on wheels, leaving my minivan at a friend's house in nearby Ann Arbor. Then another friend drove it back to the East Coast, and afterwards we put her on a train back to Michigan. It was too smooth to be believed.

As we chugged down the road I thought "Now you've done it! You've gone mad!" I was terrified that I'd regret the decision and that it would turn out to be a real albatross. But as we continued on our journey it proved to be an excellent decision. Life on the road was finally becoming more comfortable.

When the war ended I traded it in. Now there was a recession and the smaller cab-overs had become more valuable, where the bigger vehicles, known as "Class A" (one solid body), were the ones going for much less. In a stroke of luck I got a trade-in value greater than what I owed the bank, and ended up with a real, sizable tour bus. The one I own today is a forty two foot long diesel pusher with slide out sides. I couldn't ask for a better way to tour. In reality it is the only way I could continue. If I did not have my own space on the road I would have to retire as my body could not take the strain of a different bed every night, questionable food, horrible bathrooms, and other unknowns. Having once gotten locked into a filthy gas station rest room in a western state, I don't relish the idea of giving up my quiet, safe, clean space.

If I Was King Of The Forest

Today I feel regret about one important thing... the carbon footprint. The need for diesel fuel to roll down the road and operate the generator bothers me immensely. But let's consider- say I were to fly. Unfortunately passenger jets are among the top environmental offenders. They suck up oxygen at an inconceivable rate and spew out noxious fumes and pollutants which destroy the ozone layer and create toxins which sift down across the last wild spaces on earth. Why do we travel so much? I leave that to the experts to figure out. If I parked the bus there would be rental cars, hotels and restaurants. Hotels would have more sheets and towels to launder, more dishes to wash, more electrical use- and so on. Restaurants would have more cans to open, and more propane to use cooking more dinners. The rental car would require gasoline... and someone to wash and vacuum it after each use. The whole ball of wax is a mess and I don't think anyone can really say which method is better, carbon molecule for carbon molecule. The solution lies in alternative fuels- for my bus, for jets, for homes and businesses- wind, solar, and clean engine fuels. Nothing is going to change much until such things are made widely available. If I knew how, I'd invent and implement. I'd do it now, and not in "ten years."

And let's not forget the unbelievable mess created by CDs. This is a VAST source of waste plastic. It follows us all around, and almost no one complains about it. And before you tout the idea of eliminating CDs and making all music cyber- what about your computer, office equipment, in fact ALL technology? What happens to the syringes from medical waste, X-ray machines, and diagnostic equipment? The list is endless. Almost none of the mega equipment we surround ourselves with is "biodegradable" (which the dictionary defines as: "capable of being decomposed by bacteria or other living organisms"). So we have a gigantic problem which is choking out life and swallowing us whole. I try to do everything within my personal power to reduce all waste. On the road we carry recycling in the shower until it is unmanageable. We constantly search for recycling bins, asking at venues, stores and hotels. Once in a while someone takes our bags home with them to add to their own recycling. Other times we trailer the stuff all the way home! In case you were unaware, across this country, public recycling is often impossible to find. How can we reverse the environmental problems if something as basic as recycling is still a secret? In Europe they frequently have recycling bins on street corners. We MUST do this as well or sink under the weight of our own waste.

If it was up to me no manufacturer would ever be allowed to produce anything that was poisonous. But if such a material was essential to survival, then let that same manufacturer by law take back the packaging or unused portion and detoxify it in a laboratory- period. Vile toxins manufactured and handed to irresponsible humans is a problem bigger than anyone acknowledges. We find oil change refuse, gasoline and fuel, pesticides, paint, and solvents dumped everywhere on the road- in the woods- in streams- and in otherwise pristine areas. Primates eat fruit and drop the seeds. Humans drink soda and drop the cans. Nothing has changed except the nature of the trash. Primates planted seeds with their rubbish. We poison water and soil with ours.

Footprints Of Carbon

The world is filled with imbeciles...
They get up in the morning, act imbecilic,
And then, it's straight to bed.
Sometimes there's a sandwich or two,
Most likely ham and American cheese,
in the interim between waking and sleeping,
Velveeta will do, or some donuts...
then bed.
Your carbon footprint continues to swell,
Its vast proportions blotting out the skyscraper next door.
There the sun shines only on the rubbish heap,
Now incalculably large,
With your name on it.

Rory Block

Good News, Bad News

Somewhere in the Great Plains, I had a show with a good friend- an excellent musician and one of the best in his field. His travel adventures would no doubt fill several books. I got a call saying he was going to be delayed coming through some bad weather. I started the show and he arrived about half way into the first set. I think we shared the second set. This is just what happens out there. That night he told me a true story which embodies every performers restless nightmare: he was traveling to a gig and called the venue to see how the weather was up the road. The promoter answered and said, in a relaxed and mellow kind of way, "Well, I've got good news and bad news. The good news is the weather is fine. The bad news is the show was last night."

The Recurring Nightmare

I am trying to get ready for a show and rummaging through outfits-nothing seems right. Each one I try looks worse than the last. Time is passing. Suddenly I can see the venue from above. It's large- very large, and filled to capacity. I note with concern that I need to hurry as I don't want to be late. But more time passes and I'm still unable to pick an outfit. A terrible feeling of anxiety and frustration sets in. Other elements play in to create further delay. I note that some people are starting to leave, and sense a disgruntled attitude beginning to spread through the house. There is a general murmuring. For unknown reasons I am both a participant and a spectator, able to move from the dressing room and my general chaos to a bird's-eye view above the house. I watch as more and more people leave. Many are standing and milling about, yet I continue to be powerless to get ready. Now it is late, and folks are angry. In this terrible dream I have made a disaster out of the night, created much ill will, and damaged my reputation and credibility, among other things. I awake in an ominous sweat. This is a real nightmare, one that for years wouldn't leave me alone.

Color Me Wild

*T*apping, humming, singing, rhyming. If I wasn't banging on boxes I was inventing melodies with wandering narratives. My mother saw this continual flow of music as proof that I was "nervous." It was annoying, she said. Of course that made me feel terrible- but the river refused to stop flowing. When my children were born they were regaled with endless tunes, adventures and accompanying percussion. As my first critics, they gave me excellent reviews. I could see the delight on their faces. Sooner or later I would have to write a book, make a children's album, or both.

It began with *American Children*, a project which included many of my good friends- Maria, John Sebastian, Taj Mahal and others. It got me to dip into the well of material I had just sitting there from the time my children went to the Mountain Road School. Being too broke to afford tuition, I had negotiated some kind of swap arrangement, and a couple times per week I taught music, song writing, and even art classes. The song writing was a big success. Most of the kids were somewhere around eight years old, and their minds were anything but inhibited. I would cast out an idea and the kids would get excited. We wrote about an "Outer Space Elephant"- invented "Mango Man And The Papaya People", and "Billy The Bad". I would play chords and the kids would shout approval. Then I scribbled the words on the blackboard and we were off. Two of the songs ended up on *American Children*,

after which the seed had been planted and it seemed it was time to make a full album. Alcazar records was excited about the project, so we recorded in a little studio on the Woodstock side of the river. I got to go nuts and be the kid I have always been. I spoke in silly voices, made chicken sounds, and wrote whacky songs with wild words and wilder chords. The record is called *Color Me Wild* and seems to bounce from children's label to children's label. I don't even have a copy of it right now, but I meet young people who grew up listening to this record.

Art classes were another matter. I came up with various ideas for projects, and the most amazing one had to be a "draw your parents as however-you-see-them" kind of theme. It started out a very positive idea, but a couple of the kids revealed some startling images. One boy drew a large drawing of his father crying while his mother was pictured as the president. The father was deeply upset by this. Perhaps this art business was just too hot to handle.

The Man With The Brain Tumor

There will always be an endless stream of memories, some good and some bad, and many consigned to the sea of forgetfulness until some unexpected person or event triggers one for better or for worse. One such memory came back to me recently.

I received a letter from a woman on behalf of a friend of hers who was dying of brain cancer. He had expressed his final wishes, and one of them was to hear me sing "The Water Is Wide" in person- one last time. This was deeply touching to me. How could I offer anything valuable enough to be a part of someone's last wishes? It was overwhelming to contemplate. And I wondered, would I be up to the task? Would I be capable of singing a wonderful version of the song under such sad circumstances? It meant going to a hospital in Massachusetts and performing the song at his bedside.

We met this man's friend in the lobby, and were led to his room. Laid out on a bed with his head wrapped in a huge bandage, he gathered all his strength and sat bolt upright. Feeling incredibly inadequate, I tried to say something appropriate to the gravity of the situation. But what could I say that would be of any help? I don't remember the conversation- we were all pretty quiet. I closed my eyes and started to sing. The level of emotion was so intense it seemed I could barely manage, but the sound came out, and I got through the song. He stayed silent for a moment and then applauded- but I felt I had done a mediocre version where an earth shaking rendition was required. This man was about to be escorted by angels to another realm. The feeling that I could have done a better job haunted me, but when his friend later wrote to tell us he had died, she indicated that he said my personal performance to him was one of the highlights of his final days.

Sometimes life holds such overwhelming sadness I just can't contain it all, but I believe that someday, somehow, it will all make sense. If we could use the sorrow we feel from the loss of life to increase the joy of living it, that would be one valuable lesson gained. Tell people we love them, spend time with friends and family. Enjoy each moment, "For we know not the day nor the hour." I heard someone say that on a deathbed no one ever says "Darling, please bring me my gold watch. I just want to see it one last time." Instead people ask for their estranged family members, old friends and loved ones to be with them. This should help us to understand which things are of real value. Perhaps we can adjust our priorities now if we contemplate this.

Something similar happened on another occasion with this same song. A man who was dying of AIDS came to a show in a wheelchair. His friends passed me a note asking to hear "The Water Is Wide." If only my mother could have known how her little bedside song would extend outwards through the years! A pebble dropped into water sends out a ripple that continues around the world. Her song was just such a pebble.

All Things Considered

My cousin Melissa Block, youngest daughter of my uncle Danny, is now the producer of NPR's top news program "All Things Considered." She jets all over the globe covering relevant issues. Her older sister Bethany is a doctor in Cambridge, Massachusetts. When we were growing up we used to visit our aunt and uncle at their home in Brooklyn. Bethany and Melissa were four or five years younger and would run about busily with their toys.

Melissa was a cute, precocious three-year-old with large round eyes and dark hair which bounced around her face in ringlets. One day when we were visiting, Bethany and Melissa got into a sisterly row and Melissa called her older sister a "Doo doo head." This struck me as hysterically funny, and in my way of thinking was one of the most fabulous, descriptive things to call someone if you wanted to make a point; a title so cool and amusing to me as a youngster that it became a permanent part of my vocabulary. It doesn't necessarily have to be said in an insulting way- in fact I think of it as entirely affectionate.

A number of years before Melissa came to NPR, a reporter for "All Things Considered" drove to my father's house in New Hampshire to do a "Father/Daughter" tribute- a special on Dad and I for Father's Day. She brought all her audio equipment and settled in to record us for her piece. But instead of playing music with me, Dad said "Wait, let me call my son." My father had given my brother land and a house adjacent to his own in New Hampshire which was a stone's throw away by foot. He actually phoned my brother to come over and fumble with the guitar even though the interviewer had just asked Dad to play a song with me. My brother is not particularly a guitar player, but that's not the point. Dad just couldn't seem to acknowledge that NPR was there because of me, his daughter (now an established professional performer who had grown up playing music with him), and that the story was about the father and the daughter, not the father and the son (who no one had heard of). When the interviewer (now an unwitting witness to this strange dynamic) changed the direction of her inquiry to ask my father for any anecdotes from my childhood, he flatly said he couldn't think of any, as if this was as normal as apple pie. It was a stinging slap in the face, and an uncomfortable reminder of his general denial of my existence. I wondered, was this about some old cultural taboo regarding female children where you were only as important as the number of sons you had sired? Daughters around the world are marginalized, sometimes hated, even killed. Had all these negative messages favoring sons over daughters influenced our father? Very likely, yes. This was the atmosphere I endured throughout most of my life- until just a few years before Dad's senility set in. For the briefest, but most wonderful period of time, Dad did an about-face.

Ron Bach

From the late eighties to the mid-nineties Ron accompanied me on all my tours. I met him at a studio in Connecticut where he was the top engineer. With his beret and dark hair, he looked very European. Tired of having his last name incessantly misspelled, he shortened it from Bacchiocchi to Bach (which he felt would be easier all around), giving him the somewhat intriguing name of Ron Bach. He was a superbly talented engineer who had worked with an array of incredible artists like Chakka Kahn, Glenn Frey of the Eagles and audiophile Paul Winter. He was the epitome of a true perfectionist and a computer geek from before computer geeks were invented. He was beta testing the recording programs when they were in their infancy, and he was one of the very first to be using these high-tech methods. He had studied computers in college when computers were these clicking, clacking contraptions that spit out tape and filled an entire room. In his spare time Ron sat around reading bulky manuals with fine print, or science fiction and new age channeling books. As a result he knew how to use each and every program that came out the moment it was released- for Ron, there was no learning curve. He did these things in his sleep.

He was six foot one and reed thin. When I first saw him he had an ethereal quality as if he had recently survived a near-fatal illness. We were working on *I've Got A Rock In My Sock* and staying nearby. One morning Ron came out of his room with a sky blue dress shirt wrapped around his shoulders. He was holding it closed over his chest but I could see his smooth, hairless body. He had good looking features, bright blue eyes, black hair and fair skin- a startling combina-tion- and this made him look extremely interesting. At some point he must have had something like measles or acne which left scarring on his face, but it was minor and only a part of his unique appearance.

Ron and I were just friends when we mixed a song called "Lovin' Whiskey" at the studio in Norwalk, Connecticut. The shell of the song had been recorded in various stages, and the original version had some whiney, self-pitying words... the "You broke my heart and are so mean and life is so unfair poor me" kind that sounded totally amateur. Later I felt that they had to be stronger, so I pulled out a letter to a former flame which had started its life on a paper napkin and then evolved into a hand written letter which I copied and stashed at the bottom of a pile of scribbles in a drawer. I was unbearably shy in those days and was sure my little epistle was stupid, so I sent everyone out of the studio but the engineer (who by nature is often a very neutral presence), and I sang it while making endless excuses regarding the silliness of the song. At the eleventh hour I played it for Shari Kane (an excellent blues guitarist I first met on the road in Michigan- the same woman whose friend drove my minivan home after I bought the cab-over RV), and she said, in her usual uncanny, direct way "I'll kill you if you don't put that song on the record." Her keen insight turned out to be spot-on. Good call, Shari! "Lovin' Whiskey" was soon to become the biggest success of my career.

A year or so later Ron and I recorded the *House Of Hearts* album, a tribute to Thiele. At first he had girlfriend troubles and I was an outsider thinking "If only he was available," but soon they parted and Ron and I became a couple. It was one of those mellow beginnings where the lines between friendship and relationship gradually blur. At a time when I was grieving horribly over Thiele's death, Ron showed tremendous compassion. Although he had never met Thiele, he accompanied me to the tree where Thiele died and we sat there together in the grass with his arms wrapped around me in silence.

Ron probably fit the category of "Sensitive New Age Guy," and yet he had a sarcastic wit and made many astute observations and irreverent remarks. Once, in an attempt to shed some light on a particular issue, we sought out a New Age therapist, thinking this would be a gentler way to go. She was of absolutely no help, sat there mooning over Ron, and was incapable of hearing my grievance. She said "New Age women would give their 'eyeteeth' for this man." I remember thinking she was useless as a relationship counselor and had broken the very first professional rule by totally taking his side. She came off like a therapist who would cheat with your man...

With John Hall and Ron. Photo: Carla Gahr

Best Blues & Originals

Rounder Records started in someone's basement- a tiny label with the humblest beginnings. For years they had been clear about the fact that they couldn't compete in the commercial market. That took long dollars, they explained, and their resources at that time were not even close- but they gave me total artistic freedom, which was more precious than gold or a big budget. I knew early on that my career was going to be a slow and steady journey, and that it would be based on incessant touring, recording, and very hard work. The moment I accepted this was the moment my career jumped to the next level- the

RORY BLOCK

Best Blues and Originals

moment *High Heeled Blues* got reviewed in *Rolling Stone*- and the moment writer Dave Marsh said "Some of the most singular and affecting country blues anyone, man or woman, black or white, old or young has cut in recent years." This was an auspicious beginning.

One day I learned that my compilation CD *Best Blues And Originals* had been licensed in Europe. Next I heard that a single had been released. This decision was made without me in the room, otherwise I would have said something stupid that would have put a kibosh on the whole thing. I have learned this- if I expect it, or want it badly, it doesn't happen. If it's the farthest thing from my mind, it happens-

Murphy's law, or something like it. Other people don't have to worry about this, only me. The whole thing came as a total surprise. "Wow!" I thought "They really mean business!" It seemed like someone had a few dollars to spend- and then I put it out of my mind.

The humblest tune, the one I thought no one would ever care about- THAT was the single... "Lovin' Whiskey"- the little letter, at first scrawled on a napkin in a restaurant, then copied out and sent to a man with a drinking problem.- that was the song they chose! I almost didn't put the song on the record. I sang it only once in the studio as I never expected to use it anyway. It was added to the album as an after-thought. An influential Dutch radio promoter found this song person-ally meaningful and made it his special project. All of a sudden I was getting letters asking me to write out the words. The European fans wanted to understand. This was incredible. Soon a fax arrived with a hand drawn champagne glass tilting over and bubbles flying- "Con-gratulations, you have a gold record." With fingers clenched tightly against the arms of the seat, I flew to Europe and an amazing new fan base.

A Gold Record

I have to admit, the joy of being handed a Gold Record is unprece-dented. So is the joy of winning an award. In front of twenty thousand people at The Pink Pop Festival in Holland, I accepted a plaque show-ing that the record had sold in excess of 25,000 in The Netherlands. I almost died. I was the little girl who so many had counseled to give up before I even started.

But despite all, we must do it for ourselves first and foremost. We must say "It doesn't really matter"... even if inside we would love nothing more than a Grammy and a one hundred thousand dollar recording contract. We certainly do assume money is happiness, and MORE money is MORE happiness, regardless of all the warnings of this being illusion. From my point of view I just wanted to pay my bills, and after a lifetime of being broke, I finally began to make money. It snuck up gradually. One year my accounting program said I had grossed six figures. I couldn't believe this, and looked at it again and again. There must be some mistake. I said to myself, "That's what a doctor makes!" I hadn't realized that over time I found myself pretty much rolling in money, at least by my extremely humble standards. Shopping was my greatest joy and the money never seemed to run out. I even came back from Europe once and paid off the mortgage with tour cash. But that was back in the good old money days- and today is a completely different world.

Lovin' Whiskey

Well If you live in dusty twilight baby, that's OK,
There are women at the bar to greet you every day,
And you can take them back to lie with you and visit Jamie's room,
But they can never take the pain away or brighten all the gloom,
And if your hands are clenched in sorrow, may it help you ease your pain,
Though the windows have a view of city rain, city rain...

If you walk in constant sorrow and you cry for me,
And if you're hit with painful memories maybe then you'll see,
That if you drown yourself in liquor because it keeps you company,
Then just remember who you're losin' and be proud to set me free,
Because it don't talk back, it don't disagree, it just makes you see so hazily,
But in the morning light your life is scattered with the wind, scattered with the wind...

They tell you on the telephone to let him go,
They tell you he's a sinking ship, and he's trying to pull you down, don't you know,
But every time you call me up and say you want me back you know you break my heart,
You want me to come back home and try again, you want me to make a brand new start,
But if wisdom says to let him go, then it's hell, because you just don't know,
Until you've tried to love a man who's lovin' whiskey, lovin' whiskey...

My baby left me for the bottle and the lure of the night life,
Good times and crazy women and another glass of Tanqueray,
But if wisdom says to let him go, then it's hell, because you just don't know,
Until you've tried to love a man who's lovin' whiskey, lovin' whiskey!

Words and music by Rory Block

$\mathcal{T}$he song "Lovin' Whiskey" was a real life situation with no embellishments. I just took a "Dear John" letter I wrote to someone and put it to music.

Sometimes when you meet someone you feel as if you've known them all your life. What attracted me to this person was his soul- from his wavy black hair to his sparkling mischievous eyes he was an artist inside and out, and there was a look of depth and understanding in his face. We were introduced at the first recording session of *The Woodstock Mountains Review*, but at the time we were both involved and there was no thought of ever getting together. After that I didn't see him for a couple of years.

One day I was in a state of utter despair. I had just discovered my husband was having an affair with some young girl who had wandered into the Sandal Shop. I had two kids, a grand old house, and the world was falling apart around me. The phone rang, and it was that beautiful guy I hadn't seen since the recording session, and he was now single. The timing was perfect. He said "I think I should drive over to see you." After an evening of talking he said "You feel like 'old lady' material to me." This was the best compliment in the world. It meant that in his estimation I was someone he could get serious about. I had the same feeling about him.

Getting involved completely wiped out all the pain and rejection of the past. It was so much better than anything I had known before. Soon it became the deepest connection of my life. I was crazy about this man. But in time a pattern of drinking and carousing emerged that eventually led me to consider the possibility that he had an alcohol problem. It seems that we are attracted and fall in love before we realize the full extent of the issues, and by then it is that much harder to leave- but when I think back I realize there are always little warning signs we can choose to ignore- but that's another issue. So I called one of the first 1 800 hotlines in existence and bent the ear of an incredibly patient lady who clearly understood everything about this issue. She told me things I didn't want to hear, in particular she kept saying that I couldn't save him, that I couldn't do anything to influence his decision. She said he would have to "bottom out" if that's where he was going to take it. She compared him to a sinking ship and said if I stayed I would get pulled under with him. In the meantime I was clinging to the idea that I could somehow help, but she led me to understand the error in my thinking. She also said something amazing- that sometimes alcoholics are beautiful people. They might be soulful, artistic and honest- musicians, artists and so on, and that they could be easy to love- when they were sober. I felt like she knew him! Of course I don't have space here to describe the downside and all the ways you can no longer enjoy the good things because of the destructive influences of alcohol addiction. There are a wealth of books, meetings, and countless resources for that.

The breakup was one of the hardest things I ever had to do. I drove around screaming with the windows rolled up until I couldn't scream anymore- desperate screams of agony and frustration- I wanted things to work out more than anything in the world at that point. This person I loved from the deepest place in my soul was diving off into the abyss- and all I could do was "Let go and let God."

He was one of those people I just kept on loving no matter what else was going on in my life. Once or twice I contacted him and we had awkward visits- he was always with someone else though his exploits were short lived. He even met another woman named Rory- how likely is that? In retrospect both our lives were turned upside down like the little snowy landscapes under glass- tilted, the flakes swirl everywhere. The slightest movement sets everything in motion again.

I compared everyone to him for years and held him up as the unattainable standard. He on the other hand went a little crazy and lived on the edge for a while longer until something made him decide to rein in. He stopped drinking and has thanked me for it- I say no- it wasn't me. But he is kind about it. The sad business of it is that we lost each other, though we both gained wisdom.

The "Dear John" Letter

A few years after that I had an unfinished little piece of music. I had experimented with a drum machine and created a short section, a bar or two, of a pattern. Then someone looped it for me in the studio and it wrapped around this little acoustic tune, but because the format of the song changed while the loop didn't, it caused the pattern to reverse itself throughout the song, creating a strangely intriguing effect. Then I moved the words of the "Dear John" letter around a bit to fit the song, and I sang it only once- what we usually call a "reference vocal." No one would care about such a personal song, I thought. The last thing I ever expected was for this unfinished, unadorned song to become so popular. Perhaps it had some of the simplicity of "True Colors," at least in the rhythm track.

That's how "Lovin Whiskey" came to be written. It has been bread and butter to me ever since, and I am incredibly grateful to the people who bought the record, understood the problem, and who have shared their own compelling personal stories with me night after night- to this day.

The Netherlands- My Second Home

On the first tour of the Netherlands we played in someone's living room. I have never been able to get anyone from Holland to recognize the name of the town it was so small. We got off the train, were met by the homeowners, and given a room which was directly above the donkey stalls in the barn. The smell of ammonia was so strong I could barely breathe. However the place was an exceedingly charming, antique farm, and some of the people who were there that night continued to follow my career, later coming to my shows at theaters in the bigger towns.

Holland became like a second home. I knew every street and market in a beautiful neighborhood in Amsterdam where we often stayed. Job Zomer, owner of the Dutch label Munich Records, used to urge me to buy a house in the Netherlands so I would have a place of my own when touring there. Some devoted fans started "The Blockheads Fan Club," which for a while had a newsletter. Ronald Coster, who founded it, still comes to my shows. I can hardly express what considerate, polite, civilized people the Dutch are- but because they are also extremely humble, they refuse to take any compliments. I remember being jet lagged, in a foul mood, and trying to check into a hotel where the room wasn't ready. My bad attitude was met with the most gracious patience. I felt embarrassed- here was this kind person trying to do everything to accommodate me- and I didn't deserve it.

Gunther

Gunther was the Dutch road manager assigned to us by Double You Concerts, and he turned out to be the best thing I had ever found- a superbly professional, highly experienced, infinitely patient, tireless man who lived to accommodate artists on the road. Gunther was always on time, always low pressure, took care of the details behind the scenes, never got lost, always helped load in and out, and talked to all the venues. Gunther did all of this without ever driving too fast, because if there's anything I hate, it's speeding. I'm well known for this. Someone is always assigned to watch the driver like a hawk and if they don't get the message, they're yanked from the driver's seat and replaced by someone who does get it.

Gunther was tall and thin. He always wore super-tight, faded black jeans, cowboy boots that slammed the ground percussively when he walked, a short black jean jacket, and had long, tousled hair- what you could call "big hair." I doubt he did anything to it whatsoever, but he had a cool look that comes from very little fussing.

Gunther was just as good and efficient with a band as a solo artist. I remember hearing his boots clanking down the hallway every morning knocking on each door to let everyone know it was time to rise. I wrote a song for Gunther that detailed the sound of his boots, his long strides, his jiggling of door handles, and his efficient way of rousing and collecting everyone. If you've ever toured with a band, this just might be the hardest job of all. A great many European hotels have seemingly been constructed of metal and concrete, which releases an unbelievably loud pinging sound as you go up and down stairs. This highlighted Gunther's walking style no doubt.

Koko Taylor- First Lady Of The Blues

One of the first people I opened for in Europe was Koko Taylor. Koko is the powerful voice of the blues. She can out-rock just about anyone, and she makes getting older look sexy. In her red sparkly dress and boa, she grabs the mic, moves her hips, and howls like the siren call of Bessie Smith and Big Mama Thornton rolled into one. Everyone in the house goes nuts when Koko walks out onto the stage.

Koko and I have crossed paths many times over the years and had already been introduced, but one night in Germany we were the only two acts on the bill. Her band was there and watched me play. Later that night Koko called me up and dubbed me "Little Miss Dynamite" in front of the audience, a name I loved the moment I heard it. Afterwards we sat around talking about some of the challenges of life away from home- the difficulty of having family so far away, or loved ones too ill to travel- it's a part of touring we all understand.

Another gig we did together was televised- it was staged to look like a party. Later I discovered that the performance was recorded onto an early format called laser disc, which looked like an LP. Someone pointed this out to me at a record store in Paris and handed me a copy. People were going crazy that night because Julia Roberts was eating dinner in the restaurant downstairs. When I later inquired why I had

never been informed of this release, I was told I had signed a contract. Since I never had, it was clear it was some kind of bootleg for which I was receiving no royalties. I watched it once in the screening room of some high-end audio store in Connecticut just to be sure it was quality. Then we contacted the folks who released it, and they replied that I had signed a contract giving them permission to release this... royalty free? I don't think so. Then we had to hire a lawyer in the country of origin, and the best they could come up with is that I supposedly signed a contract which was entirely in a language I don't speak or understand. I don't think so. No one ever produced a copy of this contract which I supposedly signed. So there you have it, and it's out there, perhaps even now on DVD, and I make not a penny.

Bonnie's Rockin' Slide

I met Bonnie Raitt at a show in Massachusetts sometime in the '80s. I talked my way backstage, and when I got there she was totally welcoming. There we were, two women, born two days apart, both of us with fathers in the music business, both having received the exact same kind of guitar at the exact same age (eight years old, I think), both loving early blues. We even knew some of the very same rediscovered blues artists. But of course Bonnie played electric and had a commercial sound to her records I just couldn't match. I was humble around her- my stuff was so unimportant in comparison- that was my way of thinking.

I saw her again at various times over the years, once after the ghastly experience of missing the flight to Denver. When I finally arrived hours late for the festival where we were both performing, she was understanding. At her urging the festival tried to squeeze me into a different time in the lineup, but it simply wasn't possible. Some years later I stopped in to one of her shows at the Saratoga Performing Arts Center, and she invited me onto the stage. Little Feat, who I hadn't seen since the Chrysalis Records days, were also on the bill, and it was great to see my dear friend and conga player, Sam Clayton. Bonnie asked if I knew "Angel From Montgomery" and I nodded, having heard the title. I assumed my old harmony abilities would kick in- but the song was filled with the most amazing twists, turns and unusual changes, and I simply couldn't follow it. So I wandered around near one of the mics humming and smiling, but I was pretty much useless. I managed to join in the Conga line that danced across the stage, and a lot of my friends and neighbors who were there that night saw me and said that I was "great"... who knows what they meant. Bonnie, who has always been incredibly kind to me, said "That's OK, it's just good that you got up there."

Bonnie once invited me to speak at a special event to protest an environmental travesty of some kind- something nuclear I think that was going to ruin and pollute. She spoke boldly and eloquently as she always does, taking a stand for a better world. John Hall was there too and may have had something to do with politics at that point (he later got elected). Perhaps he and Bonnie had arranged a press meeting. Bonnie also invited me to join her at the Grammys a few years after her big win. I was not able to make it but kick myself often to think of the night I must have missed. Later I expressed my concern to her about how the Grammys have no category for Country Blues- in my mind the most foundational American music of all as the roots of modern blues and rock'n'roll. I asked if she could point this out to the Foundation, but she urged me to do it- I said, "they'll listen to you, they'll never listen to me." She was the one with clout. They didn't know me from Adam- witness the missing category!

The night I won the Blues Music Award for "Traditional Blues Female Artist of the Year" Bonnie was at the ceremony performing with Keb Mo. They had been touring together and made a terrific pair musically. Bonnie's presence lent tremendous credibility to the event, which had been overlooked in favor of rock awards for years. As we sat back stage afterwards with Dick Waterman and Keb Mo, she commented that I looked younger than my years. She said, "Didn't you ever do anything to dissipate yourself?" I had to laugh... no one is more beautiful than Bonnie. Dick took some pictures of the two of us that night, me waving my award about, which I've never seen. Later we crossed paths in Europe, this time after I had become well known there- but Bonnie was respectful and complimentary either way. She said nice things about me from the stage (Bonnie is known for her generous spirit and for lending a hand to other musicians). This night we were both performing in the same town, and in the same building- a multi-theater complex. Both shows were sold out- mine a four hundred seater, hers over 2,000. I remember the double doors at the back of the theater opening and Bonnie's hair highlighted with backlighting. I fell apart knowing she was there. Afterwards, I went to her show. She was gracious, introduced me to everyone in her band and invited me on the stage once again. This time it was just the two of us with our acoustic guitars. We traded verses on Tommy Johnson's "Big Road Blues." Finally, a show with Bonnie where I hadn't fallen apart. I had goose pimples as our two voices and guitars rang out powerful and clear into the darkened theater. Bonnie is truly an inspired player. She can improvise, something I have never been able to do. At the end of the song she leaned over and hugged me and said, "I love you." This is the kind of sisterhood I have always wanted.

In 1999 I asked her to play on my *Confessions of A Blues Singer* CD. She agreed and we began the complex dance of trying to connect our schedules. We finally had to settle for the remote overdub thing, and as we sat mixing Bonnie's part, I learned something about slide which I had never understood, and it unlocked the door to my becoming a better player. I always had this despair feeling about slide- I could never get it to sound like anything but a frazzle- it was always out of tune, tense, and incredibly stiff. As we isolated Bonnie's track and soloed it in the room, I heard this relaxed, funky vibrato- it was a lingering, easy-going, rocking style... and suddenly I got it. "It's so relaxed!" I said. It wasn't tense like I was playing it. So I tried the mellow, rocking thing, and in no time I found the "pocket" and started to work on it for real. It's kind of a Zen thing, like a tennis backhand. Everyone has to do it their own way. *Confessions of A Blues Singer* later won "Acoustic Blues Album of The Year."

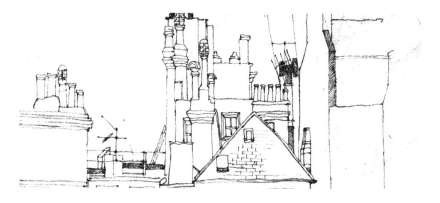

The Roots Of Rock'n'Roll

When Robert Johnson played "Rambling On My Mind" he defined the familiar pattern we recognize as twelve bar blues which connects acoustic blues to the more "commercial" sounding electric blues of artists like Elmore James and Muddy Waters. Then came artists like Elvis who used the blues format to break into a huge commercial market, Chuck Berry, and the more traditional electric blues of BB King. Song by song, the music moved from early to the modern styles we came to call rock'n'roll. Certain artists have done a great deal to make that bridge more obvious- Bonnie Raitt is one of them. Artists who brought a connecting form of electric blues to a wider audience- say like Paul Butterfield, Koko Taylor, Robert Cray, and others have helped to educate the public into the family connections between acoustic and electric blues.

Woodstock 2

John Sebastian said, "Whatever you do, get down there." The second Woodstock festival was a severe mob scene, but I made it to the festival grounds (a whole other drama) and found my way to the main stage. The event was being broadcast on Pay Per View, though I never saw it along with most of the other TV shows I have been on over the years. Bob Weir, Bruce Hornsby, Levon Helm, Rick Danko, and Jorma Kaukonen were preparing to go on stage. Jorma grabbed me and said "Come on up," so up I went and sang harmonies- "I see my light come shinin', from the west unto the east, any day now, any day now, I shall be released!" along with this all-star band. There I was with some of my favorite musicians and songwriters of all times. In front of me was a sea of mud covered bodies surging and sliding in the rain soaked soil. We had practically been stampeded getting in. Security gates were being toppled. It was the most chock-a-block, overflowing, super-crowded event I have ever seen before or since. On the way to the stage Levon Helm pulled up in a limo and I leaned in the window to say hello. Always a perfect gentleman, he smiled and said "Rory..." Later I learned that Levon was peeved that so many people were pushing their way on to the stage and somewhere during the event I heard that he left, but I saw nothing but people and cameras.

The Payne AME Church:
The little church on the hill

Perched on a hillside in Chatham, New York for over a hundred and fifty years, the Payne African Methodist Episcopal Church is a small family church with a devout tradition. Through the grapevine I had heard there was some great gospel singing there, and I became determined to go. It was my lifelong dream to sing with a choir, so I called Reverend Corinne, and she said, "This is God's house! Everybody's welcome."

The first Sunday I attended was a powerful sermon. I started thinking about Thiele, and the loss and sorrow in my life- and I couldn't stop crying. A lady in front of me handed me a tissue and I felt embraced by compassion. But my tears were no longer just about sorrow, they were also about joy- the joy of being in a place where people cared, where everyone worshipped with such enthusiasm and power- a place filled with Holy Ghost sweetness. I said to myself "This is home!"

Whenever I was not on the road I went to church. Not only did I sing with the choir, but I learned more about prayer and worship than in every other church I'd ever visited in my lifetime- combined.

It made me realize that something had been missing in my life, something I realized was there but didn't know how to find. It was as if I had been disconnected from close relationships with people- from the deeper things that made life real and fulfilling. There were always plenty of superficial contacts through business, but personal connection was lacking... and what I was missing was right there at the AME Church: warmth, love, openness, caring, and a sense of family... God's family.

Mama's Blues

There are days when every bone in her body is achin',
And she feels like everyone hates her, and she cannot speak,
And she sees herself as ugly, and not worthy of any love...
That's mama's blues (good God almighty), makes you want to cry,
That's mama's blues (said I'm talkin' about it), makes you want to
cry...

And he looks at her like she's crazy, and he does not understand,
He doesn't think she looks much different, or much fatter than before,
Yes she seems to look the same to him, and she's sad that he can't
relate to her state of mind...
That's mama's blues (great God almighty), makes you want to cry,
That's mama's blues (don't cha' know about it), makes you want to
cry...

Oh when mama gets the blues, papa tries to understand,
And he wonders what he needs to do, to be a better man,
Mama's cryin' cause she thinks she's ugly,
And the world, the world is out of hand...
That's mama's blues (good God almighty), makes you want to cry,
That's mama's blues (said I'm talkin' about it), makes you want to
cry...

Now she's lookin' at her body in the mirror,
And she's cryin' cause her waist is not as tiny as before the babies,
And she feels like the world is at an end, oh yeah,
And she thinks nobody's ever gonna want her body again,
And he wonders what she wants from him,
And he's sittin' drinkin' coffee at the breakfast stand,
And he tells the waitress that it's lonely at home,
And all the young girls, they take pity on him...
That's mama's blues (that's what I said), makes you want to cry,
That's mama's blues (don't cha' know about it), makes you want to
cry...

Words and music by Rory Block

*R*ounder used to give me the budget money and I would hand them a finished album. This worked out perfectly for thirteen albums. For the fourteenth recording the label had grown to the size where someone got assigned to your album, and suddenly I was expected to hand in a list of material, discuss all creative ideas, and send in samples of the songs- and this just didn't work for me. I understood that from their point of view staying connected to the projects on their label was important, but I was too used to artistic freedom to give any of it away. I think I create well in my own little vacuum. For me, recording an album is like giving birth- you just need a few assistants nearby to facilitate. Too many hands would get in the way.

Mama's Blues was my sixth recording for the label and I was on a roll. Largely a blues album, I planned to record my usual one or two Robert Johnson songs. The Payne Church happened to be located on a hillside adjacent to the train tracks that brought provisions and passengers into town since it was originally founded as Groats Corners in the 1800s, and freight trains still rumbled by from time to time. I had requested permission to record some songs at the church because of the great acoustics. Ron set up the mics and we prepared to record "Terraplane Blues." Just as we were starting a train rolled through, shaking the whole building. Ron started recording, and the intro of the song overlapped the huge rumble of the train. I couldn't think of a more fitting combination of elements.

The song "Mama's Blues" for which the CD was named, presented an interesting challenge. Although I had long since stopped drinking prior to live performances, I still had a habit of using alcohol in the studio to get in the mood for vocals. This is a total illusion of course as no drug ever made anyone a better singer- quite the opposite. All it really did was reduce fear, or elevate confidence- something that can be done as well or better without alcohol.

Ron and I were in the studio in Woodstock preparing to record the vocal for "Mama's Blues." Jorma Kaukonen had stopped in a few weeks earlier and put a crying, bending electric blues part on the shell of the song. Most guests and backup musicians prefer it when the words are there so they understand the meaning. Lacking words, a pro will ask what the song is about. I didn't even know this much at the time, but Jorma managed to capture a mood and set the tone for the song, no easy task. I decided to use some words I had scribbled down that seemed to match the sweet soul of his playing, and in this sense he influenced the direction of the song.

I looked around for my crutch- but there was no alcohol to be found. I told Ron we had to go out to find something to get me in the mood. Engineers don't have to agree with everything an artist does, but they do provide a nonjudgmental atmosphere which allows whatever has to happen to occur without hindrance. Patiently, Ron drove me around looking for a store, but it was Sunday and everything was closed. The very last option was a wretched-looking little roadside bar. "You could go in and get a glass of wine," Ron suggested. I looked at the place. I thought about the rotgut wine they would probably serve me in a dirty glass. No, I couldn't do it. So we drove back to the studio while Ron gently encouraged me- I could do it, he said, without alcohol. So it was a landmark vocal for me. It had a kind of sober honesty to it that actually enhanced the song- and changed everything. This dry vocal totally matched the mood and came out like a conversation straight from the heart.

When I handed in the album, Bill Nowlin at Rounder Records wrote me a note which I still have taped on the wall. "Great album. It's everything we'd wanted. Exactly on target." From my point of view all the magic came from the trust in our working relationship. I thrive in that atmosphere. That album later won the WC Handy (Blues Music) Award for "Acoustic Blues Album of the Year."

The Neighbor's Haunted House

There was once a prosperous mill on the Kinderhook Creek only a few hundred yards from my house. A picturesque covered bridge spanned the water with a tollbooth for wagons traveling between Boston and Albany. The building across the road is said to have been a stop on the Underground Railroad, and is rumored to have secret passages and chambers beneath the cellar which housed runaways during the Civil War. My neighbors often asked me to keep an eye on things when they were away because the furnace always seemed to shut down the minute they left. They had a hunch there was a spirit in the house who didn't like to be left alone. When the red light in their window came on the next day indicating the heat was off, I walked over. As soon as I opened the door I felt a whole group of souls leave the building. The women wore long dresses with fancy hats and the men had Civil War uniforms- I felt them walk across the street to my house, where I opened the door. They all came in, and I welcomed them, thinking that opposing them would not be a good idea. It was all very peaceful. They wanted to see what I had done to the house. I invited them to stop back again whenever they wished- after all, they had been here before me- and I think they must have been pleased as I never noticed anything again.

Prior to that I had experienced many negative energies in my house, particularly in one room- but after that time the tension eased and only a sense of peace remained. I felt my decision to welcome these departed souls was the reason for this. I speculated that they would have no issue with someone willing to acknowledge their right to come and go from their former homes. They just wanted to know that the new residents were tending to things in a proper fashion. Some day, as a soul drifting freely from place to place, I'm sure I will feel more than a little curiosity about the new caretakers. Or perhaps I'll be long gone and part of a celestial choir (give me the mic, please, I want to sing lead), in a place so glorious as to never look back. But if you ask me, here and there is a continuum. I try, but can't imagine a place more spectacular or glorious than this little planet.

Mother Marian

One of the first people I noticed at the Payne AME Church was Marian Van Ness. Ninety-two at the time- she sat in the same row and seat every Sunday. At her side was a powerful looking man with large hands who turned out to be her son Robert. She wore a dark blue dress, small hat, a gray tweed coat, and a most beautiful expression on her face. Marian was astute and occasionally made remarks that left everyone speechless. She was my kind of person, one who would always say what everyone else feared. She was nobody's fool. No one was more respected or venerated than Marian.

One day I decided to visit her with a small vase of yellow flowers as a gift. I found her trailer- the one with the low white fence- and knocked. A scratchy little voice from inside said "Come on in!" and there she was in her easy chair, stocking feet raised, with a fuzzy blanket across her lap. Her head was uncovered, revealing a thin layer of wispy, gray hair, and her hands immediately flew up as if she didn't want me to see her that way. She looked around for her stocking cap,

but I told her not to worry. She dropped her hands in a gesture of resignation- as if to say "Oh well..." and then she relaxed. We smiled. Instantly, we were family.

Marian and I would sit together for hours on end. She had a photographic memory and a need to recount the events of her life, and I was completely fascinated. She related a vast amount of information regarding the history of the area and the traditions of her day. She described the paths of the old roadways before they were modernized, and how she used to hitch up horse and wagon and drive for miles down the county road to the general store twice weekly. She used to read a newspaper called *The Rural New Yorker* where she got most of her recipes. Some of them, peeling and stained, were still taped to the wall in the kitchen. I learned that in the early 1900s the Welfare man used to come directly to the houses of the needy and drop off supplies- sugar, coffee, flour, bacon, meat, canned goods, matches, coal for the stove- everything needed for survival. It was a completely fair system based on need.

Marian had very clear opinions about the modern world and let it be known when she disapproved of things. With her eyes very wide she'd say, "Why, in *my* day they wouldn't stand for that!" She didn't approve of women coming to church in pants and particularly objected to the tight, stretch styles. She thought large women shouldn't wear them, saying "They be a highlightin' things they shouldn'a be a highlightin'! Look like they got the *whole world* in those pants!" I had to laugh. Once when Corinne's son Jason came over to mow the lawn, he was dressed in loose, brightly patterned shorts- and nothing else. "I told him to go home and get *dressed!*" she said "Comin' over here naked like that!" So Marian was always saying things that made us both laugh. I felt I understood and appreciated the things she loved. I was able to commiserate with her about the loss of the old traditions we both valued, and I often heard her say, when mentioning some old friend or neighbor, "They're all gone now. It's sad..." shaking her head with a faraway, misty look.

She often spoke of names in her family history while I tried to keep track. I knew that many of the area residents of African descent were closely related, with Van Alstyne and Van Ness being the most familiar family names. Marian's great grandfather had been an officer in the Civil War, and his name could have been Grimes. That would have been an early interracial marriage in the area which seems to have been part of a climate of warm relations from as far back as anyone has ever mentioned. Marian never spoke of anything indicating tension.

When Marian was four, her mother came down with some kind of fever and died. She remembers the door of the bedroom being tightly closed, and that she wasn't allowed in. "Your mother has gone on a journey," they said. She learned that her uncle would come for her in two weeks, but though she waited and watched by the window every day, he never came. "Roy," as she called me, shaking her head and looking down at her hands, "that was the longest two weeks of my life!" I felt such sorrow for the little girl with no mother. She told me how she cried when they shaved her head (in preparation for adoption), saying that "hair wasn't clean." Eventually she was taken in by a local dentist and his wife where she was raised in a household with other children. As a teenager, she met Robert Van Ness and was given permission to marry. She had good memories of this family and seemed to feel they had been kind to her.

Marian and Robert had lived in the old house diagonally across the road from mine. Jim, her first child, was born in a room I had been in. Robert worked on the farm and they must have survived fairly well as Marian never mentioned any lack. I believe Robert was a proud man who would have insisted on being a good provider. But I also think that in Marian's day there was an entirely different standard. No one had credit cards- there was no debt in that sense- maybe you owed a bill to the Country Store at the end of the month, but no one could ever go into the multi-thousand dollar debt levels people can today with cards. So you worked, spent cash on your supplies until it was gone, tucked away a handful in a box, and then made more by working. Life was simpler. Marian was always a grateful person who valued basic things in a way we forget to today. No one had technological toys, stereos, closets full of outfits, or fancy this and that- those things just didn't exist.

Marian was friends with Kate Boland, who had lived in my house, and gave me a wealth of information about the history of the building and the previous owners. I learned that the son of a former resident hung himself in a neighbor's barn across the creek, which could have accounted for some of the uneasy feelings I sensed when I first moved in. I knew that John Boland and his sister Kate didn't speak to each other but shared the house by dividing it down the middle. Kate had a violent husband and used to run across the road to Marian's house for protection when he was on a rampage. All these things had contributed to the unsettled spirits which once resided in the house. During the renovation which occurred prior to my purchase in 1979, an antique whiskey bottle was found inside the wall- God only knows all the stories behind that... someone or other had been a major lush. In addition Marian told me that John Boland had been laid out in state in the front room. One of the younger Bolands (who was referred to as *"a retard"* by the local kids) had actually, according to Marian, become impaired by a terrible car accident in which he was rendered unable to speak, and hobbled about on crutches for the rest of his life. Apparently he was teased mercilessly and eventually became a familiar fixture in the area as he walked in his limping sort of way down the road. This was all happening in and around my very home. The graves of the former owners, all the way back to what I believe was the original owner, John J. Van Valkenburg, can be found in a cemetery less than a mile away.

Marian and Robert soon moved to a nearby mill where Marian spent many years running the household and raising her children. She told me that Robert had the last word in everything; that was the deal... she raised the children, he provided. It was the accepted arrangement. After Robert died of a heart attack, she moved to a trailer just outside of town. At that time she used to walk everywhere- sometimes miles per day- well on into her late eighties.

Marian spoke to me of her dreams and longings, her childhood, her marriage- just about everything. I learned more than words can tell, more than books can contain, and more than documentaries could reveal. Our time together, which would be almost six years, was precious to us both. She was my Granny.

"I'll make a nurse outa' you yet!" she said one day. She would give me detailed instructions, and I followed every one of them happily- how to prepare certain foods, where to put things away- she was ever so precise, and I found it charming. Helping her was always a joy. Once she looked at me and said "You've sure made *me* happy." I just about died. I thought about how much meaning she had brought to my life, and how, one day at the end of my life, I will look back and feel proud of my relationship with this dear, Saintly woman. But it's not as if looking out for her was a job; it was a privilege.

After listening to a wealth of stories about the local area it occurred to me to ask if she would like to see some of those places again- and her response was a resounding "Yes!" That started the "Gals on the go" phase of our relationship, one of the best periods of my life. I would make sure the car was nice and clean, and then arrive at the appointed time to pick her up. As I pulled into her driveway the door would open and there she'd be, dressed and ready to go: coat, hat, bag and cane. I'd help her into the car, hook up her seat belt, and away we'd drive, laughing, pointing, and reminiscing. We'd just cruise around- anywhere at all that she wanted to go. I learned the history of practically every old house in the area. That was so and so's house over there, she'd say, pointing to an old house I'd passed a million times. "He was a doctor, and his wife used to work down at the hardware store." We visited the graves of her husband and son Jim, who had died in a car wreck when he was twenty-one. This would be a bond we would share as two bereft mothers. We ate lunch and dinner out. We even went to the mall a time or two, once to get her a new coat. She had boundless energy and ran me ragged. The two of us probably drew interested looks as we walked slowly, arm in arm, going about our chosen activities. I would always say "Take your time" and then we would just shuffle along. She knew I was in no rush, and that being with her was pure happiness to me. But most of all, it was the laughter. She had a fabulous sense of humor, and we were on the same wavelength. Not only was she a grandmother to me, but we were also best friends.

Whenever I had to leave I worried that she might slip away while I was gone. Once after returning from a tour, I failed to check in on her in my usual timely fashion. It suddenly occurred to me that I was overdue for a visit. When I walked in the door she looked at me disapprovingly and said *"Where* have *you* been?!" I had failed to check in, and she was upset with me. When I was leaving her house she would often say "See you on Sunday, Lord willin'!" Sometimes she would shake her head in a peaceful sort of way and say "I've had a good life." There was a tremendous sense of acceptance about her.

Marian often told me that she loved my singing. I always sang a capella- "Just like the old days!" she'd say with a smile. Marian didn't like the incredibly loud sound of a band. Patting her head with her hand she explained that it just about made the top of her head explode. She said all the singing in the early church was a capella.

One day I returned from a tour and found her in a deteriorated condition. Apparently a stomach upset had led a doctor to prescribe certain medications, and she felt (rightly so, I think), that she was now sicker as a result of the pills. She knew instinctively the antibiotic was a problem, repeating again and again that she'd never taken one before. So we assembled all the little jars, a boggling array of designer drugs, and after sorting through all of them, called her doctor. It was like pulling teeth. Suspicious, and tighter than a drum, the doctor finally explained the name and purpose of each pill. The first to go was an antidepressant. "Marian," I said, "did you know you are on an antidepressant?" She was shocked. "Antidepressant!" she said, "I'm not depressed!" So we threw that one out. Then she was on an antibiotic- a fancy one that had all kinds of side effects, from stomach irritation to other awful symptoms. When I asked why the antibiotic, they explained that Marian "might" have had a urinary infection. "Did you do a test?" I asked. No, they hadn't, but the symptoms she described over the phone sounded suspicious, so *just in case*, they put her on antibiotics. This made me mad. Without testing or even examining they had prescribed this over the phone! That was the next pill to go in the trash, particularly because Marian had no symptoms of infection, and from what I could tell, never had. Then there were overlapping blood pressure pills- pills that canceled out other pills, pills that shouldn't be taken together- something like eleven different medicines. I doubt very much that the doctor liked me after that, but I'm used to this (I get in a twist about things I think are wrong and I speak up). I finally got clearance to take her off all but the necessary few- heart related- and she seemed improved. But she had lost confidence. I correlated this in part to the introduction of a powerful medicine she had never encountered before from which her system never completely recovered. At that time I felt she needed more attention, so I began staying overnight. I put sofa pillows on the floor and tried to get comfortable, but as soon as I drifted off, I'd hear her gravely voice calling "Roy?" "Yes Marian?" Then she would need help getting out of bed. Towards the end she would say her "legs didn't work," so we'd rearrange her slowly- sitting first, then turning- and when, eventually, her legs were over the bed, we'd make our way to the bathroom.

One day she was feeling ill when a little voice went off in her head- she gestured with her hand- "You better get out of this place!" the voice said, so Marian called an ambulance. I arrived in time to ride to the hospital with her. Incredibly, we were laughing and joking the whole way. When we got there she was put in a bed for observation. I told her I was so exhausted I was going to take a bed next to hers- and she laughed. Some hours later, when it seemed like she was going to be all right, I went home to get some rest.

For several days she was in a room with another patient. Once when I stepped out of the room the woman in the neighboring bed asked if I was her professional caretaker. I said no, we were just friends. Then she said, "Well in that case you must be an Angel." This touched me deeply.

Somehow the hospital had the authority to put her in a nursing home, so instead of returning home (which she continually requested), she was admitted to a local facility- but not the one of her choosing. This is when the medical "machine" took over. Legal regulations, most likely structured to protect doctors and hospitals from lawsuits, were like an impenetrable iron wall. She was now in for life. So our visits took place at the nursing home, fortunately only a few miles from my house. She never stopped asking me to take her out of there, and she never stopped saying she wanted to die at home like her husband. I never stopped trying to get her out, but it couldn't be done. If she had died on her day trip home someone could have held them legally responsible, and that concern apparently came before an old woman's personal freedom.

Marian asked me to bring over some of her possessions- several sweaters, photos of her son Robert, and a few other comforts. Giving me careful instructions as to where I was to look and what I was to find, she provided me with a small list. It felt deeply emotional to be opening her little closet and looking for her possessions which were hung carefully on hangers or stored in neat little boxes. The window into this incredible woman's life was precious to me, and I wanted only to be a comfort to her, and worthy of her confidence.

I was sitting with Marian one day when a Pastor came into the room. We were chatting as always, and perhaps, noting our level of closeness, he inquired about our relationship. "I seem to think she is my grandmother" I said, and he smiled. "It has been an honor meeting two such wonderful women," he said.

At this same time Marian's son Robert went to the emergency room with an injury to his thumb, and for reasons beyond comprehension, ended up on a dialysis machine. I went to see him- the once-powerful son of a farmer- and he was lying there unable to speak, hooked up to all kinds of tubes. When he opened his eyes briefly I told him I was taking good care of his mother. He nodded his head appreciatively. Marian was aware that Robert was in a hospital and you could see this weighed on her. I explained that I would be keeping an eye on him, and she was relieved to hear this.

Within a short period of time Robert died. This tragic turn of events had devastating consequences for Marian. I made the decision not to tell her- at least in the short term- knowing it would kill her. I reasoned that whatever time she had left would be shortened and made cruelly painful by becoming aware of the fact. I didn't see the need, but the Pastor of the Church made the decision to tell her. I can't judge this as it is possible that my decision was wrong- it was simply what I felt in my heart. Nonetheless, the Church came over and packed into Marian's room. I stood next to my dear friend Jeanette, who Marian often referred to as "Jeanettie," and we all locked arms. I couldn't handle what was about to happen- after all, I knew this pain- Marian knew it too. I was braced for the worst. The Pastor stood next to the bed and started saying something about something- I couldn't hear anymore. All of a sudden Marian was saying "Where's Roy?" "I'm here, Marian!" I said, but I was swept back by the crowd. My heart was breaking, yet it comforted me to know that more than the Pastor, more than anyone, she had asked for me. My granny! But I knew it was coming to an end.

Over the next few days she continued to decline. She had me position Robert's picture at the foot of her bed. She stared at it constantly and made little sounds that were a kind of weeping. She began to babble on and off, dreams about angels at the foot of the bed, about a young woman standing there "flickering and flickering." She seemed to be reliving memories of her husband having a falling out with the Church. I knew nothing of the details, but she was very upset, and at times even angry. "What a terrible thing to do to him!" she kept saying. She spoke of someone who was ironing, and some other recurring memories. Then she slipped into a coma-like sleep.

After Robert's death it was revealed by somewhat miraculous circumstances that Marian had two granddaughters, one a friend of mine
from the Church, and another who lived in a neighboring state. Both
had been raised to believe they would never know the identity of their
father. Not only did it turn out Robert was their father, but they also
discovered they were sisters. With one granddaughter in tow I went to
Marian's bedside. As she lay unconscious, I held Roberta's hand and
Marian's hand. I understood that Roberta's existence had been kept
a secret to avoid the shame of illegitimacy. I had to address this, but
didn't want to upset Marian either- after all, these matters had been
hidden for many years. Roberta was overcome and asked me to speak,
so I cleared my throat and said "Marian, I'm here with your granddaughter Roberta. She needs to see you, she wants to get to know you.
None of this is anyone's fault. Times have changed and it is OK that
she didn't know Robert was her father. Everyone understands and ac-
cepts this now- and you can all be together now. Please, wake up for
Roberta, your granddaughter. She is here to see you- she needs you."

Several days before she fell asleep, Marian had asked me to become
her health care proxy and had signed a piece of paper giving me the
authority to make medical decisions. Knowing she did not want to be
kept alive on a feeding tube, I made the less drastic decision to give
her fluids. I leaned over her and asked if she would allow this. I said
"Marian, we are not feeding you, we are just giving you some fluids
so you won't feel dehydrated," and amazingly, she squeezed my hand
in recognition. She seemed to be OK with this. The next day Marian woke up. She was herself again for almost a week. Seeing that
the nursing home was giving her ridiculous foods like jello and ice
cream, shoveling them in to reach some kind of caloric quota- I made
her a mineral broth out of every nutritious vegetable: beets, carrots,
onions, parsley, celery and so on, and brought it to her in a jar. When I
explained that it was rich in minerals but probably wasn't going to be
very tasty, she opened her mouth. I gave her small sips from a spoon
and she said "Mmm- good" in a small voice.

The next day when I came over she was seated in a wheelchair,
bundled in a red plaid blanket. At first she was speaking, but soon it
became a labor. Then she stopped. I waited. Slowly, and with great
effort, I heard her say, "Roy, I'm dying." This was more than I could
bear. I should have accepted it. They brought in grief counselors to

help me accept it. But all I wanted was to take her home and honor her incessant requests to leave. Of course no one would let me.

During her last few days I felt very helpless. One evening I received a call telling me her breathing had become labored. I raced over, but when I got there she was gone. Little Marian, who we called Mother Marian at the Church, was ninety-seven years old when she died. Several days earlier she had whispered, "I thought I was going to make it to a hundred."

Mark Knopfler

1 was listening to the radio one day when the sound of the most supremely gorgeous guitar playing leaped out at me. It had uniquely beautiful tone- something I would call a chorusing effect, with a superb reverb. The notes were simple, clean, and powerful. "Who is that?!" I asked, totally blown away. "That's Mark Knopfler," was the answer, and I knew I had to get that fabulous guitar player on my record. Emboldened by my incredible experiences with musicians like Stevie Wonder in the past, I asked someone at Rounder to see if they could track him down. He was located, and we arranged to meet at a studio on the road.

Mark has beautiful instruments and a guitar tech who knows everything about the sounds he wants. He asks for this and such and the tech hands him the instrument, ready to go with all the right effects and EQ. Mark sits there calmly playing this earth-shatteringly beautiful music, melodies- soaring, diving notes bending into each other-lingering reverb tails, and washes of chords. I think he is the best and most tasteful electric guitar player I have ever heard, more emotional and evocative than anyone else. He is also a master of dynamics. Listening to him gave me ideas- the power of starting slow and then bringing things to a fever pitch of volume, then pulling way back again for the drama of it. Kind of like James Brown when he tells the band to drop way down... from a gallop to a walk, wham!

Mark put a solo on "Faithless World," a song with unexpected chord changes, but as I have found before with great electric players, no one knows the neck better... key changes and jazzy chords didn't slow him down a bit. I admire this knowledge of the neck- the ability to play in any key without a capo. I'm a capo freak... that way the arrangement stays the same. When he was done, I asked him why he had agreed to play on my record. His answer blew me away. He said, "Because you're great." I hardly knew how to respond to such an amazing compliment.

I later spoke to Mark's manager to see if he might be available to manage me. He explained that he was overextended but made it clear that he thought I had done very well without a manager. He was extremely supportive of my career and what I had accomplished, which he said in no uncertain terms was admirably solid. If Mark Knopfler's manager approved of my career, that meant the world to me. He also gave me some advice on how to find a good manager. He said, "Enthusiasm is more important than experience." I keep that little tidbit of wisdom in mind all the time. Finally, he paid me the ultimate compliment, saying, in the most charming British accent, "I'd swim the Atlantic for your hair!" He had one of the early promo photos of me which showed my hair cascading over my shoulders.

Later we were able to stop in at one of Mark's shows in Paris. There were rows of ambulances there and medics carrying women out on stretchers. Mark was wearing a headband and a sleeveless shirt which featured his nice shoulders. I'm not the fainting kind, but he is pretty charismatic.

Alan Gorrie

"Pick Up The Pieces" was a monster song for The Average White Band- an anthem for R&B fans. It was interesting that these fantastic musicians were from Scotland, and they brought a refreshing edge to their interpretations. Ron introduced me to Alan Gorrie, bass player and one of the lead singers for the band. They had worked together in the studio in the Connecticut area where they both lived. I was a little intimidated, not because of anything Alan said or did, but because the AWB were R&B Gods to me and I was in awe. Alan joined us for one of the European tours, Freebo style. I got to listen to some of the best bass playing in the world every night during the shows.

Alan is hilariously funny, and this was one of the most entertaining tours I have ever done. We went from town to town doubled over with laughter at his witty remarks. If you ever had the opportunity to go backstage at an AWB concert and were able hang out with the band, you'd be laughing so hard you'd need a back support to keep your stomach muscles from tearing. You don't know humor until you end up with a bunch of brilliant, wiseguys on the road. Tour humor is a life saver, and I try to get right in the middle of it if I can- not an easy task around some of the best.

Alan and I started a project in the studio for a European label which we were never able to finish. It was several totally smokin' R&B tracks, but in the end the label decided to go with the blues and song-writer material over this highly commercial sound Alan had produced. I really want to hear these songs again as I guarantee they would sound great next to anything on the radio today. I don't know who has a copy of these now- maybe Alan.

Ron and I ate dinner one night at Alan and Jean Gorrie's house, and

I brought along a pumpkin pie I had made. My recipes are always adjusted to make them healthier, substituting one hundred percent maple syrup for sugar, olive oil for butter and so on. At that point I hadn't discovered a way to make a decent pie crust without the use of saturated fat (now I have a major handle on it), so at one point I found a frozen pie crust which had simple, reasonable ingredients- no lard- and I began to make my pies with these moderately healthy shells. After dinner we were eating the pie, and Alan couldn't stop talking about how terrific it was- in particular the crust. He never out and out asked what it was or how I had made it, so I did something not at all my style- I said nothing. Advertisers make a huge deal out of this idea- that you should take credit for things you haven't done by concealing the source and smiling and nodding "Thank you." Having never done this before I can say it feels bad, at least to me. I said nothing, but felt totally dishonest. Indeed the filling was my special magic recipe that everyone always compliments, but his main point was the crust.

I didn't set out to make this book a true confessional, but I suppose this story fits the category. Because I tend to be compulsively honest, this pointless little ruse felt all the more uncomfortable to me. I tried to reach Alan recently (not about this, but I intended to mention it), and found he had moved. I thought about the friends who knew him that might help locate him. Most obviously, I couldn't call Ron (I jump ahead). Then I thought of guitar player/studio owner Brian Keane, but his number was also disconnected. Then singer Sarah Brooks- same deal. Alan, if you're out there: it was an Oranoke Orchards frozen crust!!

I Give Jack Elliott A Haircut

It's hard to imagine anyone nicer than Jack Elliott. Soft spoken and incredibly gracious in an old-fashioned kind of way- with a sweet, never-ending smile, Jack is the gentle giant of folk music. In his unassuming way he carries the mantel of Woody Guthrie and the music of an era squarely on his back. Gentle, because he never raises his voice in self importance or thinks of himself as the keeper of the flame. He simply plays, sings, and tells the stories that might otherwise fade into an image on a parchment colored photo. Jack was one of the Village regulars and we knew each other the way a grown singer and someone's daughter (who played the guitar) might. Friends of friends of friends- out for an evening of music- there were many ways to pass each other in the park or brush by an elbow in the backstage of a folk venue. After that years rolled by without walking much in the same circles.

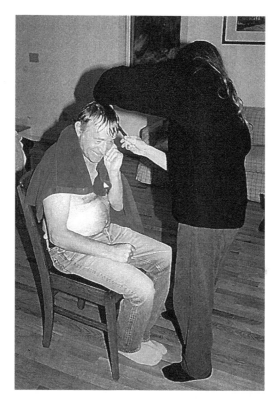

Then one night my friend Rick Robbins and I went to a venue in Woodstock, and there was Jack. Whether it was my show, or Rick's, or Jack's I can't recall, all I remember is Jack's set. I hadn't realized how funny he was, how entertaining, and how earthy. After that Rick would say "Jack's in town" and we would go catch his set somewhere. Jack used to roll up in a motor home and that's really how I got the idea that an RV was something to consider. Running my hands across the overhead cabinets and listening to Jack's stories about pulling up to Jack Nicholson's latest movie set, knocking on the door of Nicholson's trailer and having Nicholson say "Jack! Come on in!"... contemplating the rooms and creature comforts- kitchen, bathroom, bedroom, closets... the idea of actually owning one of these babies first settled in as a solid concept.

One time Jack was staying at Rick's and we all went over to Arlo's. We sat on the grass and had a riot of a time reminiscing about everything and rolling out tales of our last great adventures. There was some long, drawn out saga about a boat Jack had been renovating for the last twenty-five years, but I forget the details. After that Rick said that Jack always asked about me whenever they spoke.

At one point Rick walked into Ron's little studio looking to record a few of his favorite old songs for posterity. He would give a copy of his music to his grandchildren some day. As soon as Rick had done a tune or two I got an idea. "Rick," I said. "you sound as good as a lot of

With Rick Levine and Jack Elliott backstage at The Sweetwater

people making records... better, actually. Have you considered making a real record?" Rick was dumbfounded. No one was less aware of his own abilities. So I talked Rick into making a debut album which I offered to produce. Ron got on board, volunteering studio and engineering, and we proceeded to make an extraordinary album. I sang harmonies on a number of songs, and played guitar with Rick on almost everything. Rick sang in a dusky, rich voice that sounded like he had been doing this his whole life. I was happy to be stretching out in another style, having focused solely on blues and contemporary in recent years. We called in people like Garth Hudson from The Band, Larry Campbell (then touring regularly with Bob Dylan), and John Sebastian. Rick's old friend Arlo Guthrie sang a duet with him, as did Jack.

For this part of the recording Ron and I went to Rick's house. Jack was his usual sweet self and never more shy and humble about performing. He had to be coaxed a bit, but then there was that evocative, signature voice. We all ate spicy Indian food that night which Jack later explained wrestled with his innards all night, and then the next day I was somehow volunteered to give Jack a haircut. I've given haircuts all my life, so this was a natural for me. Either Jack trusted me totally, or, like my father (who had been my first customer, giving me scissors and carte blanche from the moment I was old enough to hold a comb), didn't care what his hair looked like. But it came out great and Jack, like almost all the men whose hair I have cut over the years, openly celebrated the new light and airy feeling. Women were more likely to anxiously check in the mirror, where men were well rid of the hair and could barely be tempted to glance at the results.

Rick's solo album got fantastic reviews, and this guy who had no expectations suddenly had a fair amount of acclaim and people requesting that he go on tour. But Rick was a family man and had no great need to travel. After all, he had never intended to make a record. When you think of all the people who struggle and starve to death just to make one album with important guest stars, Rick was walking in golden shoes. However, since that point he has gone on tour with Jack a number of times, proving that the call of the road is in him after all.

Jack and his friend Rick Levine came to a show I did at the Sweetwater in Mill Valley, California some years back. Someone snapped pictures of the three of us in the green room- but when we asked for a copy the photographer refused, claiming journalistic privilege. By some quirk of fate someone found a copy, and this photo came back to us by this circuitous route.

Music And Intimacy

When I was working with Ron we were mixing a song called "Heavenly Bird." The words of the chorus are "Heavenly bird, beautiful bird, your love is like the golden morning sun." It's meant to be spiritual, and not really a love song, but in the ride-out I was improvising and one of the last things I said was "I love you." I left the room while Ron was mixing, and when I walked back in he had my vocal soloed in the room. He seemed flustered and mumbled something about how it was beautiful. He kept playing back my voice in the room saying "I love you." I wanted to disappear it was so vulnerable. We were not a couple at the time, but that could have been the moment he decided to pursue me.

Numerous times in the past I have been up all night in the studio. After hours of working side by side with the engineer, you sometimes begin to feel like you're in a relationship. Understanding the medium, the familiar language and shared purpose can become sexy- even erotic-some time around two in the morning. This could be why so many people who work together end up in relationships. Breathing side by side and crossing arms over the console is personal. The proximity and nature of the working relationship has a tendency to eliminate barriers. I think one has to be careful of the aphrodisiac effect. It is possible for someone otherwise of no interest to become attractive. After all, your voice, often with deeply intimate words, your most personal thoughts, and your art is laid bare before another human being who is getting inside your world. You climb in together. You tend to start laughing and having a great time and everyone knows humor is sexy. Great musicianship is sexy. Guitar playing is sexy. Someone once put it this way: competence is sexy.

Roundabouts

Whoever invented "Roundabouts" should be taken straight to jail. They are like an infection that spreads. We thought we'd seen the last of them when we flew home- then noticed a year or two ago that they've started to appear in the United States. Someone must have brought them over on an airplane. Nothing could be more ridiculous, misguided, and wasteful. The concept, I was told when I inquired, is "to keep traffic moving." The reality is that a once quiet intersection with a stop sign or an unassuming light is transformed into a madhouse of swirling maniacs, a bumper car ride for aggressive drivers. No one has any idea when and where the next predator will appear, and it's everyone for themselves, twirling, whirling, growing dizzy, desperately trying to read the signs while attempting to avoid impact... then circling again because you missed your friggin' turn. This is just plain madness. It's one thing if it's only a trip from home to the local market. Then it could fall into the "Oh look, we have to spin for a while" category. If you're feeling well, and are not having an overly stressed day, you might be able to gird your loins and make the rotations, avoiding all comers, and get to the market, knowing you'll endure it again shortly. It's a kind of obstacle course, a video game if you will, and we're all being forced to play.

Suddenly I feel the urge to invent a joke (let it be known this one is mine): How many weary band members does it take to navigate a roundabout? Four: one to drive, one to call out town names, one to read the map while frantically trying to determine which town corresponds to the desired direction, and one to violently gesticulate at other drivers to keep them at bay. This may not be as funny as it is true. Nothing could be a more difficult and dangerous deterrent to smooth progress on a long journey. You can probably take the mileage-to-travel time estimates from the USA and more than double them for a tour where there are roundabouts. The Europeans deal with this by driving ever faster. Of course certain countries have no speed limit at all, something that is a frightening, horror movie scenario when you envision what that would mean on this side of the ocean. With the dangers of auto travel already at maximum levels, the idea of no rules is unthinkable.

Then there's the question of real estate. We began to calculate how much land was needed to create one of these monstrosities, and we noted that some of the mega roundabouts required vast tracts of land- maybe a hundred acres or more- to be dug up and rearranged in these gigantic patterns one could probably only visualize from outer space. Then take the smallest roundabout. One roundabout connecting two or three possible choices takes up far more land than a simple intersec- tion... maybe three or four times as much. And, hello, it's ugly. If this is the wave of the future it is very much in line with general global decline. Logic, sanity, and reason have swirled away down the drain. Speaking of drains, how many millions of tax dollars does the duct- ing system under this complex take as opposed to the simplicity of the familiar ditches, the pleasant channels found alongside traditional roads? No doubt they'll have to create underground control stations to monitor their engineering extravaganzas with computerized screens indicating traffic flow and areas of impedance.

The last shock was learning that some places did not always have these. I assumed there had been roundabouts from antiquity. But when I asked I found that they were a recent concept. I had envisioned me- dieval foot traffic entering the roundabout methodically, circling, and continuing on their way... OK, I thought, they've done this since time immemorial. No big deal. But this was wrong. Of course the chances are that I am the only one who has ever been annoyed. My responses to things are so different that I can never be sure if I am from earth or simply from a dust pod that arrived here on an asteroid.

It should be noted that as with other things like smoking and the con- sumption of rich foods, the Europeans do not seem sicker or in greater danger. It appears to be related to what we are used to. Humans adapt and develop skills equal to the task. As far as these latter two issues, I think it's quite possible that in Europe, eating and smoking are done in a much more relaxed setting. Meals are celebratory rituals, and as a result are far more drawn out. This in turn aids in digestion and me- tabolism, and no doubt offsets most of the unhealthy potential which to us, with our fast-food lifestyles, would be disastrous.

Digesting Toilets And Observation Platforms

After a long and stressful flight, Ron and I arrived at the hotel and fell into a jet-lagged trance. We were jolted awake by an incredibly loud grinding, whirring, clacking noise that emanated from the wall. It happened frequently and lasted several minutes at a time. Sleep was out of the question. When we called the front desk to inquire, they calmly explained that this was the "Digester" in the hotel bathroom... what on earth?! As you might imagine that became a central theme of the tour. Every tour has one, and they're all funny. I'll spare you some of these ghastly names.

Another type of toilet we couldn't stand was the old design: box suspended above, waterless platform, and pull chain. The Allan Block Sandal Shop had one of these, a relic from the past. There's no polite way to discuss this, but we've gotten used to our water-filled bowls which swallow contents quickly. These Euro toilets do nothing to absorb whatever lands on the flat porcelain surface. And then, when you pull the chain, some of these gawd-awful contraptions don't quite flush. The stuff rocks around and falls back. You'd think these could be updated. Ron used to find this hilarious. He called them "observation platforms."

Upstaged By A Red Sports Car While Choking On Cake

Ron also found the fact that soap is called "zeep" in Holland hysterically funny. You never know what will strike you when you're sleep deprived. Fun is a huge part of touring, especially with a band. Imagine five or six exhausted, hungry, irritable people with nothing to do but sit in hotel rooms or travel to shows. The wit becomes finely tuned and each one plays on the next until some kind of documentary about the birth of humor could easily be filmed.

On one of our tours we were in a part of the world where fast driving is synonymous with masculine power (OK, so that's actually most of the world). The driver had been admonished repeatedly to drive "slowly," which in his mind meant eighty miles per hour instead of over a hundred and ten. With no speed limit, it's like traveling in outer space- projectiles exploding all around- being passed by rockets- sheer madness.

Our driver lived on cake. Every morning he would stop at the bakery and pick out an array of pastries of the most extreme, sugary kind- and that was his food for the day. We had given him a top speed limit comparable to sixty-five miles per hour on the open road. All of a sudden a little red sports car came out of nowhere and pulled up next to us. He locked eyes with our driver for a moment as if to say "You wuss- you're hardly moving! Are you a man or a worm?" Then the sports car took off like it was shot out of a cannon and our driver almost choked to death on his cake. "What was *that* all about?" I asked. He explained in his broken English that the driver of the red car told him he was "not a man" because he was driving too slowly.

A New Level Of Intensity

One night at a festival in Belgium security guards were assigned to my back room. That evening there was a commotion- a woman was crying and trying to get past the guards, pressing against the barrier and begging loudly to have my towel from the stage. This was a new level of intensity- someone wanted my sweaty towel. I decided to have security bring her into the back room to say hello, which they did. She turned out to be a single mother trying to raise a child on her own, and with tears in her eyes she explained that my music made her feel very emotional. I gave her the towel and we talked for a while until she calmed down. To me, fans like this woman are beautiful people. I never take anything for granted, and I appreciate each and every person who likes my music.

The Birth Of A Song

Silver Wings

Two houses were born in a very different time,
And I saw one from above as I circled in a cloud, I was flying in a
cloud,
It had white porches and small windows,
It had a wild front yard, it had a wild front yard,

And I was flying, trying not to fall too hard,
And I was flying, trying not to fall down too far,
But my faith, faith can pull me up on silver wings...

I heard a voice and it was Wendy saying,
She said a soul wants to be born, and you will be its mother, you know
you are its chosen one,
I was nursing a baby, he was my own little child,
And then he looked at me so wild, and he had laughter in his eyes,

But I was crying, trying not to fall too far,
I was crying, trying not to fall down too far,
But my faith, faith can pull me up on silver wings...

I had a friend and she was wise and patient,
She had raven black hair and her eyes were morning blue, you know
she always spoke the truth,
And she rode white horses that she raised on a farm,
While many birds were singing, and there were birds everywhere,

And she was flying, trying not to fall too far, She was flying, trying not
to fall down too far,
But her faith, her faith could pull her up on silver strings,
Silver strings, silver, silver wings...

Words and music by Rory Block

While touring overseas I discovered a fascinating phenomenon. My dreams were incredibly vivid for the first two weeks- so clear I remembered them all day, and sometimes much longer. I came up with a little theory (totally unscientific) that I believed could be a factor. Because of the time difference, our sleep cycles are shifted- perhaps by the five to eight hour time differences- and this means the active dream portion of our sleep occurs at a time when we might be required to rise and go about our day. I think, at least for me, this means I wake up in what would have been the active dream cycle back home, and it yields a wealth of imagery. This is a gold mine for songwriters, and you don't have to keep a recording device by the bed- these dreams don't fade. So I delighted in this until my body has adjusted to the time change, and then things would go back to normal- darn it!

One morning in Holland I awoke to one of these power dreams. Although I hate flying in airplanes, I love the other kind of flying- arms outstretched, drifting on currents, soaring about surveying the world below. This has been a recurring dream throughout my life from the earliest memory. As a child these were escape dreams where the air was as thick as oatmeal. I climbed- groping, grabbing handfuls of air, kicking my legs in a frog-like fashion, struggling to rise- barely escaping evil enemies intent on destroying me. These were terribly frightening dreams. It began with being chased. "I'll just take off," I decided. This seemed a logical idea, and I remember the sense of launching into a new realm. As soon as I was aloft I was pleased to find I could navigate and swim in this thing known as air- while just below, menacing, grasping hands reached to pull me down. With great effort I rose above them.

Then I had another revelation. In a flash I knew I could go higher, much higher- I no longer needed to struggle. "I can soar around if I want to," I thought. This was a joyous breakthrough. I was weightless and agile like a bird. I reached great heights and had total control. "Silver Wings" was born out of this feeling.

Wendy Stewart

"For what is your life? It is even a vapour, that appeareth for a little time, and then vanisheth away."
James 4:14.

"Silver Wings" is in large part about Wendy: "I had a friend and she was wise and patient... she had raven black hair, and her eyes were morning blue, you know she always spoke the truth..." As a young woman she had married race car driver Jackie Stewart and kept his name after they parted. Wendy and Nathalie were my dearest friends at the time. In retrospect there may only be a few people on earth who we can truly call our best friends, particularly as we get older and more guarded. We remember them from childhood, but we lose touch and suddenly there is no one. Wendy was one of those rare people, perhaps even more so than Nathalie, to whom you could say anything, and who could say anything to you, and it was all understood. You could laugh about the same things, and nothing was too private or sacred a subject. Everything was on the table. Ah, how I miss these friends! She died of breast cancer, and even when I sat in the front room of her house next to the open coffin with her little daughter Arabella on one side of me, I still couldn't understand how she could be gone.

At the end of her life I kept hoping there would be much more time-time to get back to our friendship, time to relate again. The days when we had laughed about men and shared details of our sex lives were past. I had allowed too many opportunities to escape, and then I got the call... "Wendy's in the hospital." I squirmed, I procrastinated, I hoped she would come home, I went into denial, and she died- and I dreamt about her constantly. Sometimes she appeared as a ghoul in a rainstorm with lightning flashing. I thought with horror, my God she's angry at me... I failed her! But other times we were in her beautiful country kitchen baking bread together, chickens wandering in and out through the open door. We stepped over duck poop in the yard but didn't care. Wendy was from England and had the most natural, earthy lifestyle ever, and I was as comfortable with her as I was on the hillside in Neshanic, New Jersey in 1950. Her upper class British accent and clear voice was a joy to listen to, her measured insights, her astounding perceptions- Wendy was one of a kind. I could write a chapter devoted to the wise and amusing things she would say that always cut to the core. I used to write down her comments to contemplate them later.

The guitar part started during a sound check. Live drums take forever and we were getting bored, so I started playing a little ditty in a freaky drop C tuning. I'm a person who turns the pegs wildly until I like what I hear, then I experiment and ultimately let the tuning write the song. I don't read music anymore (as Louis Armstrong once said when asked if he read music, "Not enough to get in the way")... so I have to remember the tunings later, a huge challenge which I usually fail. I started playing this ditty, and suddenly Neil Wilkinson began clicking and clacking on the rim of the snare. Neil played with the British band Everything But The Girl at that time and was the consummate song-writer drummer. I had gotten a plum gig at a festival and an English band was called in to back me up, and that's how I met Neil. Then Scott Petito, bass player and owner of NRS Studios (where a number of my albums have been recorded), started sliding around on his fret-less, and before you know it the song was pretty much written. I raced back to the hotel room to put my dream to the song, and the band sounded so tight we rented a studio in Holland and recorded it on the spot. The rest of the album was done in Woodstock at NRS. "Silver Wings" is on the *Ain't I A Woman* CD which was nominated for the National Association of Independent Record Distributors (NAIRD) Award. This is the same award, in the "Best Adult Contemporary Al-bum Of The Year" category, later won by the *Tornado* album.

My First Handy Award

In May 1997 we traveled to Memphis, Tennessee for the W.C. Handy Awards. I had been nominated for "Traditional Blues Female Artist of The Year" and was invited to be a presenter. As much as I would have loved to win, I was fully prepared to accept the honor of nomina-tion. That was a significant form of recognition- just to be mentioned among names like Ruth Brown and Luther Allison. So I had no expec-tations. I had never won anything- I was used to that.

About a week before the awards I had a powerful dream. I was at the Orpheum Theater, and through some miracle, I won. As I stepped up to accept the award, my heart was filled to overflowing. The feeling was so intense it woke me. I knew the joy of winning, if only as an illusion... but it didn't matter now, I thought- I had already had the experience, and that's what mattered. It gave me a completely satis-fied feeling.

That evening Luther Allison took home practically every award. Slender and extremely good looking- reminiscent of Chuck Berry- he leaped off the stage and ran up and down the aisles of the theater swinging his electric guitar and bringing down the house- it was probably the most dynamic live performance I have ever seen. When I heard that he died shortly thereafter of cancer it was almost impossible to believe. He seemed totally healthy. I continue to wonder what would happen if we simply didn't know we were sick- if no doctor told us, if we had no warning. It seems to me we could live a much better quality life for much longer.

My category wasn't going to be announced for a while so I went out to the bus to relax. When I stepped outside briefly to talk to a fan I saw Bob Vorel, publisher of *Blues Review Magazine*, coming towards me. "Congratulations!" he said, and I responded "For what?" (I had no idea). "You just won!" he said. "Won what?!" I thought. So that was a shocker.

With Guy Davis, Honeyboy Edwards, Robert Jr. Lockwood, and Henry Townsend at the Awards ceremony. Photo: Tom Burnham

Television

Italy, Germany, France, Switzerland, England, Scotland, Belgium, Holland, Norway, Australia, Poland... these are some of the places I have played. Japan, Ireland, Romania, Czechoslovakia, New Zealand, Hawaii- these are places where I have been invited but haven't yet toured. It's a question of getting on an airplane. For years I flew overseas about twice a year. The travel was traumatic- but the tours were always fantastic.

In Europe I have done numerous television shows, particularly in the Netherlands. In the USA not quite as many, but all great shows- CNN

Showbiz Today, NBC's Weekend Today In New York, CBS Night-watch, QVC, Austin City Limits, and various cable shows- and I began to understand how to go into a space where nothing but energy and emotion existed. In this way it didn't matter how many people were (or were not) watching- I learned to treat an intimate venue or hundreds of thousands watching by television with equal respect. I learned to take eyes riveted on me as a source of energy which can-celed fear. I stopped worrying about judgment. Most people who come out to hear you play are already your "friends-" fans who love your music. Sometimes people are dragged to the show by a friend who wants them to see me play- those people often come up after the show to say they are my newest fans. This is an openhearted and enthusiastic atmosphere in which I have surrendered fear and received confidence. It's not a perfect science of course, and there are excep-tions- but fortunately not that many these days.

Wilderness Survival And Dreadlocks

Don't tell your teenage children to cut their hair unless you want them to resent you- but if you force them to cut their hair they will hate you for life. The art of waiting cautiously, pretending not to notice, even being deceitfully complimentary, is much more effective. Eventually they tire of whatever extremes they have manifested. In Jordan's case I thought dreadlocks looked good on him. He showed me that in order to form the proper tangles, they could not be washed with soap and had to be worked between the fingers and twisted into knots- but eventually not washing became a far bigger issue than hav-ing long, hopelessly tangled hair. Nonetheless I knew better than to mention the issue. We all quietly hoped something would change and he would crave a shower.

One day Jordan announced he was going to shorten his dreads. He planned to do it in the natural way, explaining that some Native Amer-ican tribes would burn hair instead of cutting. So he disappeared be-hind the barn with matches and held a flame to the ends of the dreads. Needless to say I freaked out thinking his head would go up in a ball of fire, but he showed me that the tangled hair would smolder and then fizzle out. Of course I hated this and couldn't relax until he stopped.

Jordan was on one of the cross country tours when he decided he wanted a haircut. Ron had commented that he smelled something strange in the bus, and Jordan started contemplating the possibility that it might be the long unwashed tresses. I held my breath when he asked, thinking he'd change his mind. Better not show too much

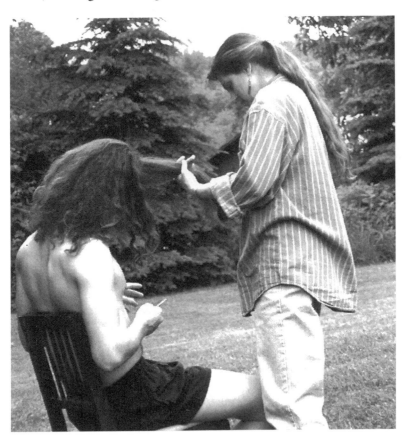

enthusiasm. So we set out a chair and the process began. Years earlier I had learned that baby oil applied to hopelessly tangled horse mane helped in the process of burdock removal. I oiled his hair and worked on it for hours with a wide tooth comb, and eventually he had a huge, heavily frizzed head of hair. Next came the shampoo, and soon, the clean hair was braided, and Jordan said "Aaah" in an apparent sigh of relief.

Jordan was to do numerous interesting things in the coming years which were all about survival and self sufficiency- extremely good things to know. He studied basket making, mediation, emergency rescue in the wilderness, and other life-saving techniques.

One time we pulled into the driveway after a long tour. I stepped out of the bus and heard an odd buzzing sound. I looked up to find a large, hairy piece of animal hide, covered with dripping blood and flies, draped over a nearby branch. I screamed- I thought some sick individual had left it there to send an evil message or put a hex on me- I felt like the guy in the Godfather movie who went to bed to find a severed horse head under the covers. I called Jordan, who told me that he had been traveling on the Mass Pike when he encountered an elderly couple who had hit a deer. They were pulled over and there they sat, somewhat stunned, beside the dead animal. They didn't seem to know what to do, so he offered to help. He got them on their way and removed the carcass from the road. Having been studying about Native American leather tanning techniques, he decided to try out his skills, so he actually put the deer in his trunk and carried it home, where he skinned it and stretched it over a tree branch to dry. He was not exactly squeamish, but neither were Native peoples who did exactly the same thing. It was Jordan's goal to create clothing and footwear from the leather. I can't remember how the project ended.

Then there was soap. He took my best giant stock pot and combined coconut oil and lye (God knows where he procured this), and sat on the floor stirring this witches brew for hours on end. The splatters from the evil liquid left permanently bleached spots on the floor, but the end result was incredible, huge hulking blocks of good quality soap which he cut into bars and gave as gifts.

How I Smashed My Guitar

Some years ago I appeared in concert at the NAAM show in Los Angeles representing Martin Guitars. Ever since my travels with Stefan in the 1960s I thought they were the best guitars on earth. Because I play so aggressively, I doubt very much that there are many builders who would want me to slam their guitars around the way I am known to do. I have heard the story of another artist who actually beats his guitar with a hammer, and although I am not THAT bad, I am in fact very, very tough. I once played someone's new guitar on stage and afterwards, with shaking hands and beads of sweat dripping off his forehead, he inspected the guitar for damage. It happens that I was sitting backstage at NAAM five minutes before showtime, and as I looked down I had a strange hallucination- I thought I saw a six-inch gash from the widest part of the guitar all the way to the jack at the bottom. As I focused, I realized that I could see straight through this gaping hole into the interior of the guitar. I also realized that something had to be done immediately as I then had four minutes left till showtime. Someone ran into the audience to get Dick Boak of Martin Guitars. Acoustic builder and old friend Michael Gurian was there as well as a number of other experts, and after hastily considering the options (declining Roy Rogers's kind offer to borrow his beautiful Martin guitar- you can see how I felt responsible at that moment not to)- Dick came up with a bold plan. Snapping his fingers in the air, I heard him say, "Bring me some duct tape!" A roll of wood-grain duct tape appeared from nowhere and Dick firmly and expertly taped the break together, though by that time it had spread around the entire back- the pressure from the strings pulling the neck was literally separating the sides. With everything held together by tape, I wondered aloud if I should skip my set. Dick said he wanted me to do the show regardless. When I asked if I should go easy on the instrument, he again boldly said "No, do your normal show." I would just wing it and if it turned ugly we could make other arrangements. Roy's guitar was still an option (what a gentleman), so, after Dick went up on stage to introduce me, I almost managed to do my normal show. In the first two songs the guitar shifted with a series of pinging sounds as the strings slipped into various tunings, but after that it stood the test and actually sounded excellent until the end. As I took my bow I spontaneously kissed the guitar and someone recorded it all on film. This is how passionate I feel about my instrument. The next day Martin took the guitar (we all figured I musta' slammed it against a cement floor somewhere along the road), and gave me a brand new shining cousin straight off the wall from the Martin booth at NAAM. The new guitar has proven to be yet more fabulous than the other dear old friend, which has since met its death. After being shipped home it was laid out on the diagnostic table at the Martin factory and it was determined that it would eventually be consigned to the Martin Museum along with a short story about the night I split open my guitar.

The Robert Johnson Tribute Concert At The Rock And Roll Hall of Fame

Robert Johnson was starting to become well known. Tribute concerts, festivals and compilations were now fairly common, soon to be all the rage. A large concert was being held at the Rock and Roll Hall of Fame in Cleveland and I had been asked to participate. Big names were going to be there and it promised to be a banner event. We often have a challenge finding a flat, wide parking space for the bus, but this was one venue where that was not going to be a problem, so after docking with shore power and making our way inside the complex, we got swirled up into this interesting scene. No doubt movies like *Spinal Tap*, with crazed bands running around in the maze of sub-basement corridors, could have been filmed here.

When I went up to do my set it was pretty daunting. Both sides of the stage were lined with blues and rock dignitaries, venerable writers, historians, family members, you name it, and they were directly in my line of view. This was like a personal concert to everyone and anyone who was an insider. Television cameras pressed upon me from every angle. Suddenly the lights were blinding and the air was suffocating. The experienced performer in me melted and I felt totally intimidated. There were stars everywhere, and I was a nobody. I started playing and then suddenly stopped. I can't remember why, just that I was a super jerk. I looked up and thought "Now you've done it- you ruined the LIVE broadcast!" I envisioned them angrily editing out my set in the cutting room while making derisive remarks. After mumbling something about nerves, I started up again. Obviously they took that part out. But by some miracle, I was part of the final package that turned into a DVD called *Hellhound On My Trail*.

Afterwards I received a letter from someone who saw *Hellhound On My Trail* in a theater in New York. He said that when my set finished, the whole theater jumped to their feet and gave me a standing ovation. I have never watched this video- being too afraid to see myself- but to know that it was perceived in some positive light by the public was deeply touching to me.

Blood And Gore

Bleeding fingers. Flesh separated from the nail. Skin sanded down to the raw... bruises from pounding... damaged cartilage from stomping- tweaked shoulder muscles from supporting the guitar. The things that can happen to the body from playing are downright gory. I once met a doctor who specialized just in injuries to musicians caused by repeated stress to certain areas of the body. He said it was akin to sports injuries in athletes.

With the exception of foot pounding and the trauma to my left leg, most of the injuries are to my hands and happen at the beginning of a tour. I need rock-hard calluses to play, and that comes from repeated wear and tear. It's impossible for me to maintain my hands between tours. Every dish, shower, or bath softens and eliminates calluses as does skin lotion. How I love hot baths and how I hate soaking while holding my hands above water! But to rest my arms down in the water means softened calluses. I often go out on stage with my hands look- ing as much like alligator skin as ever because softening them just to look good would be instant death to my fingers.

The formula that seems to work is two shows, followed by two nights off. After the first two nights my hands get sore and need a night or two of rest. Then I can do another two shows, with another two nights off. After that I'm usually good to go, although humidity and perspi- ration can make things much worse and could require another day for healing. If all things go well, by the end of a long tour my fingers are like iron. If I don't get the time for my calluses to build properly, unbelievably bad things happen.

More than several times I've had the string go under the nail of the middle finger on my right hand and pull the nail away. I was perform- ing in France when I felt something sticky. There was no pain- it was

318

past that. I looked down to see blood spattered across the face of the guitar. I left it there for quite some time after it dried as a kind of badge of something or other- perhaps the things we do for the love of music.

In England I found a large bruise on my arm right where the inside of the elbow wraps around the guitar. I couldn't figure out how it got there until I did the next show and realized that part of my arm was taking a beating from the thumping. I've also had bruises on the inside of my wrist mostly from the Charlie Patton or Robert Johnson songs. I should probably wrap my palms in tape the way Conga players do, but almost anything, long sleeves, jewelry, tape and so on, can get in the way.

Prairie Home Companion How To Fix Torn Fingertips

*T*he night before Prairie Home Companion I knew my hands were sore, but during sound check the problem got severe. I managed to sand off the flesh of the first finger of my right hand, the very finger I need for songs like "Crossroad Blues". I wandered around the stage asking band members if anyone had any solutions. It was a desperate situation and I finally had to resort to duct tape to cover the injury. Unfortunately that completely destroys the friction on the strings and turns everything to rubber. I later discovered that black electrical tape works a bit better- a thin strip over the tip, and a band wrapped around it sideways to hold it firm. This black tape has better traction and allows some semblance of playing to occur. Crazy glue, or some other kind of solvent-based skin sealer (as suggested by my old friend and fiddle player Andy Stein) would probably not work for me... if it bonds flesh together but then intense pressure rips it apart again, I figured it would take a good chunk of my hand with it.

I have discovered that Carmex, the stuff designed for chapped lips which comes in a tiny round jar- is the absolute best thing for repairing torn fingers. Dunk your finger directly into the Carmex at the first sign of trouble, then wrap it thoroughly in skin tape- leave overnight. The

319

next day it will have improved. Two days might be required. Don't waste your time with creams, or even Vitamin E. I've tried them all, and Carmex is the only thing that works. Gently remove all the sticky material from the skin tape and allow the hand to dry before playing.

In regards to other injuries resulting from aggressive playing, I almost had an operation to repair compressed, worn cartilage in my left knee, an injury resulting from incessantly stomping my foot. I declined at the last minute when I heard they wanted to put me on a breathing machine during the operation. I knew that would be too much of a shock for my system, so I just go easier now if I can. The doctor was extremely upset with me for declining the operation- seems he was counting on poking around in my knee cap. He even read me the riot act about how I was an "uptight" kind of person. I looked at him with his obvious hair piece, his Hitler mustache, and his army of nurses who catered to his every whim, and I had to chuckle that he would use these kinds of techniques to intimidate patients into surgery. That was over ten years ago and my knee is just fine.

Nathalie Becomes Mary Lynn

For reasons absolutely no one has ever been able to explain, Nathalie changed her name suddenly to Mary Lynn. She had different phases of musical interest; there was the easy listening, elevator music phase, and then at the end of her life it was country music. She became a line-dance enthusiast, and it seemed to me that "Mary Lynn" was a way of reinventing herself as an American. Up until then she had been exceedingly English; her lifestyle, way of dressing, eating and speaking were all recognizably British. Suddenly I was supposed to call her Mary Lynn, but I just couldn't get over the idea that her name was Nathalie. She told me a confusing story about Mary Lynn being her original name, but then I had to wonder why she had changed it to Nathalie.

After years of not seeing her, we ran into each other one day at a local mini mart and our friendship started up again immediately. We had a lot of catching up to do as a number of years had passed and she now had five children- two from her first marriage, and three with her second husband. She was in generally good spirits and spending a great deal of time out with friends.

Nathalie on her wedding day

A group of us went to dinner on various occasions. She came out to my area shows. We scheduled time to take long walks together. But things had changed, and as subtle as it was, I detected that something was eating at her. One evening she called to say she had gotten a bad test result. Some old cervical cancer had returned, and the doctors had given her conflicting, confusing reports. This was when I saw most vividly the deterioration caused by hearing the word "cancer." This vital, freckle-faced girl, line dancing and spirited, almost always flushed and laughing- suddenly went into a hospital for surgery, and from there it was a swift decline.

During her illness Nathalie and her husband traveled to the East West Institute. They had a consultation with Michio Kushi, a world renowned authority on macrobiotic healing. "What went wrong?" she asked. "I live on a farm in the country, I eat organic food, and I don't smoke." He said the most chilling thing which resonated to the core of my being. "Too much medical intervention," he said in a matter of fact way. How simple. Don't get tested so much- or if you're me, not at all. Of course they'll find something. Give them your body to poke and probe and they'll find something malignant, and then you'll have the hex on you. Studies have proven that if you think you're dying you're more likely to die, plain and simple. For myself I'd rather live happily in oblivion to the last, wandering about enjoying life until one day I simply keel over. Then they'll open me up and find all the diseases that should have killed me years earlier. For me, not knowing would probably add ten or more years. The plan is to get a foot rub everyday and feel tremendous gratitude- seize the day and the moment. Grab it by the reigns... and sing, Kushi said, "Sing a happy tune every day." He gave Nathalie a list- walk barefoot, laugh, take a warm bath, feel grateful, avoid doctors, and so on. Somehow over the span of my lifetime I have instinctively known these things.

Nathalie got thinner and thinner. She lost all sense of modesty, undressing in front of whoever was in the room without concern. She had somehow embraced the idea the she was dying yet at the same time fought it with the most intense kind of anger. I would stop in and find her in bed, depressed. She was in more and more pain, so I rubbed her feet and showed the technique to her husband. At other times she would be lying out in the hammock in her beautiful yard. She and her husband had an utterly lovely historic home on two hundred acres, and over time it had been landscaped beautifully with stone walls and perennial gardens of every description. As she lay in the dappled light, we reminisced about our many adventures. Suddenly she was crying and saying "We've been through so much together!" It was wrenching to see her this way- and myself as well, losing another dear friend.

Yes, we had been through so much. I just kept telling her she was going to make it.

She called frequently to ask if I knew of anything that could help with pain. I wracked my brains. I had heard of the use of magnets and bought her something which ended up not working. I also brought over a feather bed which she loved and sank into with a huge sigh. I gave her my reflexology sandals which she apparently wore, but I always had this feeling that ultimately she would reject all efforts to help- and it was frustrating. We still took walks like we used to, but now she was very weak. On our last walk together she became unexpectedly forceful and started moving faster and faster as if in a daze. Suddenly she collapsed. I looked at her lying in the dusty road. She looked like a bag of bones she was so thin. For a moment I had no idea what to do. I knew I couldn't carry her- but I had to get help. As she lay there on the shoulder, I ran back to the house as fast as I could. I found her oldest daughter and we jumped into the car and drove back to where she was resting- peacefully, in a way. I could see she had given up. The road was as good a place to lie down as anywhere. We were able to get her into the car and brought her home. I felt helpless and totally inadequate.

After that she went in and out of a kind of coma. I sat on her bed and read to her from the Bible. There were tears rolling down my face. Her husband sat nearby in silence. I felt for him- this must have been beyond awful. He seemed so devoted, so totally willing to do whatever it took.

She woke from time to time. In the end it was all about pain. She wanted more and more medication, far more than was advisable or safe. At one point when I was on tour I learned that she had asked for me. Apparently she needed three signatures from people close to her, authorizing something or other that might have led to her legally ending her life. I was glad I was not there, as I could never have agreed. I was torn because I knew she would have been angry at me had I said "No, I can't do that." I hoped I wouldn't someday be begging someone to help me leave this world to escape pain. It was confusing.

She died while I was away. Once again, through my grief, I felt angry. "Nathalie, come back!" I screamed. That was over ten years ago and

I still have this nagging feeling that she wasn't meant to leave. I still expect her to come back. It seems she left with much unfinished business, and I often feel her looking on with disapproval, as if I am being asked to go and set things right for her. She wants her flowers tended, her walls rebuilt, her business organized, her children mothered... I did try, after she died, to look in on her children and offer as much help as possible. But ultimately my friendship and concern would never be able to fill her important shoes- and I had to "let go and let God" all over again. Thankfully her children are all incredibly capable, talented and intelligent, just as she was. I think this competence, which she instilled in them, has helped them to survive the tragedy of her loss with greater resourcefulness. I will always feel like Aunt Rory.

Sometimes I find it hard to make friends like I used to. When we were younger we were naturally carefree and strong- confident that the world rolled out before us like a broad path. We had no thought of death or disease. We could laugh about our lives and at other people's lives. We never intended to give up. Now the weight of understanding fragility and impermanence pulls on us. We must be careful not to sit back and wait for things to decline.

The Video Experience

The voice was asking "Is this Rory Block?" "Yes," I said. "THE Rory Block?" "Ye-es!" I heard a lovely clear voice- it sounded familiar, like someone I had known for years. It made me so happy I almost started to laugh, but that would have made no sense. Film director Merle Worth was on the line, and she was calling to see if I would like to write a song for a video that was in the planning stages. Always up for a challenge, I wanted to hear all about it. The American Bible Society, she explained, was doing an educational series geared towards young people who were raised watching video and film and were less inclined to read than the previous generation. They had decided to put Bible stories into a kind of rock video setting to make them appealing to a modern generation accustomed to the format. A panel of experts had come together to create a new, extremely modern translation of the "Prodigal Son" Parable, and they were looking for an artist to

324

write a song and perform in the video. The project would involve a cast of actors and would be filmed just outside of Atlanta. I would be expected to ride a horse. This sounded incredibly cool.

"What made you think of asking me?" I inquired. Merle said that when she heard me sing "Walk In Jerusalem" she knew it had to be me. That song was still exuding some kind of transcendent power- it seemed to have an energy all its own. Even one of the most intense

Photo: Catherine Sebastian

atheists I know cried when I played it for her. This was the song that made my mother raise her weak little arm on her deathbed. For me it is not so much about my performance, though I knew it was inspired, but the fact that it was an incredibly emotional musical collaboration with my son Jordan. We were singing this powerful song together, and people would ask "Who's the brother?" when they heard his voice... and I would say "That's my son!"

Merle had called the record company to ask for my recordings. The label rep kept urging other singers on her. No, Merle was firm, she wanted Rory Block. The rep was saying "What about this one? Or "How about that one?" Merle said she had to get aggressive... she needed a copy of "Walk In Jerusalem." Maybe they had grown so much larger at that point that some of the down home atmosphere had given way to major label thinking- or maybe that day she got someone new who didn't know I had been with the company for fifteen years. But no matter, she got the record, played it for the execs at the ABS, and I got the job. All I had to do was use their translation word for word and make the song five minutes long. I loved the challenge- I was sure I could do it.

I used to have a process for writing songs- Ron would implement by recording whatever I came up with on the spot. This was in the thick of my songwriter days and I was sometimes writing more than one per day. I was on a roll at the right time, and somehow I came up with this epic song that fit all their guidelines. Jordan did a fantastic job singing the male voice. Merle was thrilled, the song was to be called "A Father And Two Sons," and it was off to Marietta, Georgia to make the video.

When we got there I realized this was a big deal. There was the equivalent of a festival site filled with lights, cameras, tents, equipment, actors, and crew, and even an animal or two milling around. The father was played by a great looking actor named Muse Watson. He exuded this wonderful, calm feeling which would be perfect for this role- he had to radiate paternal energy without being old or square. His face was filled with warmth and character, which had to be why they picked him for the role. Then there were the two sons, handsome young actors who looked to be in their twenties.

The first couple of days were orientation. We went down to the stables to check out the horses and meet the white stallion I was going to be riding. As we headed out on the trail with a long line of horses nose-to-tail, I learned that the stallion I was on was hated by the others. They wanted to kill him, explained our trail guide, because he was an unfixed male. I began to feel uneasy.

I was not inexperienced with horses. When we moved upstate I had purchased a horse and become a good rider. I got him from a teenager named Betty who used to barrel race, and had a stack of blue ribbons to show for it. Prince ran away with me the very first time I got on him and nothing ever felt so fast as clinging to this frenzied atomic powerhouse of a huge animal stretching his legs against the ground like a freight train. When we pulled up there were tears in my eyes from the wind, but I held on. I bought him, somehow wanting the challenge. My riding instructor got angry, saying I had made a bad choice- but Prince was beautiful, and I had this strong feeling about wanting him. However he ran away with me again as soon as I got him home. It became a pattern. I always stayed on, but I got more and more frustrated. He was taking control in this heady kind of way and I hadn't figured out how to stop him. Then several things happened which took me to the next level. A group of us were riding in an open field when someone suggested we run. Most trail horses will step up the pace but will not often bother to go all-out. They lope along or even gallop, but it doesn't get out of control. But Prince took off. He passed the others like they were standing still and suddenly I got it. Prince was a racehorse, and winning meant everything to him. He had the spirit of a warrior- he was a wild creature who loved to run. It was a beautiful thing. I leaned forward and gave him his head, and for the first time I wasn't scared. It was a "Wahoo" moment.

Betty was the best rider I have ever seen. She never used a saddle and would just leap lightly onto his naked back from the ground. She was fearless, totally relaxed, and perfectly in control. There was no yanking at his mouth, no battle of wills. "Watch this!" she'd say, and then show me some amazing move that belonged in a rodeo. Once she took Prince sideways down the edge of a steep gravel pit. I thought surely horse and rider were going to have a deadly accident, but she just rocked in the saddle until he went to the edge and started down, lightly alternating his feet in pairs, each one slipping down the hill through the gravel, then the other foot, down, down, tilting slightly, Betty tilting with him- all the way to the bottom. I couldn't believe my eyes. Another time she asked if I wanted to see how to stop him from running away. Of course I wanted to see, so she leaned forward lightly while lifting the reins gently and he took off like he was shot out of a cannon. Then she sat upright, just like that, and he stopped dead in his tracks. No pulling, no yanking, just sitting up straight- and he stopped on a dime. It was easy. I tried it, and it worked. Just lean forward to start, sit up to stop.

Back to Marietta, Georgia and the white stallion. I knew from experience that "kill" energy between large animals is nothing to trifle with. I wondered if the stable hands were a bit too casual, and if we were compromising safety just a little.

The following day we went out on the shoot. It was predawn and the mist was rolling across the grass as the sun peeked over the horizon- and then we heard a thundering sound. The earth started to shake. My horse, who had been totally calm, began to leap and prance, almost bucking in agitation. Suddenly a herd of horses roared towards us across a hillside and went straight for my stallion. Surrounded by an angry sea of whinnying, bucking, frenzied geldings intent on killing my horse was more than terrifying. He was being bumped, kicked, and bitten from every side. I was clinging for dear life knowing that if I went down I would be trampled to death, and if I stayed on I was likely to be severely injured by a kick or a bite. I don't quite know what happened, just that eventually the other riders and perhaps the camera crew managed, with much shouting and swinging of riding crops, to shoo this angry group of roving bandits away. I was unhurt but terribly rattled. Then they wanted me to canter across an open field through plumes of smoke from a machine- with this other herd of horses standing off in the distance glancing our way from time to time and fully aware of our presence. "Don't worry!" they kept saying to me "It's all under control now," while I kept repeating that we should wait, knowing that the adrenaline was still high- but they had to catch this scene during sunrise. So somehow I managed to get through it- or should I say the horse managed- and it ended up looking totally relaxed on film. I kept thinking that this must be what actors and actresses go through on a daily basis.

There were other scenes where I was singing in different locations and in different outfits. Merle kept on shouting "Beautiful! Beautiful!" as she cupped her hands over the camera. She was a fabulous director and clearly the energy behind it all. The final result was excellent, and we went to the screening feeling totally excited about the project. The song "A Father And Two Sons" ended up on my *Ain't I A Woman* CD.

Muse Watson

By some stroke of luck, the actor who had played the father in the video also had a trucking company that moved performers and gear. Between movie projects, Muse briefly became available as a driver, and no one could possibly have done a better job. Utterly road-savvy, Muse had the gift. At my request, he drove 55 miles per hour at all times. He never complained, never varied, and never made me feel uneasy. He was a natural at guarding and stood near the CD table with his leather vest and pipe with his arms firmly crossed. He patiently assisted load-in, and was an expert on the CB.

Muse's deep Louisiana drawl was the quintessential trucker voice. I learned more about the rules of the highway from listening to him converse on the radio than any movie, road novel or instruction manual could possibly reveal. Truckers can be mean, horny, and ruder than junkyard dogs, but also funnier and more entertaining than professional comedians. No one has a better natural sense of humor than a good-ol'-boy driving a truck.

Sometimes on a long run two semis double-up in a kind of buddy system. Late one night we were making some midnight miles when another voice joined up behind us. "Ya got cher ears awn, Camper?" The truckers usually called each other "Drah-ver!" but campers had a different name. When Muse answered, the banter started. The trucker asked why we were going so slow and said,"If ah owned that baby a'd be dravin' ninety mahles per awer down the hahway throwin' hundred doller beels out the winder at the cops..." Muse calmly answered- "Well, you know, the little lady's got all the doilies owt..."

The David Letterman Band- Paul Shaffer and Will Lee

Will Lee and I met many years ago through drummer Rick Marotta. Rick was part of a band assembled to back me up for some shows when I was on RCA. We became friends, and he took me to meet his buddies- some of the world's finest musicians- Steve Gadd, Will Lee, The Brecker Brothers, Richard T, the guys in "Stuff," Anthony Jackson and others. These were the top session guys who also did the jingles in New York, and watching them hanging out was totally entertaining- they had incredible camaraderie. No one gets a musician's life like another musician. After that I called Will from time to time to do sessions, and he brought Paul Shaffer with him. When recording *Tornado* we worked in the same building as the David Letterman show so they could do the session, run back to the show, then come back to the session. We'd take a break while they taped, then work again when taping was over. I had recorded with Paul Shaffer once before and knew he was a total gentleman. When he walked into the studio he bowed and kissed my hand. I thanked him for being so kind as to play on my record, and he told me it was his honor. He even wrote a little blurb for my press kit.

"Rory Block is one drop-dead gorgeous babe, and she can sing, too."
Paul Shaffer

Finding Aunt Frances

With Aunt Frances, her daughter Janice Randall
and granddaughter Sara

*P*erhaps my mother's youthful rebellion explained why none of her family stayed in touch after she ran off, and why I was raised without any awareness of the many relatives that remained on her side. It took my mother's first cousin Frances to approach me at a show in Phoenix, Arizona. I had no idea she existed until that moment, and I was in my 40s at the time. This brave little woman opened the door to a lost side of my family which turned out to be one of the best discoveries of my adult life.

Great-great-grandmother Martha Woodin with my grandfather's brother Roy Keller, my great-grandmother Ida Estelle Rogers Keller and Aunt Frances

After spending time with Frances (who was technically a cousin, but being closely related to my mother and of the same generation, felt distinctly like an Aunt), I learned that she was into genealogy, and she presented me with a large book resulting from her personal research that traced our family back many generations. Incredibly, after examining some of her records, I noticed that a great Aunt, a woman married to Alson Keller (one of my Grandpa Robert's brothers), was not only alive but living in the same county as I was, and in fact only about twenty minutes away! This was a revelation of the most amazing proportions. Alice Bloomer Keller, who lived in Hudson, had no date next to her name in the deceased column. This meant she was alive!

After returning home to Upstate New York I contacted Alice. She answered the phone. This was amazing... I just couldn't believe my good fortune. We arranged a visit, and as I walked down the hall of her assisted living apartment building and she watched me coming towards her, she said something amazing. She said "You look just like your Grandpa Robert- tall and slender." How this tugged at my heartstrings! The Grandpa I had never met- who died before I was born- whose amiable face smiled in antique photos- the long lost father my mother so loved and grieved when he died- I looked like him! It's hard to describe the emotion. Suffice it to say it's important to us all to be connected.

Alice Keller had some kind of machine which she wheeled around- perhaps it was oxygen, and I felt bad to see that she was so frail. But how precious, how incredible to have met her and learned of my likeness to my grandfather, and how deeply I appreciate Aunt Frances and what she did to bring us together!

Soon I located another of my mother's first cousins, Gertrude Keller, right up the road. She and her husband Robert (come on now, how can this be)? came over to my "Little Green House" and even my sister joined us. Gertrude, who reminded me of my mother, commented that my sister looked like Aunt Trudie, another interesting revelation. As much as Robert was the repeating name on the male side, Gertrude was the same on the female side. There were so many Gertrudes that each had a variation- Gertrude, Trudie, Gertie, etc. Then I met Helen, another of my mother's cousins. Next I got a letter from a Keller of my generation. Instead of my mother's cousins I was now meeting my mother's cousins' children. Grandpa Robert Keller had numerous brothers and only one sister (Gertrude, of course). Some of the Keller brothers had children, and I was now meeting Roy Keller's grandchildren, Carol and Michelle. This meant that our grandfathers were brothers. I think that made us second cousins, but these technicalities barely matter. They seem like sisters to me. They are fabulous women who feel like cookie-cutter versions of myself. We seem to think alike, and I feel totally comfortable around them even though we have only recently met.

If you haven't had this same experience it's probably difficult to convey the emotion one feels discovering relatives. We find in them a living, vital, mirror-image of ourselves. I will never know exactly how and why our family got so spread out or why we were raised without the knowledge of their existence, but perhaps this is like so many other things we do- purposely or accidentally- which we are greatly impoverished by.

Ron's Journey

1 thought Ron and I would last forever. I couldn't believe things ended the way they did. His words, which tore my world apart, inspired an entire album called *Tornado*. The demise of the relationship is a story I relate almost every show, but I think the it bears repeating with a few new details.

I believe it started to unravel the moment I got pregnant. Unfortunately, we were scheduled to leave on a long European tour and I knew immediately that flying overseas and continuing my grueling schedule was a bad idea. I had read about how flight during the first trimester was risky, but the tour was booked and there was no way to get out of it gracefully at the eleventh hour. So I boarded the plane feeling nauseous and exhausted. On one particular night off, we went to a movie with friends. People smoke their heads off in Europe, but I wasn't expecting it in a theater. I was spinning. All of a sudden I began to bleed, and I knew it wasn't good. We ended up at an emergency room where they did an ultrasound. There was bad news; the baby had no heartbeat. They offered to check me into a hospital and perform the operation right there, but I refused. The only alternative was to finish the tour and fly home. The doctor warned me that it was dangerous to board an airplane under the circumstances. She said I could start

bleeding over the ocean and not be able to get help. Miscarriages are not always easy, predictable events. There was a danger of bleeding to death if I couldn't get help in time. I continued the tour knowing that at any moment this event could begin. By some stroke of luck I ran into Bonnie Raitt on the road and she was immensely comforting. I cried when I explained my situation, and she was kind and understanding. That night I sang on stage with her with a dead baby inside me knowing I would be having a miscarriage in the near future.

The return flight was uneventful, and I was very relieved to be home safely. But soon afterwards contractions began and I was taken to the hospital in an ambulance barely able to lift my head. I had no idea it could go this badly- I thought miscarriages were like periods. I wasn't prepared for severe blood loss, near heart failure, and major trauma. I came home shaky and deeply depressed. I felt like the emptiest of all vessels.

Two weeks later I was in my flower garden and a shadow passed over me. I looked up and it was Ron. His lips were moving, and I thought he was saying something like "Don't take this personally, because I love you very much, but I'm leaving." It didn't compute. "What do you mean you're leaving? When are you coming back?" I stammered. I heard him say something about two or three weeks, but I knew right then and there that it was forever. He went away, I went into shock, and night after night I had harrowing visions of his face. I knew something was wrong. This was a different kind of breakup. I kept thinking "This is worse than forever."

You know how it is when someone you love is at someone else's house cheating... I'll spare you the details, except to say I called her up and got a load of bull about how he wasn't there- this, from the friend I took care of when her husband left for another woman! Betrayal is always ugly, and there is no defense against it. However, she was only a brief diversion, and then he met someone else.

One night I was weeping and clutching the pillow when a little voice said "Go get your guitar." I perched on the edge of the bed and wrote "Like A Shotgun" at two in the morning, and as I sat there rocking and singing this new song, my feeling of total despair changed... to total joy. I tell people at shows "That's what the music is for." A song can save your life. You've probably got one- I've got one: Bruce Hornsby's "Fields Of Gray" which I played incessantly at breakneck volume for well over a year. I had to have that song to survive. No other song would do.

Eventually I tuned out and started seeing someone else. But we have to be careful because the drug of a new relationship can bring a certain kind of blindness with it, and we may end up realizing that we compromised wisdom to avoid being alone. But no matter, a year passed.

Ron and I had been making one album almost every twelve months for a long time, so we went round and round- could we handle it or not? We changed plans a dozen times. I knew it would be difficult on many levels- for one thing every song on the album was about him, and seeing him would be painful, particularly since he was now living with his new girlfriend. I have no idea what was going on in his head as he had become a total stranger. It's as if he was trying to create a brand new personality. It all seemed so artificial. In retrospect he was having second thoughts and was not sure he had done the right thing.

I could tell that Ron was in pain. The songs on the *Tornado* album are hard-hitting, one right after the other. "Rosaline" is about the miscarriage, "Like A Shotgun" is the story of him walking away. He must have felt utterly naked the entire time, but somehow we got through it. It got so raw that I wished we could have hugged- but we never did. I knew all of this had a direct connection to the miscarriage, but this is something he would never acknowledge. *Tornado* later won the NAIRD Award for "Adult Contemporary Album of the Year." At least my pain had added up to something...

At the one year mark Ron had a small walnut-sized lump on his forearm. We all asked about it and he said it had been looked at and that it was nothing. But a year later when we assembled to make another album (which turned out to be our last), he was a changed man. His hair was long and pulled back into a pony tail. His skin was gray, and I could see he was very sick. His eyes looked apologetic. He was having problems with the new relationship and portrayed her as an ice princess. He began confiding in me. He wanted to talk about her, so I listened. This was fascinating in a weird kind of way. One thing was clear, she wasn't there for him.

A couple weeks after the record was completed I got a call saying Ron was in the hospital. This was scary. For one thing, I still loved him. We can armor ourselves all we want, but real love lasts forever, and I could feel the same tears that had plagued me when Uncle Bob died, when the little animal perished in the bathroom on the Cape- my incessant, out of control, humbling compassion- welling up. How I wished I could control this and make it go away, but it's not meant to be. What would I say? What would I do, what would I wear, what would I bring? I panicked all the way to the hospital. Everything was wrong. My shirt color was too bright and cheery- inappropriate, I thought. My choice of photos too happy- they would only depress him now. They showed us happy, in love, busy, without a care in the world. My words would be wrong. Then I realized: BE WRONG- BUT GO. The same temperature changes, bursts of heat followed by flushing, cooling, then heating up again that had accompanied signing of the adoption papers so many years ago was happening again. This was emotional, not physical in origin.

I walked towards the room and there were Ron's parents in the hall-way. We all fell apart immediately. It was incredibly bittersweet to see them. We understood the gravity of this loss. Ron's mother in particular knew how much I loved him and how I would have tried to prevent this from happening had I been able. In retrospect, I wondered if Ron left because, on some deeper spiritual level, he knew he was dying- and that I would have interfered. I would have taken him to every specialist and stopped at nothing to save his life. Ron must have made some kind of decision about this being his time. He never really seemed to resist what was happening to him.

Ron lay on the bed a virtual scarecrow. He was a shadow of his former self, yet his eyes were crystal clear and very blue. It was like my mother's eyes after Will died- 100% open, without guile; a doorway to his soul. Eyes have incredible ability to communicate- or they can glaze over and atrophy, sending out no message at all- this is when the owner of the eyes is totally blocked, and thus, I instinctively feel, dangerous.

"Please forgive me... nothing was gained. We could have worked it out." He said every touching and kind thing. "You were the love of my life"... "I made a mistake. I know I hurt you." These precious healing moments don't always materialize in a given lifetime. Sometimes im-portant people go to their graves with no closure and without forgive-ness. I knew this difficult time was of immeasurable value to us both.

I stayed with him for two weeks, night and day. The nurse opened a fold-out chair where I slept next to his bed. He kept saying "Please don't leave me," and "You are the only one here for me." Although I was wearing a ring for my new relationship (the one that later turned out to be an illusion), and although he was asking me directly if I was happy with the obvious implication that he wanted me back, I clung to the ring and what I hoped it represented- some imagined security, and some ill-placed confidence. I should have followed my instincts, called the other person to say goodbye, and married Ron in the hospital. Marrying Ron was a long term goal, and I had pursued him relentlessly against all his "new age" objections.

At the last, Ron left the hospital and I drove him to his parents. I had seen him through many tests and surgery. The other woman never showed up. She really was an ice princess. The "interim fling" lady phoned once while I was sitting there, and in a loud, edgy voice that you could hear across the room, asked "Right NOW?" when he told her I was there. I thought she sounded like Foghorn Leghorn, the rooster in the old cartoons with a blast-furnace voice. It's funny how people who seem to have so much power one moment have no consequence the next. She never showed either.

The ice princess began demanding career assistance and various professional guarantees from Ron as he had apparently promised to train her as an assistant. The whole thing started to seem like it was a business deal to her. We were aghast, but no one could say anything to him. He was clinging to straws.

Jordan, who was in his twenties at the time, loved Ron very much. He considered Ron a friend, brother, and a father figure rolled into one. He respected Ron's accomplishments and talents. Jordan was on his way to see Ron at home, but by the time he arrived Ron was in a coma. There were no words spoken, but I'm sure Ron appreciated Jordan's presence.

Ron loved Jordan and was there for him through the transitional and complex teenage years. Being a successful engineer, Ron always had a cool sports car, and young boys gravitate to these like supercharged magnets to iron. Somehow, Ron allowed Jordan and a very shady friend to borrow his little red car for a short spin, and when they returned Ron knew something had happened. As Ron circled the car suspiciously, Jordan and his lock-picking, jail-baiting friend denied

338

all. "No, nothing happened!" they protested. But when Ron opened the trunk he saw that all the contents were tightly pressed into one corner, which could only have happened as a result of some extreme burst of speed or violent braking. Years later Jordan revealed the harrowing truth of the story; how his friend had urged him to ramp up and pass another car, how the other driver had done battle on a narrow road, not wanting to be left in the dust by two teenagers in a shiny red sports car. So a race began, and the faster they went, the more the other car sped up. They found themselves in the passing lane hurtling towards an oncoming vehicle, and with the closest of margins, escaped a head-on collision. They were shaken up when they returned, but realized how important it was to act completely cool.

When Ron died I couldn't bear to go to the funeral. I sent a hand-written note with a friend who read it at the service. I had my special time with Ron; we said our goodbyes and had come to terms with each other. Before the funeral I met Ron's parents on the highway and brought numerous framed photos of him to be displayed at the service. Beautiful, bright, happy pictures of a handsome, outstanding-looking man who had been such a steady, kind presence, such a skilled and artistic expert, and such a source of happiness and hope in our lives.

Afterthought

A therapist said it, and I wrote it down on a piece of paper: "After a miscarriage, the man frequently takes off." The note was lying out by the phone, and the next time I saw it, these words had been added: "all his clothing." Thus it read: "After a miscarriage, the man frequently takes off all his clothing." Don't ask me why this seemed so funny, or charming- and how can I explain that this note, with its light hearted humor, made me decide to go out with the person who wrote it, only to find that what seemed like charming humor was actually a total emotional disconnect. But the humor helped me greatly at that moment. I had almost bled to death and my blood count was very low. The grief and emptiness of losing a baby and being abandoned was excruciating. I followed my broken heart into another brief relationship which ended in a chillingly similar way, yet with much less time and no deeper connection, thank God. I found myself saying "I will not let anyone destroy me," and that was the turning point. I have not become bitter, just less likely to lay myself open to attack.

The Research Project

Some time after Ron died I endeavored to read the entire Bible again. This time I read it twice, reading the Amplified version. This was a huge research project, but I never lost interest or ran out of energy. I couldn't wait to start reading again the next morning over coffee. The Amplified Bible sends you back and forth between related texts so you can understand the source and learn where things repeat themselves. I found myself reading it in a scholarly way, something I never dreamed I could do. After all, I was the kid who hated school... so I was surprised to find I was capable of incredibly involved study. I went through this entire process of tagging pages and making detailed notes, and discovered that I was totally wrong in my perception that Jesus could be separated from the Old Testament. He tells us clearly that he is the fulfillment of the prophesies: *"These are the words which I spake unto you, while I was yet with you, that all things must be fulfilled, which were written in the law of Moses, and in the prophets, and in the psalms, concerning me," Luke 24:44.* "Think *not that I am come to destroy the law, or the prophets: I am not come to destroy, but to fulfil," Matthew 5:17.* The first five chapters of Matthew have over a dozen references to scripture being fulfilled: *"Now all this was done, that it might be fulfilled which was spoken of the Lord by the prophet..." Matt 1:22.* Jesus quoted repeatedly from Psalms, Isaiah, and many other Old Testament books. His death on the cross and final words are all foretold clearly. Psalm 22 gives accurate details of his crucifixion: *"I am poured out like water, and all my bones are out of joint," Ps. 22:14.* Scientific studies show this is what crucifixion does to the joints. Jesus said *"I thirst"* when he was on the cross. *"...my tongue cleaveth to my jaws," Ps. 22:15. "...they pierced my hands and my feet," Ps. 22:16.* After Jesus's death the Roman soldiers divvied up his clothing: *"They part my garments among them, and cast lots upon my vesture," Ps. 22:18.* Psalm 22 contains an exact transcript of Jesus's last words:*"My God my God, why hast thou forsaken me?" Ps. 22:1.* Thus Jesus tells us directly that he cannot be separated from the Old Testament, but when we read casually, it's easy to miss this. The Amplified Bible reveals these powerful connections. However the Bible does say this about the Old Testament: in 2nd Corinthians, chapter 2, Peter says that there was a veil over the understanding of the Old Testament which was removed by Jesus.

I should point out that this is not about me trying to convince you- any more than *When A Woman Gets The Blues* attempts to convince you to play guitar and go on tour. This should be about intelligent people having an interesting conversation. I wouldn't want to leave out something that influenced me- say, meeting Son House- any more than I would leave out the Bible. I personally find it interesting that someone raised to be as left wing as I was- taught to be skeptical, suspicious, and intellectually rejecting of God and spirituality- could be so moved and changed by the Bible. I never expected that to happen in a million years. But after studying it, I just don't find intolerance, unfairness, inequality, or hatred in this book. I find enlightened instruction of the highest kind: *"But the fruit of the Spirit is love, joy, peace, longsuffering, gentleness, goodness, faith, meekness, temperance: against such there is no law," Gal 5:22-23.* It's not like there are a bunch of disparate, inconsistent teachings contained in its pages. To the contrary there is a supernatural level of consistency that can't be explained intellectually. Recently there have also been computer based discoveries such as Bible codes. It's something to ponder.

Michael Hedges: The Guitar Summit Tours

One day I was invited to be part of a terrific series of shows called "The Guitar Summit Tours." This was no doubt someone's very cool brainchild and always featured four guitarists of differing styles traveling together and performing in the best, most upscale venues. I was honored to be included on two of these tours- the first with Herb Ellis playing jazz, Sharon Isbin, classical, Michael Hedges, contemporary- and I was there representing blues. Every night each performer did a solo set- two opened, followed by an intermission- then the other two closed the show. The evening ended with a four-artist finale, and each was expected to do a solo. I was devastated. I couldn't solo, I explained... I was the kind of guitarist who did the old arrangements note for note, and that was it. I had never had the ability to improvise. Besides, I didn't see myself as a "real" guitar player. Anybody could do what I did, they just didn't want to. Michael Hedges later took me aside. In a hushed tone he told me I was flat out wrong. He called me a great guitar player, and wouldn't hear of any supposed insecurity. He said "Of course you can do it!" Then he leaned over and said something that touched my heart. "You're the reason I came on this tour," he said. "Ask my manager if you don't believe me." I was dumbstruck. Here was this superb musician, a world-class player who refused to look down on me. I said, "Anyone can do what I do." But he said "No way- if you think what you do is easy, you're crazy. Just because someone plays great electric guitar doesn't mean they can get a handle on the complexities of Country Blues. It's a whole other animal," he stated. I never thought of it that way. He made me feel fantastic- my confidence grew that night. Later, with his encouraging words in my head, I played a solo and it came out better than I expected. "See?" he said, "I knew you could do it." We sat there in the back room in our stage outfits contemplating where life had taken us. "Those are cool," he said, pointing to my leopard leggings.

Imagine my horror to learn that only about two weeks after completing this tour my friend Michael died in a car accident. No one could believe it. He had been winding up a narrow coastal highway in northern California to see his children when he went off the road. It took a while for the authorities to locate his car. Devastation upon devastation! I became ever more aware that we are here one moment, gone the next. Nothing is guaranteed, and every second is what we have. I reminded myself again to be grateful and make something positive out of each moment of existence, because it is so fragile and fleeting.

Band On The Road

Jordan, Peter O'Brien, Mike DeMicco and Rob Leon in Europe

In 1997 we went on tour with a band to support the *Tornado* release. The band was comprised of some of the most highly respected musicians on the east coast, and despite the fact that I was a solo artist and not an experienced band leader, they carried the day, having played together for years. I floated about on the stage virtually unable to hear my vocals, unsteady with the guitar shifting about on the end of a strap. I have always anchored myself on a chair where my two feet can stamp, with the guitar resting securely on one leg. Being upright with an instrument swinging wildly was totally foreign to me- and I could barely play. It felt like the time I drifted about aimlessly on stage with Bonnie, not knowing a word of the song, and generally making an ass out of myself. The band held it together beautifully, and eventually I started to relax and enjoy the feeling of having powerful musicians supporting me- there's a sense of "Got your back!" which I never knew before. "I could get used to this," I thought as I danced around. Soon we began to lock-in and I learned I could make eye contact with Rob Leon, a powerhouse bass player from the jazz band The Dolphins (a group founded by Dave Brubeck's son Danny). Rob was like a security guard. His vibe was intense, and his bass playing could bring

343

down the house. No one had better attack, technique, tone, or sensitivity. Rob was a monster player, and a master of every style. Want a little Jaco? No problem. Want jazz? How about some super funk with snapping? Or maybe some gorgeous harmonics. For all his formidable presence he had an incredibly gentle spirit, and he was one of the most comforting people on the road. He talked about his little daughter all the time, and he was aligned with the emotional content of every song we played. He watched my solo set each night and complimented me repeatedly, and his attentive, kind remarks helped me gain confidence. He always noticed my perfume. He would walk over, sniff my neck and sigh with approval. When he died some years later in Florida we were all bereft. The vacuum left by the death of a great musician is incalculable.

Guitarist Mike DeMicco is an excellent jazz player with solo albums and extensive touring experience. Remember the cereal commercial where the older brothers pass the bowl to little Mikey the fussy eater, and in suspense, they wait for his first bite? When he smiles, they cheer and shout "Mikey likes it!" This is where I got Mike's nickname. Mikey is one of the best people on the planet. He's a good soul with the ability to cut to the bone with remarks that kept us all in stitches. His guitar playing regularly brought tears to my eyes.

Peter O'Brien is a fabulous, slammin' solid drummer. I saw him on stage with Orleans at a festival in Vermont and thought he was one of the sexiest men on the planet. Musicians seem to have a charisma that drives women wild, and Pete had it. I've always loved someone who can hold down the beat (remember, my dad valued that above all else), so Pete was a hero to me immediately.

He was also one of the funniest people I have ever met, right up there with Alan Gorrie of the Average White Band. Pete and Rob Leon often told me they were brothers. They were quip-masters, along with Mikey, and we roared with laughter all the way down the road listening to their routines.

These were accomplished jazz musicians and I always considered jazz to be way over my head. Being around players who understood such a sophisticated art form was humbling. I used to record regularly with piano player Warren Bernhardt, who always left me reeling with his intricate rhythms. Warren plays everything- just ask, no problem. But I particularly love Warren's understanding of early blues piano. Very few people can handle a song like Skip James's "If You Haven't Any Hay, Get On Down The Road," but Warren can play it perfectly. If you want your head to spin, listen to the original.

The Sound Clown From Hell

You'll never know and I'll never tell, but there was someone who earned this nickname. Every tour has to have a title, and every memorable road experience takes on epic proportions. I've worked with some of the best engineers on earth- and some less than that, shall we say. In the early days of touring I understood the challenges inherent in showing up at a new venue and having the house engineer, who had often never heard your music, try to mix the pounding, snapping sound of a Willie Brown or a Charlie Patton song. House mixers invariably tried to notch out the thumping frequency. Most had been trained to smooth out the sound, not enhance the slam. A lot of sound systems in small venues are jury rigged to the max, and some are run by rank amateurs. So I spent many years being blown off the stage by shrieking monitors or regaled by disappointed audience members complaining about the thin, shrill quality of the house sound (as if it was anything I could control). Eventually I started bringing my own engineer. Jim Gallagher, who also worked with Stevie Wonder, brought the audio to a whole new professional level that allowed me to perform, not struggle with bad sound. He drove, set up and tore down, ran the board, and gave me credibility. After Jim there were others, notably Ron, of course, who was the ultimate stabilizing factor on the road. But when Ron left it was back to the drawing board. I desperately needed an engineer for a particular tour and only a day or two before departure, one was located. It's not easy to just take off down the road with someone you never met before. You can find yourself in a tight situation with no alternatives, and this happened with two engineers in a row on a tough band tour. I will spare the details, but one of them got the little nickname above while another shut the tour down every hour to get out and pee. Eventually the band members took his iced tea bottles away from him. They told me all he did was sit there

345

and suck these down and then pull over to pee. We had to make five hundred miles per day and this guy was shutting down the tour.

After this Rob Leon and Peter O'Brien started talking about a guy named Rob Davis. He was "the man" according to them. Rob Leon made the call and put me on the phone with Rob Davis, and from the beginning we started laughing. When he heard about the tour shutting down so the other engineer could pee every hour on the hour he said, "You've got to be kidding me! That's not going to work at all!" The next gig we did was at the Bottom Line in New York City, and that was the first gig where Rob did the sound.

BB & Bobby At The San Francisco Blues Festival

The San Francisco Blues Festival is one of the most prestigious festivals. The first time I was booked there BB King and Bobby McFerron were performing. When I walked back stage I saw a crowd of journalists clustered around someone. It was BB King in all his glory, and there was something very moving about seeing him up close. I must have had an expression of reverence on my face and didn't notice another awesome person standing next to me. Suddenly I realized Bobby McFerron was looking at me. Startled, I said, "He's beautiful looking" referring to BB King. "You're beautiful looking" he answered with an incredibly sweet smile. I was floored, but being shy, I had no idea what to say. I mustered a "Thank you." His compliment touched me deeply.

Straight To The Hospital

The next time I was booked at the San Francisco Blues Festival was in the midst of a long west coast tour. The previous evening I had performed in Davis, California and during the show I began having sharp abdominal pains. It was not like indigestion, it felt like something inside me was torn- like an injury. Later that night it got progressively worse. In my hotel room the pain was so intense I was doubled over and knew there was a serious problem. I called Rob, who had now begun taking me on the road, to tell him I thought I was going to have to go to the hospital. I don't remember much after that- I know he had to prop me up in the elevator as the pain was so excruciating I started to faint. I was lying across the back seat of the cab in agony. At the hospital they injected me with pain killers and I went into some kind of twilight sleep. Doctors banged in and out of my room every so often. Someone said intestinal problems were showing up throughout the city that night. I was too drugged to care. Rob managed to stay with me for the first two days until he had to fly home, but I don't remember anything about that time. He later told me he had to confront a few people about something or other- I think he said they were ignoring me for hours on end as I lay on a table by myself in a stupor. Afterwards I was transferred to a room where I was pumped full of intravenous antibiotics. I had a raging fever and some unidentified internal issues which could have been a burst appendix, diverticulitis- or any number of other grim possibilities. As I lay there depressed, alone in a strange hospital on the west coast with an unknown condition and unable to make it to the festival- nothing could have been more discouraging. Several doctors voiced completely different opinions. One suggested exploratory surgery, to which I flatly said NO. In addition the nurses seemed worse than incompetent. More than once they forgot my medicine, and another time someone brought me pills that turned out to be for another patient. I figured it out because they kept calling me Kate. No one was able to get an intravenous line into my veins, and after poking me repeatedly, someone did something which caused extreme pain and a large swelling from internal bleeding. Eventually they stopped the intravenous medication and switched to oral. By this time I was determined to get out of there before I was killed by a nurse- to heck with the unidentified internal problem.

On the second day the promoter from the festival showed up with flowers. He had some ideas about what might have happened to me- perhaps diverticulitis, he suggested. His wife had experienced it and the symptoms sounded exactly the same. I was greatly cheered by his visit and was touched that my situation warranted the honor of his presence. Then Maria Muldaur, who lived nearby, arrived with bags of lovely things from the health food store. It was an incredible boost to see my dear friend. Finally Marc Silber came over. He sat on the bed, played guitar and sang to me. Nothing could have made a bigger difference.

In desperation I started calling all my friends back east. Old friend Bill Knight suggested I call my cousin Bethany Block. I ran the situation by her and she immediately made some suggestions for simple tests no one had thought of which seemed obvious. She was also able to negotiate my release to continue any necessary treatment at home, and my travel agent, a wonderful lady named Pike (pronounced Pee-Kay- who also did all the flight arrangements for Taj Mahal), offered to fly with me to the East Coast so I would have a chaperone. The only requirement was that my fever had to break.

The next day Marc came by. My fever was still raging and I was totally discouraged. But then something amazing happened. Marc was singing- his wonderful voice and beautiful guitar playing was like chicken soup to me- as I lay there washed in the sentimental, soothing cascade of notes, I decided to get rid of my fever. I concentrated, determined. First, I got hotter and began to sweat. My face was flushed, my cheeks turned beet red, and I felt like a furnace. It was scary because for a moment I was getting worse. Then it happened. It was as if the top of my head blew off, and in just a few minutes I cooled down to normal. Miraculous. So again I say this- you can control your body functions. How do you think Buddhist Monks are able to sleep outdoors in the thinnest cotton garments in the ice and snow while Westerners are huddled in their high tech winter clothing trying to keep warm? It's the mind. I believe we make the choices, and the body listens. My homeopath Dr. Incao says the body has its own wisdom and is making adjustments constantly in the background. What an amazing system.

Hooray! Marc picked me up in his old truck, we went to the pharmacy to fill the prescription for some antibiotics which I tossed in the trash, and within a day, Pike flew home with me. At the local clinic I was told I had to have a barium enema. As I sat on the table sipping horrendous radioactive pink stuff, my body rebelled again. "I can't drink any more of this," I said. "You have to," they insisted. "No," I said, "I can't do it." So they did their little put-me-in-a-tube routine until I couldn't take it anymore and no one was the wiser. They still couldn't tell what had happened, but they did say there was no walled-off abscess (which might have indicated a burst appendix), so that was a relief. The doctor at the clinic suggested a few things like "take fiber." I felt delicate, but so glad to be home that nothing could prevent me from rejoicing. Shortly afterwards, with no one able to say what had happened, and with the simple knowledge that I was still alive, I put the whole thing out of my mind.

Later Rob came to visit me with his two children. It was so nice to see them. Even though Rob was just my friend at the time I was starting to think he was pretty terrific.

Walk In Jerusalem In Pennsylvania

I am always surprised and delighted when fans know my songs. I love it when people call out song names- but this night was unusually special. We arrived at a wonderful little listening room called The Common Ground in Bryn Mawr, Pennsylvania, and discovered that a group of local singers had worked out the entire arrangement (including vocals and keyboards) to "Walk In Jerusalem" and were offering to perform it with me. As if this wasn't great enough, they wanted to know if Jordan would be singing the male vocal. Unfortunately Jordan wasn't on that tour, but this group of enthusiasts didn't stop there. They offered to send a helicopter to upstate New York to get Jordan and bring him to the show to sing, and then fly him home. Someone knew the pilot, and we almost made it work- if he hadn't been out on another job, it would have happened. That took top honors as the most effort any fans were ever willing to expend just to hear a song.

So I sang "Walk In Jerusalem" with these local singers anyway, and it was beyond beautiful. These were professional level voices and they knew every note. The piano player had the part written out and all that was left was for me to sing. The support of beautiful background vocals cannot be overstated. This was the best I had ever performed the song live. Angels sang it for me, really- I just stood back and listened as if in a dream.

Rob, who was now working with me full time, fastened my necklace in the back room before the show. He walked me arm in arm across the snow, carried everything in and out of the venue, and did incredible sound. Driving to and from shows hour after hour, day after day, I began to confide in him. This is what I call romantic, and this is how our relationship started.

Practice, Quantum Leaps And The Art Of Resisting Progress

1 don't generally practice, warm up, or rehearse. I suppose I am still the rebellious child refusing to cooperate- just like when I was forced to study classical guitar. It's possible there are many things we do in life simply to subconsciously assert our will, which defeat the entire purpose and hold us back... and doing this for rebellion's sake would be just that. But it's possible there is a different element: a flighty brain which leaps to new pursuits- wanders out of doors, finds a pile of clutter to sort through, or simply glories in the art of avoidance. Some things feel like they require walking over glowing coals to accomplish- that's how entrenched the resistance can be.

In the recent past I have had to come face to face with this closed door, and the ridiculous assumption that I had already acquired enough information. I used to feel my style of playing was complete, and that I knew the things I needed to know to carry on, most of my innovation and struggle having occurred at fourteen years old. Then I began to notice how useful it would be to play slide and not just a close facsimile done with the fingers... that had stood me in good stead for some years, but it was becoming one dimensional. Bare hands have no shimmer, no sparkle. I was becoming too precise. One day a European writer stopped in to the house in Upstate New York. He wanted to show me something. He too loved the old blues. With my permission he grabbed my guitar and started playing slide. This was irritating. He was pretty good. #$%^&! If he could do this, perhaps I had better look into it! I had been avoiding it for a while, years even, and this was the catalyst that pushed me over the edge. Everyone and their uncle was playing slide, I reasoned, and I can't afford to get left behind. Slide was no longer an eclectic oddity for a few specialty players. I had to get on board. This was going to mean practice- that dirty word.

My reason was originally that in 1964 you couldn't buy a slide, nor could you find a bottle narrow enough to fit a small hand. Stefan Grossman, John Hammond, and a few others could break any standard wine bottle, sand off the end and have a perfectly good slide. If you were really super funky you could go with a jackknife like Fred Mc-Dowell, who also managed to use a beef bone, and later glass- but for myself I gave up the search. I had another reason as well- that Robert Johnson's playing was so clean it almost didn't sound like slide. The modern attempts with jangly, buzzy tones awash with multiple fre-quencies just didn't sound like the old records. It was too modern, too bright. Maybe it had to be an old recording, a dusty back road, and a rusted old piece of metal to get it right. So I had allowed it to slumber.

John Hammond provided the information that led to the change- he told me to "Go out and buy yourself a socket wrench, they come in all sizes." I would have no more excuses. I rummaged through a friend's tool box and found a fourteen millimeter deep well socket which fit the third finger of my left hand- it went on only far enough to cover the first half of the finger, allowing me to bend at the knuckle the way Fred McDowell did it... same finger, same idea.

Knowing with a sense of aggravation that I had to put in some seri-ous work, I picked up the socket. Man, it sounded bad. I tried this and that, but my attempts were all pathetic. All I could produce was a thin, edgy, out-of-tune note. It felt tense, very tense. This was going to be a real problem, a challenge I wasn't sure I had the energy to tackle. Yet I knew that avoidance was not going to work anymore.

There were stages, small advances, but mostly frustration. I want to say this went on for almost five years, and I was making little or no headway. Then came the breakthrough listening to Bonnie's playing. The easy, relaxed, rocking attitude was pure revelation. The informa-tion she imparted was priceless, and pointed me in a new direction. This is what many guitar players crave. Finding themselves stuck at a certain level, they seek a key which will open a new door of informa-tion and allow them to move forward and grow musically, and this is what motivates many players to take a lesson or attend a workshop. Being stuck is boring, and if you are bored everyone who hears you will be bored. Boredom is death- so we need to seek these inspirational jolts.

One evening I was sitting in the back room of Godfrey Daniels, a great little folk club in Pennsylvania. Back home I was preparing to record a Charlie Patton song that required slide, and as I sat there doodling, it fell into "the pocket"- just like that. A friend was standing nearby and said "Awesome." Awesome, I thought- how is *that* possible? Then I tried it again. It seemed like something had changed. I grabbed onto it for dear life, and suddenly I had a handle on it. It was relaxed, and had a really super slippery attitude. For a while it was still illusive, and this "pocket" could sometimes disappear- but within the next year or two my hand finally learned it. Now I love nothing more than slide. I can almost say I live to play slide.

The Signature Model Martin Guitar

Much to my shock and surprise Dick Boak called one day to say that Martin wanted to design a signature model guitar for me. I had been forgiven for cracking the last one! I was beside myself with excitement. So many great things had come to pass, and this was one of the best. After all the years of borrowing guitars from friends and coveting other people's instruments, I would actually have a Martin guitar with my name on it!

We went to an area sushi restaurant where we drew ideas on dinner napkins. First, we came up with the concept of the neck as a highway- the black top road seemed like a bluesy theme. Then we added passing and no passing zones that would be done in mother of pearl inlays. We designed a railroad crossing to signify Robert Johnson's "Crossroads," added "stop" and "yield" signs, and Dick created a fantasy Terraplane car to celebrate the Johnson song of the same name. It took a while- there were more months of discussions, brainstorming, drawings and prototypes, but eventually the guitar was unveiled at the NAAM

Photo: Sergio Kurhajec

354

show in Nashville. I was flushed with pride and ridiculously happy as I stood next to my brand new guitar.

The instrument became the ultimate combination of everything I had always loved about Martin Guitars. I chose the classic body shape and size so it would be a good fit for a man or a woman, a rowdy player or a mellow finger picker- every range of style and approach- so as not to limit the function of the instrument in any way. I asked Martin to design extra strong bracing and durable frets for the way I play- case hardened steel. It could be that someone else out there would also want to slam the guitar.

It is Martin's policy to invite each artist to pick their favorite charity, and to arrange for 100% of the artist's share of the proceeds to be donated to that organization. What a wonderful opportunity this was for me! After careful consideration, I chose Best Friends Animal Sanctuary. I later spoke to the people at Best Friends and found they had received some thousands of dollars as a result of my guitar, and even though it's only a small contribution to a very large problem- that of neglected, abandoned and abused animals- I know that every little bit helps.

A Near-Death Experience Without The Enlightenment

In my mid-forties I decided to try In Vitro fertilization. It was a complex process requiring a huge amount of planning and preparation, and although I ended up pregnant with twins, one of the embryos was not viable and was the cause of another severe miscarriage. After these two life-threatening events I was traumatized. I had almost bled to death for the second time in my life and was being told I could hemorrhage again. I had received six pints of blood under pressure in addition to multiple bags of fluids. I've never been so weak, exhausted or aware of what dying by blood loss really feels like. As I was being raced into emergency surgery, I remember saying, "Take my uterus, it's trying to kill me!" which was probably mildly amusing at the time. But I knew I didn't want to go through anything remotely like that ever again. The last thing I remember is the doctor telling me that would be a bit drastic- I don't suppose people are encouraged to make

By Rory, 3 yrs old. Originally printed by DoubleTake magazine, 1999.

life changing decisions under sedation. After the surgery I was ordered to stay in bed for two weeks. I lay motionless on the couch in complete terror without sleeping for fourteen days and nights. At that point I became a television addict. I had to take my mind off my situation and Colombo reruns helped immensely. With the TV tilted towards the couch I watched one show after the other around the clock. I don't think my eyes ever closed once until the two-week limit was reached and I was out of the woods. Every day I would count down... seven more days, six more days to go... it was pure hell. In addition there was the grief to deal with. A new life, in which you invested all your emotion- love, hope, anticipation- is now gone. Miscarriage may sneak by as a bad period, but in fact it's a real death with all the accompanying emotions.

As a result of these two extreme bleeding events I can now add the sight of blood to the list of things that terrify me. At the onset of the first miscarriage I thought all the bleeding was somewhat interesting. I had no idea how limited the supply of blood in our bodies really is or the true implications of losing a fair amount of it. That particular sense of weakness is very frightening- not being able to lift your head for instance- because you can't fight it. It's like someone pulled the plug. The blood in our veins is life, and the less we have the less alive we are in a sense. By the time the first miscarriage ended in surgery, I was learning about what I should have done. Jordan, who had taken some intensive courses in wilderness survival and how to deal with life threatening medical emergencies, said "Mom, you only have only 13 pints of blood in your entire body- you can't mess around with blood loss, you have to go to a hospital immediately."

Live On QVC With Steve Bryant

It was at this time that I discovered QVC and the soothing, comforting effect of listening to inconceivably polite men and women talking about fashion or chatting away about vacuum cleaners, non-stick pots, and sleep number beds. I found it totally encouraging. I noticed that other listeners called in, and it seemed like many were convalescing just like me- some were housebound, some elderly. It was actually touching hearing various people say QVC felt like family to them. Some people left it on all the time just for company. It's pretty much what I was doing, and soon I was familiar with every show, every product and every host. My absolute favorite was Senior Host Steve Bryant. Cut from an entirely different cloth, Steve was rip-roaringly funny. I know he gave the suits a nonstop headache as he always played things his own way. He talked about guys drooling in their sleep while he was selling pillows, mentioned his "partials" falling out while selling toothpaste, and smushed the pancakes on a cooking show advertising a nonstick griddle. As he pulled the tray of squashed flap-jacks and slid them out of sight on a lower shelf, the camera zoomed in behind the counter. "That's it guys" he said, "Follow me down!" Some people probably missed the humor, but I noticed that this guy was hysterically funny and totally together.

One day Steve was selling kitchen gadgets when he pulled out an acoustic guitar and began playing in a style somewhere between Dave Van Ronk and Lightning Hopkins. I couldn't believe it. "Wait a min-ute!" I thought. "I'll have to call this guy up and say, 'Hey, you don't know who I am, but I play guitar, and I'd like to be on your show!'" A crazy idea, but I had learned that crazy stuff sometimes works. However I never made the call as I didn't think I'd ever be able to get through.

It was on the second Guitar Summit Tour (where Stanley Jordan had replaced the slot vacated by Michael Hedges), and we had just played a theater in Wilmington, Delaware. As I stood at the CD table greeting a line of fans, there he was in all his glory- Steve Bryant on line to buy a CD. "Hey, you're the QVC guy!" I blurted. Wouldn't 'cha know it, I suddenly couldn't remember his name. But Steve is a gentleman to the core. He had come to pay his respects, and suddenly I was paying mine. I explained the idea about being on his show. He said "I would love to have you on my show!"

We had a series of follow-up calls discussing his idea about how to package my product. He wanted to create a compilation of Country Blues. I offered a songwriter CD as an option thinking that middle America might be more open to Adult Contemporary than early blues, but Steve was determined. He said "Before I leave this place I want to do something that feels good in my heart. This is the music I love." So he went to bat for me in a big way. He said to his boss "If I can't sell this, you can fire me." Of course they didn't know he was planning on leaving.

It took about a year but Steve made it happen. The record company got on board and a two-CD package containing *Gone Woman Blues* and *Confessions of A Blues Singer* was shrink wrapped together with QVC's brand name on it. We went on air sandwiched between two other products: Hippopotamus shaped ice cube trays, and Twirly Towels, useful little items to wrap over long hair after a shower. The show was called "Gifts For Her." I wondered how many of the people shopping for gifts for the women in their lives- mothers, grandmothers, sisters, friends, wives, or sweethearts- would be likely to pick up my Country Blues CD?

Can't explain how it was possible, but I was supernaturally relaxed. I think it was Steve and his gracious hospitality. I was dressed from head to toe in QVC attire- an art to wear silk shirt, pants, boots, jewelry from QVC- and Steve was the masterful interviewer making me feel totally at home. I played from the heart, not caring that seventy or more million viewers were watching. Country Blues speaks for itself, and if someone doesn't get it, that's not my responsibility. I present the music that was written to the best of my ability. This is my life's work. It's not necessarily for everybody. It's for the discerning listener. Robert Johnson is a bit like your first taste of whiskey, or your first toke on a cigar. Coffee takes a while to love, but when you get used to it, "you got to have it."

The label rep was walking around backstage at QVC trying to line up other acts. By this time they had grown much larger with a bunch of folks from the majors who had joined on through some kind of merger. In the hallways I saw a lot of the QVC hosts walking around who had kept me alive after the miscarriage.

Steve probably has no idea how deeply his generosity touched me. I went down to QVC several other times at his invitation to be a guest on his "Jammin' in the Kitchen with Steve" program- intros, segues, that kind of thing. And there was something else he did that brought tears to my eyes. While selling computers to gazillions of viewers, Steve would do a close-up while explaining operation- more than once I heard him say "Here's how easy it is. Let's open a web site... say, Rory Block's web site..." and then he'd open my site for the world to see. There is no way to estimate the positive publicity and huge exposure this sort of thing provides. Steve knew this of course- but he didn't know I was watching- now that's something I would call a "random act of kindness." If I didn't know that all humans were flawed, I'd say Steve Bryant is a Saint.

The Extracted Tooth

Dental emergencies on the road are a drag. No one wants to take you spur of the moment no matter how much you pain you are in. "We do have an opening in three weeks..." "Thanks, but I'm only here overnight."

At home I discussed my situation with the dentist, who said I needed another root canal. But having had a couple of bad experiences recently, it seemed like something to be avoided at all costs. With my mouth stretched to the breaking point with some metal torture device, choking to death and buzzing with medication, I survived the endless process, eventually leaving the office feeling poisoned. As the dentist pronounced my sentence, I asked the price. He mentioned four figures and I groaned. I asked what alternatives there might be. Extraction, he explained, would be two figures. I made the decision to say goodbye to the stupid tooth, so he pulled it out. There would be a healing period before a bridge could be built- and of course we hadn't discussed that price which would bring the whole thing to even more than the root canal.

I wandered about with a missing tooth, careful not to smile. I was given a temporary pop-in which had a large, unwieldy plate. It was impossible to eat, speak, or sing. I sounded like the "Pepperidge Farm remembers" guy. Finally I took a utility scissor and cut the thing down to size, at which point I could pop it in as needed. During this interim period I used to carry it around in the front right pocket of my jeans and would lightly tap the pocket to be sure it was there before going out. In the supermarket, if I saw someone I knew coming down the aisle, I'd quickly hide behind my hand and insert the thing to become presentable.

Of course touring had to continue- and the permanent bridge hadn't yet been installed. Shortly thereafter Rob, Jordan, and I were in

England, and every day Jordan would ask "Mom, do you have your tooth?" I'd tap my pocket to confirm. One day I tapped, but there was nothing there. I tapped again- this wasn't good. We were on the way to the next show three hundred miles down the road with no time to turn back. So I called the hotel and the kind proprietor listened respectfully while I described that I had left a tooth in the room, most likely in a glass by the sink. He would ask the cleaning lady, he said. They would even check the little screen in the dishwasher drain. But it was no use, the tooth was gone- gone to wherever one sock, pens, keys, and other daily necessities disappear to- perhaps into a swirling parallel universe, or into a specialized black hole which swallows these items only. Some day a time traveler will find themselves in this dimension, surrounded by everyone's missing possessions, all the owners long dead.

I called the dentist from England. This presented a formidable challenge because there were virtually no cell phones at the time and overseas calls meant a world of inconvenience- some years prior in Germany they had to be made from a post office, a very strange reality to me. I reached the dentist in the USA and asked if he could make another tooth for me from the plaster cast of the other one. "Uh, we don't keep those," he explained. What was I thinking, that there would be miles of warehouses where dental impressions, each tagged and labeled with their owner's names, were kept for a century? Come to think of it there just might be such a place- but now it would be for the purpose of forensic science and not customer convenience. But my dilemma was this: I explained to the dentist that we would arrive home from Europe on a Sunday night. On Monday morning I had to leave to appear on QVC. They needed me there by noon, so an early morning appointment seemed impossible as it would have been before business hours. The dentist said he'd think on it and that I should call back in a few days. In the meantime he suggested I search for a suitable non-toxic material- perhaps taffy of a similar color- which could be molded into shape. This led to a most amusing search throughout the city of London where we discovered that salt water taffy is an unknown item in England. We eventually found a soft candy of the appropriate color that even held its shape when fashioned into a tooth, but predictably, when installed, it melted away immediately. I suppose I completed the tour without smiling. The missing tooth was not in front anyway.

When I called back, the dentist had a plan. He would take me first thing Monday morning- seven AM (unprecedented in all of dentistry), and would install an acrylic tooth with a temporary bond. Monday morning arrived soon enough and as he cemented the tooth in place he said, "Don't eat until after you get off the air." It was OK- I knew about fasting. I could do this.

I performed on QVC with this temporary tooth in place, all the while wondering if, in front of 70 million unsuspecting viewers, my tooth would come flying out during a high note. Mercifully, the tooth held and in fact remained for several months until I had a permanent bridge installed.

Around this time I was invited to submit a story which embodied life on the road for a book which would be called something like *Rock'n' Roll Road Stories*. I presented three- two I thought would be contenders, but the third was an afterthought, thrown in "just because." This is my style, and that's always the one that does well... so they chose the extracted tooth story- go figure. It's in a book out there somewhere, and now, it's right here in this book. I haven't seen the other version for some years, and don't remember what I wrote, so this version is brand new.

I'm Every Woman

*T*his was my fourteenth album for Rounder Records. For this one they made it clear that they wanted a duet album with every song a collaboration with a different artist. I began by trying to contact some of my favorites, but when I realized the full scope of this project- the complexity of trying to reach and assemble all these special artists who were zooming all over the globe on completely different schedules- I decided to change my direction slightly. There are so many quality collaboration albums out there, I reasoned, that there wasn't much need for me to do another one- at least not at that particular time. So instead I assembled a great band in New York City- a special treat for someone so used to making solo acoustic albums. Engineer Larry Alexander was introduced to me by guitarist Jeff Miranof, and

Photo: Shonna Valeska

Larry has now worked with Rob and I on every album from *I'm Every Woman* onwards- six thus far. We consider Larry an essential part of our team.

When a terrific band starts to lock in together in the studio, there's almost no greater magic. The power is immense- emotionally, spiritually, and musically. As an artist I just stand there with my hair on end waiting to sing. With this album the idea to cover some great R&B classics made a lot of sense. The band was there and could create superb tracks. I chose "I'm Every Woman," one of my old favorites performed by Chakka Kahn, to which I later added an acoustic slide lick that created an entirely unexpected juxtaposition of styles. This became the title track of the album as it had an unusual, intriguing strength. I also chose Al Green's "Tired Of Being Alone," Teddy Pendergrass' "Love TKO," "I'm A Fool For You" by Curtis Mayfield, and Marvin Gaye's "Ain't Nothing Like The Real Thing" which ended up as a duet with my friend Keb Mo. I also did a contemporary R&B/gospel song called "Hold On" with Reverend Herb Sheldon of the Payne AME Church. Herb is the piano player for the choir and has a terrific, resonant voice. He did an ad lib speaking part at the top of the song about his son's death that was so moving we could barely continue working.

Keb Mo and I met a number of years ago at a Robert Johnson tribute festival on the west coast and he gave me a cassette of what may have been his first record prior to release. Here was this enormously good looking, sweeter than sweet man with the blues energy all around him. I liked him immediately, and the music was fantastic. Later I called the number on the cassette and left a message saying how great the music sounded, and of course Keb went on to become a sensation. From time to time we cross paths- at the Bottom Line, at the Troy Music Hall, and I think I saw him last in Norway- and we always do a few songs together on stage. Keb is funny, charming, and extremely gifted. He has a timeless texture and depth to his voice that sets it apart.

Not wanting to leave out roots and acoustic music, I decided to do duets with some other favorite artists of mine- Kelly Jo Phelps, Gaye Adegbalola, Paul Richelle, Annie Raines- and my son Jordan. Gaye and I sang "Sea Lion Woman" together, a haunting little a capella song performed by two little girls on a Library of Congress recording. Kelly

Jo and I played guitars and traded verses on "Pretty Polly." Paul and Annie joined me for an old version of "The Rock Island Line"- Annie played harp while Paul sang bass. Jordan and I did "Ain't No Grave Can Hold My Body Down," another a capella piece, recorded in a church to capture the natural reverb. The album now had a most unusual mix of commercial versus unadorned roots material- but this is something I have always enjoyed- I think it makes for an interesting, startling kind of contrast.

The Long Black Dress

Every gal's gotta have one. A long black sequined gown was not exactly the image I had been projecting for some years, but I brought it to the photo session anyway just in case we decided to have a little fun. We were finished with the pictures and packing up when I remembered the dress. I slipped it on and suddenly there was this wonderful mood. Rob stood behind photographer Shonna Valeska, smiled and made a few silly faces, while I lit up like a Christmas tree. I was twirling and dancing, lost in a reverie. I felt like Cinderella going to the ball. These pictures turned out to be the best and ended up not only as the cover but also as a veritable gallery of choices.

Last Fair Deal

After my enduring adventures with Rounder, I got signed by Telarc, a solid label with great taste in music. Tab Benoit, Eric Bibb, and Maria Muldaur were all recording for them at the time and it seemed like a logical transition. *Last Fair Deal* was my first outing for the new label and I could feel things moving to another level. This was the first time I had ever dared to improvise, something I believed impossible until Michael Hedges so kindly told me I could do it. The creativity level ramped up and suddenly this acoustic album was turning into multiple levels of blues, gospel, and originals with a touch of jazziness thrown

Photo: Shonna Valeska

in. My guitar playing got better- the energy of being in a new environment brought excitement and inspiration to the table.

Back in the Rounder days I had added a little wacky speaking segment to one of the records. It was something that just happened in the studio. There are always going to be things on tape which are later deleted- communications with the control room- jokes, repartee, preparation- the "Rollin' Bob" kinds of remarks. I suppose now that we live in a world where people are secretly using photos and recordings of each other to harm, or for personal gain, this would be something to be incredibly careful about. I just thank goodness my records are made at home now and I don't have to worry about this- because I always go a little nuts in the studio, or at least I used to. So this comedy moment got left on the record- temporarily. It was the kind of thing you might expect to find on a Monty Python recording... footsteps entering the room, someone clearing their throat into the mic, followed by a bizarre comment or two. Nothing lewd, mind you, just silly. But I got a call from Bill Nowlin, and he was tweaked. He wanted this silliness off the record. "Never do that again!" he admonished. OK, no problem, no more getting silly!

With *Last Fair Deal* my crazy side surfaced again. My husband Rob had recently gotten the Harley Davidson of his dreams. He's a Harley kinda' guy, and I knew how much this meant to him. Rob is a hard worker- perhaps the hardest working person I have ever known- and he needs certain breaks or else he'll work himself into the ground. I wanted him to have this motorcycle- he needed a way to leave everything behind and just roll, and this was it. So he brought the bike home, and it was in the trailer. I went out to see it in all its glory with a microphone in my hand. I had to capture his excitement as he started it up for me for the first time. And that's how the record begins... Rob is talking, the motor roars, we start laughing- and then the song begins. I kept thinking that this was something Bill wouldn't have liked.

Bottom line, *Last Fair Deal* was fun to record, the photo session and artwork seemed to reach a new high with another slew of photos that I loved, and the CD got outrageous reviews. I felt like I was on a roll.

Photos: Shonna Valeska

From The Dust

Everybody's askin' me, why I sing the blues,
They're lookin' for a Hollywood sign,
Ain't no little woman from way up North, can understand the soul of
the blues...

But let me tell you somethin', that you don't know,
From the dust of this earth we were formed,
And when he made us, good God, He gave us strong emotion,
And He breathed into each body a soul,

When you're standin' on a corner, with no place to go,
And your mama calls you crazy then you'll know,
When the child that you raised in your arms up and dies,
When a man grabs you when you're sayin' no, no, no,

But let me tell you somethin', that you don't know,
From the dust of this earth we were formed,
And when he gathered up dry bones from the floor of the valley,
He breathed into each body a soul...

It ain't just the feelin' when your baby says goodbye,
The blues ain't no outward thang,
It's not your age, it's not your size, it's not the color of your eyes,
No the blues ain't a hat that you wear,
It's the heart that he gave us, and the legs that he formed,
For walkin' on that long and dusty road, come on children...

I said let me tell you somethin', that you don't know,
From the dust of this earth we were formed,
And when he made us, good God, He gave us strong emotion,
And He breathed into each body a soul...

Words and music by Rory Block

Photo: Shonna Valeska

$\mathcal{P}$erhaps some people got a little nervous after I released *From The Dust*, a bluesy mix which leaned heavily towards gospel. An interviewer asked me if I believed in God. The question was carefully phrased so as not to mention Christianity, but the implication was clear. I said "I didn't get to be fifty years old without noticing that something greater than me is in charge."

Musically I was still wailing on the concept of making the guitar an orchestra. I love layering rhythm parts, which seem to come flowing out like a waterfall of textures once the basic part is recorded. The Country Blues style lends itself to percussive overlays. With each one, the bounce just seems to increase. I'm not sure this kind of percussion can be taught as much as felt. I always make a major effort to explain the technique I have developed for using the hand as a drum, but not everyone wants to throw themselves into harm's way. However this was a signature element of early blues, and if you try to play in a polite, cautious way you won't capture the spirit of the Mississippi styles. Because the guitar became the instrument of choice for blues, it stands to reason that a player with an instrument would want to stretch the options as far as possible, so that one instrument could cover multiple bases.

Shonna Valeska

$\mathcal{R}$ounder had connected me with a photographer named Shonna Valeska at the time I was recording *Confessions of a Blues Singer*. Shonna was recommended as someone who had just done a great job with Ruth Brown's latest cover. At the time I was in a foul mood about being photographed and was explaining my despair to Shonna- how the last thing I wanted to do was get all dressed up and stand around posing- but Shonna didn't seem worried. She brought along an assistant and makeup artist Peter Brown, and they started rummaging through my closet. This was different as no one ever had made "wardrobe" suggestions before. Shonna and Peter picked out a large white men's dress shirt and paired it with my oldest jeans- we stood outside a rundown brick building and took pictures with everyone staring as they drove by. The session turned out extraordinarily well and I ended up having so many good choices that I could barely decide. This boosted my confidence greatly at a time when I was feeling low. I continued using Shonna for the Telarc releases and beyond, and she just kept getting better and better results.

Shonna is a successful New York photographer who is not exactly a prude. She likes sensuality and encouraged more revealing shots than I was used to. She would end up getting me to remove my jacket and I always thought, "It's OK, we won't be using these anyway." We always ended up using those, as Shonna's eye was setting up the shots with the greatest visual appeal every time. On the cover of *Last Fair Deal* I am wearing the support garment that belongs under the jacket- but somehow it made for a striking photo, and since lingerie is now in vogue as outerwear, we were not really doing anything shocking. However the *From The Dust* cover was even more unexpected. The lacy thing I was wearing was only supposed to be a peekaboo from underneath a jacket. Of course Shonna got me to take the jacket off again and ultimately, the photo was so revealing the lace needed some retouching. But the cover shot just jumped out it was so intense. Rob glanced at it as if it was a bit too hot for public display. He said "I don't know if you want to use that photo." He thought it was too sexy. Of course we ended up using it anyway.

A tall, bearded fan at a festival told me that he and his friends loved the photos on *From The Dust*. He actually had the nerve to say "We use it as porno" directly to my face. I was a little shocked. But then I thought that there will always be someone saying something about something or other, and there will never be a way to predict or control everything. A little risk here, a little artistic statement there- it's all a part of it. I just feel a little awkward when people I know show up at one of my gigs and pick up *From The Dust*. I feel a little naked.

Becoming A Teacher

1 used to be convinced that learning blues meant becoming an apprentice. You had to follow around a master watching their every

372

move. You had to be quick, intuitive, and savvy. You needed an excellent ear- nothing would ever be handed to you on a platter- just like studying with Reverend Gary Davis. You played and practiced around the clock. This is how I learned in 1964. The idea of teaching the secrets I had discovered made no sense to me. They were just that... secrets.

Stefan acknowledged that I had a good ear and often placed me in front of a speaker to figure out certain songs that resisted transcription. I was obsessed. I stayed up all night and worked out an arrangement of "Mississippi Blues" by Willie Brown which Stefan then put into tablature form and began teaching it to his students. This arrangement eventually went around the world and is the standard that is taught today. I did the original transcription. Figuring out what was going on in the D7th section was a major breakthrough. This is not to claim that if I hadn't done this transcription that no one else would have later been able to come up with a similar version- no doubt someone would have, but mine was the first to crack the code. Today a lot of people claim old arrangements as their own. I never did this. Finally, after years of seeing "traditional arrangement" by this one or that one and learning that they were paid royalties for this, BMI advised me to send my version along with the original, and their experts would assign a percentage for originality... perhaps a small portion, perhaps nothing at all. So I register all songs as instructed- but if it were up to me no one could ever claim a penny for copying someone else's arrangement. The surviving family members would receive everything.

It's Murphy's law that when you resist something, you keep stumbling over it. People kept asking me to teach. They kept requesting lessons and workshops, and I kept declining. Then one day I had a break-through: if I (who have spent my entire life transcribing this historic art form, music I learned from some of the most important rediscov-ered masters, most of whom were now dead and gone) failed to teach-then some of the old music could die out. If I have something of value and do not share it, that could be irresponsible, not to mention sad. My perspective then changed totally. Sunshine Kate, the shy little girl who wanted information kept secret, died- and a different person was born.

One day Artie called to suggest I make a teaching video for his brother's company. I was convinced I wouldn't be able to do it, but he said "Don't worry, I'll be there. I'll show you how- it'll be great." His support and kind assurance helped me get started, and I decided to give it my best shot. It was labor-intensive sitting in front of the lights and cameras all day, but the end result got extremely positive feed-back- people were saying it was very clear, the last thing I expected. I would imagine the skilled editors at Homespun Tapes had a lot to do with this, but it also built my confidence and enthusiasm for teaching. Now I get so many requests for private lessons and workshops I could teach full time.

For a number of years I have been doing guitar workshops at Jorma

Kaukonen's Fur Peace Guitar Ranch in Pomeroy, Ohio. Jorma, originally of Jefferson Airplane fame, went on to form Hot Tuna with bass player Jack Cassidy. Jorma and his wife Vanessa had this wild idea to build a place in the mountains where people could spend an entire weekend hanging around and studying with their all-time favorite guitar heroes- jamming after hours, watching a full-length performance by the star instructors in the lovely new theater, eating home-cooked, healthy meals in the dining room, and participating in a student concert (hosted by Jorma) at the conclusion... so they moved from Woodstock and all things familiar to the rolling hills of rural Ohio. It was a big leap, but it paid off. Vanessa's organizational wizardry and Jorma's charismatic star quality and legendary humor established this as the place to go to stretch the limits of your playing while having a life changing weekend retreat.

I started my workshops with solid Country Blues techniques. The students were astounding, and, though some years have passed since the first class (taught outside sitting on hay bales), many of these original students still stay in touch and even come to my shows around the country.

At one point I decided to make things a lot tougher. I named the class the "Wilderness Survival Course for Guitar Players." Warnings were emailed to everyone in case anyone wanted to pull out. Surprisingly, no one did. I explained that in 1925 there were no teaching DVDs, electronic tuners, or other resources we take for granted today- blues was not written out in any tablature. You had to be singularly driven, to apprentice, to figure out stuff by ear- you had to struggle, and fight to learn and carve out your own style. I said, in essence, we are soft and spoiled- used to being spoon fed. We've become complacent, expecting the teacher to place the material in our laps. We might not even feel like practicing. I told the students this year I was going to ask them to start from scratch. We were going back to the organic methods of the old days.

Everyone brought a stack of Country Blues CDs. We passed them around and each student took one they'd never heard before- the honor system, no cheating. The first assignment was to take this to the cabin overnight, listen, figure out the tuning, transcribe the song, and perform it for the class the following day. As you might imagine there were many groans. The consensus was that they didn't have the ability to figure out tunings or songs, and most didn't feel comfortable about performing for each other. I explained my secrets regarding easy techniques for all the above, and by the end of the workshop there was resounding success for this approach. Some of the students even continue to apply these methods to songwriting, something else I am determined to support in people. Creativity is a delicate matter, and it can be crushed easily by careless criticism. In my way of thinking each person has completely unique abilities possessed by them alone, and support can nurture this enough to bring out what I have convinced my students will be their very own trademark style. Take your "weaknesses" and make them into your strengths. The old players knew this well.

The Lady And Mr. Johnson

I like to say that since 1964 I have been meaning to make a tribute album to Robert Johnson. From the moment I heard his evocative, edgy voice and supernaturally fast, percussive guitar it was clear that he was the embodiment of the greatest elements of the music- to me he was the all time genius of early blues- and maybe all blues. I have over twenty releases and have included a Robert Johnson song or two on most of them. For me this has not been a fad, or a jump-on-the-band-wagon kinda' thing.

Remember the old Barbara Mandrell song "I was country when country wasn't cool"? Replace the word "country" with "a blues musician" or even "a Robert Johnson fan." Maria once affectionately said that I live in a comfy little bubble- she keeps up with stuff where I have no idea what's going on out there- so she's totally right. Long ago I discovered that my level of vulnerability made it hard for me to compete. If I have to come up against the world and all its trends, I fold, a wound I carry from childhood. I'm better off focusing on one project at a time and immersing myself in the old music, the source of my inspiration. If I went out and bought a stack of CDs of everyone who has ever done Robert Johnson covers I would simply lose my ability to play. I can't compare myself to others in order to create. This is probably not a great quality, but it's the way I am. I'm kept up to date on the road, where I meet everyone else on the circuit. In that setting it's always comfortable to enjoy what other musicians are doing, but specifically checking out other Johnson covers to compare- I don't do that. So I didn't know how many people had covered Johnson (other than John Hammond, who was one of the very first- and Eric Clapton since the '60s)- and I went into the studio in a deep immersion bubble. This would be the culmination of my life's work.

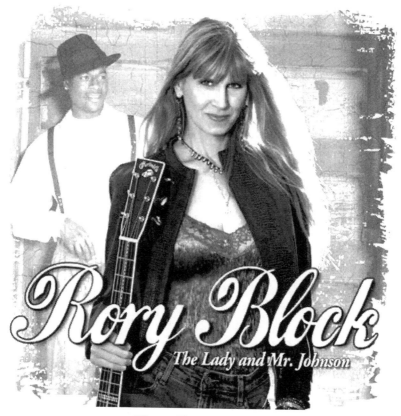

Photo: Shonna Valeska

A Ph.D. In Life

7 decided to make this recording as close to the original as possible. I felt compelled to crack the code. I wanted it accurate measure by measure, no compromise, no shortcuts, no sweeping the hard parts under the rug. It was a research project of extraordinary proportions, my personal Ph.D. This would be a form of redemption for dropping out of high school- a degree in life, if you will.

People have asked the following silly question many times: "Why do you try to play it like Robert Johnson? Why don't you just improvise and do it your own way?" For me the answer is simple: "Because his way is better." You see, to me Robert Johnson is Classical music. The level of accomplishment is on a par with the great composers. It has every subtlety, every watermark that distinguishes the best. In Classical there are numerous terms for things that can't be written down- a slight slowdown in tempo, additional emphasis- decreased volume, added emotion- Robert Johnson does all these things, yet most people miss it when they interpret him. When you play songs like "Walkin' Blues" with an even beat or a band, it becomes a different song- because the steady tempo of the drums loses all the feel. The tempo is meant to breathe, and this can't happen with a band. This is not a criticism of band interpretations, it's just different.

When people go to see Handel's *Messiah*, they pay money, walk in and sit down. If the orchestra comes out and starts jamming, or playing it their own way, this would be a travesty. I say this: play it as it is written (Classical or Robert Johnson), with deep feeling and emotion until people weep. If it were not possible to do this then no one would ever go to a Classical concert again. No one would ever be heralded as the greatest new violin player from out of nowhere. No one would care. But we seek a fresh, new, powerful interpretation of the very same notes. It's no good unless each and every interpretation is uniquely inspired. This is the challenge, and this is my goal. This does not diminish someone else's choice to do the music their own way- it simply defines my personal approach.

One more point in this regard: No one will ever be Robert Johnson, but it's good to try. Why not seek to emulate the master, to climb the mountain?

Meeting Robert Johnson's Family

With Robert Johnson's son Claud Johnson. Photo: Shonna Valeska

One day while in the midst of the tribute recording, the phone rang and I heard a voice saying "I just got off the phone with Robert Johnson's grandson, and he wants to speak to you." It was Lisa Rich, my gifted guitar student from Connecticut. She put in the legwork, looked up the number and made the call, and for this I sincerely thank her. But was this coincidence? Here I was working on the tribute album. It seemed surreal. What grandson? What family? I was utterly astonished. You see, in 1964 we didn't know Robert Johnson had living relatives. I wasn't even aware of the search many years hence that located Johnson's son Claud. There was a trial, and the estate was awarded to Claud and his family. But I hadn't heard of it- clearly, I had some catching up to do.

Robert Johnson came into the world like a flame burning brightly- only to be extinguished suddenly. We assumed he had left this world without an heir- with no one to carry on the tradition. We used to say

"Man, what would Robert Johnson be playing now if he had lived?" Would he be playing electric, like say, Muddy Waters and Elmore James? This was something we loved to debate in the '60s, and of course no one could ever win because it was pure speculation.

So here is this genius who records only one album- an album that goes on to rock the world and win a Grammy sixty eight years after his death. He dies under mysterious and contested circumstances, no one knows for sure where he is buried. Legend and lore surrounds his short life. For many years accounts of his death vary greatly- was it shooting, stabbing, poisoning, or complications? Was it a jealous husband or an angry woman? Some had woven tales of Johnson at the crossroads selling his soul to the devil. They quoted his contemporaries as evidence. Movies were made, rock stars were inspired. I visited two grave sites after my first release for Rounder leaving signed copies of *High Heeled Blues* to Robert Johnson on both graves. When I returned shortly afterwards the CDs were gone. Maybe someone took them to sell someday- Ebay or whatever- or maybe the grounds keeper chucked them in the dumpster to keep the clutter down.

Insiders say the trial was unusual. Someone testified they had seen Claud's mother having an affair with Robert Johnson. The judge questioned- how could they be sure? The witness stressed they had actually seen the affair, and the Judge said "You mean you watched?" The witness answered, "Ain't you never watched?" There was a ripple of laughter through the courtroom. It was ultimately established that Claud was Robert Johnson's son and rightful heir. But where had he been over the years? After speaking to the Johnson family I learned that via this union, a young woman gave birth to Robert Johnson's child. People didn't talk about that sort of thing in those days. As it happened her father was a minister who didn't want his daughter hooking up with a "blues singer,' it being widely considered to be the music of the devil. Twice little Claud saw his father coming up the road. Looking through a window he could see Grandpa and his father talking, but Robert was turned away. The last time Claud saw his father he was around six years old. Once again it was through a window. He saw Robert coming up the road, and Grandpa going out to meet him. They talked. Robert wanted to know if he could marry the minister's daughter and take his wife and son with him. He tried to do the right thing, but again, Grandpa turned him down. Then Robert gave Grandpa some money for his little boy, and Claud watched helplessly as his father (the monster all time genius soul-singing blues man Robert Johnson who changed the world), walked away forever. Shortly after that Johnson died. It doesn't get much sadder.

Soon his mother married, and Claud was absorbed into a new family. The other kids probably knew the rumor, but no one spoke of it. Once, when Claud picked up the guitar, it was taken away from him. He was forbidden to play.

Robert Johnson's great-grandson Richard... wow!
Photo: Shonna Valeska

A Voice From Mississippi

I dialed the phone with shaking hands. This was beyond emotional for me. A beautiful, mellow voice answered from Crystal Springs, Mississippi. I said "You don't know me, but to me, you're family. I feel like I'm meeting long lost kin." I had reached one of Robert

Johnson's five grandchildren Steven Johnson. We struck up a friendship immediately, and our conversation moved to the myth and lore surrounding his grandfather. Steven Johnson is an Elder and a Preacher in his church. I said "That's interesting. You must have been raised around the stigma about blues being the music of the devil- then you come to find out you're related to the greatest Country Blues genius of all time who supposedly sold his soul to the devil- you must have had some reconciling to do." He confirmed this. Then I said, "Well I don't think blues is the music of the devil-

Robert Johnson's grandson Steven Johnson. Photo: Shonna Valeska

I think blues is anointed, spirit filled music." Our conversation went deeper. He said, "Well you know all that myth about my grandfather selling his soul to the devil- that's just Hollywood. He never sold his soul to the devil. My grandfather was singing gospel." He said, "Listen to the words he sang- 'I went to the crossroads, I fell down on my knees, I asked the Lord above for mercy, he said poor Bob if you please... If I had possession over judgment day, Lord I wouldn't have no right to pray.' Those are not the words of someone who worships the devil. No, my grandfather was a man of God." This was deep- this was opening doors for me and ringing bells. This was exactly my thinking. I said, "I see your point. What do you tell the detractors who say "Well, Robert Johnson wrote 'Me and The Devil' and 'Hellhound On My Trail'?" In his calm way Steven said "That's easy... when you're talented, when you're on a mission, the devil hates that. He tries to take it away from you. You just might have a hellhound on your trail." So we decided together that the devil had failed miserably. He thought he had won when he took out Robert Johnson, but the story didn't end there, did it? That old devil made a mistake, because Johnson went on to become a world wide phenomenon with people revering his music around the globe. Claud has been restored to his proper place as Robert Johnson's son, and was there to accept his father's Grammy in 2006. Now that's what I call a blessed ending to an otherwise tragic story. "What the devil meant for evil, God will use for good." Amen.

Journey To Crystal Springs

I knew I had to make my way to Crystal Springs as soon as possible. I arranged to fly Shonna and Peter Brown to Mississippi to capture the meeting with Johnson's family on film. This was a once-in-a-lifetime event for me. Rob and I met Shonna and Peter at a bed and breakfast on the green. Then we called Michael Johnson, Steven's brother, and he was the first to arrive. I have never felt so much joy in meeting any-one as I did meeting Robert Johnson's family that day. Even the great grandchildren came down. Steven arrived, bringing his two children Stephen and Bethany. Then we met Claud. I took one look at him and said, "You're Robert Johnson's baby boy!" He said "I'm Robert John-son's only baby boy."

Steven recommended I take photos with great grandson Richard. He said "Everyone in the family thinks Richard looks the most like grandpa." When Richard showed up my jaw dropped. Steven was right- Richard is a supernatural likeness- he has the spirit of Robert Johnson everywhere around him- he virtually vibrates with a powerful presence- blues, intrigue, history... twenty-five year old Richard has it.

With Richard Johnson. Photo: Shonna Valeska

And beauty, did I mention beauty? We brought a white shirt with some suspenders, Richard brought an old hat, pleated pants and some shiny shoes. He stood behind me in the photos and his aura wrapped itself around the record like strong arms from the past. This was not lost to some of the reviewers who later wrote about the release.

I stood next to Claud and Shonna took pictures. I rested my head on his shoulder. He couldn't possibly know how emotional I felt about him- I must have seemed like any number of other crazy fans and cling-ons who followed him around just to pick up some of the mystical blues energy surrounding him. In the meantime Claud is straight as an arrow, a hard-working, devoted family man who forged his way in life and became the patriarch of a large family, all before the Robert Johnson thing hit.

Robert Johnson's great-grandson Richard.
Photo: Shonna Valeska

Down At The Crossroads
Blues Meets Gospel

Sister Jackie Frasier. Photo: Shonna Valeska

Steven and I have remained close. We share a fervent belief that Johnson's legacy is sacred, not profane. In one of our many conversations about the intimate connection between blues and gospel an idea was forged. We would put together a tour with Steven's choir from The Straightway Ministries Gospel Church. We'd call this "Down At The Crossroads- Blues Meets Gospel." It would be an evening of music featuring my opening set of Robert Johnson, followed by a second set of rip-roaring-roof-raising gospel from the choir. Steven would introduce. Claud would come down to the show in New York City. I thought someone should film this. We had rehearsals, got ourselves ready, handed it to the agent and the label- and nobody got it. No one wanted to think about blues and gospel being related. People love to tell the story about Robert Johnson selling his soul to the devil- and this was messing that right up.

We ended up making it happen ourselves. Passing the info to friends and venues personally, we managed to put together a tour of four major cities- New York, Boston, Portland, and Charleston. We had no idea what would happen. Our first show was in West Virginia. When the Straightway Ministries Gospel Church bus pulled up straight from Utica, Mississippi and the choir stepped out onto the sidewalk, I almost fainted. Nothing could have been a greater honor. Family members, husbands and wives, grandparents, a few babies and small children, Elders, Preachers- all had put aside jobs and lives to come out for these shows. This was glorious. I reached my arms around as many people as I could grab at one time and said "You are my family."

But there was one question- would a gospel choir at a blues festival be a problem? Would some artist be offensive, or vulgar, and make everyone sorry they showed up? I talked to Apostle Butler as we sat behind the stage. Dinner was served and everyone was either seated and eating or filing past the food trays. I asked her if everything was OK, and she looked at me and said, "I don't hear anything I have a problem with." If Apostle Butler is happy, I'm happy.

Our show began as planned- the two sets, blues followed by gospel. We might have been a little tentative as this was the first night of our experiment. Everyone did their job well but we were still testing the waters. The next night was New York City. On the way, everything that could possibly go wrong occurred. First, my bus broke down. We called Bishop Frasier from the side of the road. He was well ahead of us and making good time through the mountains, but he turned around to rescue us. Bishop Frasier is not only one of the most powerful bass players I have ever heard, he is also the tireless bus driver, he owns his own company, and used to take the Mississippi Mass Choir on tour. In addition he is a mechanic who can take apart the bus and put it back together again. Bishop Frasier's wife Jackie is one of the strongest and best gospel singers ever- watching her passionate performances taught me a tremendous amount, and she was a sweet spirit that became like a sister to me almost immediately.

Eventually we got roadside assistance and with our bus up and running, I called Bishop Frasier to let him know he could turn around. By this time we were late and exhausted, and we knew the trip into the city would be a challenge. Needless to say the venue provided no parking. When we entered New York the streets were jammed. We finally found a restricted parking space right across the street from a major television network and my son agreed to stay in the bus lest we get flack from anyone. We explained our situation to the security guard and he was OK with it. We had one advantage. Our vehicle looked like a guest on a TV program had arrived. Then Bishop Frasier called to say he had found an empty space a few blocks away in front of a large church. He said no one would bother his choir bus there, and he was right. That struck me as a brilliant call.

The name of the venue sounded like a small theater, but it turned out to be an underground bar. Despite the many phone calls confirming details, suddenly no one claimed to have gotten the rider saying they would provide a multi-course meal for a forty-person choir. This was a serious disaster. Claud Johnson had flown in for this event, Michael Johnson and his wife and daughter were there as well- they were VIP's, honored guests- and there was no food. The record company guy who showed up threw his hands into the air- he didn't have anything to do with it. As the choir filed in, exhausted and famished, I stood in the doorway apologizing to everyone as they passed me. No food, a long and grueling ride, and a lowly basement bar to sing in. It wasn't looking good. Rob cornered the little rep from the label: get the meal, have it sent, put it on the company card. Finally it happened, and pasta was served. Everyone from the choir looked at this Nouveau Cuisine and wondered when dinner was coming. I felt worse than ever. How could so many people have dropped the ball? Countless phone calls had been made and everything was cleared and checked- and now this... I felt like all was lost. I couldn't believe the ineptitude that had led to this fiasco. This was supposed to have been a theater with velvet seats. Robert Johnson's son was being handed a plate of cold pasta for dinner.

Don DeVito, one of the engineers who had assembled the gold Robert Johnson reissue on Columbia had come down to see the show. I did my set as he sat in the front row with some friends and family. They cheered me on and recognized everything that I played. Thank God they were there. Then it was time for the choir. Somehow Steven found some kind of podium and pushed it onto the stage. He said "I'm Robert Johnson's grandson" and then he started to preach. He used the setting as part of the sermon. He started to sweat, things got heated up, and people started to shout. Then the choir came up and tore down the house. A little cocktail waitress dropped her tray of drinks and said she had never witnessed a show this great at the venue. Later that night Bishop Frasier said, "This is what we love- to take our message to the streets."

Claud Johnson, a man who deserved (and could have demanded) all the creature comforts, was kind and humble. He politely explained that he had a chance to see Times Square with his son and was perfectly happy. All he asked for was a few signed copies of my tribute album *The Lady & Mr. Johnson* for some charity event he was hosting.

The 2007 Blues Music Awards

In spring of 2007 I was in Memphis to perform at the Blues Music Awards (formerly known as the W.C. Handy Awards). *The Lady & Mr. Johnson* had just won "Acoustic Album of The Year." I walked out onto the stage in front of every contemporary, fellow artist, record company, booking agent, radio personality, reviewer, writer, fan, worldwide internet listener, and all those who would see the film of the show forever and ever throughout eternity. I sat down and started to play. Then something went terribly wrong with the monitors. My guitar made a distant, high-end frazzling sound- like the last gasp of a dying electric toothbrush. The volume and EQ were way off. No time, no time! If there is anything unattractive, it's whining all night from the stage about monitors- believe me, I know- and I have learned to say nothing and play. I've become an expert at performing whether I can hear or NOT. That evening the cameras were rolling, the timer

Photo: Irene Dudek

was clicking, and the red light would flash after three songs. The hook would come out. No, adjusting the monitors was not going to be possible. It would take way too long- I would make a spectacle of myself and hold up the show. I had no options, so my brain simply shut down.

I was sitting there under the lights with zero recall of every song I had ever played. I started singing "Crossroad Blues" a capella. I eventually began to play but it was not the music I was so familiar with, it was some strange quasi-slide fumbling I didn't recognize. It was surreal. This is why big stars sometimes use lip sync and prerecorded tracks for television- to prevent this kind of disaster at all costs. Frankly, I had passed the stress test so many times before I never expected shut down, but as usual, God throws a little embarrassment into the mix. It keeps us honest, on our toes, and prevents arrogance. I want to be humble. I understand the pitfalls and dangers of ever being otherwise.

Gay Adegbalola, lead singer of "Saffire, The Uppity Blues Women" fame, solo artist and educator, pointed out to me that in simplifying "WC Handy Awards" to "The Blues Music Awards" we have removed the name of an important, venerable African American. Historically significant people should always have a sacred place in our collective consciousness. I agree and am concerned lest we get too far from the roots. I would say this- before changing this we could have done more to educate. I can't tell you how many times I heard "W.C. Handy" called everything from "W.C. Dandy" to "W.D. Tandy"- after a while I got tired of correcting this when walking onto the stage. Not enough people understood and recognized the significance of the name "W.C. Handy" a man who has been called "the father of the blues."

The Road To Damascus

One day I was driving and listening to letters written by Saint Paul to various churches (these coming from the pen of a man who had started out as a persecutor and hater of Christians). He used to round them up and behead them. But on "The Road to Damascus" he experienced a conversion through a shocking experience. He saw a bright light and fell to his knees blinded, and then heard a voice saying, "Saul, Saul, why do you persecute me?" When Saul asks who is addressing him, the answer comes "Jesus of Nazareth." Later Saul is renamed Paul and becomes one of the greatest witnesses for Christ of all times. The words of his letters are personal, intelligent, and passionate. He never expected them to become part of a book. He was just giving counsel, training and guidance to new believers. The fact that his letters were included in the Bible was not a motive for him as he could never have known.

As I was driving, a funny thing happened. The words I was listening to became a letter directly to me. I heard every word as if they had been written only moments before. They revealed themselves in incredible clarity and intimacy. Time and distance disappeared. There was no such thing as two thousand years ago. I had never understood it so well. This was an amazing experience. I told it to a friend who said, "That's because you were ready to hear it."

I wonder, how many people who know me (or know of me) are shocked, offended, and ready to put this book down? If you continue, be assured that I never expected to feel this way. I was the last person who would have ever suspected myself to be vulnerable to something I once had such disdain for. But isn't it sad, that after all I have come through to get to this moment- after overcoming obstacles, losses, and trials- that I would now have to fear people hating, misunderstanding, or rejecting me because I read this book that gave me such comfort? What sense would that make? And where is the tolerance with which we as a society pride ourselves? Is there a double-standard here? Is tolerance for certain things and not others? Is something so gentle as being encouraged by the beautiful, loving, life-changing words of Jesus so likely to anger otherwise open-minded people? Have you read the Bible to know whether or not you really disagree with it? When I raved against it, I had never read it. I have learned something amazing: most of the people who debate the meaning, rail against the Bible, and have the greatest contempt for it, have never read it. So I suggest: read it, and learn what it says. Don't comment on something if you are uninformed. Do the research, then comment. But do the research thoroughly- don't skim. How many other things can we make authoritative remarks about that we haven't researched? Almost nothing, guaranteed. Can we become a lawyer without studying? Can we write legal documents without knowing the facts? Can we become experts in anything without training? Thus to earn the right to put out your plaque and open your business, you need experience. I think of the really funny TV advertisement featuring a busy command central of mission control landing a spacecraft where something goes terribly wrong. Suddenly a geeky guy with a donut in his mouth starts giving orders to the rocket scientists at the computers, and a life-threatening emergency is averted. They look at him and say "Hey, are you new here?" And he says "No, but I did stay at a Holiday Inn Express last night." So the guy with the donut doesn't exist. I wonder why so many people have opinions about Christ and the Bible without ever knowing the facts? Read the book. Even if you don't believe, read the book, just to be accurate and informed. This is what I did. Read it to have extensive knowledge of history. Read it for the magnificent poetry. Read it to be qualified to comment.

My sister is yelling that my beliefs bother her. She is outraged because she thinks that I might be Christian. One wonders at her point. I never push it on her. I never even mention it to her. She continues on: "You probably watch Fox News, that right wing conservative news station!" This is the sort of completely uninformed, inappropriate anger this Book seems to stimulate. Why not be unbiased, and tolerant? Why such passionate objection to a person's beliefs? I suspect this is because Jesus pushed so many buttons. "*And ye shall be hated of all men for my name's sake...*" *Matt 10:22.* "*And a man's foes shall be they of his own household*" *Matt 10:36.* If the world loves us too much, we can be fairly sure we are at odds with God. This is strong medicine along with many other radical things Jesus said.

Why does Jesus piss so many people off? I was taking a walk with a friend who considers himself Jewish, yet he has no particular religious belief. He is an atheist who thinks of himself as culturally and genetically Jewish. Somehow the subject of spirituality came up. He asked if I believed in Jesus, and I said yes. He went silent, as if I had said something terrible, or perhaps betrayed him. Finally he said, "That's heavy." We kept walking. "Why do you say that?" I asked. "Jesus was Jewish. He was the fulfillment of the Jewish tradition. He did not set out to start a new religion, just to be the completion of the existing one. It was his followers that gave it a new name. Even if you don't believe in him, at least be proud of him," I said. "The most famous man on earth was Jewish."

Dutch Television Joins The Tour

*I*n December of 2008 a Dutch television crew flew to the United States to interview me about the writing of "Lovin' Whiskey." This was for a year-end event in which the top 2,000 songs of all times were voted on by the public, then played in reverse- like a countdown-during the two weeks prior to Christmas. Twelve of the 2,000 were filmed and made into short pieces for television, and mine was one of the twelve.

Although we had five dogs on board and warned the producer that they might wish to avoid all the hair, they responded, "We love dog hair." With bags of excellent Dutch coffee for Rob, and some little blue and white Delft pottery for me, they met us and boarded the bus with all their equipment. The interview was filmed on the bus and in the back room of The Ark in Ann Arbor, Michigan. In addition they filmed the show. A year or two earlier, a Dutch pop artist named Anouk had recorded "Lovin' Whiskey" and the song became a hit once again, thus keeping it very much alive in the minds of the public. I was shown excerpts of her performance in the back room and was impressed. "You go girl!" I said as she sang her heartfelt version.

You can find "The Story of Lovin' Whiskey" on YouTube. I've never put anything of mine up there- I wouldn't know how. But performance after performance, despite nightly announcements prohibiting photography- another song is posted. Of course I can see the little red lights as people hold up their cameras. Nowadays when you speak, perform, or just go about your life, chances are you're on film. So I know that each show is a performance to the entire universe, which beats the 70 million QVC viewers I once performed to.

The Family Of Musicians

*A*rtists and performers are an extended family. We cross paths with everyone sooner or later. Despite the fact that the biz creates a competitive atmosphere which often pits us against each other, the artists themselves rarely operate this way. The nicest people are almost always other performers. Person to person is where we form bonds- dealing with managers and agents invariably creates bad feelings- it's their job to slam doors and drive away superfluous requests- to represent their artist as exclusive and above the crowd- when in fact most musicians are humble and would do almost anything to accommodate each other.

James Taylor has always had the best backup singers, and that's how I first heard of Valerie Carter. One day a wonderful remake of an old soul classic came on the radio and a beautiful voice wailed, "Oo wee child, things are gonna get easier." I discovered, to my delight, that it was Valerie Carter's solo debut. Whoa, this was good. She had broken through the old marketing barrier which I had encountered- that of being a "blue-eyed" soul singer in an industry that loved stereotypes. At the same time *Cashbox Magazine* had reviewed my RCA release saying, "Rory Block was born white but oozes forth such a soulful delivery as to forever lay to rest color boundaries..." (if I had a stated goal, this would certainly be one of them- remember: credit the writer and the founder, celebrate the source, and then open the field, where humans inspire other humans). A few weeks later I noticed that Valerie was appearing at the Bottom Line in New York, so I went (feeling small and unimportant), to see her show. I managed to make my way to the back room to pay my respects and introduced myself apologetically. "Rory Block?!" she exclaimed. Then she started singing one of the songs from my Blue Goose release- "I got a man, who treats me the way I want to be treated!" I was blown away.

A couple years ago, a promoter at a venue in the UK told us he had just read an interview with a world famous guitar player. He told us this artist had mentioned me as the number one interpreter of Robert Johnson in the world. I was deeply honored and extremely curious to see the article, but the promoter soon drifted off and never emailed the quote to us- so I can only wonder at exactly what was said, not being much of a googler.

I have a friend who tours and plays with major stars. He was on the road with one of the most famous household words in the world, and in the back room he noticed the man playing something interesting. He asked "What's that?" and the star said, "It's a *Rory Block* thing."

At a festival a few years ago a woman came up to me insisting that she was a friend of Keith Richards and that he was a "big fan" of mine. Keith baby, if this is true, give me a call- I'd like to open for you guys! Rob's been trying to call you but you keep changing your numbers! P.S- Keith... Eric... how do you like my teaching DVD's?

Carrying On The Tradition

The glitzy, super publicized world of the music biz can be daunting to the people who carry on the tradition. I may not be a household word, but two years ago a friend called to say my name went by on the scroll bar at the bottom of the screen on CNN. It said something like: "Blues singer Rory Block is 58 years old today." Somehow I made it into a database of "celebrities"- or it wouldn't be news, I suppose, so I felt pretty cool about that. I called my dad in New Hampshire, and he said "I know you're famous!" The fact that I have won any awards, have any fans, and have developed any kind of a solid career is way beyond my expectations, and to have built it largely on acoustic pre-war Country Blues is all the more unexpected... miraculous, really. So for me this is a triumph, and not something money can buy. Not even a hit record can assure the kind of status you may crave or the kind of fans you'd appreciate. I expected nothing so it's all icing on the cake. And every day I feel grateful, which is probably why I am happier now than I have ever been.

When you think about where you could be- six feet under with many of our contemporaries- when you wake up to a new day, can get out of bed, dress yourself, and are in your right mind- not in a hospital in a coma, not breathing your last or broken to pieces in an accident but able to walk around in the fresh air, not doing prison time- these things are miracles as far as I am concerned. It becomes clearer that those able to get around need to take care of those not able to get around. I feel a sense of solidarity with anyone struggling to survive and make a name for themselves. I know how hard it is, and what a life-long battle it can be. I want to encourage, not discourage- as I was so often dis

Photo: Art Tipaldi

couraged. When things get sweet, the past no longer hurts. It becomes a badge, and if we never forget what it took to get where we are, we will have earned the opportunity to assist others. The greatest thing of all continues to be the people I meet at the shows, and the moving, affirming things they say. This has turned out to be more than enough positive reinforcement for a lifetime.

The Golden Agers Club

After reaching fifty I began to reevaluate my life. I considered the possibility that the first half century had been largely about taking. When we're children we are entirely dependent, then as young adults we think the world is our oyster and run about "taking care of Number One." We might be arrogant, thinking ourselves to be "all that." We might treat people in ways we later regret, though at the time it barely had significance to us: burning bridges, inviting conflict, and thinking there would never be consequences. We had experiences, we learned about the world from countless angles, and lots of caring friends and family bailed us out. If we survive to fifty, I concluded, it's time to give back.

My main goal is to do something good for people through the music, and I recognize the power songs have to comfort and heal. If I fail to be helpful then I'm just taking up space and creating garbage.

At a certain point I began fretting that I wasn't doing enough, and that I could do more by retiring, giving away my worldly belongings, and walking the globe advocating peace. Virgil Brallier said in response to my concerns, "Ah, but you already have a bully pulpit," a way to reach people directly from the stage. So at least for the time being he was right. We all have a calling in this world. If you think you know what it is, go for it. Other times, if you follow a door that has opened for you, you find it. One thing I know for sure: I was put here to play music.

Despite the fact that I have had my share of pain and sorrow, I am incredibly lucky to have followed the path which has satisfied my soul, and in doing so, I have been given the opportunity to touch others. I consider the ability to reach a wider audience a privilege, and something I would never take for granted. For one thing you're only as famous as the people willing to come out to your shows and buy your recordings. If that dries up, it all dries up- so gratitude is a huge factor.

"Lovin' Whiskey" with it's unlikely beginnings, has helped more people than I will ever know. Night after night, year after year, people tell me that the song brought them through the hardest of times- even "saved their life." Someone actually wrote me a letter saying they were about to commit suicide, and then they heard "Lovin' Whiskey" and changed their mind. Again and again I hear "Thank you for that song- my father was an alcoholic," or, "My husband/wife/child is an alcoholic," and perhaps the most moving of all- people who come up and say "I am an alcoholic." This takes courage, and that's precisely why the social worker told me that alcoholics can be beautiful people- that they can be honest, soulful, artistic, deep people- that they can be "easy to love" (when they're not drinking). Humans have a problem letting go of someone once they're in love. No relationship begins bad. It starts great, and *then* deteriorates (not always of course- but *if* it's going to). We seek partnerships that get better, not worse. But if you're in a damaged relationship that you've been warned to leave, you are not alone. I've learned that when a song is personal (far from my original concern that no one would get it), it generally resonates with most people and reaches into their own intimate experiences. I've also noticed that you don't need to have the exact experience to understand someone else's pain- we have good hearts- we're made that way. No one wants to feel alone with their problems, and music helps us understand that we're in this together. Feeling totally alone and isolated makes us feel "crazy," something I am sensitive to as a result of my upbringing. Being labeled crazy is a horrible, frightening feeling. Music is the healing balm I can use to undo my own sorrow- and thus other people's as well.

For The Love Of Animals

We have five dogs and eight cats, or should I say, they have us. I love them dearly- they are my family, children, and grandchildren. They are the most extraordinary beings whose abilities and skills, in my opinion, far exceed our own. They have language, but we are too dense to understand. We hear a bark or a meow, when in fact there are a myriad of subtle tones which convey infinite meanings our brains are too dull to decipher. The sounds are there, but our abilities to hear and learn are just too limited. They on the other hand understand us. They comprehend our words and body language. Don't think that when a dog or cat fails to come when called that they are stupid- far from it. Do they know you are calling them? Yes. They simply make a conscious choice not to allow whatever you had planned for them next- most likely confinement. How do they know your intentions? They are psychic, skilled at reading every bit of body attitude and mental energy you are emitting.

Animals have been shown to have telepathic abilities, such as sensing when their owners are heading home from halfway across the globe. This makes them more aware and finely tuned than us on just about every level. Why would it follow that with all these heightened abilities- smell, hearing, intuition among them- that their emotions would be limited and dull? The bottom line is that our failure to comprehend them causes a world of mistreatment and devaluation of animals as we mistakenly look down on them as a subspecies.

Anyone who has truly come to know an animal realizes the nobility of the other kingdom. They share the full range of emotions we do- love, joy, grief, disappointment, sorrow, humiliation, pride, envy, excitement- they show these feelings in their eyes, their demeanor, and their actions as we do. The most horrible thing we can do is treat them as an inferior life form whose feelings don't matter. To think this way is to grossly misjudge them- thus putting ourselves on a precariously false pedestal.

It is a priority to give our animals the best life we possibly can, a huge but not impossible challenge for touring musicians. I would retire before I would give them away or cause them unhappiness. That would be the worst kind of betrayal. If I could, I'd have more, but there is a limit to the space we can provide. So our lives revolve around animal care. We spend more money on their upkeep than we do on ourselves. Between vet bills, food, pet sitters, and related equipment, the costs are huge. And it takes a continual dance to keep the dogs and cats separated from each other at the appropriate times. We've spent thousands and thousands on fencing to protect them from the road and each other. Beau is a fox hound and his instincts tell him to catch and kill small animals, where Ranger is a gentle cat lover, and they all know the difference. Ranger can curl up with the cats without a problem, but if they see Beau in the distance, they scurry into hiding.

When our dogs are with us on the road, everything waits for their care. We arrive, park, and walk the dogs... then we do sound check. If I told you how many times we stop to take them out you might think we were being extreme. It's our policy to take them out before they get anxious. We estimate all our travel time based on the additional time it takes to make regular stops at rest areas and parks. We have happy dogs, perhaps as much as the restrictions of our lives in the music business will allow.

Every day we take the dogs across the road to a hundred acres where they run off leash. Recording sessions stop, building projects cease-this pilgrimage is sacred. The oldest dog is now fourteen but is so healthy that people often ask if he is a puppy. Running is what dogs need, and running is what they hardly ever get. If it was within my power to do so, I'd make it a law that every so many city blocks a full-sized dog park, fenced and designed just for canines, would be required- so that city dogs could have this wonderful off leash time as well. Then I'd make it a law that every dog had to go there two times per day for a certain amount of time so they'd get significant exercise and social interaction with other dogs. We see more of these "dog

parks" popping up around the country and applaud them wholeheart-edly. This is the humane thing to do, and certainly people benefit as well on so many levels, not the least of which is freedom from the other side of the leash, enjoying low-stress-down-time with other people at the park (for God's sake shut down that damnable little gizmo), the relative peace of a green area in a city- and the benefits of a happier dog.

If there's anything that makes it hard for me to sleep at night it's the suffering of animals, almost entirely at human hands. Animals have no voice. They can't say, "Help me, please, I'm being locked in a swelter-ing apartment around the clock. They don't give me fresh water, and I have no way to relieve myself. When they come back they beat me for making a mess. I have no life. Please, get me out of here!" You see the grief, sorrow and resignation in the eyes of animals every day. Lost souls, confined and living on the end of a string. No stretching, no running, no freedom. Then we take them to shelters, often because we don't feel like caring for them anymore, and put them in boxes. I have heard of the most trivial reasons given for dog drops at shelters. There the animals lie, confined day in and day out, month after month, even year after year- like trash, the cast offs of human society- knowing that we intend to kill them. And then we "euthanize"

them, a euphemism for murder. It's unbelievable how many people have convinced themselves there is something kind about this. Cesar Milan, the "dog whisperer" says, "Killing a dog is never an option." I couldn't agree more. In my mind it's no more acceptable than the idea of putting human beings down.

I ask, what are we doing to animals? Would we want to be kept in a pen? Would we want to separated from others of our kind? Would we want to be yelled at and dominated morning, noon and night? Would we want to be "put down" if no one cared about us? Imagine the emotions experienced by the dogs every time people come to a shelter and walk from cage to cage, trying to choose one of these frightened, betrayed animals. Imagine the hope, and the desperation- "Please, choose me! Get me out of here! They're going to kill me!" Imagine the heartbreak when the people pick a different dog and leave. Imagine yourself in this position controlled by another predatory species.

This is an unprecedented time in history. Humans now dominate the entire planet. We are beginning to understand the environmental disaster this is causing, not the least of which is total confinement of animals both wild and domestic. Because we are obsessed with driving fast cars, dogs are no longer safe off leash. Deer and other wild animals are routinely mowed down and left to suffer horrible, agonizing deaths on the side of the road. One hundred years ago these dangers didn't exist.

Today we are workaholics and playaholics, and we have no time for animals. We keep them because they are cute, or because they guard our apartments- then we babble on cell phones when we are walking them. If you think about the life of a city dweller, this is most likely the only time the dog is taken out all day. I've seen more animals dragged along by brainless people on phones while the dog is trying desperately to pee- bouncing on one leg, being pulled along, while the babbler just keeps walking. Animals get locked indoors for obscene amounts of time. Eight hours in a crate is not OK, no matter what your fancy trainer says. "They love their crates," "It's their special place," or "They feel safe there"... come on- that's no life! We think a four foot by five foot pen is a "run." And of course holding in waste material all day leads to cancer, not to mention pain. Would you choose this for yourself every day of your life?

We are killing animals faster than you can say "No more jack rabbit." It's uncivilized, it's thoughtless, and it's cruel. Ghandi said that you can tell the health of a nation by the way it treats its animals. We would be well advised to heed this. But how do we rate in this regard? Animals like racehorses and dogs are treated like royalty while they generate income, but then are discarded like so much trash when the cash flow stops. This is a stain on our civilization.

Courage- did I mention courage? You know a dog will go to its death defending you. Do you think it doesn't realize the full implications when it puts itself between you and harm's way? It understands death and values life just like we do. Dogs, cats, and animals are heroes. It is my personal feeling that there will be powerful punishment for people who are cruel to animals. If you not a believer in heaven and hell, but are a believer in karma, then it will be karmic punishment.

Perhaps it is simply a matter of education. In my city days I thought of dogs as a lower life form. I assumed they had no "feelings." They were scary, smelly, wild animals, and I wanted nothing to do with them. When I moved to the country and got my first dog, I almost never let it in the house. I fed it of course, but otherwise expected it to fend for itself. When it turned up at a shelter I considered, and then left it there, thinking someone else would take over its care- as if it wasn't my responsibility. I cringe now to realize that through my ignorance I was guilty of causing this terrible suffering. The one thing this tells me is that I need to understand when others inadvertently mistreat animals, and that the best approach is through education. If people can understand who animals really are, they are very likely to change their attitudes. After all, that's what happened to me. I wasn't cruel- I didn't beat or mistreat- but I did abandon a dog at a shelter. I misjudged the true importance of the life of another being and no doubt caused its death through ignorance. I was a part of the problem, but now I need to be a part of the solution.

Taking Care Of Number One

We can no longer just strive to "take care of number one," the haunting refrain of the woman who cheated with Ron- after all, what does she have now? *Certainly not Ron-* and that kind of thinking leads to a total breakdown of society with everyone clambering for personal gain. At some point there will simply not be enough perks left to go around- at times it seems we have reached this very juncture, the possible silver lining being that all of us will have to call upon increased self-sufficiency, personal responsibility, ingenuity and creativity. When- and not if- the lights go out, I don't want to get an anxiety attack because internet access is down. I hope that will be a seamless transition where we will light the candles and wood stoves- as windmills, waterwheels and solar panels do their work. Maybe even those inventions will be still, and we'll have to become like our cave ancestors again- something I am not incapable of valuing. If we still have books we will read them. We might choose to take up an instrument and play. All the things good enough for human kind since the dawn of time will still be good enough for me.

Stepping Back In

There are times I am so exhausted with traveling I don't even want to walk to the mailbox. Having nothing to do and nowhere to go is pure luxury. But as John Hammond once said to me: If you retire you'll eventually go crazy- and I would add this: I'd miss it so much I'd become like a lost soul. I would feel there was a selfishness to my existence.

Bottom line is that when there's doubt, or fear, or insecurity, I throw myself into touring and making records. This is the real drug for me, the greatest high, and the best place to channel energy and life experience. For me it doesn't get any better than this.

I have also become a storyteller over the years, and miraculously the fans tolerate this- even appreciate it. People say "We love the songs, but we love the stories too..." I'm always so pleased. "That's a good thing," I answer, "because I can't seem to help myself." Sometimes I explain that it's hereditary- how my dad talked so much on stage he forgot to play. No doubt this is in my future. Sometimes I ramble, and once or twice over the years someone has shouted "Play music!" (shut up and play). Rare, yes, and rude, but I am not above being corrected.

My Paintings Make The Long Journey Home

One December evening I performed at a small venue in Woodstock, New York. It was just eight months before Artie died. As I walked in, there stood my dear friends John and Catherine Sebastian. Next, Artie and Beverly arrived. Jordan and his girlfriend were also there. John and Artie joined me on stage, making the night one of the most wonderful experiences in recent memory. Artie, who must have been quite ill at the time, played more beautifully and more spectacularly than ever. His artistry came straight from above- no description would do it justice. I heard his music as never before. Then John joined the set. John is still one of the only people who can make every note gorgeous without ever overplaying. His performances are the soul of brevity. Each note breathes, and each note is more beautiful than the last. Nothing could have made the evening more wonderful except for this: an area resident who had purchased several of my oil paintings years earlier left a note saying that she had decided, after owning and enjoying these paintings for twenty years, that she had to cut back on her possessions, and she wanted these pieces to be back in my collection. There they were, carefully wrapped, and as I opened each one, it would be impossible to describe the joy I felt at seeing my old friends again.

Fleur Today

$\mathcal{T}$oday Fleur lives in Hawaii and has been adopted by the Native people. She is as productive and artistic as she always has been. She raises birds, has published books of her spectacular nature photography, and is a devoted animal advocate, a passion we obviously share. We are also both deeply concerned about Native American causes and the environment. She is the perfect mother.

She sent me this letter recently about a rooster she adopted. I had been following his story through many letters.

Dear Ro and Rob--
Little Hana rooster died yesterday during an operation in Kona by the wonderful veterinarian Shannon Nakaya, to see what had been hurting him so the whole past month. The bones in his head had broken down, "like termites have been there." She thought it might've been cancer. "The bacteria in his head just wiped him out." He fought it as long as he could.

I'd brought him home for the two days before the operation, and, under the pink shower tree, he gave his "come quick see what I've found!" call to his hens, and they all came running. I've never seen such sweetness between chickens in my life. He revisited all his favorite spots in the yard. I'd brought his favorite hen, plump Lo'i, to be with him for several days in Kona; she fussed over him and pecked bits of stuff from his face and ears, and even dropped bits of food to the ground in front of him, as if she were trying to feed a baby chick.

He'd landed in my yard three and a half years ago, spinning like a top, and almost dead, and Shannon saved his life by draining massive amounts of pus from his ears and cheeks. He not only achieved his balance, he fathered many little ones, who now live with friends of mine in Kohala, and who continue his line.
love, Fleur

This letter explains who Fleur is more than any glowing description I could come up with.

Last year I wrote to one of Fleur's friends in Hawaii who has worked her entire life struggling to restore Native lands to the rightful owners. This dedicated woman is up against the tourist industry, which is locked in with the usurping government- the same people who ousted the Native inhabitants years ago. There is an ongoing battle to return sacred sights to the original owners, but as you might imagine the entrenched industries do not want to budge. The battle to acknowledge the rights of Native peoples continues. It is an issue far from the national consciousness, yet it is one of the greatest all time travesties which exists right under our noses. While people are busy demanding personal rights and suing over hot cups of coffee, we have all but forgotten this shameful injustice to an entire nation of people who lived here before we did. Are we aware of and concerning ourselves with the fact that much of this continent was settled on land taken from people who have a legal claim to it, and that untold numbers of treaties have been violated?

two little roosters who are growing up in my library

Photo:© Fleur Weymouth 2010

Full Circle

"Bralph" came to one of my shows the other day in Virginia. He is still an amazingly vital person who exudes the same wholesome, contagious enthusiasm. Ralph is the first person I called when I decided to write this book, and it turned out that he had founded a publishing company, eventually handing it over to others to run. Someone at the company explained that they mostly publish things like dulcimer manuals- and this book was pretty far from a dulcimer manual- but nonetheless Ralph's support and encouragement gave me the confidence to continue writing. In addition, seeing his face again was incredibly comforting and filled me with a sense of certainty that somehow, over the years, everything good comes back around- that my life had come full circle.

Alienation and Healing

Even in the darkest moments of pain and despair, I always thought the day would come when my dad would apologize and want to make peace with me, and incredibly, it did. It happened at the Altamont festival about five years ago when he reached out and completely healed the damage from the past. This was the day he said, "I have a genius for a daughter." Frail, and in a tender state of mind, he touched my hair very softly. He looked at me intently and asked my age. I said, "fifty-five." He said "You look twenty-five." This was the day he said he loved me and wanted to walk arm in arm, and as we shuffled slowly towards the food tent and he said, "Now I feel complete, because you are here." I was totally overcome with emotion. People stood on either side of the pathway looking at us, some taking pictures. Jordan waved them away saying this was a private moment. But I didn't care because I only saw Dad, and felt the two halves of my torn heart coming together again. His words, those healing and loving words, changed everything. It's not that the past is of no consequence- it will always exert a strong influence. But now I can truly say that those challenges made me far more determined. For all I know his rejection really did make it more likely that I would succeed- just to prove it was possible.

Photo: Fleur Weymouth

A Father's Love

Now I have received my father's tender blessing and acknowledgment. I am aware that this sort of reconciliation might never occur in one's lifetime, and that it is a priceless gift. Of course Dad still makes odd remarks. As my sister and I sat on either side of him, he said "I don't know which one of you to love more." In the past this would have caused division and competition. I can understand his old self inserting itself from time to time- it's just that now I know I am not competing with anyone for my father's love. It has arrived at

412

the perfect time- and in a way that no one can take away. So eventually everything falls into place- not on our schedule, of course, but in God's time. But when God's time arrives, it's like no waiting ever took place... it's always right on time.

Dad lives at home as he would wish. My brother and sister- who are both available with no conflicting demands- are sharing in his care along with a local woman, for which I am grateful. I often crave to be able to drop everything- tours, recording, writing, the animals- and go stay with my dad. I would play music for him all day long, and I would read poetry. But the responsibilities of my current life allow zero time to disappear. Or perhaps I fear the pain of not being recognized, my sister's posturing, or some other imagined ill. I cling to my father's love as shown to me so openly on our last visits when his mind was still intact... and a great mind it is and was, filled with astonishing poetry, uncanny observations, child-like humor, and a tremendous love of life, nature and of course, music. It seems far too soon for him to forget... but I am told everyone's chemistry is different. It's just that I want to cling to that sweet feeling he has shown me, and bask in his approval just a little bit longer...

My 60th Birthday Party

$\mathcal{T}$he phone rings, I pick it up and hear something hard to identify- some fumbling, and then a whisper. The caller ID reads "Allan Block." I call out "Dad! Dad, it's Ro!" Then the phone goes dead.

I told Rob that Dad tried to call- we thought he'd call right back so we waited. Sure enough the phone rang again and it was the same- some rustling, some whispering- and then I detected the softest words, almost like inside-out breathing. Then it went dead. In a panic I called my brother- was Dad alone? Was he having trouble breathing? Had he had an accident? Was he calling for help? My brother's machine came on. I called uncle Danny, but no one knew a thing. Then the phone rang again and it was my sister. She said Dad had been trying to call me for several days. He was very determined. It was my 60th and he was calling to wish me happy birthday. What was this? Did he remember? Just as before, my sister related how Dad had been asking for me. My heart raced... my dad remembered me, he was thinking about me, he wanted to call me! She said he was not able to hear well and couldn't tell that someone had answered. I got on the phone "Dad!" I shouted. "Dad, it's Ro! Dad, I love you!" Then I heard him. He was saying happy birthday. He was saying come up and see me. He said, after a long pause "Bring Rob." The following day was my birthday, and I told my sister Rob and I were coming. Dad kept saying he wanted to take me to dinner and a movie, and my sister kept telling him there were no movie theaters in the area.

We drove up the next morning. It was a gorgeous, cloudless November day. When we arrived my sister came out and we greeted each other happily. It's funny how human emotions can run amok, yet at the bottom line all is well. I walked in and looked around for Dad. There, in the cradle of his bed, covered by a new goose down quilt my sister had picked out for him, lay my dad- a cocoon. Next to him was the warm glow of a table lamp, some glasses and a pile of books. I went in and knelt by the bed. He took my face in his hands, and with an expression filled with both wonder and overflowing love, he said my name again and again "Rory... Rory... you're beautiful."

Dad laughed when I read my poems to him. They were not as great as his by any stretch. We went to the living room together and sat side by side on the couch. I read to him from his own book of poetry called *Unopened Mail*, a book I cherish and read often. I said to Dad "You have a great mind." He seemed pleased. As I read these poems he gently touched the pages of the book. He looked thoughtful. We stopped briefly- perhaps to digest many unspoken words- the time he had taken to craft these incredible poems- the fact that his daughter was reading them to him- or maybe some other meaning he wished to express but couldn't.

I brought my guitar as usual. Dad reached for the fiddle, so I opened the case and handed him this ancient, paper thin, weightless instrument- Dad's old fiddle. He began to play the one song my brother says he plays often these days, "Sailor's Hornpipe." We played it again and again. While this was going on Rob took his iPhone and set it on a nearby shelf in a record mode. There it sat quietly with an old microphone pictured on the screen. A few moments later I got up to see what my sister had done with the upstairs bedroom, and as I left the room my dad quietly said, "Let's play another one." I was unaware that Dad had said this until I listened to the recording after we got home.

There were other songs, and there was a late birthday present I brought for my dad's 86th, which had been on the 6th of October. It was the inside foldout of my latest CD framed and signed to Dad-thanking him for inspiring me to play music. He looked at the photo of me on the cover with professional makeup on and said, "This doesn't look like you." Dad has never been one for artifice or ornament. He's the original "Mr. Natural." No wonder I have no idea how to apply makeup- Dad would have hated it, so I never learned.

We all sat around the dinner table with our various organic offerings. I brought my famous vegan apple pie, and my dad ate his own special chicken and gravy: mashed, because he can only eat soft foods. He had been staring at us for some time when he pointed his fork across the table and announced, "Someone's missing." I realized he meant my brother. I was deeply encouraged. This was not someone incapable of reasoning and understanding.

Although Dad asked me to stay, we had to get home for our five dogs and eight cats, two of which were sick and in the care of the vet tech who doubles as the pet-sitter. She called to say all was well, but we had planned to be back later that evening. As we drove away I said to Rob, "That was the best birthday of my life."

The Ninety Year Old Man

There is a ninety year old man,
Who digs a trench outside my window.
Slowly, methodically, he places the shovel,
Presses a mud covered boot against the edge,
Pumps it three or four times,
And tilts it slowly to secure a small amount of soil.
Carefully, he lifts the shovel,
Shaking it slightly to keep the contents from falling,
Then gently deposits it onto the rising pile of rubble.
He is uncomplaining. He does not think it unfair
That he should throw his body into the work.
He goes at his own pace,
And finishes the job without flourish.
Squinting,
He stands back and smokes a cigarette.
Stop whining, I say.
We are soft, pale, and childish.
We expect compensation-
Services, breaks, perks, and overtime...
We want our work as light as possible.
We often hate our jobs, hate those we work for.
Better to be like this ninety year old man,
Grateful in his way for being alive.

Rory Block

416

Ro, Dad and Mo, New Hampshire, 2010

Table of Contents

418